Finding Beautiful

Finding Beautiful

Book 1, The Beautifully Broken Series

Amanda Kaitlyn

Gavin

He is a ladies' man.
The CEO of a multi-million dollar company.
He thought he had it all. Until, Aria.

Aria

I was damaged. Broken. I had given up on men. When I stumbled upon
a sleek Jaguar and a man beneath the hood of it, I was drawn to him
instantly.
He was electric. He was undeniably attractive.
But worst of all?
He wanted me.
I knew I was in trouble.
But somehow, I trusted him.

"Breathe, Aria. Christ, please, just breathe for me."

Gavin came into my life like a hurricane, turning my world on its head.
I didn't want to fall for him, but it was inevitable.
From the moment, we met, he claimed my heart.
I knew he would do whatever it took to protect it.
When the shadows I fought so hard to escape, threatened to tear us
apart, could the love we'd found be enough to persevere?
Or would our fight be in vain?

"I'm going to give you the world, beautiful. This is only the beginning."

This novel contains adult content, graphic violence and sexual
situations. It is only meant for those 18 years or older.

Finding Beautiful is the first book in a series of stand alones by Amanda
Kaitlyn. Each novel includes a guaranteed HEA and no cliffhanger.

Dedication

To every person that encouraged, nurtured

and pushed me to pursue this dream of mine.

I am immensely grateful.

Prologue

"Aria, look," Farrah whispered from our adjoined desks, as we sat towards the back of Mr. Nelson's history class. Her hazel eyes zeroed in on someone across the room, her slim eyebrows raised and her eyes wide with curiosity.

"What?" I whispered, peering down at my notebook filled with the lecture notes I needed to memorize by next class. My overly excited best friend kept nudging me, even as I tried in vain to ignore my curiosity at who caught her eye. The last guy I would be interested in was some jock that Farrah had her sights set on, but hell, I was curious. Aggravated, I turned to where she tilted her head, only to gasp when a pair of chocolate brown eyes collided with mine from three desks over.

I was right. He was a jock. A LAKERS cap was drawn low on his head and three girls surrounded him, wanting his attention while he had his sights set on me. He wasn't staring, at least not in that way boys looked at you with only one thing in mind. He was just looking at me. With curiosity. With wonder.

I knew who he was, practically everyone at Beaumont High did, Bryce Williams, a senior. He was the quarterback on our football team. Chocolate-brown eyes, tousled black hair, and a muscular frame—he was any girl's dream.

And he was looking at me? No way. My cheeks flamed red at the thought. I hastily turned my head to see if there was someone behind me, but there was no one. Oh goodness, it was me. Why the hell would he be looking at me?

"He's looking at you!" my best friend gushed as I turned to see her biting her thumb in excitement.

When I looked back at him, his brows were raised and a wide smile played on his full lips. I knew I should look away. My sister warned me about boys like him, especially given what people said about him. They said he was dangerous; that his last girlfriend, Kristy Jenkins, fled to private school after only two months of seeing him. Looking at him though, I wasn't sure I believed those rumors.

Chapter 1

I clasped the locket in the palm of my hand and took a deep cleansing breath. Dancers glided elegantly over the wooden floors, masses of grace and beauty. I had bonded with these women over three weeks of brutal training. From the wings, I watched them, hoping I'd be just as confident when I took the floor.

I approached my coach, mentor, and dance partner of six years, Eli Jones, and tried to cover up my trembling hands with the wrap I was holding. I didn't know why I was so nervous. Dancing was like walking to me. I'd done it ever since I was old enough to put one foot in front of the other. It had been an outlet for me through the lonely nights of middle school, the stressful, exam-filled days of high school and especially through my four years at Julliard. It had been my relief from everyday life. But this would be my first-time dancing in front of an audience since my hospital stay four months ago.

Oh, shit. What if I fell on my face? With my hands shaking terribly, that was a possibility.

My errant thoughts were interrupted by a hand on my shoulder, squeezing me from behind.

"You're going to do fine, Aria," Eli whispered in my ear with another squeeze to my shoulders. I smiled because I was afraid that if I spoke, I wouldn't make it to my dance before I talked myself out of it.

I had to do this. For me. For everything I'd endured and every person that had lifted me up the numerous times I had fallen.

The slow instrumental of a Celine Dion melody began, and I slipped the gold-bowed ballet flats on my feet and pulled my wavy black hair into a bun.

I drew in a deep breath as I glided onto the floor. It felt as if every moment leading up to this enhanced my already frazzled nerves. My body was strung tight from my toes to the tips of my fingers. I hadn't done this in so long, I was terrified that I'd mess up. What did they say about riding a bike? Learning to drive? If you learned once, you'd positively remember how to do it no matter how much time had passed. I really hoped that was true.

I stretched my fingers to the ceiling, and as I did, my eyes flicked over to see my supportive dance coach looking at me. When he nodded his head, I knew I could do it. I had this. Taking another deep breath, I began to move, making sure to stay in sync with the lyrics playing in my mind.

> *Once more you open the door and*
> *you're here in my heart*
> *and my heart will go on and on.*

I moved to express everything inside me, and soon I didn't even have to think about the rhythm or the steps or the people from my academy's dance program watching my every move. I was one with my body, the soft music, and the heartbeat inside my chest.

My right leg lifted as if in a trance while my other rose in front of me in a perfect arch. I held that position through a few strains of the violin and then glided back into position for my finish. When the violin ended, I went for my big ending and landed it with easy grace as the audience applauded for me. A larger-than-life smile spread my lips, lifted my cheeks and made my eyes burn as I took in the number of people avidly applauding and celebrating.

This was my world and my love. All I needed, I realized. All the pain, grief, fear, everything faded when I danced. It was the only place in my life where all the bad feelings didn't overwhelm and crush me.

Everything had finally crashed down on me four months ago, and I almost never danced again. Thank God, I lived to dance once more.

A pair of skinny, but muscular, arms caught me as soon as I was within reach and I giggled as Eli hoisted me off my feet, laughing in my ear. He squeezed me gently as he hung on a little longer to our hug.

"You, my mistress, are back."

I met his gaze and nodded, knowing I truly was back. Eli let me go as I saw my sister, Kel standing by the locker rooms. Hastily I ran to meet her. Instantly she drew me tightly into her embrace.

"You were amazing, Aria. I'm so proud of you, honey." She grinned against my head and I sniffled into her Rolling Stones tee. I blinked a few times so she didn't think I was sad today, because I was not.

"Thanks for coming, Kel," I murmured, hooking one arm through hers. As we filed out with everyone else, she spoke only for my ears.

"I wouldn't have missed it for anything in this world. I'm just sorry Mama wouldn't come."

I closed my eyes and reminded myself to be strong. My mom hadn't talked to me ever since my older brother, and her beloved son, died years ago. I still remembered the moment he flat-lined.

I was at Jeremy's bedside with my arm in a sling as he fought for every breath. A drunk driver hit his truck cab and he suffered internal bleeding along with broken ribs and massive head injuries. We had no idea whether he'd wake up, and even if he did, would he remember us? Would he be our Jeremy? Or would he be a vegetable for the rest of his life?

In the end, though, his heart wasn't strong enough and he passed exactly one hour and twenty-two minutes after he was brought into the emergency room. It crushed me. Hell, it broke me. My mom took it the hardest and placed all the blame on me amid her grief. The pain got to be too much for her and the only way she could cope was to be angry. At the world. At me. But God, did it hurt.

I didn't realize tears were falling until they stung my cheeks. Kel wiped them away, her amber eyes filled with worry. I missed him so much.

"It's okay," I whispered, struggling to rein in my emotions.

Kel wrapped her arm around me and led me to her car, knowing that I had to move, to do something other than relive those terrible moments. We walked across the parking lot and I spotted a canary yellow sports car with a black pinstripe detailed on each side. I could tell from the make that it was a newer Jaguar. I didn't know all that much about cars, but this had to be the sexiest car I'd ever laid eyes on. Every inch was sleek, painted in the brightest shade of yellow, the designs up one side in thin lines of navy and black was a stark contrast to the bright yellow. Then I caught sight of the gorgeous man leaning against it staring at his phone.

I lost my breath when a pair of piercing blue-gray eyes locked on mine and I swore my heart stopped beating. It felt as if the air around me was charged with something as I met his gaze. My breath faltered as I took in the man standing no more than twenty feet away. With brown tousled hair that begged me to run my fingers through it and a look in his eyes that made me stop where I stood, I was mesmerized. His eyes captivated mine, two clouds of brilliant blue and gray. His lean cheekbones and nose complimented his face perfectly. His mouth was sculpted and tilted into a half-smile. Somehow, it made my blood heat in anticipation. Gradually, my eyes swept down his body. The man was wearing a white dress shirt, unbuttoned at the top that hugged his chest in the best way and black jeans with black dress shoes to match.

When my eyes returned to his, he cocked his head to one side as if to ask *are you checking me out?*

I couldn't help the butterflies that took flight in my stomach. He was … beautiful. My brain seemed to catch up with my eyes and I immediately asked myself, what the hell was I doing? It was not as if I'd never seen a good-looking man before. It just felt like my eyes were somehow drawn to him. I watched as he pulled a wrench out from under the hood of his car, straightened up, closing the hood with a loud thud. The way he carried himself was like sex on legs. It dawned on me that he didn't seem cocky or full of himself like most guys with his looks were, but he did have a sense of self-awareness and power in the way he moved.

I drew my eyes back to his and he stepped forward. The smile he gave me made me weak in the knees.

God, what was happening to me?

Aria, calm down. He was just a man.

"Like the view?" he asked, his voice gravelly. The sound seeped through me, through the space between us, through my overheated skin.

I opened my mouth to speak, but I ended up just taking in a breath and attempting to gather my thoughts. He watched me quietly, eyes trained only on my face.

I tried to reason with myself, to get in the car and drive away, but I couldn't truly think of anything that would cause me to run.

Okay, he was just a man, who was sinfully beautiful and had eyes that drew you in like a moth to a flame …

"Oh … um, yes. Is this yours?"

He nodded and took a step forward, startling me a tad when he took my hand gently in his. The simple touch was like a spark between our bodies, sending tingles over my skin.

"She is," he said, that half-smile lighting up the dips and shallows of his face. I could see at least one day's worth of brown stubble across his jaw, my fingers itched to touch him, feel the roughness I knew I'd find along his jaw. I bit my lip as he admired me with those eyes of his. God, his eyes were so deep, so full of mischief.

"She?" I cocked my head to the side in confusion.

"Yes, that surprises you?" he teased me, eyes narrowing a bit.

My mouth stretched into a shy smile, and I felt my heart flutter as he gazed down at me. "Let me guess, you named her, too?"

"I did. Jasmine, after the girl that broke my heart years ago. I'm hoping history won't repeat itself. I can't imagine she'll run off with a French exchange student. You think?"

It made me laugh, his naming his car, but it also saddened me knowing he had felt heartbreak. I could relate. Heartbreak was something I knew intimately, but didn't everyone get their heart broken at one point?

"I hope not."

I didn't try to take my hand from his. The skin contact was just too intense for me to want to. Beside me, Kel tugged on my arm and smiled knowingly as she looked at our joined hands. Oh goodness, what did she have in mind?

Leaning closer to me, she whispered in my ear, "Shall I invite him tonight?"

I narrowed my eyes at her and hastily shook my head, though I did want to see him again. My sister insisted on having a party. She said it was to celebrate my performance today, but she just really loved parties and any excuse would do.

Kel stepped in front of me, blocking me from his view while she looked at him. I watched her lean in to whisper in his ear and I vaguely wondered what he must smell like.

"Of course, I'll be there. Thank you."

I met his eyes intentionally, wondering what he must be thinking of her taking a such quick liking to him. His eyes sparkled with mischief, and they didn't leave mine while he talked with my sister.

My heart was in overdrive for the first time ever and it was due to this man. I had to remind myself to focus on something other than his beauty or the speed of my heartbeat in my chest. He was just a man. I kept telling myself that.

"You don't have to come, my sister is just being nice," I half-whispered as he moved a step closer to me. I swore the heat in his gaze could burn me in two.

Shaking his head slightly, he gave me a smile that just about melted my heart. I wondered, could he possibly want to see me again? Did I want that?

"I'd really like to see you again. You're beautiful and mysterious, and you intrigue me." Beautiful and mysterious? *God, what was I doing ... ?*

Still, I found myself nodding. I turned to the car before I said something else. My thoughts were rattled and all I could think about was how soft his lips looked and how those eyes captivated mine.

Suddenly, he caught my hand again and immediately my heart sped up as the hairs on the back of my neck stood on end. His touch resonated through me and when I saw the sincerity in his eyes, I gasped audibly.

"Can I at least have your name?"

This man's voice knocked my heart into overdrive again. His eyes searched mine for long seconds. I wondered what he was thinking as he trained his eyes intently on my face. A strand of my hair flew in front of my face from the breeze and he deftly lifted it away, tucking it behind my ear. When his fingers dipped to my cheek, a blush spread across my skin, fireworks sparked underneath the touch.

"Aria," I whispered just loud enough for his ears.

He nodded, his eyes heating with something I wished I had a name for, as his finger grazed my cheek, my eyes never leaving his.

"Gavin," he murmured, giving me his name.

I bit my lip at the sound of his name off his sinfully attractive mouth. I found myself wanting to lean into his touch as his hand brushed against my cheek, still. The name fit him so well.

Gavin.

"I'll see you tonight, Gavin." I breathed, feeling lighter as he smiled that crooked smile at me and took my hand in his once more, not letting go as he stepped away until distance pulled our fingers apart.

"Tonight," he said.

"You're blushing, Ari. Holy shit," my sister said, chuckling as we pulled away from the curb where I could still see Gavin leaning against his car. She looked at me and I inwardly sighed. I couldn't stop thinking about the way he seemed to focus completely on me. A man I had never met. I had never felt that with anyone I had dated. Undivided attention.

"That was … intense," I mumbled to my sister as she started the car.

"I'd say. And that car had to be expensive. Like something out of a movie."

She turned left and grinned at me.

"It was a Jaguar, one of the most expensive foreign automotive brands out there."

She looked at me as if I had two heads and shook her head.

"Forget the car, he was beautiful! You should have given him your number, honey. He was looking at you like you were water and he was thirsting for a tall glass."

I burst into giggles at that and she joined me as we pulled into our apartment lot.

"You're horrible, Kel. I swear I don't know where you got your sense of humor."

She smirked at me, giving me that look again. She knew I was stalling, diverting her attention. From the mysterious man, we met today. About how I felt about seeing him again.

"Oh, come on, you couldn't take your eyes off him. I've never seen you react to a man like that. I think you should get back out there, Ari. Don't you think it's time?"

I sighed, feeling both terrified and excited at the idea of seeing him again.

"I don't know, Kel. It's been years and honestly, I have no idea how to put myself out there again. I'm not ready to make a fool of myself or get hurt."

"I know, but if you don't try you could really regret not taking the chance."

Her bright eyes implored me to say something, but I was speechless. I hadn't—no, I couldn't—let myself think about giving someone the power to hurt me, break my heart again. I couldn't be hurt again. I wouldn't let that happen.

But Gavin … he looked at me like no other man had and it confused me. Was I ready?

"I don't know. It was like he saw me, the real me. Not the ballet dancer or the rich girl or the heartbroken teenager that everyone else saw when they looked at me. But you saw him, Kel. He probably has a girlfriend or a wife! I can't compete with God knows who."

She didn't answer me, shaking her head as she got out of the car. She leaned back in through the window to meet my guarded gaze.

"I didn't see a ring on his finger. And you're beautiful and mysterious, remember?"

I folded my fingers in my lap, trying to clear my thoughts. She was right. He did say that. The thoughts and emotions inside me had me tangled up, confused, hesitant. I didn't know if I was ready. Would I ever be?

"We both know I'm not cut out for relationships!" The words tumbled out of me, voicing my insecurities. My eyes stung with emotion and I turned my gaze away from the window.

I got out of the car and met her on the other side. I hoped that maybe she would just let this go. But I felt her brown eyes on me as I took the steps. Taking my hands, she tugged me down to sit on the top step with her. My determined-as-hell sister looked at me, imploring me to listen, and it was not the first time today.

Sighing, I squeezed her hands in mine so she knew I was listening.

"Ari, it was never your fault what Bryce did to you, and it doesn't mean that you aren't just as deserving of love as anyone else in this world. The problems in that relationship were not you, they were his issues. You can't use that bad relationship as a measuring tool to determine your ability to function in a relationship."

No.

With the sound of his name, my voice died in my throat. I didn't want to think about him. Not. Ever. Again.

My chest ached with the memories that flooded me from the sound of a single syllable, a name I hadn't heard in years. A name I wanted to erase from my vocabulary—Bryce.

Kel didn't let it go, though. She took hold of my wrists and pushed up the sleeves of my sweatshirt revealing the yellowing bruises, and cuts marring my pale skin. Shame washed over me, and my eyes closed briefly as I fought to push down the sadness that tried to make its way into my thoughts. For years, I had been able to suppress the pain. I had a rigorous routine leaving little time for dwelling on anything outside of dance and my studies at Julliard. But one day when the pain had gotten to be too much, when I believed I was just as useless as he had made me feel back then, I found a way to take away the pain in my own way. It was the lowest point in my life and I couldn't see my self-worth. I saw it now, though.

"Look at me," Kel said with tears in her eyes.

In her eyes, I saw how much she worried about me. She knew just how much I had gone through, how long it had taken me to feel whole again.

"You. Are. Beautiful. Aria. It wasn't your fault what he did to you and you should never let the fear of getting hurt again stop you from going after what you want, honey. It's been years. Just keep your heart open, okay? You deserve happiness. I found it with Lucas and I know you can, too."

I nodded, unable to speak as my heart swelled with love for my remarkable sister. Kel kissed my forehead and squeezed my hand, giving me strength. Taking a deep breath, I decided to give myself a chance. A chance for happiness. One date never killed anyone. Right?

"Let's go get ready for this party, huh?" I grabbed her hands and pulled her to stand, hooking my arm in hers as we headed upstairs to plan a celebration.

As we turned the corner near the apartment, we saw Lucas, my sister's fiancé, leaning up against our door. With messy blond hair, a lip piercing, topaz green eyes and a lopsided smile, he was attractive in the most rugged way. But more than that, he was the sweetest and kindest man I had met in a long time and just from the way he looked at my sister, I knew he adored her. When I saw them together, I could see how happy he made her. He looked up and smiled when he saw us.

"Hey, sweetheart." Immediately Kel stepped into his arms, a smile brightening her face as she tipped her head back and he kissed her forehead.

"You don't have your key?" she asked.

"I do, just thought I'd wait for you. How did it go, Aria?"

Lucas wrapped an arm around my sister's shoulder and then released her to give me a bear hugs, lifting me off my feet easily. I grinned and laughed, wiping the moisture from my eyes before he saw it.

"It went great," Kel said for me as Lucas took my keys to unlock our door. The minute I made it to the couch I set my dance bag down and plopped down where Kel joined me.

"You were amazing," Kel said, obviously seeing my doubts after the performance. I knew she was right, but sometimes I couldn't help doubting myself. After that night, all those years ago, I didn't know if I'd ever be able to love myself and believe in my abilities again.

Four Months Ago

For years, I had pressed all the pain and anguish down as deep as I possibly could. I danced to escape the feeling of worthlessness I felt each waking moment. When school demanded my whole focus, I had no choice but to ignore all the ugliness I carried inside.

I didn't used to feel so insignificant.

But years ago, *he* broke me.

Bryce Williams.

My monster.

My worst nightmare.

My darkest mistake.

Even now if I let myself think about it for just a second, I could hear the sound of a loud crash and for a moment, it all came rushing to the surface and I remembered the night that changed everything five long years ago.

After he broke my heart and my spirit, all I had left was dance. The intensity and competition at Julliard demanded all my focus. It let me escape the ugliness I carried inside. The day of my graduation, when I should have been pirouetting on top of the world, all that pain and ugliness rushed to the surface. It was all I could see and feel. After graduation, I got a job dancing. For a while, it was a good distraction, proving myself outside the academic world. But then my escape abandoned me, so I tried to abandon my miserable existence, my life as I knew it.

I finally reached the end of my rope.

A couple of quick slices and I watched numbly as the pain and ugliness seeped out of me. I closed my eyes and welcomed the peace that came with the darkness. I gave no thought to anything but leaving the pain behind. The memories, dark and loud, smothered me as I sat there, the pain jolting my body. The intense physical pain of the cuts in my arm overpowered the tears in my heart from that night five years ago, that forever changed my life. I closed my eyes then and I watched as the events of that night played through my mind.

The sound of a loud crash coming from the kitchen made my eyes fly open in a mixture of surprise and panic.

I had fallen asleep waiting for Bryce to come to the cabin where we were staying for our holiday vacation. We were only supposed to stay for a few days but Bryce had insisted we stay and enjoy New Year's here. After getting a call from his father early that morning, he dashed off to meet him, promising to be back that night. My eyes flitted down over the pillow to see my cell phone lit up and numerous missed call notifications showed upon the screen. I didn't have to check to know they must have been from Bryce.

Shit.

I hoped he wouldn't be mad at me for drifting off. Though, lately it seemed that he was always angry at me for something or another.

"Where are you?" Bryce yelled, making me jump. Then I saw his cold eyes and clenched fists as he stalked toward me with loud, sure footsteps. I lifted my head and searched for any sign of humanity in his eyes, but all I saw was anger. The boy I met and fell in love with years ago, was gone. He had slowly been replaced by this stranger bearing cold, dark eyes of anger and hatred.

"I ... I was sleeping, Bryce. I'm sorry." My voice shook unintentionally.

He narrowed his eyes at me, raising the empty whiskey bottle and throwing it past my head, making me flinch and jump back from him.

"Do you know how worried I've been?" he asked, a quiet venom in his words as he backed me into a corner and forced me to look into his reddened eyes. His hand gripped my chin tightly, making me whimper at the force of his hold.

"I'm sorry ... I ..."

He didn't let me finish before his fist came down hard on the side of my face. The pain spread across my skin. I cried out and fell back, my head hitting the hardwood floor with a smack. I felt the blood trickle down my face and my body trembled in fear. He looked down at me, his brown eyes almost black with anger as he cursed and kicked me in the stomach. Once, twice, three times ... I lost count as each blow melted into the previous one other. Searing pain low in my abdomen caused me to shake with tears falling down my face. I struggled for breath as he grasped my hair in his fist. My eyes drifted closed and the darkness overwhelmed me, the pain finally ceasing as I blacked out.

The pain woke me up and I found myself lying face-up in bed. A quick glance around revealed my clothes in a messy pile on the floor. I felt my panties being slid down my legs and his mouth nipping at my neck. No, God, no! He couldn't be doing this. This wasn't happening...

"No ... No ... Please ... Stop ..." I pleaded, having no strength to struggle against his hands trapping me against the mattress. Bryce grinned against my skin and ground against my hips, making my body tremble in fear. There was a time once when I thought I loved him. I would have

done anything to please him. But now I was only a game to him. This was the man I knew now. I felt rough, merciless hands digging into my waist while his knees pressed against my sides. The last of my laced underwear came off my legs and I pulled my knee up, attempting to buck him off me.

"No!!" I cried out, making contact with his stomach instead of his nether regions. I continued trying in vain to push against his hold, kicking my legs in vain.

"Oh, I love it when you fight me, princess. So, feisty."

I felt the rub of his lips against my jaw, my collarbone, my neck, and then my mouth. A whimper escaped me when he pushed his tongue in my mouth and took.

"You. Are. Mine. Ari." He growled each word into the space between our mouths.

His chuckle was empty and cruel against my ears. I kept struggling, forcing my head to the side trying to escape his weight, his voice, his cold, clammy hands gripping my thighs.

And when he took and took and took, there was no one there to hear my cries of agony. The sobs broke through my chest and I cried silently, willing it to be a nightmare. My skin crawled with a dirty, horrid feeling and my eyes closed, willing myself to die instead of live through this torture.

"Aria, sweetheart, open your eyes," my sister's voice whispered as I forced my eyes to open against the numbing pain. She was sitting next to me, kissing and squeezing my hand in hers. When I saw her tear-streaked face and heard the beeps of a machine next to me, I realized where I was.

"What happened?" I choked out the words through a dry throat. My head was pounding and I could barely open my eyes to see my sister and an unfamiliar man standing next to her.

Kel leaned forward and kissed my forehead. I heard her intake of breath and waited for her to tell me what happened. Why was I here? In a hospital?

"Dad found you in Aspen this morning. He got the address of Bryce's cabin from his father. He knew something was wrong when you didn't call to say goodnight like you always did." She took a breath and I saw the fear and worry and anger in her brown eyes.

"God, Aria … You were beaten … and …" Her voice trailed off, as if she was unable to finish her sentence. I saw tears build in her eyes as she asked me in a broken voice, "Do you remember what happened?"

I took a deep breath, trying to lift my body that was numb from the medication I must be on. Pain speared me in the chest as I remembered his face, my cries for him to stop, and the pain down there and throughout my whole body. I just didn't understand how I hadn't seen him for what he really was until that moment. I was so blind. I covered my face with my hands to gather my scattered thoughts.

"He came into the cabin really angry … I tried to talk to him, but then he hit me and I must have blacked out because when I woke up I was in bed. He … Oh, God …" My voice cracked as I realized the three words that I couldn't seem to wrap my head around. He loved me, I know he did, but last night, God, he was just … a monster.

I had met Bryce Williams when I was a junior in high school. He was one of those people that dominated the room. He was eccentric, largely liked and kind to everyone around him. He made me laugh, even when I was in the worst of moods. After my brother, Jeremy passed a few months after my high school graduation, we grew even closer. He became my rock and we fell deeply in love, or at least, that was what I thought had happened. The following fall, I enrolled in the dance program at Julliard and Bryce went to work for his father at his law firm. I knew he wanted to do more than work for his father, but money was tight for us and his father planned to promote him if he proved himself. My second year in college begun on a high note as we moved in together and planned a life together. But it turned worse as the months went on. The man I fell in love with became angrier, the kindness in him bleeding away as more and more was asked of him at the law firm. I think that was when Bryce changed. In therapy, I was taught that often, people present a side of themselves that they want to be seen, even if they don't know it.

I saw the good, the kind, the gentle, the funny side to him but in time, his bad side came to light. On Christmas break of my sophomore year, we went on vacation to Aspen, where his family owned a cabin. The longer we were there, the more fear of him set in. I hadn't wanted to believe it was true but the Bryce I knew for so long was a monster. I had planned to end things before he could really hurt me. But I didn't get the chance.

My sister squeezed my hand, her eyes full of sympathy and love, an-durged me to continue.

"He raped me, Kel," I said in a shaky voice, grasping onto her as she wrapped her arms around me and hugged me tightly, allowing me to finally let go of the overwhelming emotions that threatened to smother me.

Present Day

My hands shook from the force of the memories, the darkness that loomed around me from my broken past. Lucas squeezed my shoulders from behind, bringing me back to the here and now.

"You okay, Aria?" Lucas asked over the rim of his Corona Light. I blinked, shaking my head to clear all thoughts of the past. I looked to see Kel setting out party platters, hanging streamers from the ceiling, and placing buckets of beer bottles on the tables in the living room. That made me smile. She was in her element right now. Planning a party, making the platters, and setting the decorations up were things she loved to do.

"Wow, she's excited."

He laughed. When he handed me a Blue Moon from the cooler, I looked over at him and grinned.

"She loves a party, huh?"

"She wouldn't be Kel if she didn't love this, right?" His eyes went to my sister, softening when she winked at him from across the room. He was so good for her. Just what she deserved.

I nodded, lifting the beer to my lips.

"We invited someone today. We met him at the studio."

Lucas was in the middle of raiding our fridge when he looked up, raising an eyebrow at me. His eyes narrowed at me. He thought I was kidding, since for years, I had refused to even think about men. But now I wanted to. I wanted to be open to the future if that happily-ever-after was still a possibility for me. I was just so terrified of being hurt again. I wasn't sure I could piece myself back together one more time.

"What?" His voice was incredulous … And then, his face erupted into a wide, no-holds-barred smile. One I'd never seen before. Setting his beer down, Lucas wrapped me up in a hug and squeezed too tight.

"You're finally getting back out there! That's great, Aria. Who is he?"

I blushed and looked away, not wanting to think about how badly I liked Gavin, how close I came to leaning into his touch today. It was crazy and it scared me how much I reacted to him when we met. I had never felt that way before.

I didn't trust men. And for good reason. The man who I had thought was my prince charming turned into the worst thing to happen to me and five years later, I still had the scars he had left me with. Not only physically, though the cuts marring my skin were evident. The deepest scars I had were purely emotional. Most of the time, I could hardly stand being close to a man, unless he was close to my family or a friend. But when I was with Gavin, I was put at ease. I wasn't afraid.

He brought out the strangest feelings in me and *that*, scared me.

"His name is Gavin. I don't know … after what happened with Bryce, I don't …" He stepped up to me and squeezed my shoulders in reassurance.

"Any guy would be damn lucky to have you, Aria. Okay?"

I nodded, giving him a smile, and ran to catch up with Kel as she balanced two trays in her hands. I hastily grabbed one from her and set it down on the kitchen island.

"Careful, sis"

"You ready, Kel?" Lucas called from the living room.

She grinned at him, narrowing her eyes. She'd never say so, but she was totally smitten with that man.

An hour later everything was set up and the DJ had arrived. Needing a minute of fresh air, I opened the doors to the balcony and closed them behind me, taking a deep, fortifying breath. Then my phone rang.

"Hello?" It was an unknown number, which made me nervous, as if Bryce would call me after all these years. *Would he? Would he come back and look for me after all this time? God, what would I do ... ?*

"Hello, my name is Peter Piers. I'm with Grayson Dance Academy. I'm calling about a spot in our program. How are you today, Ms. Morgan?"

Relief and elation swam through me. This was the call I'd been waiting for, praying for. Excitement quickened my pulse. I auditioned for his dance company, the very company that was known throughout the performance arts world as the most esteemed dance company in the country.

"Yes, thank you for getting back to me. I'm good. How are you?"

I was proud that my voice didn't crack with the nervousness I was feeling at that moment.

I remembered how nervous I'd been all season about this program. It was a modern dance fellowship and at the end of it I could possibly have a position with any one of their world-renowned studios. It had been my dream since high school, hell, since the very first time I danced.

"I wanted to speak with you about a position. Are you still interested in a full-time spot with our Modern Dance program?"

I beamed in excitement, practically jumping in the heels I wore.

"Absolutely."

"Good, we're honored to have you. The footage I saw of you was phenomenal. You're a very talented dancer, Ms. Morgan."

His voice was filled with awe and I knew he meant every word. Having the praise of the Peter Piers meant so much.

"Thank you, Mr. Piers," I said, closing my eyes against the sting I felt from the tears that threatened to fall.

"I'll send the orientation paperwork to you as soon as I can. Welcome to the program!"

"Thank you. You won't regret this." It was a vow.

I hung up and jumped when I saw Kel at the door. She beamed with happiness and I knew she heard everything.

Chapter 2

"Did you hear?" I asked.

Kel smiled a proud smile that I'd only seen twice before as she nodded in answer.

She grabbed my shoulders, laughter ringing in my ears as she hugged me tightly. We basked in the moment.

"I knew you'd get it!" Kel squealed, squeezing me once more. She let me go, a wide grin still on her face. She was happy for me, like I knew she would be.

Swinging her arm around me, she whispered in my ear, "He's here, you know. He's talking with Lucas now."

A blush rushed to my cheeks in anticipation. Joy in my news was quickly replaced by the excitement of seeing Gavin again.

"Do I look okay?" I nervously rubbed my hands down my lavender, mid-length dress, and bit my trembling lip. I didn't want to mess up. Kel was right; it was time to live again, not just exist.

Kel's hand reached out and squeezed mine.

"You're perfect, Aria," she said tucking my hair behind my ears before pushing me toward the door. I stepped inside, quickly grabbing another Blue Moon before veering towards some friends.

I greeted several of mine and Kel's old friends, groaning inwardly at how little their superficial ways had changed in the years since high school. As I made the rounds, I grabbed the bowl of pretzels from Lucas, all the while glancing around inconspicuously for Gavin.

"He had to make a call, Aria." Lucas stated with a knowing smile. I must not have been as discreet in my search as I had thought.

"Have you seen that man? The one who was looking for you earlier. You might have to stake your claim before one of us snatches him away!" Sasha squealed, nursing a cranberry martini, while smoothing her hands down her too-short, leather skirt.

Immediately, I imagined kissing him in front of all these people, ruining him for her and all these other girls. But I wasn't not ready for that. For all I knew, he was taken. What was going on with me today? It wasn't like he was the first hot guy I'd laid eyes on the past few years. A few handsome faces had caught my eye, but none had made me contemplate risking my heart again. But, Gavin with those eyes and the chiseled sculpt of his lean chest, and narrow hips … oh my, it put him in a league of his own.

My thoughts were interrupted by a hand on my shoulder, igniting a shock that lit up my skin. I knew he was behind me. I turned, meeting his crooked smile. My heart skipped a beat as I looked up into his eyes, feeling drawn to him. It was almost like gravity only somehow stronger.

"There you are! Do you want to dance?" Sasha chimed in, batting her lashes at him expectantly. Gavin gave me a wink, his stormy blue eyes never wavering from mine. Never had a guy shown interest in me over someone like Sasha. After what felt like a lifetime of gazing into his eyes, I noticed the song changed to a slow beat that I instantly recognized as ColdPlay.

"A dance, Aria?" his soft voice resonating through me in the best way. I placed my hand in his and nodded as he led me onto the floor. He turned to me and wrapped an arm around my waist. Linking his right hand with my left, he swept me to him, leading us in a graceful slow dance. I looked up at him with a smile on my lips.

"You showed up."

Gavin's face spread into a wide, dimple-bearing smile making me feel lighter somehow. Then I realized he dipped me in the circle of his arms, causing my heart to beat impossibly fast. I grabbed his biceps for balance and watched amusement blaze in his eyes. I could feel every line of his muscled body against every one of my soft curves. When his warm-hand pressed at the small of my back, my heart hammered in desire. God, how long had it been since I'd desired or truly wanted a man? Years. I hadn't felt like this since my high school and early college. I couldn't help but think how naive I was back then.

"Of course, I did, Aria."

He pulled me back into his arms, hooking them around my waist as he balanced me again. I linked my hands around his neck, sucking in a tremulous breath at the sight and feel of him.

Wow, he was toned. His body was distracting me and jumbling my thoughts. I tried to sort my thoughts into words.

"Why? I'm sure a guy like you had plans tonight before I gawked at your car and my sister invited you to our party."

Gavin dipped his head, his mouth only inches from mine.

"I did, but seeing you again was more appealing. You look beautiful, by the way," he explained in a deep voice.

"Thank you," I whispered breathlessly.

When he pulled me to his chest, I rested my head against his shoulder. My heart pounded so hard at his nearness. It wasn't fear or nerves that kicked it up a notch. It was desire for him that was wreaking havoc on my system.

All too soon the song ended. Without the song, I no longer had an excuse to stay in his embrace. I lifted my head and gave him my best smile, hoping he couldn't see my disappointment at the song's end. Without the cloak of the song, nervousness began to seep in. I was terrified of opening to this guy I did not even know.

WasI ready to do this?

"I have to go refill the refreshments. Save me a dance, will you?"

Gavin's dark brown hair fell into his eyes as he loosened his arms from around me and nodded. His eyes locked onto mine. I could see uncertainty in their depths.

"Are you okay?" he asked, his hand brushing my cheek. I sucked in a breath. My heart stuttered and stalled at the brief contact of skin against skin.

"I'll be back, I promise."

I just needed to take a breath, get some air to sort myself out.

Reluctantly, he let me go and I tried to calm my heart as I pulled my best friend, Farrah outside with me. She was the only girl I knew that would never sugarcoat things for me. And that was what I needed right now—a dose of reality.

"What the hell, Aria, are you okay?" Farrah asked as she grabbed my hand pulling me down on the steps.

I took a deep breath and turned to her. She had been my rock for as long as I could remember. I didn't know what I'd do without her.

"I don't know what I'm doing, Farrah," I admitted. "I met this guy today and he's, … God, so gorgeous. Like … his eyes captivate me, holding me hostage. And when he was holding me just now, it felt so right, you know? Am I being stupid?"

She grinned and squeezed my hand reassuringly, her knowing eyes seeing right through me.

"Then go with it, Aria. Don't start over thinking it! It has been long enough, don't let HIM take anything more from you."

"He called me beautiful, Farrah. I mean, I don't even know his last name! This is insane. Right? Is this crazy?"

She shook her head and looked into my eyes, her gaze forcing me to be honest.

"Do you like him?" She cocked her head to the side, pinning me with her stare.

"Yes," I whispered cautiously.

"Then stop thinking about it. I can tell he likes you."

I grinned at the thought and narrowed my eyes at her.

"Really? How do you know?"

Her eyes gleamed with a smile as she threw her arm around my shoulder.

"He couldn't keep his eyes off you. He asked us what your favorite band was so he could request it. Trust me, honey, he's into you."

Farrah gave me another hug before she stepped back inside, leaving me on the steps for another minute. With resolve I decided to give this a chance, whatever it was. I knew that if I shied away from him, I would always wonder what could have been.

"Are you ready for that dance?" Gavin's smooth voice spoke from behind me, causing my heart to race just from the sound of it.

"Yeah." I lifted my head and took the hand he offered to help me up. A boyish smile danced on his lips as our fingers linked.

"Can I ask you something?" I asked, my hand still wrapped around his.

He nodded, not letting go of my hand and steadying me further with a hand on my hip.

Trying to organize my jumbled thoughts, I briefly looked up at the sky, glittering with stars. When I looked back into his eyes, I laid it all out there.

"Why do you like me? I mean, maybe I'm misreading this, but I … I like you. But why do you like me?"

He gave me a sexy, lopsided smile that made my knees weak. He cupped my cheek with his hand as I stepped closer to him.

"I just want to get to know you, Aria. You're beautiful and kind. And when you danced, I saw this passion inside you. It was amazing, as if you lived for each step, each movement, and each spin. Aria … you take my breath away." His eyes filled with some unnamed emotion that managed to stir something deep inside me.

I sucked in a breath as my body leaned closer to him. "You saw me dance?"

He nodded, gliding his thumb over my cheek, leaving tingles everywhere he touched.

"Yes, I saw. You were incredible, Aria. It was elegant, yet modern. Every move amazed me. The entire audience was captivated. Then when I saw you in the parking lot, I just had to talk to you. It was like fate or maybe just sheer luck. I don't know what this is, but there's something about you that draws me to you. I want more."

A delicious shiver ran up my spine at his words. And when he placed both hands on my face, tilting it up so my eyes collided with his, I felt like I was drowning and being resuscitated at the same time. "More?"

"Do you have a boyfriend, Aria?" he whispered, caressing my cheek achingly slow.

I gasped, shaking my head. My heart pounded sending the blood rushing through my veins. I felt alive and vibrant, as if my every breath lit my body anew.

"No."

He smiled and leaned his forehead closer to mine. I could feel his breath upon my lips.

"I want to kiss you, Aria," he said, his voice so deep with lust and desire that it took my breath away.

Yes, please.

"Gavin ..." I whispered, my voice breathy in anticipation.

He leaned back, meeting my gaze making it was impossible for me to look away. His blue-gray eyes captured mine and in that moment, I was his.

"Yes or no, Aria?" he whispered, urging me closer to him with a hand at the small of my back.

His other hand cupped my cheek so gently. All I knew was that I wanted to be closer to him. I didn't want to worry about whether this was the right thing for me given my past. I just wanted him closer. NOW. I needed it more than my next gulp of oxygen.

I nodded, feeling his breath on my face. He smelled like mint. His touch felt like a dream as I wrapped my hands around his neck, pressing my chest against his. My fingers tangled in the soft, smooth strands of his unruly hair.

"Yes."

He smiled, one hand moving across my cheek and down to my neck so he could tilt my head up. He wrapped his arm around my waist.

When my eyes met his, the desire I saw blazing there took my breath away.

"Tell me if you want me to stop, beautiful."

I moaned deep in my throat at the sound of that single word on his lips. The sincerity in his voice at that word let him slip past the last of my defenses. Then his mouth closed softly over mine. And all coherent thought left my head. I was aware of only sensations—his heat engulfing me, his soft hair as I tangled my fingers in it, his sensual lips.

I opened my mouth to his. My leg came up of its own volition and wrapped around his waist. I gasped against his ardent kiss. I had never been kissed like this. Savagely, yet gently, all at the same time.

I heard Gavin groan, sending tingles up my spine. One of his hands grasped the bottom of my dress. His tongue slipped slowly into my mouth, licking, tasting, and exploring every corner as I did the same. A moan slipped out when he nipped my bottom lip. A jolt of aching desire shot from my lips to my core. Hot, piercing passion ran through my veins.

God, I couldn't get close enough.

"Aria," he whispered against my lips, pulling back an inch to look in my eyes, searching them for a moment before that gorgeous smile graced his mouth.

He leaned his forehead against mine as we tried to catch our breaths.

"That was … wow," I whispered, smiling excitedly.

His hand brushed my flushed cheek and his mouth ticked up in a smile that lit up his ruggedly handsome face.

"Amazing," he said, pressing his lips to mine once more softly before leaning back and grasping my hand. "Do you want to dance?"

I grinned and nodded as he led me back inside. My heart beat fast and erratically in my chest. We walked back to the almost empty dance floor. He swept me around gracefully to the soft Shania Twain melody. Then he turned me around so that my back was pressed to his lean chest. His arms wrapped around my hips, swaying us easily to the beat.

I closed my eyes, just enjoying the feel of his gentle touch. And I knew, from that moment on I'd be completely and totally his.

Three songs later, Gavin turned me to him and tucked a curl behind my ear. His finger grazed my cheek making my breath hitch.

The things I felt both scared and excited me.

"Take a walk with me?" he asked.

"Of course. Let me go change into something more fitting for walking and let Kel know. You want to meet me outside?"

He dipped his head and pressed a kiss to my lips, trailing a finger across my chin before pulling back to look in my eyes.

"Sure, take your time."

I smiled and pecked his lips once more before stepping back. I spotted Kel talking with Elliot, our cousin, over by the beer coolers.

"Hey! Going somewhere?"

I nodded, unable to keep the smile off my face. I hugged her, waving to Elliott.

"I'm happy for you, Ari. You deserve some happiness," she whispered before leaning back to kiss my cheek.

"We're just going to take a walk. I'll be back later for cleanup. Okay?"

She nodded. I beamed at her, hoping that she was right about opening myself up to love again.

I found Gavin leaning against the door frame as I stepped outside. Breathing in the cool Chicago air, I couldn't keep a smile from gracing my lips as I stared at him for a moment without his knowledge.

"Ready?"

He looked up from his phone and gave me a heart-stopping smile when he realized I was staring unabashedly at him. Seeing him with his phone made me think that I might be pulling him away from something important. Doubt clouded my thoughts as I stepped toward him.

"I hope I'm not pulling you away from anything or …"

He gazed down at me, biting his lower lip to hide a smile.

"Do you really think I would've kissed you if I had anyone waiting on me?"

I let out the breath I'd been holding, hearing the sincerity in his voice. He placed his hands on my face and pressed a soft kiss to my forehead.

"Sorry," I whispered, my hands on his chest.

I rested my head on his shoulder. It felt so natural, as if I'd known him much longer than a few hours.

"No worries, we hardly know each other. Let's take a walk. There's a hiking trail not far from here."

I nodded as he interlaced our fingers. We headed down the road leading to Marley's Cove, a hiking trail I had frequented a lot as a child.

My feet brushed against the dirt road, the sound filled the air between us. I looked up to see Gavin gazing down at me, running a hand through his messy brown hair.

Our hands brushed against one another as we approached the hill leading to my favorite spot in the city. It was a calm little spot just by the large hill, nestled between two old oak trees. We turned toward where the cove lay and Gavin tugged my hand gently. We carefully stepped over the stream. Minutes later, we settled in under the branches of the oaks.

Gavin sat on a boulder while I perched against the tree trunk a few feet away. I was unable to look away from him. I memorized the messy brown hair that fell over his eyes, the intensity in his eyes. I couldn't stop looking at him.

"Penny for your thoughts?" he asked.

"I was just thinking that I'd like to know more about you," I said.

He smiled and reached out his hand to me. I stood and stepped to take his hand. He scooted backwards and pulled me up on the rock with him. I settled in between his legs, pressing my back to his chest. His large hand linked with mine across my thigh.

"Ask me anything you want, Aria," he murmured, pulling me closer to him.

I took a deep breath, thinking of all the things I wanted to know about him. I started with an easy one.

"Why do you call me beautiful?"

I felt his smile against my neck as he sucked in a breath.

"You're beautiful to me, Aria. I call you that because it's how I see you."

I couldn't help the stutter of my heart and the wide smile on my lips as I placed my arms on top of his arms, reveling in the feel of his skin against mine.

"My turn," he whispered. He placed a kiss on my neck, moving his lips in a circular motion as he spoke against my skin.

"When did you start dancing?" he asked, his deep voice in my ear.

"When I began preschool, my mom enrolled me in a toddler dance academy. My love for it grew from there."

"Is your mom a dancer?" he asked as his hands skated down my arms, causing goose bumps.

I giggled and pressed closer to him. Being in his arms felt better than I could have imagined.

"That's two questions, but no, she isn't. She's a model and travels a lot."

The last thing I wanted to think about was my absentee mother, but he asked and I wanted Gavin to know me.

"Did I upset you?" he asked, turning me so that I faced him.

I hastily shook my head, laying it against his shoulder. His hand stroked comfortingly up and down my back.

"No. And I actually haven't talked to her in a long time."

Deftly, Gavin lifted my face with a gentle finger under my chin and peered into my eyes.

"I'm sorry, Aria."

My heart skipped a beat at his heartfelt words as I leaned my face into his touch.

"What about your parents?"

He gazed down at me, smiling softly.

"My mom and I have always been close. She's the glue that's always kept our family together. My dad, well, he passed away five years ago. It was cardiac arrest."

I gasped, my hand instinctively going to the locket resting against my chest. The pain of losing someone important, so vital to you, never healed completely. My chest tightened at the thought of his pain. Leaning forward, I kissed his neck urgently, hating the thought of him losing his dad. He rubbed his hand up my back.

"I'm so sorry, Gavin. I can't imagine ..."

He pressed his lips to my temple, silencing me. His arm tightened around me.

"It's okay. I miss him. We all do, but he had a great life and I have to take some comfort in that."

He leaned back, a look of reassurance in his eyes.

I couldn't imagine losing one of my parents so tragically, though I'd felt the pain of sudden loss before.

Jeremy ...

As if he read my mind, Gavin pressed closer to me, giving me his warmth as a breeze blew.

"Do you have any brothers? Sisters?" he asked, his eyes focused on mine.

"Yes, Kel's my sister. She's older by three years. And um ..." My voice trailed off as I wondered if I should tell him about Jeremy. Though it had been years, each time I had to speak of my loss the wound ripped open again. I was unsure if I could get the words out without having my emotions get the best of me.

When I cast my eyes downward he tilted my face back up and searched my face. Worry stretched over his face.

"Tell me," he whispered, holding me close, giving me strength.

"My brother Jeremy. He was four years older than me and the best brother I could have asked for. He was my rock."

Gavin ran a hand over my cheek, never taking his eyes off mine.

"Was?" Gavin's eyes filled with concern as he regarded me.

"Jeremy and I were on our way home when a semi sped through a red light and crashed into his side of the car. They ... um ... couldn't save him. He died from the blood loss."

My voice broke twice. A tear fell to my cheek as I closed my eyes, bracing myself for Gavin to make an excuse to leave. One day with me and I was already a mess. The tightness in my chest felt as if my heart was being squeezed by a fist. My worst pain being voiced made me feel naked and exposed in front of him.

Would he pull away now? Would it be too much, too soon for him to deal with?

Would he see a damaged, unlovable girl in front of him or would he really and truly see me?

Gavin's thumb caught a tear against my chin and his lips pressed against my forehead so very lightly. A feeling of relief came over me when he squeezed me. I buried my face in his neck, letting myself feel the pain for the moment.

"I didn't mean to tell you all that. I'd understand if you walked away right now. I know, I'm a mess," I whispered, not daring to look into his eyes for fear of what I'd see there. Pity, regret, sadness, concern, maybe panic. I couldn't bear that so I just pressed closer to him as he whispered in my ear.

"You're not a mess; you're so goddamn strong. I can see how hard it is for you to talk about him. I'm so sorry that you had to endure that. How long ago?"

I gazed up at him then and let out a breath as I saw fierce devotion in his face, not pity.

"May third will be the seventh anniversary of his death. I'm okay though. He's in a better place now, and I have to believe that." He nodded and pulled me back to his chest, stroking my back soothingly. It felt so good that my eyes drifted close. After a moment, Gavin pressed a kiss to my forehead.

"I have a sister, Callie. She is why I was at the studio and was able to see you dance. She was there to watch a friend."

I smiled and leaned back to look at him.

"Yeah? How old is she?"

His eyes filled with joy when he talked about her, his mouth turning up into a smile.

"Sixteen years old as of April twelfth. She's a dancer, like you. Does some gymnastics, too. She's my mom's pride and joy, of course."

I grinned and swept locks of brown hair off his face, my touch lingering.

"What do you do for work, Gavin?" My voice teased, but I genuinely wanted to know.

He hesitated, gauging my reaction before he opened his mouth.

"My dad passed Thomas Corporations down to me, the family company. He'd been priming me for it since I was fifteen years old. I own and operate it now, along with my mom."

My breath caught. I struggled to imagine how much money he must make, owning a growing computer technology corporation like that. Mom always told me to follow the men with gold, but it didn't make me want him any less or any more. It was just a surprise.

"Wow. I mean I figured you had a high-end job to afford your Jaguar, but I didn't expect that. What do you do? It's computer technology, right?"

He nodded looking into my eyes.

"We try to innovate mobile and computer technologies for modern-day society. After Windows 8, our system was in almost every PC in America."

I gave him a smile, assuring him that I was only curious about his work and not trying to pry.

"Windows 8?"

"Yeah, once we put together the idea, software, and patent for it, we sold it for quite a lot to Microsoft. It took them a while to give us a viable offer, though now we have access to almost any software or technology information program we'd ever need. Trust me; it was well worth the wait."

My eyes lit up hearing him talk about something he was very passionate about. I leaned in to him to give him a quick kiss on the lips. He grasped the back of my neck to deepen it causing me to lose my breath. His touch lingered along my oversensitive skin and I leaned into it.

"What was that for?" he whispered as he pressed a kiss to my temple and ran a hand through my hair.

"Just wanted to let you know that you didn't scare me off."

He smiled that shy smile at me, showing off how handsome his features were.

"Did you read my mind?"

"No, but I saw it in your eyes."

I bit my lip as he pulled me to him and began kissing my neck, licking as he went. I felt heat in my core and wetness between my legs as my arousal grew.

"It's getting dark. I probably should get back … " I whispered breathlessly as he groaned against my skin.

He didn't seem to want to let me go yet.

"I don't want to push you but … "

Something in his voice urged me to look into his eyes and I saw a vulnerability there.

"I want to see you again, beautiful. Your sister told me that you might be a little gun-shy concerning a relationship because of something in your past … "

I gasped, feeling a little betrayed that Kel spoke with him about that. But I did want to see him again. I wanted to be near him, just like this.

"But honestly, Aria, I want to be with you. You take my breath away; I don't think I could stay away, not unless it's what you wanted."

I sucked in a breath, letting go of my fears. I struggled to find words.

"Gavin, I like you. I think anyone else would have been running for the hills by now, but you're still here. And you take my breath away, too. The way I feel about you, it's so new to me and, honestly, it scares the crap out of me. I mean I've spent the last five years being afraid to get too close to anyone for fear of being hurt. But with you, I want to take that chance. I want to be with you, Gavin."

I held my breath trying to read his expression. Instantly his eyes light up with relief. His hands clutched my face, banishing the shivers on my skin as I laid my heart out to this man I'd only known for a day.

His face stretched into a crooked smile, and his lips collided urgently with mine. Our mouths moved together in perfect unison and when his tongue licked into my mouth, I moaned into his mouth. He softened the kiss, his lips slowly and reverently pressing to mine as if he was memorizing the feel of me. He just kissed me, groaning deep in his throat. He pulled away, showering little kisses on my parted lips, my cheeks, and then my temple.

My, oh my.

Need zipped through my body. His kisses awakened a yearning deep inside. But I was still so fearful of being hurt again. I had to slow this down.

"Oh, beautiful. I like you too," he whispered, leaning his forehead against mine, both of us gasping for breath.

I smiled, not trying to hide the jubilant giggle that parted my lips.

"Gavin, I think we should take this slow, get to know each other and spend time together. There's no rush, right?"

He leaned back and nodded, kissing me on the nose. His eyes filled with want when he peered down at me.

"No rush, okay? Can I take you out sometime this week?"

I blushed and nodded eagerly. I was thankful that he was willing to go slow. I wanted, no, I needed to see him again.

"I will call you tomorrow and we can figure out dinner for later this week."

I kissed the side of his mouth and heard the catch in his breathing. "I'd love to."

He stood, reaching his hands out to help me up. He wrapped his arm around my shoulder, holding me close to him as we strolled back to my apartment.

Once we reached the porch, I looked at him and smiled, feeling more at peace knowing I'd see him soon.

Amanda Kaitlyn

"So, I need your number?" he asked, his voice reverberating with that sexy drawl that made my heart stutter.

I laughed a little, pulling out my phone as I leaned back into his chest.

"God, I love the sound of your laugh," he whispered, running his hands up my arms for warmth against the evening chill.

"Doesn't this feel a little backwards? I give you my number after we make out like teenagers."

His husky laugh made my voice all breathy and I turned to him, giving him my phone. He handed me his. I programmed my number and handed it back to him.

"It does, huh? Well, this way I don't have to wait three days to call you for a date."

I giggled, gazing up at him. He traced his hand over my cheek, lighting my skin up in flames.

"Would you have been able to wait three days?"

He laughed, shaking his head and grasping my hand. He towed me to the door.

"No way, maybe one, but not three, beautiful."

I got out my keys and unlocked the door before turning back to him.

"Come here, Gavin," I whispered, my voice raspy with desire. He stepped up to me, wrapping his arms around the small of my back and lifting me off my feet in a whoosh. I giggled happily when he crushed his lips against mine. His kiss was sweet, slow, and lazy as his tongue invaded my mouth and his lips adored me. When he pulled away, once again I was breathless.

"Talk tomorrow," he whispered, lifting our joined hands to his mouth and pressing his lips to my palm before stepping back.

I smiled, my lips still tingling from the kiss. I closed the door behind me and sighed while I put down my keys. I headed to the fridge for something to eat. My mind was still reeling from all that had happened, but I was happy.

Chapter 3

As I made my way into the kitchen the following night I saw my dad hugging my sister. I squealed and a huge smile spread on my face because I hadn't seen him in weeks. Excitement bubbled up inside me when he turned to see me.

"Pumpkin, come here," Dad said, pulling away from my sister. I ran into his arms, happy to see him. He lifted me off my feet and kissed my cheek.

"When did you get here?" I asked, pulling back to look at him. I laughed with joy at seeing him. My eyes cataloged the changes since I saw him last. His beard was coming back. He had some new lines around his eyes and mouth, but his deep amber eyes, were as bright as ever.

"You look happy, Aria," he said, twirling me in a circle like always.

"Dad, you seriously need to shave!" I laughed through the words.

He threw his head back and laughed. He made his way to the table where Kel placed three plates of mac and cheese. My sister loved to cook. It was a godsend she did because no one else in our family could make a decent meal, other than Mom. Kaelyn was amazing in the kitchen, though.

"I'll take it under advisement, pumpkin," Dad winked at me.

Turning to my sister, he said, "This is great, Kel. Thank you."

I sat down next to Dad. Silence filled the space as we dug into our dinner.

"Oh, my God, this is amazing, Kel!" I gushed, enjoying her home-made food.

After dinner, we went into the living room and watched reruns of *Full House*. Dad told us all about his trip. He had gone down to Boston to look in on the garage he owned just outside of the city. He had been gone a few weeks and it felt so good to have him home.

After a while my sister went to bed, but I stayed up and decided to tell him about Gavin. I just had to figure out how to broach the subject. I glanced at my phone, hoping for a text. He hadn't called yet.

"You okay, pumpkin?"

He reached for my hand and squeezed it.

I looked up from my phone, and gave him a smile.

"Yeah. I met someone yesterday, Dad."

He grinned wide, kissing me on my forehead. There was caution and relief in his eyes. He had been worried about me. He wanted me to be happy.

"Yeah? Kel may have mentioned that. You like him?"

"Yeah, so much. I didn't think it was possible for me to open up to a guy ever again after what happened with Bryce, but I really like him."

He pulled me into a hug, rubbing my back. I took in a deep comforting breath. He smelled like gasoline and cigarettes, like always. My dad had worked in his auto repair garage since I was a little girl. The smell of it always lingered on him and smelled like home to me.

"I'm happy for you, pumpkin. Just take it slow, enjoy the chase. There's no rush, Aria. You deserve a guy who treats you right, who treasures you, like I treasured your mom while we were together."

Tears filled in my eyes. I remembered growing up and seeing how much they loved each other. My mom stopped modeling when Jeremy was born, but she still did occasional shoots for local magazines and spreads. She loved her job, loved modeling. My dad always supported her dream. He stayed home with the three of us on the nights she had to work when we were young.

We were a happy family, but everything went up in flames after the accident. Nothing was ever the same. My mom just broke, emotionally and physically. I knew she loved my dad with her whole heart, but after burying her child, her heart wasn't whole anymore. She just couldn't take the never-ending pain of losing her son. She ran from the support of our family, from what happened, from everything. I'll never forget watching my dad's heart break when she left us.

I rested my head against his chest. I needed this reassurance from my dad about starting something new with Gavin.

"Do you miss her, Daddy?" I asked, my voice clogged with tears.

He sighed and nodded, his eyes filled with a trace of sadness. "Every day pumpkin, but she made her choice. And no matter how much it hurt me and you girls, we have to accept that."

His thumbs wiped my tears away and he kissed my forehead. I'd be lost without him. My dad's strength put us back together after we broke apart. But I knew he'd never truly gotten over my mother. She was his one true love. When she left a piece of Dad's heart went with her.

I rested my head on his shoulder again, not wanting to think about Mom.

"Can we talk about something else?"

"Sure, pumpkin. What's mystery man's name?"

I lifted my head, narrowing my eyes at him. I loved my dad, but ever since high school, he had run background checks on every one of my boyfriends or any boy I had an interest in. It was like he was trying to protect me before I got hurt. I think he felt guilty for what I endured at Bryce's hands. Even with his protectiveness and caution, he wasn't able to prevent me from being hurt.

But none of us saw the real Bryce, we only saw the handsome, popular guy from school. Underneath it all, Bryce was a monster. I shuddered, thinking of his face, but Dad kissed my forehead for comfort as if he read where my mind had wandered.

"Just in case, Aria. It would put my mind at ease. After what happened with Bryce, I can't fathom the idea of you getting hurt again. I couldn't bear it, pumpkin."

I exhaled, remembering my dad's broken face in my hospital room years ago, when I came to after the last and most damaging assault I endured at Bryce's hands.

"Gavin Thomas."

He raised his eyebrows skeptically at me.

"You mean the billionaire, Thomas Corporations' CEO?"

I gasped, shocked that my dad knew who he was.

Oh, crap.

"Yeah, I think he said something like that."

My dad threw his head back laughing and then smiled knowingly.

"Sweetie, do you realize how successful that man is? He has taken over a very successful software company AND helped increase the value of their stocks. He is never portrayed negatively in the news. I think you have chosen a nice man to capture your attention. You might not believe it, but your mom would be really happy for you too."

I inwardly cringed, not wanting to think about how much money he had or what a "catch" my mom would say he is.

"Don't tell her, please, Dad. I just met him. She would only care that her daughter found someone successful. And that doesn't matter to me. I only care that he makes me feel treasured and beautiful and … alive" I whispered, looking anxiously up at him.

I didn't want my mom to sully the wonderful thing I was just finding with her shallow expectations.

He nodded after a moment, giving my shoulder a squeeze.

"I won't. I promise. Just be careful with him. I'll let you know what I find out."

He got up and headed to the fridge, grabbing a water. He picked up his duffel bag off the edge of the couch. He crouched down and hugged me tightly, kissing my forehead.

"Love you, Daddy," I whispered into his neck before he leaned back and smiled warmly.

"Love you more, pumpkin."

After a nice hot shower, I put on a pair of gray yoga pants and a tour tee of The Band Perry. I crawled under the covers, grabbing the remote and flicking through channels until I found a police procedural that I liked.

My mind was racing with curiosity and worry about what Dad could find on Gavin. I was desperate to build something with this man who stole my breath and awakened something I thought long dead inside me. But I didn't trust myself anymore. Just one more thing Bryce forcibly took from me. I was afraid that I wouldn't see another monster lurking in the shadows until it was ready to devour me.

I glanced over and saw my Mac laptop screen flash with a new email. I reached over and pulled it onto my lap. I opened it up and after seeing it was just a reminder of my hair appointment next week, I clicked out of it and opened a new tab in the browser. I pulled up Google Search and with only a small amount of hesitation, typed in "Gavin Thomas."

I knew I should stop myself, but in all honesty, I needed to know what I was getting myself into by pursuing a relationship with him.

When the results came up across the search engine, I slowly scrolled down. There was a picture of Gavin and a blond, skinny woman with brown eyes. His hair was slicked back. He looked dashing in a gray Paul Smith, three-piece suit tailored perfectly to hug his lean chest, arms, and toned thighs, and a dark green tie. I turned my attention to the woman on his arm. She wore a silver dress showing off her prominent chest and long legs. He had to be only twenty in this photo and I wondered vaguely how old he was now because he looked so young in this picture. His arm was wrapped comfortably around her shoulder and she was smiling brightly up at him. I felt a little jealous that he had been so happy with this girl.

Oh, my God! What if he still loved her?

The caption read:

"Young prodigy, Gavin H. Thomas left at the altar by his high-end, fashion model fiancé of two years, Jasmine Elliot."

The date underneath read almost four years ago.

Oh, no.

I felt both relief and sadness as I read more. Then it dawned on me. Jasmine, his Jaguar, this had to be the woman who had broken his heart. I shook my head as I moved down the search page. There was a lot about his business.

"Billionaire, Gavin Thomas takes the technology world by storm!"

And …

"Thomas spotted with younger sister Callie Joy at Raymond's in North End, Chicago."

I scrolled through the list of articles. It seemed that he was an interesting subject for the media.

Then I saw something else that made my heart hurt. It stuttered while I read on.

"Son, Gavin Henry Thomas, devastated after tragedy strikes the Thomas family. At the young age of twenty-three years old, he finds father, James Thomas, suffering from cardiac arrest. He died later that night, leaving Thomas Corporations to his only son, G. H. Thomas."

I closed my laptop, feeling sad for a young Gavin, lost after his father's death. He must have felt so alone, having to be strong for his mother and sister while grieving his father's death. Top that with all with the added responsibility of caring for the legacy his father had created in the software world.

I watched television and had almost fallen asleep when my phone finally vibrated with a text. I smiled, my sadness vanishing when I opened the message and saw it was from Gavin.

You still up, beautiful? I had a very interesting day yesterday with this gorgeous ballet dancer.

I giggled, warmth erasing the shivers across my skin. I texted him back as I leaned against my pillows.

Really? Do I know this dancer? She sounds wonderful.

I waited, switching off my television and pulling the red covers over me as I laid down. My eyes were getting heavy as I awaited his reply.

I think you might. She's your twin.

Hmm, I don't have a twin, Gavin. Could she possibly be me?

He only took a minute to answer this time.

She's definitely you. How was your day?

Good, spent some time with my dad. He just got back into town today. Hard to text when I'm this tired. Can I call you?

Not even thirty seconds later my phone rang loudly in my hand. I smiled, feeling giddy as I answered.

"Hello?" I murmured, biting my bottom lip nervously.

"Hey, beautiful."

My heart raced at the sound of his husky voice.

"How was your day?"

He laughed, sending tingles over my body.

"Busy. That's why I didn't call earlier. I'm actually just driving home from work. I didn't wake you, did I?"

"No, I'm just falling asleep now. Isn't it a little late to be ending your day?"

He chuckled again. I recognized the sound of a car engine in the background.

"It is, but I had a crazy day. Did I mention the dancer I met yesterday and thoughts of her distracted me all day today?"

My heart sped up and I smiled widely, even if he couldn't see me.

"I think you did. I actually told my dad about you," I said, feeling a little unsure of how he'd react.

"Yeah?"

"Yeah, he said you're a billionaire CEO with high ambitions."

"That's true. Does my job bother you at all?"

I was surprised by his question, but I took a breath and answered honestly.

"I'm not sure. It surprised me when you told me what you do for a living, but I already liked you at that point. So, for me, it doesn't really change anything between us. If I knew before I spent any time with you, I would have been too intimidated to talk to you. But you are just a normal man who happens to run a highly successful company."

I could almost hear his smile at the other end of the line.

"Happy to hear that. How about dinner tomorrow night?"

"That sounds perfect."

"You have any preferences?"

I thought for a moment, but knew it wouldn't matter to me where we ate as long as I was with Gavin.

"No, I just want to spend time with you."

"Same here."

Then I yawned loudly and blushed embarrassment.

"Get some rest, Aria. I'll text you tomorrow."

I smiled, surprised by his thoughtfulness.

"Yeah?" I asked.

"Yeah. Goodnight."

I giggled and snuggled deeper into my pillow.

"Night, Gavin."

I hung up, placing my phone on the charger face up so I'd hear the alarm at ten for my studio session in the morning. Soon I closed my eyes, hoping for sweet dreams.

Chapter 4

"Mine, Ari," he whispered, sending terrible shivers down my skin as I writhed against his hold. I found myself trapped against his heavy, unyielding body.

His cold, hard eyes stared down at me. He grasped the edge of my panties and roughly pulled them down my legs as I sobbed. I felt helpless against his weight and greedy hands.

"Please, stop. Stop, Bryce ... you're hurting me ... no!" I whimpered and screamed fearfully as he held me down.

He showed no mercy as I clutched the bed covers and sobs racked my body. The pain was relentless as I feel his lips press hard against mine. I couldn't get away. It hurt so much!

"No! Get off me ... It hurts!!" I squirmed and yelled, crying out for help as he slapped me hard across my cheek. I whimpered in pain. I yearned for it to stop, but no matter how I struggled and protested, I couldn't keep him from viciously taking what I used to give in love so freely.

He chuckled then, his hands roughening as he took me again. I screamed against his movements andI felt my sex spasm painfully against his punishment. I had no way of getting him off me with his death grip on both my hands.

"Shut up, bitch."

"Stop!! Please ... no!" I began to beg.

Then I heard a faraway voice filled with panic and fear.

"Aria! Christ, please open your eyes, beautiful."

My eyes flew open, my hands grasping onto the sheets as the terror of my nightmare ran through my veins. My body trembled, aftershocks from the horror of the memories assaulting me.

God, I couldn't breathe.

A sob escaped me, then another as tears fell down my cheeks. Even with my eyes open, all I remembered was his face and the pain.

Oh, God, the pain.

I couldn't seem to stop shaking. I had been having these nightmares on and off since the attack. They were different sometimes, yet still the same. In all of them I was under him, his abhorrent scent filling my lungs. They weren't the same as my memory of the attack but they were just as painful. I relived the attack of that day in a dozen different places and ways and I hated them and him, to my core. My skin crawled as I recalled the terror of my dream as my body slowly calmed itself.

"Aria! Are you okay?"

I looked up through my tears and saw Gavin sitting on the edge of my bed. His ruggedly handsome face was etched with panic. He gazed down into my eyes, his own storming with concern causing the blue gray color to darken. Gavin's large, warm hand held mine tightly, anchoring me.

I shook my head no. The sobs took over my body, my face fell into my hands. My body shook with loud sobs coming from my chest. I couldn't stop them. The agony swallowed me whole.

"Beautiful," he said, and without another word, he pulled me to his chest, lifting me as he sat against the headboard.

He wrapped his arms tightly around my shuddering body. He settled me in his lap. I buried my face in his neck, clutching his shoulders for support. I let my emotions take over my body, feeling the pain and terror and then the relief of being held.

"I can't ... " I stuttered, trying to talk through my tears.

His hand ran up and down my back, banishing the cold, dirty feeling that lingered on my skin from the dream.

"Shh, baby, I'm here. Just breathe," he whispered, kissing my forehead and tucking me closer to him.

I took a breath, then slowly let it out.

"Again, Aria," he continued to whisper, watching me while I took another full breath and released it.

I felt myself calm down from his warmth and intoxicating scent, a mixture of mint something uniquely Gavin. He placed his palms on my cheeks, tilting my face up so his eyes met mine. He gasped at my distressed state. I saw his forehead crease with worry even as he wiped my tears away with his thumbs and showered my face with soft kisses.

"How? When did you get here?" I whispered in confusion.

I found comfort in his unwavering eyes and gentle touch on my lower back as he hugged me slightly. He brought one of his hands up to rest on my cheek. His touch was so light it was almost as if I imagined it.

"I was on my way to work and I wanted to bring you flowers to surprise you. When I got here, your sister let me in to give them to you. I found you lost in a nightmare. You looked so scared, so helpless, I had to wake you. I can't stand to see you like this, hurt and afraid, Aria. Are you okay? Please be honest with me."

I couldn't seem to form words so I rested my forehead against his. I took a deep breath to steady myself.

I'm okay, it was just a dream. I'm okay.

"I'm okay. It was horrible, but I'm okay," I finally whispered.

Gavin exhaled, not letting go of me. He traced a pattern across my thigh, calming me.

"What do you need, baby?"

I got butterflies despite my nightmare at the sound of him calling me that. I might even like it better than beautiful.

"I don't know, Gavin. I can't fall back asleep after that. Can you just hold me for a while?"

He leaned back, smiling warmly at me. My chest felt a bit lighter when he did that.

"That I can do."

His arms enfolded me, his hands gliding up my back to soothe me. Pressing my face to his chest, I focused on breathing in and out. God, he felt so good.

"Do you remember your nightmare?"

I lifted my face from the solace of his embrace as he pressed soft kisses to my forehead and temple. His warmth, deep voice and touch were so comforting. And even though I was sure I wouldn't see him again after this, I couldn't bring myself to let him go just yet.

"I don't think I can talk about it right now, Gavin. I'm sorry, I just can't."

He gazed down at me and nodded with understanding in his gaze.

My face flushed in shame and I realized what he must think of me.

"You must think I'm a basket case. I'm so sorry. I didn't mean to break down on you like this."

He ran his fingers through my hair soothingly, and despite my embarrassment, I relaxed into his chest.

"Don't think that, beautiful. I like you. I want to be with you."

"Morning!" I heard Kel say as she sprinted down the stairs with Lucas close behind her. I sat on a stool at the kitchen island. Gavin looked ruggedly sexy, standing next to me, drinking a cup of black coffee.

"Hey, sis. You remember Gavin, don't you?" She gave me a knowing smile as she walked up to hug me. Lucas stepped up to Gavin and shook his hand.

"Of course, it's great to see you again. Would you like an omelet?"

She began to get out ham, eggs, American cheese and milk, along with a pan and four plates.

"I'd love one, thank you," Gavin said in a, smooth voice.

I still couldn't believe that he stopped by to bring me flowers. We watched the news and talked about our favorite movies and music. It felt so natural to be with him. There was no pressure.

His phone rang. He leaned close to me causing my eyes to dart up to meet his. His smile made me weak in the knees.

"I have to take this. Do you mind if I step outside for a minute?"

I shook my head and pulled his mouth down to mine. He smiled just a little bigger.

I pressed my lips against his again in a slow and tender kiss. He groaned, tucking my hair behind my ear before he pulled away.

"No need to rush; I feel like I'm taking too much of your time anyway, Gavin. I know you were on your way to work when you stopped by."

Gavin shook his head and leaned forward to press a soft kiss to my cheek.

"I'm glad I stopped by to see you and that I could be here for you."

I smiled, satisfied with his answer as he stepped away and headed toward the door with his phone pressed to his ear.

"You guys are so cute, honey. What happened this morning at the crack of dawn?" Kel asked, sitting next to me while the pan heated on the stove.

"He brought me flowers on his way to work, he held me, and we talked. It was the best."

She smiled approvingly and handed me a glass of orange juice.

"That's really great, Aria. Did you guys … ?" Immediately, I knew where she was going. I jumped forward and put a hand over her mouth, hastily shaking my head.

"No! No, not yet. We just talked and kissed and watched TV, had coffee. He's so much more than I could have imagined. I mean, he listens, and I think he really gets me. Which is crazy because I've only known him, what? A couple of days?"

She just shook her head and went to start the omelets.

"I knew Luke here three hours and I knew he was different. There isn't a rule saying you need to know everything about a guy to start falling for him."

Lucas looked up from his tablet and narrowed his eyes at Kel.

"You're such a liar, sweetheart. You were a goner from the moment you laid your eyes on me."

He gave me a wink as my sister turned around, setting the burner on low before walking over to Lucas. She sat in his lap and smacked his arm.

"You're so full of yourself!"

Nuzzling her face into his neck, she smiled up at him.

He grinned wider, chuckling as he kissed her on the head.

"You know you love me, sweetheart."

"I do, smart ass."

As they began to kiss I headed over to the door just as Gavin came in. His brow was creased with worry as he pushed his cell phone back into his pocket.

"Everything okay?" I asked, walking into his arms as he kissed my cheek.

"Just a problem that I need to fix. We've been trying to merge with Alcatraz Industries for the last quarter and it just fell through. I'm sorry, baby, but I have to head into the office for a few hours."

I could see the stress on his face and I nodded hastily, not wanting him to feel bad for leaving.

"It's all good, Gavin. Thank you for staying with me this morning. You didn't have to, though. You're late for work."

He grabbed my hand in his and lifted it to his lips, kissing my palm.

"I loved spending time with you, Aria. And I'm the boss, so I'm not late."

I doubted that was true, but I smiled and wrapped my arms around his shoulders. He kissed my forehead and I found my eyes closing contentedly.

"Dinner tonight?" I whispered. Gavin pulled away and smiled, nodding his head.

"Absolutely."

Chapter 5

As I slipped into my dance shoes, my cell rang. I skipped over, almost falling as I reached for it. I saw Gavin's name on the screen and smiled. It hardly seemed a week had passed since the morning he rescued me from that horrible dream. We'd gone out to lunch almost every day, growing closer with each shared moment.

I found so many big and small things I liked about him, his laugh when I tried to impersonate my family members and friends when I told stories, his passion for his father's work, his fierceness when he talked about his sister, Callie. I learned he only drinks when he was with people he trusted. Though it was a lot to take in, Gavin was much more than a billionaire or a CEO or even the owner of a very large, very reputable, technology development company.

He was more.

"Hi."

Gavin's husky laugh made my heart beat faster in my chest. I loved the sound of it in my ears.

"What are you up to, beautiful?"

"Just stretching before my dance session with Eli."

He was silent for a moment, making me wonder what he was thinking about.

"Eli?" His voice hardened just a bit.

I didn't understand why.

"Yeah, he's my dance coach, Gavin."

"How long have you been working with him?"

I gnawed at the inside of my cheek, unsure why he seemed upset.

"A few years. You're not jealous, are you?"

"No. I mean, not necessarily. Aria, I think we need to talk."

My heart just about stopped at those words and I dropped my bag on my foot.

"Shit! Shit!" I cried out, forgetting that he was still on the phone.

"Aria, are you okay?" he asked, as I cradled my foot like a baby.

"Um, yeah, I'm fine. Can we talk later? I have to go."

"Sure. I'll see you tonight?" His voice was still filled with concern.

"Of course." I hung up and decided to walk off the pain while I searched for Eli.

What was going on with Gavin?

God, what if he changed his mind about us?

I tried to work off my anxiousness by doing my normal exercises with Eli. After 25 minutes, I began to wind down from my worries.

"Great job, Aria. Perfect. Now once more," Eli said over the music.

I took a deep breath, balancing on my feet before I closed my eyes, finding my center and beginning again.

This time I took it slow, going through each move on pace with the violins overhead.

When I finished my last step, I opened my eyes and sank to my knees. I took a swig of my water.

"You did great, Aria. You feeling okay?"

I nodded, letting Eli pull me up. I gave him a smile and a side hug before making my way to where I left my bag and cowboy boots.

"See you next week?" Eli called from the back of the gym, ducking his head under a beam.

"Sure thing! Have a good one!" I called back, waving as I moved into the locker room to change out of my leotard and ballet flats. I put my dance gear in my bag. Then I pulled on my fleece jacket and boots along over a pair of dark wash jeans and a light blue blouse.

I got into my car, and realized how much I missed Gavin. As I pulled up at home, Sarah Bareilles,' "Brave" rang from my phone. Farrah was calling. I grabbed my cell off the dashboard.

"Hey, Farrah."

"Oh, my God!! I talked to Kel. Tell me everything!!!"

I giggled at my friend's excitement. Pulling my ballet bag over one shoulder, I headed up the stairs of my apartment building.

"Shit, I wanted to tell you myself!" Damn that sister of mine …

"I know, but I have to know now."

"OK." We hadn't spoken all week and I was surprised it had taken her this long to find out about Gavin and me. The next words she spoke, made me grateful I hadn't put her on speaker as I walked into my apartment.

"Okay, so sex scale with 10 being the best and 1 being the worst, how was he?"

I burst out laughing, earning a surprised glance from Kel as I stepped through the door of our apartment. Her glare followed me as I sat on the sectional. I tried and failed to give her the evil eye.

"Seriously! I've only known him a week! I haven't slept with him, you slut!"

She laughed hard and I could hear Jaden, her boyfriend, laughing, too.

"Oh, my God, I'm on speaker?" The blood rushed to my face.

"Well, duh! He's laughing his pretty little ass off!" She was still laughing too.

Ugh, how embarrassing. My cheeks flamed.

"Hanging up now, bye!" I ended the call.

Having heard my side, Kel, giggled and put down her book.

"You told Farrah?" I asked.

She laughed again, giving me a squeeze.

"Yup!" She laughed her ass off, the smart ass.

I was so ready to have another dinner date with Gavin. Though we had met for lunch several times, having dinner together felt more date-like. By 6:10, I had showered, blow-dried my hair, and braided it so it was out of my eyes. I dressed in a light green dress, stopping just above my knees. I looked in the mirror and sucked in a breath. I slipped on a pair of brown flats and my silver locket. It was a pendant with an emerald in the center. It was a birthday present from my dad. He gave it to me after Jeremy's funeral almost seven years ago. Now the emerald represented my birth and the month I lost my rock. But I knew Jeremy would be happy for me as I started something new.

I grabbed my phone and sat on my bed. There were three new messages from Gavin.

Can't wait to see you tonight, beautiful.

You sounded a little off on the phone. You okay, Aria?

I got out a little early. Are you home?

I texted him back, thankful that I would see him later. The unsettled feeling in my chest hadn't left since our very brief phone call earlier.

I'm home, no worries. Are we still on for dinner?

Absolutely, I'm on my way over. I brought your favorite movie.

I smiled at that and stepped out of my bedroom, still feeling a little unsure of this "talk" he wanted.

Kay, see u soon.

I slipped my phone into a silver tote. As I grabbed two beers from the fridge, I heard the roar of his Jaguar outside. I could barely contain myself when he knocked. I pulled the door open and gave him a smile. Those blue-gray eyes gazed down at me, blazing with eagerness.

"Hi," I said, my eyes sweeping over his sculpted frame.

He looked yummy in black jeans and a blue Billy Joel tee that rivaled the color of his eyes. His hair was messy. Just a trace of stubble lined his jaw.

"Ms. Morgan, are you checking me out?" he asked, giving my hand a tug so I stumbled into his arms. I pressed my face to his neck, inhaling his minty scent.

"Most definitely, Mr. Thomas. You look edible."

Instantly Gavin grasped my head in his hands and pressed his lips to mine. I moaned in surprise and desire. His tongue ravaged, my mouth. I threw my arms around his neck while his hands gripped my waist.

"When you say stuff like that and I just want to stay in with you all night, beautiful."

At his statement my breathing became erratic. I realized that I really wanted to make love to him. My first time was when I was sixteen years old, lost and naive, seeking love in a man that was never capable of it. I wasn't lost or naive anymore. The intensity of my attraction to Gavin was beyond anything I had ever felt before. So, with Gavin, I knew it would be more than sex. It would be making love, and that made me happy and terrified at the same time.

"Hey, come back, beautiful," he said, his eyebrows drawn together.

His thumbs traced my jaw. I leaned into his touch as my epiphany settled in my mind. I wanted him. For the first time in my life, I wanted more.

"What?" I asked as my mind returned to the moment.

"You just got this faraway look, Aria. Where did you go?"

I shook my head, not wanting him to think something was wrong.

"Thinking. What did you bring me?"

He grinned and showed me the Blu-ray.

"*Final Destination 3.*"

I squealed happily and pulled him into the apartment. I told him that was my favorite movie. Suddenly, he swept my feet from under me and carried me to the couch plopping me down with a husky laugh. He leaned forward to peck my lips.

As he put the movie in he asked, "Your favorite, right?"

Nodding, I smiled and settled my legs on his lap. Gavin placed a soft kiss on the palm of my left hand before interlacing our fingers.

"Hmm."

He smiled crookedly and switched off the lamp. I cuddled closer to him. He pressed his nose into my hair as the credits rolled.

"Mm-mm, you smell good, Aria."

I rested my head on his chest and breathed him in, loving his solid warmth. It felt so right.

Chapter 6

Even after the movie ended, we sat staring at each other in silence. His hand rested at the small of my back. He took a deep breath and I felt him stiffen a little.

"What happened earlier on the phone?" I murmured, trying to read his expression.

"I don't want to scare you off with what I'm about to say."

I gazed up at him, a little uneasy about what he thought might scare me away.

"Look, if you're changing your mind after my nightmare meltdown, I'd completely …"

He halted me with an index finger to my lips. His eyes burned and I couldn't look away.

"I want us to be exclusive, baby."

My heart stopped and then immediately sped back up, soaring at the sound of those words. He hadn't changed his mind. He really did want to be with me. I could see it in his eyes.

I was rendered speechless. His hand cupped my cheek, his eyes clear of the darkness I saw before.

"Are you sure?" I whispered, resting my palm over his erratically beating heart My chest filled with the desire. I placed my other hand beside my left on his chest. Just absorbing his heartbeat, his breaths.

Gavin smiled then, and placed his hand over mine.

"You feel that?"

"Yes."

"You have such an effect on me. When I'm away, all I see is your emerald green eyes and soft, vibrant smile. I want to be with you in every way possible. I don't want you to do this with anyone else, just me."

I couldn't help the way I smiled at him. I clutched his hands in both of mine, hastily nodding my assent.

"No one else, I promise."

Then he kissed me. With a hand curled around my neck and an arm wrapped tightly around my waist, he devoured me with his mouth. He groaned when I sucked on his bottom lip. I nipped lightly at it before I pulled away.

"Ready for dinner?"

I beamed, unable to stop the joy this man incited within me. He helped me to my feet. It felt so natural holding hands as we walked to his car.

God, I loved this car.

"Jasmine, right?" I asked, running my hand down the hood of the car.

I saw something pass briefly over his features. The look told me he didn't want to talk about it. Maybe the car, but not the girl.

"Hey, will you tell me about her?" I asked, squeezing his hand in mine, gauging his reaction.

Gavin slowly turned to me and ran a hand through his hair. He opened the passenger door for me like a gentleman. I couldn't help thinking that his mother must have raised him right.

"Soon, okay?"

I nodded, settling in the seat before he closed the door. A minute later the engine revved to life. It vibrated underneath us eliciting a shiver of excitement. I wondered what it would feel like if I unbuckled my seat belt and slid onto his lap right now, with the rumble and tug of the Jaguar's engine underneath us. I bit my lip as the fantasy took hold of my mind and my body.

"What are you thinking about, baby?"

"W-what?" My eyes darted to his, my cheeks flushing at being caught with my dirty thoughts.

He narrowed his eyes at me a bit and then shook his head as his mouth turned up in a mischievous grin.

"Careful, please."

He winked, provoking goose bumps to break out over my skin in anticipation of what was to come.

"Hang on tight, Ms. Morgan."

A delicious shiver ran through me at his deep voice. The engine beneath us just excited me more.

When we pulled onto a dirt road off Eastern Avenue in South End, my eyes darted to Gavin. He was the picture of calm with one hand on the steering wheel and the other interlaced with mine across my lap.

"What are you up to?"

He grinned, not taking his eyes off the road.

"I'm taking my beautiful girl to dinner."

My heart skipped a beat and I smiled. I bit down on my lip to keep it from showing how much his touch revved me to life.

"Oh, okay. I was just making sure you weren't taking me down a deserted road to hack me to pieces like in *The Texas Chainsaw Massacre*."

He threw his head back and chuckled. His eyes briefly flicked to mine as we entered a grassy clearing with lilacs everywhere.

I, wondered where we were and how he could possibly know what my favorite flower was.

A small brick building came into view. It had a white door and small-town charm. A gravel walkway led to the door. Glass windows reached the entire height of the building. The lights inside were dim. A sign above the entrance was in the shape of an Italian pasta dish. It was lit with twinkling lights and read Amore per La Casa. I was speechless. My eyes blinked in disbelief as I took it all in.

Gavin looked over at me, smiling in amusement. He gently held my face as I leaned up and pressed my mouth to his.

"This is beautiful, Gavin," I whispered, leaning away and gazing into his eyes.

He chortled and kissed my hand softly.

"Wait till you see inside, Aria."

I grinned and kissed him again, deeper this time.

He kissed me back, anchoring my head in place with one hand and gripping my hip with the other. I felt a tightening in my core. I was overwhelmed with wanting to kiss every surface of his skin. Breathlessly, I forced myself to pull away, my mouth tingling in aftershock from the kiss.

"How did you know?" I asked as he led me up the walkway, his hand in mine.

"What?"

I leaned down and picked a lilac, cradling it in my palm.

"That this is my favorite flower. Did Kel tell you?"

He stepped back, his eyes filled with confusion initially and then excitement brimmed in them.

"Really, beautiful?"

I nodded, my face stretching in happiness.

His eyes locked on mine and he pulled me into him, wrapping an arm around my waist. He pressed the sweetest of kisses to my temple.

"I've noticed you always smell like lilacs, Aria. It's intoxicating and sweet, making it impossible for me to stay away from you. So, I hoped you would like this place surrounded by lilacs."

Oh, my. How could a guy like this exist and actually like me? My head was swimming with excitement, and worry that this was all a dream.

Gavin opened the door for me. The charm of this quaint restaurant took my breath away.

"Do you own this?" I asked.

He smiled lopsidedly at me, nodding his head.

"I'm a silent owner. My grandmother founded this place. Now my cousin, Anthony and his wife, Stella run it. All I do is help financially. It's amazing, isn't it?"

I agreed, pulling him to the reception desk where an older woman with red curly hair and gray eyes welcomed us.

"Hey, Gavin. How are you, honey?" she said with a warm smile. Gavin took her hand and smiled.

"I'm good, Stella. You look happy, as always. How's my cousin these days?"

She grabbed two menus and led us up to a balcony table for two.

"He's good, working hard. I swear he never stops!" She laughed lightly. Gavin smiled at me, pulling out a chair for me. Before I sat down, he grasped my hand.

"Excuse my manners, please. Stella, this is Aria. Aria, this is Stella. She's part owner of this restaurant."

I smiled and shook her hand. "A pleasure. This place is wonderful, Stella."

"It's an honor to meet you, Aria. "

"Thank you," I said as she placed menus in front of us and headed back down.

"She's delightful, Gavin."

His eyes alight with easy contentment as he answered.

"She is. I'm glad you got to meet her, Aria."

I smiled back and looked at the menu. Each day I discovered a little more of the mystery that was Gavin Thomas. We ordered after getting Stella's recommendations. I nibbled on bread and cheese as we waited. It wasn't long before she reappeared with the most amazing looking dishes.

"Here you go guys. Fresh from the oven. Do you need anything else?"

Stella set two steaming plates of food in front of us and refilled our waters.

"No, thank you so much Stella. This looks amazing."

Gavin reached across the table to take her hand in his, giving her one of his charming smiles.

"Enjoy and please come back soon, OK?" she said.

I nodded around my first bite of pasta. Gavin spoke to her a minute more before he dug into his dish.

"You're quiet, " Gavin said after Stella went to serve another table. I looked up from my fettuccine Alfredo with basil and saw his eyes considering mine.

"Oh, sorry, I was just thinking about how much I love this place. It's so quaint and the food is delightful."

He didn't smile like I expected. He put down his fork and looked into my eyes. He picked up my hand. His stare made it impossible for me to hide.

"I don't think that's all it is, Aria. I want us to be honest with each other. This is new to me and I don't want to mess it up with you, beautiful. Please tell me what's wrong."

I sighed, putting down my fork and wiping my mouth a little before his eyes captured mine again.

"I don't know, you're just so … unexpected. You make me feel different, happy, worthy, even beautiful. I like being with you so much. It is all so amazing, Gavin. I am halfway convinced this is all just a dream."

He exhaled, a small smile playing on his lips.

"I want to make you feel all those things and more. I feel the same way. I didn't plan to be so drawn to you, to feel this way. But I do and it's amazing. Can't we just enjoy it?"

"I want to. I just can't help feeling like the floor's going to come out from underneath me at some point. Gavin, good things don't usually last for me."

Letting my hand go, he placed two bills on the table and got out of his seat to kneel beside me.

"Can I take you somewhere, beautiful?"

I nodded, getting out of my seat. Gavin took my hand in his and kissed my palm softly as we made our way out of the restaurant. But instead of leading me to the car, he walked toward the shoreline.

There was a white cotton blanket laid out across the sand with a single red rose in the center of it. When I saw it, my lips twitched into a widening smile. Gavin lifted me easily into his arms. He sat down and settled me on his lap so I faced him. The need I saw reflected in his eyes took my breath away.

Chapter 7

"I know you say that good things don't last for you and I can't promise you this will. But I can promise I want to be with you, baby. I want to kiss you, touch you, cherish you. If this is moving too fast, tell me and we can slow down. I'll never push you, but I need you to be honest with me." His voice was deep with emotion.

I sucked in a breath, not wanting to slow this down but needing to be completely honest now.

"I'm sorry, Gavin. I want to be with you. This is fast but ... it's what I want, more than anything. I don't want to slow this down." Opening my heart to him, I decided I trusted him for better or worse

He exhaled lifting his hands to my cheeks, holding my gaze to his. He searched my eyes, and saw right through every defense I had, and cut through them all to the very heart of me. In that moment, I gave myself to him in my heart. I lost the words I wanted to say when he laid his lips on mine.

I breathed him in, tangling my hands in his hair. My tongue slipped into his mouth and tangled with his in a passionate dance. He held me tight to his chest. His hands gripped the hem of my dress. When he sucked my bottom lip, I moaned.

My sex clenched in desire. Pulling back, he nipped softly at my lip before deepening the kiss once more. I wrapped my arms tightly around his neck. I needed him now. I needed to be his. His hands urged my legs around his waist as he continued to ravage my mouth. His scent, taste and touch engulfed my senses. My head swam with longing for him. This deep need was new and exciting.

"Aria, we should stop. I don't want to push you," he murmured into the dip of my shoulder, laying light kisses and nips of his teeth over my neck and bare shoulder.

I shook my head, pulling his lips back to mine. I bit down on his lip when he tried to pull away. With a deep moan, he stood, still holding me to him. With my legs tight around his hips and my arms clasped around his neck, he carried me to the car and put me in.

"Can I take you home?" His voice was velvet to my ears, so tender and soft.

I shook my head, knowing Kel and Lucas were home. I didn't want any interruptions when we finally made love. I wanted it to be special when I gave myself to him. I wanted it to be right and perfect. With Gavin, I knew it would be.

"My place?" he asked, skating his hand down the slope of my neck. I nodded eagerly. Gavin dipped his head to kiss my lips quickly. His eyes alighted with a smile as he closed the door. As he revved the engine to life, he placed a hand on my leg. His gentle squeeze sent jolts of arousal sparking from head to toe. My blood heated with anticipation as Gavin turned onto Rodrick Boulevard in East Side. He pulled up to an upscale apartment complex that looked to be filled with penthouse condominiums. The sign read Jordan and Sons.

"You live here?" I asked in awe.

"Yes, I have a penthouse on the 23rd floor. It has a great view of the harbor."

Gavin parked behind the complex. I noticed a back entrance in the dimly lit alleyway. "Thank you," I whispered when he opened my door and wrapped his arm around my shoulders. He led us toward the entrance.

"I use this door so I can avoid the crowds of reporters. Trust me, it's not fun to be the center of the tabloids. "

I knew firsthand what he meant. Whenever my mother returned from a trip overseas, our house was bombarded by reporters and photographers looking for a story on the world-famous, Andrea Candice Morgan. It was exciting when I was younger, but now it was just a hassle that I'd rather avoid.

"I know how that feels. Whenever my mom came home we were surrounded by tabloid reporters. My house, the studio, everywhere was swarming with them."

He met my eyes. His eyes were clear as he smiled down at me.

"What's your mother's name?"

"Andrea."

I saw the understanding register in his face as he realized who she was.

"I had no idea. She's very successful. Did you ever want to be a model?"

He led me down a corridor to a bank of elevators.

"No, dance has always been my passion."

He shook his head, pulling me into the elevator and kissing my temple. He wrapped his arms around my waist from behind.

"You're an amazing dancer, beautiful. What does your dad do?"

I snuggled into his embrace as the elevator ascended.

"He's a carpenter and a mechanic. He's always worked for everything he has."

Gavin ran his hands over my back, making my skin tingle in response.

"You're proud of him, I can hear it in your voice."

"Yes."

How could I not be? My dad was the best man I'd ever known.

The elevator stopped and Gavin took my hand. We walked toward a black door with a brass doorknob.

"This, is you?" I cocked my head to the side in question.

He nodded. I was excited to see his place.

Gavin deftly unlocked the door and took me inside. He massaged my shoulders as I took in his place. It was nothing like I expected.

I walked over and ran my hand along the mantle as I let my gaze peruse the space again. Nothing screamed "bachelor pad." From the modern art, simple decor, and pictures on the mantle, I saw what he valued. A close examination of the pictures showed the first held a photo of him in dark jeans and a black V-neck tee. His arm was wrapped around a girl who looked to be about sixteen. She had long light brown hair and blue eyes a few shades lighter than his. She was beautiful and favored Gavin. It had to be his sister.

"Is this Callie?" I asked, my eyes darting to Gavin's before he stepped behind me and nodded, a warm smile across his face. I could see his love for her.

"Yes, that was at her birthday party last year. We took her to Paris."

I turned around and placed my hands on his chest.

"This place is very you. I like it."

We stared in silence for a few heated moments. He smiled and ran the back of his hand against my cheek.

"We don't have to rush."

I nodded. I wanted him in every way. But I feared that the horrible memories of Bryce and that night would come back to me. I didn't know how I'd handle that.

"Can we watch a movie?" I asked, hoping he didn't notice my uneasiness. He pulled me over to the couch. He sat behind me, his arms wrapped around my stomach. I could feel the warmth of his skin. Without a word, he placed the remote in my hands.

"You don't want to pick?" My eyes went to his, narrowing in suspicion.

"All yours, beautiful." His warm voice encouraged me.

As I flicked through the movie listings, I saw *Marley and Me* and clicked on it.

"Will you hate me if we watch a chick flick?" I teased, snuggling into his arms. Gavin chuckled softly.

"Not at all."

I started the movie, turning my body into his to rest my chin against his chest.

"Hmm, I like this," I whispered, peeking up at Gavin through my eyelashes. A slow, sexy smile spread across his face as he nuzzled my neck. Soon the movie began. Midway through the movie, my eyes were heavy so I let myself start to drift.

The pain radiated as he hit me hard across the face, his rings scratching me under my eye. He shoved my legs open and bit my neck. I cried out in pain, fighting to get away. He hit my face again. Then he slammed himself into me, his strong hands keeping me beneath him.

"No! No!" I begged for mercy, cried for him to let me go, but he covered my mouth with his hand and took my body forcefully. The force of his hand on my mouth kept me quiet initially, but when he slammed into me, I screamed and screamed, praying to be heard.

"Stop! Stop ... "

Tears coursed down my cheeks as my eyes flew open in panic. Gavin's hands shook me gently. His blue-gray eyes filled with worry as he wiped the tears from my cheeks. He grasped my shaking hands tightly, not letting me go.

"Aria, you had a nightmare."

Dipping his head, he showered my face with soft kisses.

My body was still shaking from the terror of the dream. I couldn't seem to pull air in through my parted mouth.

"Breathe, beautiful. Please just breathe."

Gavin placed one of my hands on his chest. I felt his slowing heartbeat. The steady thrum beneath my fingers anchored me to the present. I closed my eyes and timed my breaths with each beat of his heart. Feeling the beat of his heart calmed me.

"You feel that?" he whispered.

"Yes." My voice was frail with the aftershocks of fear.

"I'm right here, baby. I'm real." His soothing voice broke the weight in my chest. When I finally looked into his deep eyes, I felt safe.

"This has to stop, Aria. I can't see you hurting and be helpless to stop it. Please, talk to me." His voice begged me. I peered up into his fearful eyes and crawled onto his lap. I buried my face in his neck and breathed him in. My tears soaked his tee shirt. Gavin wrapped his arms around my back and let me clutch him as the remnants of the nightmare played through my mind. He kissed my cheek and stroked my hair while I breathed in and out.

Once I calmed down, I knew that I had to tell him about Bryce. It terrified me because I feared he would judge me or pull away from me after knowing the reality of my nightmares.

I leaned away from his chest and wiped at my tears.

"Just let me get this all out, okay?" It was a plea.

If I didn't get it out, I feared I'd never have the courage.

His body tensed, his hand came up to caress my cheek as he acquiesced.

"I won't judge you, beautiful. I promise."

I nodded and prayed it was true. I was thankful for his nearness. I drew strength from his hand holding mine. And then I began to tell him what happened five years ago.

"In my junior year of high school, I met Bryce, a senior. He was the quarterback of the football team, an A student, and I couldn't believe he noticed me. I liked him a lot, and for a while things were great. I was convinced that I loved him so maybe I didn't see the warning signs that I should have."

Gavin's blue-gray eyes took on a hardness as he saw where I was leading, but I had to keep going. He squeezed my hand in reassurance, silently urging me to continue.

"The first couple of years he was so sweet, gentle, kind, and perfect. He was patient with me, waiting until I was ready, and when we finally had sex, it felt right. We continued dating as he began working for his father. He supported me when Jeremy died, was really the perfect boyfriend. I started at Julliard and things continued to go well for a little while. Looking back, I see that he started showing signs of jealousy and possessiveness, wanting me to account for every minute of my time. But I didn't see it initially. We took a vacation during one of my breaks my first year at Julliard. It was then that I started to notice the changes in his personality and treatment of me during that week together. At first I attributed the changes to work stress. As the vacation went on, he started to change even more. He wouldn't even let me leave his sight. He got angry easily. One night over the break, I slipped out to see Kel, trying to get some distance from him. I needed to gain some perspective. But when I got back, he'd been drinking, a lot. That was the first time he hit me."

Gavin went stiff beside me and pressed his forehead to mine. His soft, tender eyes never looked away from me. His sincerity bound me to him at that moment.

"I'm so sorry, beautiful."

He kissed my forehead, my cheek, and my nose, cradling my head in his hands. I knew I had to tell him all of it, so I smiled weakly and continued.

"I remember the pain more than anything else. And his eyes ... they were brown, but when he got angry, they went dark. He became a monster. He didn't see me at all. The rage was all he saw. His eyes looked black as he hit me. Afterward, he cried and begged me to forgive him. Since I loved him, I did. I hid my bruises the best I could from then on, trying to be the perfect girlfriend to him. I learned his triggers, did everything I could to keep from setting him off. Things settled down. Then we moved in together the start of my sophomore year and that seemed to reassure him. But then on his birthday, he saw me talking with his cousin, Shaun, and he lost it. He beat me so hard that night that eventually I blacked out. I was so confused and I blamed myself, thinking that I provoked him like he said. When he proposed the next morning, I was so afraid of what he'd do if I rejected him, so I said yes. He bought me a ring and told me to never take it off. It was a reminder that I belonged to him. Then we made plans to spend some quality time together at his parents' cabin over Christmas. I arrived there first. He wasn't supposed to be there until later that evening after work. I had decided I couldn't live like that anymore. I took the ring off and planned to talk to him when he arrived. I laid down for a nap. I wanted out. But I had no idea how to get away from him."

I sobbed. I hadn't spoken about any of this, not even to Kel. It was all too much, but I needed to say it. All of it.

Gavin's eyes blazed with concern as a tear fell from my eye. I didn't want his pity. I didn't want him to look at me and see how truly broken I was.

"It's okay. You can tell me." His hands wrapped around my shoulders, rubbing circles with his thumbs. His touch was like a salve. I didn't hesitate to lean against the press of his hands.

"I thought I had time to figure out what to say to him before he arrived. But he got off early. He came raging into the bedroom. I knew what was coming. I tried, I promise, God, I tried to get away. I tried to calm him down, but he punched me and I fell backward. B-Bryce … he …"

I stopped. The emotion was drowning me as I pressed my face into Gavin's warm chest. I was a mess. Tears gathered in my eyes and fell down my face. I couldn't do it, I just couldn't … I was not strong enough.

"My beautiful, strong girl. I've got you. I have you." Gavin drew me up into his arms, holding me to his chest as he pressed his mouth to my forehead. He waited for me to calm down, and then I lifted my face to his. His blue-gray eyes were all I saw, all I needed. I bit my lower lip in an effort to quell the sadness that was simmering under the surface.

A sob escaped me when I let my mind drift back to where I left off. I remembered his eyes, and the pain.

So much pain, so many times I could have stopped the events from happening. I should have walked away from the man I thought was right for me when he began to change and treat me like less. But I didn't. I thought it would change. How could I have been so wrong, so dreadfully wrong?

Sometimes I still blamed myself for it all.

"You can stop if you need to. You don't have to …"

I shook my head and summoned the courage to keep going.

"I need to," I whispered, grasping his shoulders and holding onto this man that I knew I was falling in love with. After tonight, he'd have my heart forever. My broken, battered heart would be his. I knew it in my heart, even though the notion scared me. I trusted him with my painful past and that freed me to give him all of me. I hated that the bad stuff had to come first, before we could move on from it.

"I-I don't know how it happened but he was on top of me, his hands ... were holding me down. I couldn't get away."

Gavin shook his head in anger, tightening his fists at his sides. His body was strung tight and his muscles were tense under my hands. I held one of his hands in both of my much smaller ones. Though his eyes were soft and concerned, I saw the rage in them.

"God, no, Aria ..." His voice broke then, emotion taking over every gorgeous angle in his face.

"He r-raped me," I choked out in a whisper. I began to sob, hugging my knees in an effort to calm myself. Gavin shifted so his knees surrounded mine and then, thank God, he scooped my palms to his lips. He kissed each of my knuckles gently before he wrapped his smooth fingers around my nape. He covered my face in soft kisses, from the creases under my eyes to the bottom of my jaw, no spot of skin was untouched. He stood and swept me against his chest. Gavin held me tightly in his arms as he walked. Wrapping my arms around his shoulders, I clutched onto him, drawing comfort in the warmth of his neck.

"I'm sorry ... Aria, I'm so sorry," Gavin murmured, setting me on the bed while still gripping my hands. My heart raced in sudden panic. What did he think of me now that I told him all that had dirtied and shattered my heart?

"If you want me to leave, I will. I know you didn't sign up for this when you met me. I understand if ..." Gavin silenced me with a tender kiss on the lips, his hands smoothing my hair.

"Shh, I want you to stay. This doesn't change anything, Aria."

I leaned back, shocked. I saw the emotion, the need in his eyes. But was he just saying that because he felt bad for me? Or did he truly mean it? I shifted closer to him, opening his tensed fists. Anger wouldn't solve anything and I refused to let him be hurt by my past.

"What are you saying?"

I ran a hand over the stubble along his jaw, afraid to hope. Gavin's arm held me close as if he was afraid I'd disappear.

"Stay. We don't have to do anything, but I don't want to let you go yet."

"But … you can be honest, Gavin. You didn't sign up for this. He broke me … I-I don't know if I ever healed from it."

My damn voice broke when I said the last word. Before I knew what was happening, Gavin's mouth covered mine, his tongue in my mouth. In his kiss, I found solace and tenderness that I didn't expect.

"My beautiful, strong girl. You are not broken. You are amazing."

I smiled up at him, finally believing the honesty I saw in those blue-gray eyes of his. He meant it. He understood. He accepted me. I showed him my brokenness and he still wanted me.

"You're sure?" I whispered, pressing my palm to his heart.

I felt its steady beat under my fingers. The smile Gavin gave me chased away the shadows I had lived in for so, so long. He leaned his forehead against mine.

"Yes." He just held me to him, then.

"When?" Gavin whispered in my ear after minutes of just holding me close.

"Five years ago. I haven't even gone on a date since then."

"If this is moving too fast, Aria, just tell me. Your sister told me you had an ex, but, God, I had no idea."

I snuggled closer to him, pressing my head against his shoulder.

"It's not, I promise. I'm with you, Gavin."

This was all I wanted, all I needed.

Chapter 8

"What happened next?" I heard Gavin's voice brush against the shell of my ear, soft like velvet but laced with concern.

I turned to face him. His eyes darkened with worry as they locked onto mine.

"I woke up in the hospital. The night they found me, I was in bad shape. When I didn't call my dad that night, he came looking for me. My dad found me a shattered mess in the bedroom. He attacked Bryce, but he never got in trouble for that, thank God."

Gavin nodded, a simmering anger in his eyes. He wanted to protect me and it made me feel safe knowing he felt that way.

"Is he …"

"Bryce—he went to jail, but he's out now. I have a restraining order. If he steps within five hundred feet of me, he'll go back to prison."

I looked up to see a stark, determined look in the eyes I'd come to know so well. I could see what he was thinking and I hastily shook my head.

"I need a last name, Aria."

So, he could track down the bastard that hurt me and do what?

"No."

I wouldn't let him do that. It wouldn't change anything. His chest tightened, the muscles clenching under my fingers. Finally, Gavin sighed and stood up, pacing the length of the room. I could see the

74

tension in his shoulders, his muscles flexing and moving as his fists clenched at his sides.

"I need to protect you, Aria. I can't live with the idea that he might find you again."

I got up and wrapped my arms around his neck.

"You're not going after him. I won't let you."

He cursed and hugged me tightly.

"I won't let him hurt you. I promise you."

I nodded, safely encased in his arms.

"I know. Thank you."

The strains of a building melody began and my feet glided across the floor. My steps graceful as I closed my eyes and surrendered to the rhythm of the music. I spun and took the last step before the music faded and the lights dimmed.

I grabbed my bag and saw Gavin with a soft smile on his face. My cheeks flamed. I didn't know he was watching. I hoped I didn't take any missteps.

God, he was sexy. He wore a gray sweater with black slacks, his hair slicked back from a shower. His stubble was still there, though. I smiled inwardly, knowing how wonderful it felt under my fingertips.

"That was so beautiful, Aria," he said, handing me a water once I reached him.

"I didn't know you were watching." I felt my blush.

He grinned slowly, grazing his knuckles against my jaw.

"You were flawless as always," he murmured, pulling me to his chest before placing his lips over mine, breathing me in.

I was lost in thought on the ride back to my apartment after a delightful picnic with Gavin. A delightful three weeks had passed since that night in his penthouse when I told him about my ugliest parts. We went out almost every night, but he hadn't invited me up again. I knew why. But I wanted him so badly, I'd gladly take him on the studio's hardwood floors, the grass where we picnicked just before sunset, even on the hood of his oh-so-sexy car. But that was not possible, unfortunately.

"Can we get takeout tonight?" I asked as we entered my apartment.

I headed towards the bedroom to get out of my green knee-length dress. I had practiced in my dress today in preparation for a small job. But I wanted to be comfortable at home and this dress wasn't it.

"Where from?" he called to me.

"You choose. I'm just going to change."

"No rush. I'll pick a movie, too."

"No horror movies!"

"But those are the best kind!" I heard the low sounds of his chuckle.

The chicken parmesan made me moan in appreciation. I felt Gavin's eyes on me as we watched the comedy he selected. Somehow, he arranged both while I was changing. When I asked how, he just winked as if it was nothing. I looked over and saw his eyes trained on me.

"You're not watching," I said, pouting.

Gavin muted the television and leaned forward to take my empty plate.

"I know. I'm watching you."

I leaned in and kissed him softly on the side of his mouth before taking our plates to the kitchen to soak.

"Come here, Aria," Gavin called, his voice smooth as I walked toward him.

Every time I looked at him, I had to remind myself to breathe. He stood there barefoot with his perpetually messy hair and took my breath away. He pulled me into his arms and dipped his head, his mouth hovering over mine.

"I want you tonight, baby."

I gasped, biting down on my lower lip to stifle a moan.

He wanted me.

"I want you, too, Gavin. But I thought after I told you … maybe it changed …"

He shook his head, his eyes blazing with desire.

"Nothing could change the way I feel about you."

Then he kissed me. Gavin's hands gripped my hips as I tangled my fingers in the silky strands of his hair. His mouth was hungry against mine, his breath whispering against my lips. I opened my mouth to him. My heart raced in excitement and my tongue licked impatiently into his mouth. He groaned, nipping at my lip and sucking on it, eliciting a moan from me. When he pulled away, his eyes filled with pure lust.

"Are you sure? If we need to take this slow or to wait a while, then we will, Aria. You're in charge here." His voice filled with softness, waiting for me to decide.

I hastily shook my head. I wanted this so badly with him. I didn't need to wait. I needed him. His touch.

"I want this, Gavin. Make love to me." My voice pleaded, raspy with need.

He exhaled and slowly an enigmatic smile spread over his face.

He grabbed my hand and I followed him to my dimly lit bedroom.

I moaned when he came behind me and kissed my neck, his teeth scraping over my sensitive skin. His fingers moved lower and he barely lifted the hem of my shirt. I felt his hand slip underneath the fabric. His touch was warm and gentle against my back, sliding up my shirt as he went. Gavin turned me around and locked his eyes on mine, blue-gray to green. He pulled my shirt up slowly. When he pulled it over my head, he sucked in a breath. His eyes roamed over my body. His shoulders tensed a little and I realized what he saw.

Shit! Why didn't I just keep my shirt on?

I closed my eyes briefly until I felt his fingers run across a long pink scar on my lower abdomen. The memories assaulted me and I tensed instantly. What should have been a fun night, turned into a nightmare when Bryce pushed me down the stairs of the cabin the night of his birthday party. I had to get seventeen stitches on my torso.

"Oh, beautiful," Gavin whispered and suddenly he fell to his knees in front of me. Leaning forward, he pressed a kiss to the side of my scar, his lips gliding up the length of it. I felt as if he healed my soul with just a simple kiss. With another kiss to my hip, his hands came up to cradle my face.

"You're so goddamn beautiful" he growled, blinking up at me.

I bit my lip to stop from saying the words that threatened to tumble out. With eager fingers, I pulled him up to me, desperately gripping the bottom of his shirt with my hands.

"Kiss me," I whispered, pulling him closer to me.

My fingers unbuttoned his gray sweater, revealing his golden skin. A smile, took over his features as he lifted my face and took my mouth in a soft, passionate kiss. I moaned as his hands moved to the top of my yoga pants.

"You first," I whispered, pushing the fabric from his torso with greedy hands. Gavin stood before me, chest bare, smoldering eyes filled with desire. I sucked in a breath of air at the sight of him.

Oh, my God.

He was just as toned as I imagined, with a chiseled chest and a six-pack. I ran my hands down his chest, reveling in the feel of his smooth skin under my fingers. The muscles rippled and tightened under my touch.

His mouth closed over mine again. Gavin swept my legs from underneath me and parted my lips with his tongue. His scent overwhelmed me. I wrapped my arms around his neck as he laid me on the bed with my head on the pillows. He began to kiss slowly down my neck, licking my flesh as he went. There was nothing rushed about the way he kissed me. He took his time. God, I wanted him.

"Gavin, babe, please ... " I skated my nails down his bared shoulders in need.

He lifted his head and smiled seductively at me.

"Impatient?" Gavin asked against my skin.

I nodded eagerly, reaching for his belt buckle.

"Aria ... " he whispered when I pressed my lips to his jaw, teasing it with slow licks.

"I want you, Gavin. You. Here. Now." I punctuated each word with a kiss.

He stopped my hands tracing his skin and pulled them over my head. His soft eyes danced with want, mirroring my own. Gavin kept my hands still while he gazed down at me.

"I want to take this slow, okay?"

I nodded, succumbing to his lovely weight on my lower stomach. After a beat, he released my hands and kissed along my jaw. His teeth nipped at my collarbone. I wrapped my legs around his hips as his mouth traveled lower to suck at the top of my breasts. He deftly unfastened the front clasp of my black lacy bra and slid the straps down my arms. I moaned in ecstasy as his mouth closed over a nipple. It hardened under his urgent mouth. He sucked and nipped on it, creating a tightening in my core. I felt the warmth between my legs. My hands clenched the sheets as desire coursed through me. I whimpered and let my head fall back.

"Oh ... " I whispered, feeling his mouth gliding over to my other breast. His tongue adored the skin and teased that nipple slowly before sucking it deeply into his mouth. His mouth on me was making me impatient. I groaned through my parted lips as he continued to torture me.

"Please ... " I begged, pulling his head to my lips for a kiss.

He smiled against my mouth as he sat up and ran his hands down my chest, cupping each breast, before sliding them to the edge of my pants again.

Gavin slipped his hands under my waistband and slowly pulled them off. He kissed his way down my torso as he revealed my skin. He lavished kisses on my stomach, my thighs, and my calves. All that was left on my tingling body was a pair of black, lacy boy-short panties.

"If you need to stop at any time, Aria, just tell me and we'll stop." His voice was against my ear and his arms caged either side of my head keeping most of his weight off me.

I nodded, taking his face in my hands. I saw hunger and lust in his eyes, but more than that, I saw care for me in them, too. He didn't want to push me, which only made me want him more.

"Don't stop. I want this, Gavin."

Gavin sat back on his heels. His eyes never left mine as he undid his belt buckle and unzipped his jeans. I was breathless, watching him move from the bed to drop his jeans on the floor leaving him clad in only a pair of navy blue boxers. My eyes swept from his ruggedly handsome face to his chiseled chest, down to his firm abs to his toned hips and thighs. I felt that ache between my legs deepen at the sight of him. My heart stuttered in anticipation of making love to him.

I reached out my hand to him. He grasped it, kissing the palm as he hovered over me.

"Aria, you take my breath away."

I pulled his mouth to mine and kissed him until I had to come up for air.

He slid down the bed toward my ankles and kissed the left one softly. His mouth glided up my calf, over the knee, and up my thigh. I shivered with desire and need to have his mouth at my center.

"Gavin …"

I moaned impatiently, as he repeated the process with my right leg, his hand stroking up my thigh.

"You feel so good," he whispered.

My eyes closed from the sound of his husky voice and teasing touch. Impossibly, I felt like a virgin, experiencing each sensation as if for the first time. But the way Gavin worshiped my body with his touch and kisses made me realize that his adoration made this different from any other time before. All the other times were merely sex, this was making love. Coherent thought began to flee as I felt his warm breath on my thighs. His fingers slipped under the fabric of my panties and I sucked in a breath.

"You okay?" he asked, forcing my eyes open with a hand on my cheek.

"Please don't stop, Gavin."

"I won't, baby." He pulled my panties off and his boxers joined them a moment later.

I wrapped my arms around his shoulders and pressed my mouth to his as he parted my legs with his knee.

Anticipation curled deep in my belly. Gavin licked the seam of his lips as he hovered over me. My core clenched. I pulled those delectable lips to mine, groaning in need as he bit down gently on my lower lip.

He pulled back, sliding his hands up my thighs. He pressed his forehead against mine.

"My beautiful girl," he said, sliding a palm up and over my aching center.

"Please …"

When his fingers entered me, I moaned loudly and let my head fall back deep into the pillow. I felt myself tighten around his fingers. God, it felt so good, so right.

"Oh, Gavin."

He slid his body down mine until I felt his warm breath between my legs.

Oh, yes. My core tightened as his lips closed around me, his tongue licking slowly into the folds, fingers sliding in and out of me, working me. Fireworks shot over my skin, burning into the depths of my body.

"Don't stop …" I whispered, tangling my fingers in his hair when his mouth pulled at my clit.

"Gavin! Aah …"

Something built inside me as his mouth teased my clit relentlessly, his fingers going faster. In. Out. In. Out. It was perfection and torture all in the same motion because, though I needed to fall apart but I didn't want the sensation to end. I didn't want him to stop loving me.

Loving me. God, was that what he was doing?

Yes, we were making love. Together, right now. And it was the best thing I'd ever felt.

"Gavin!"

Hard waves of intense pleasure engulfed me making me see stars. I wrapped my arms around his neck, not wanting to ever let go.

I called out his name over and over, louder and louder as the orgasm crashed around me. My body trembled with the force of it. I felt wetness between my legs as Gavin pulled his fingers away and slowly kissed his way up my hip, my stomach, my chest. My skin tingled in the aftermath, my heart trembled with my feelings, and my eyes closed as tears gathered on my lashes. I felt loved. Loved by this man so completely.

My desire returned, as I felt myself come down from what I was convinced was my first orgasm. How was that possible? It never felt like that before. My eyes opened and were immediately captured by Gavin's.

"Wow. That was different." I blushed deeply as I admitted that.

"Do you have … ?" I flicked my eyes down to where he was nestled between my legs.

He nodded, sliding off the bed as he retrieved two condoms from his wallet. I felt the bed dip when he crawled over me again.

He began kissing my neck, as he teased my opening with his length. His breath was in my ear as he whispered against my skin.

"Do you need to stop?" His voice was strained with need.

I rubbed my fingers over his stubble, drowning in the desire I saw in his eyes. I shook my head, kissing his lips impatiently. He grabbed the back of my neck and kissed me hard on the lips and slowly slid into me. I moaned at the feeling of fullness and the slight burn as I expanded around him. I groaned into his neck, before moving my lips to his mouth so I could kiss him passionately. I wrapped my legs around his hips and in a matter of seconds, pleasure consumed my body. His mouth closed over mine more softly.

Gavin cradled my face in his hands. I wrapped my arms around his back. I couldn't help but clutch him as he slowly moved out of me and back in again. I could feel myself build again and I lifted my hips, moaning in pleasure at the heavenly feeling of him inside me.

"Please, Gavin, faster," I murmured, chanting his name in hot desire.

He slid out of me and squeezed my hips in his large, delightful hands. His lips pressed to my collarbone.

"Jesus, baby." His voice shook with the gravity of the moment.

"Yes, Gavin. Please," I begged, my mouth whispering against his.

He pushed into me once more and I felt myself tighten around him. I called out his name in ecstasy. I found my release in the stars. The pleasure rocked through my veins, making my skin tingle and my eyes flutter open as I watched his face. His mouth parted with a groan.

He whispered my name against my neck. He stilled inside me and I felt him let go as his body trembled. I drifted down from my high. I pressed my lips to his, passionately.

My soul was ripped open, my heart healed. My head was not able to stop my heart from falling irrevocably in love with him.

Gavin smiled and tugged my mouth back to his once I caught my breath. His kiss left me breathless again. He sat up and pulled me into his arms, pressing his face to my hair. I wrapped my arms around him while he did the same. He leaned back, cupping my cheeks. I felt the connection between us.

"Gavin," I whispered, holding onto his waist. We both panted, breathing into each others skin.

"Amazing," he whispered, kissing my forehead and laying me down on the mattress once more as he wrapped me in his embrace. I rested my head on his chest and gazed up at him through my lashes.

"Thank you for making tonight perfect, Gavin. It was amazing."

He smiled boyishly and pressed a kiss to my temple. His hand stroked my hair.

"Sleep, baby."

Chapter 9

My eyes fluttered open to sunlight pouring in through the blinds. I felt as if I had slept for days. Things had been going wonderfully since the first time we made love. I felt our connection grow with each passing day. I saw my gorgeous man lying peacefully next to me with one hand stretched across my stomach and the other arm hugging the pillow. I snuggled closer into Gavin's chest, enjoying the warmth of his skin. His face was so peaceful while he slept.

I couldn't help gliding my hands down his happy trail and across to rest upon his hip. I kissed his jaw softly, rubbing my lips over the stubble there. I climbed out of bed, intent on finding something in his kitchen to make us for breakfast.

I pulled out a pan, then grabbed eggs, milk, grated cheese, and sliced ham from the fridge. I also took out bacon and sausage links to make a grand breakfast for Gavin. I turned on the radio, keeping the volume low and singing to myself. Carrie Underwood's *Cowboy Casanova* had me dancing around the kitchen in my bare feet.

Once the omelets were made, I started on the bacon and sausage, swaying my hips to the music. I heard Gavin's approach so I flicked my eyes over to his sexy bed hair.

"What do you think you're doing?" he whispered against my ear as his arms wrapped around my waist. Gavin let his hands glide up the front of the shirt I wore. His shirt.

"Um, isn't it obvious?" I murmured, in a breathy moan as his mouth closed over my earlobe. I hummed and closed my eyes as he reached around me to turn off the burners. He pulled me hard against him. I felt his hard length and bit my lip in arousal. I wanted him again. He was just so damn beautiful. And sexy …

"You should've stayed in bed with me, beautiful." His voice rumbled low against my neck.

He reached down and squeezed my ass, making the ache in my core intensify. His lips on my exposed neck made my head fall back against his chest and my eyes shutter closed. He turned me around and picked me up. I wrapped my legs around his hips, needing to feel his hard body against my soft one.

He sat me on the counter.

"You look so hot like this." His voice was a caress, a promise of things to come.

Running my hand down his faint chest hair, I pressed a kiss to the skin there.

"So, do you."

He mashed his mouth to mine, parting my lips with his tongue, tasting my mouth. I tasted him back, pulling him closer and sliding his boxers off as his hands cradled my face. His kiss was hungry yet gentle.

"I want you, Gavin. Now."

He grinned against my urgent lips. Without a word, he slid into my damp sex, groaning. My mouth fell open in response. God, he felt like heaven. He filled me perfectly.

"Christ, you feel good, Aria." His voice tingled against my skin.

I touched my lips to his chest as he slid completely out and then filled me again, moving faster and faster with each stroke. I cried out, my body buzzing with building orgasm.

"Gavin … Gavin … Gavin!" I repeated over and over, my mouth insistent against his neck. I felt myself so close to coming.

"Come for me," he whispered against my skin, igniting my blood as I screamed his name in pleasure. Then I fell apart, waves crashing around me as I trembled in the aftermath.

"Oh, beautiful," he groaned, burying himself inside me as he called out my name like a prayer.

I watched as he found his own pleasure within me.

"Aria," he whispered, taking my mouth in a tender kiss that took my breath away and made me long to go back to bed.

"The food is getting cold," I spoke against his lips, pouting. I felt his laugh rumble in his chest and I leaned back to look into his deep eyes that sparkled in the sunlight.

"You are too good for me, you know that?"

I smiled, not believing that at all.

"Why? Because I made you breakfast?"

He nodded, running his mouth along my jaw, teasing the skin.

"All I wanted to do was make love to you again and here you were making me breakfast. You amaze me."

I pulled him in for another kiss. We were interrupted by a hard, demanding knock on his door. His face fell to my shoulder and he chuckled into my hair. I blushed, pulling his lips to mine for a quick peck before he set me on my feet. A crooked smile danced across his face. God, I'd do anything for that smile.

"Get dressed. I'll answer the door."

I held up a finger, telling him to wait. I ran back into the bedroom and grabbed his jeans. I came back and handed them over, before dashing back to get dressed myself.

I looked through the drawers in Gavin's dresser and found a blue and white button-down shirt that was a bit too big for me. I yanked it on and was immediately engulfed in his musky scent. Finding my yoga pants folded on the bed, I pulled them over my legs and I slipped on the silver flats I wore last night. I grabbed my cell phone, dance bag, and Gavin's phone off his dresser. I checked my phone as I walked out of the bedroom. There was one missed text message.

Kel—Hey. We need to catch up!

I stopped when I saw Gavin hugging a young girl with reddish brown hair. He wrapped her tightly in his embrace, cooing softly in her ear as she cried.

Oh, poor girl. It had to be his sister, Callie.

"What happened, sweetheart?"

"He didn't show up. I'm sorry. I just needed to talk to someone. Is it OK that I'm here?" she whispered just loud enough for my ears.

My eyes met hers and I nodded, giving her what I hoped was a look of reassurance. Gavin leaned back and softly wiped away her tears.

"I'm sorry, Cal. I know you liked him. Why don't you sit down? Aria made breakfast and you should eat."

She nodded, sitting on the couch and wiping away her tears. Gavin crouched in front of her, and kissed her knuckles as he assured her everything would be alright. My heart lifted just watching how he took care of his sister.

"Hey, I don't want to interrupt, babe," I said as I stepped forward, giving Callie a small smile.

Gavin grinned at me as he stood up and pulled me to his side.

"You could never be an interruption, Aria."

He looked almost apologetic as he gazed down at me.

I nodded, kissing his cheek. I mouthed the words "it's okay." He shook his head with the smile I knew he reserved only for me.

"Callie, sweetheart, this is the girl I told you about. Aria, this is my sister, Callie."

She stood and gave me a warm smile as we shook hands. She looked so young.

"Callie, it's great to meet you. Do you want to stay for breakfast?"

She nodded. I went into the kitchen to finish cooking. Once we all were stuffed, Callie went to watch TV while Gavin and I cleaned up the kitchen.

"I'm sorry. I didn't know she was going to just show up like this, Aria," Gavin whispered as he helped me.

I hastily shook my head.

"It's okay. She needed you, Gavin. And she seems wonderful. I'm glad to meet her."

He smiled, relieved, and glanced over at Callie, watching TV and nursing a Pepsi.

"Look, I have a meeting this morning so, I'll probably just drop her off at my mom's. I wish I could take her out and spend some time with her but with this merger …"

I placed a hand on his mouth and shook my head. I bit my lip, having an idea that might cheer Callie up.

"I could take her to the studio with me today. It might cheer her up, right?"

Gavin's eyes lit up and I took my hand off his mouth.

"You wouldn't mind?"

"No, of course not. Maybe I can get to know her, distract her for a bit. She loves to dance, right?"

He nodded, a smile on his lips. His palm skated over my cheek, his face brightening.

"She's going to be thrilled, Aria. Like I said, you're too good for me."

I grinned and gave him a soft kiss on the lips.

"That's too bad because you're stuck with me, babe."

His eyes heated and he pulled me in with his hands around my neck. I felt his hot breath against my parted lips.

"Oh."

Gavin brushed his mouth to mine urgently and parted my lips with his tongue as one of his hands tangled in my hair. He nipped softly at my bottom lip eliciting a moan from me. I gripped his shoulders while my tongue licked salaciously into his mouth. God, I'd never get enough.

I pouted when he pulled away and leaned his forehead against mine as we both struggled to catch our breath.

"Dinner tonight?" he asked, a suggestive smile crossing his lips.

I leaned back, remembering that I made plans to have dinner and drinks with Kel.

"Actually, I promised Kel I'd have dinner and drinks with her tonight. Do you want to join us? Luke will be there, too."

He smiled widely and kissed my temple.

"Sure, baby."

"Gavin?" Callie called from the living room, interrupting.

I laughed softly and pulled away from Gavin's mouth.

"You want to meet for lunch?" Gavin's mouth traced down my throat with the question.

I hooked my hands over his shoulders and nodded.

"I'm there."

He kissed my knuckles. His eyes were bright with a joy that I hadn't seen before as he took his sister into his arms again.

"Sweetheart, do you want to go with Aria to her dance studio?"

Callie's smile was infectious as she nodded. "That would be great, but can you tell Mom? My phone's dead."

"Sure. I must go. I'll see you later, Sis. Stay strong, okay?"

She grinned, hugging Gavin before he pulled on the shirt I had grabbed from the bedroom and picked up his sneakers.

"See you soon, beautiful," he whispered, giving me a lingering kiss before leaving.

My heart raced and my cheeks heated. I made small talk with Callie as I finished up in the kitchen.

"What kind of dance do you like?"

She smiled, a dimple appearing on her cheek, reminding me of Gavin.

"Modern ballet. I do some tap, but I never got that into it. It was more of my mother's forte. You know?"

"I can definitely relate to that. Come on, let's go."

"Aria! Where have you been?" Eli asked as we made our way into the studio.

"Sorry, Eli. Traffic. This is my friend, Callie. She dances, too."

Eli came up to her and shook her hand, smiling charmingly.

"Okay, let's get started, Aria. If you want to do a session too, Ms. Callie, I'd be honored."

He winked and took us onto the floor without another word. After a trying session, I sat cross-legged on the floor and watched Callie take the mats, her hair pulled up and a pair of white ballet flats on her feet.

An instrumental of a Cindy Lauper song played as Callie closed her eyes, finding her center. She moved across the floor gracefully, never missing a step. She was one with the song. She effortlessly glided through her routine, surprising me with how intricate her style was. She was so young, but when she danced, it was effortless.

"That was perfect, Callie," I said, handing her a water as she sat next to me.

"Really? I was nervous, actually."

"It was great. I can't believe how graceful your style is. How old are you?"

"Seventeen."

I pulled her in for a hug and then leaned back. I was surprised and awed at the talent of this girl.

"You're really talented, Callie. Truly."

"Thanks, so are you!"

We both laughed, comfortable with each other.

"So, what happened with this boy?"

She sighed and her eyes became sad.

"My boyfriend, Jude. We had dinner plans for our six-month anniversary and he didn't show up."

Oh, my God, this poor girl.

"Oh, sweetie. It's his loss. Don't let him upset you like this. You have so much ahead of you, okay?"

She nodded, giving me a small smile. I checked the time realizing it was almost one o'clock.

"Do you want to grab some lunch? Gavin and my friend Farrah want to meet us downtown."

She nodded and stood, pulling me up with her.

"Thanks for cheering me up, Aria."

I grinned as we headed out to my car.

"No problem, we girls have to stick together. Right?"

She laughed, agreeing.

I dialed Gavin's number as I pulled out of the parking lot. It seemed like just yesterday that I met him here outside the studio. I was so closed off to love. And now I was falling for him. I was breathless at the realization that I was falling in love with Gavin Thomas. Impossible to believe after such a short amount of time. But, here we were.

"Hello?" His gravelly voice shot through me instantly.

"Hi, Gavin."

"Hey, beautiful. How's it going?" I felt an ache in my chest from missing him. And it terrified me.

"Good. We're on our way to Johnny's now. Your sister is such a good dancer; I couldn't believe it."

He laughed and I heard a horn on his end.

"She is. She trained in Paris, after all. See you soon, okay?"

"Okay."

I hung up and a few minutes later parked the car. I turned to Callie who stared intently at her phone.

"Hey, stop waiting. He'll call. If he loves you, he'll call you. Let's go eat."

She nodded and smiled, hopping out of the car and heading inside the restaurant. I sighed, feeling badly for her heartbreak. The normal waiting by the phone was a long, sad process that all teenage girls went through at some point.

Gavin leaned against the railing leading into Johnny's Grille. When he caught sight of me a smile crossed his face.

"Better stop staring, handsome stranger. My boyfriend is going to be here any moment."

His smile widened and his eyes blazed with hunger.

"Is that so?"

He walked up to me and caged me against the car door. His eyes filled with lust and mischief.

"You're such a tease, Ms. Morgan," he whispered, trailing kisses up my jaw.

My blood heated in anticipation of his mouth on mine.

"So are you, Mr. Thomas."

He grinned, finally closing his lips on mine, igniting my blood and taking my breath away as he sucked lazily on my lower lip, nipping the skin. When his tongue coerced my lips apart and slid along mine, I moaned softly and I gripped his hair.

"Is it weird that I missed you, beautiful?" he murmured as his forehead leaned against mine.

"If it's weird then so be it. Because I missed you, too."

He pulled back and cupped my cheeks, smiling boyishly. I was falling in love with him. Hell, I'd already fallen.

Chapter 10

"You look gorgeous, by the way."

Gavin's blue-gray eyes were all I saw. A shy smile came to my mouth at his compliment. He took my hand and kissed my wrist. He pulled back and looked down at my wrist for a long moment. A pit of fear formed low in my stomach.

"I wanted to ask you about these, baby."

My eyes dropped to the four long cuts along my wrist from a few months ago, when I became overwhelmed by grief from Jeremy's death, blame from my mother, and Bryce's assault. The self-inflicted pain helped at the time, but I'd never told anyone that. They were starting to fade, but they'd always be there to remind me of my weakness.

Gavin's hand gently grasped my chin and lifted my gaze to his.

"Aria?" I saw the concern and hint of anger in his eyes. One hand held my wrist while the other cupped my cheek.

"Can we talk after lunch? Do you need to get back to work right away?"

He exhaled, shaking his head. He wanted to talk. I knew it. "I'm free 'til five. We do need to talk."

I nodded, placing my hand over his on my face.

"We will. I promise."

We went inside to find Callie and Farrah. Lunch was pleasant and uneventful. Callie seemed to be in a better frame of mind by the time we dropped her back at her vehicle.

Gavin was quiet as he drove us to my apartment. His hand in mine was our only contact. The pit in my stomach felt like an abyss that only got deeper over time. I was terrified of hearing the words I knew were true. This was too much, too soon for him to deal with.

"Babe?" My voice shook, betraying the fear lingering inside me.

His eyes darted to mine. My heart raced and I bit my lip, afraid of the inevitable. We'd only met a few weeks ago, and he kept finding piles of my baggage. I didn't expect him to want to keep tripping over my mess. I was certain he wanted to end it. As I realized that I could never hold on to a man like Gavin with my broken past, tears stung my eyes and I forced myself to look away from him.

"Never mind," I murmured as I closed my eyes, preparing myself for the blow that would shatter my fallen heart.

"Is anyone home?" Gavin asked as he pulled into my complex. I flicked my eyes over to his and shook my head.

"Are you okay?" His voice was soft with worry. I grasped the handle next to me, not answering.

He stopped me when I pushed the door open, pulling me to him. His hands cradled my face while his wide eyes pierced mine. I couldn't hide my emotions from him when they showed so clearly on my face.

"You've been crying?" Gavin's smooth voice caressed me.

I couldn't look him in the eyes. I dipped my head, dropping my gaze from his to my scarred wrist, wondering what he thought of me now that he'd seen them.

"Beautiful, no." Tears welled in my eyes as he held my face in his hands and pressed his lips to my forehead. He left them there as he spoke softly.

"I'm not mad at you or judging you, baby. I'm just concerned. I thought you told me everything. Why didn't you tell me about this?"

I nodded, wringing my hands as I lifted my eyes to his.

"I didn't want to scare you away, Gavin. You're just about the best thing that's ever happened to me and I don't want to ruin it with all my baggage."

He bound me up in his arms, not allowing me to hide. Then he brushed a kiss on my knuckles as he looked into my eyes.

"You don't have to worry about scaring me away, Aria. Trust me, when you meet my mother you'll see I'm not perfect. I have an ex in Rome and quite a few friends who will bore you to tears. I get jealous easily, I work way too much, and I can't stay away from you. You can take your pick. You aren't the only one with baggage and a less-than-perfect past. It's okay. We just need to be honest with each other."

I couldn't look away while he caressed my face. "I thought it would be too much, Gavin. I don't want to mess this up."

He laid a tender kiss on my mouth, not speaking for a moment. Slowly he dipped his head, and grabbed my wrists to trail his mouth along the marred flesh there.

"We won't, baby. Come on, let's go inside."

Gavin crawled onto my bed and pulled me onto his lap, kissing my hair. "Tell me why, Aria."

I sighed, finding my words.

"After each tragedy in my life, I pushed the pain down. When my brother died and my mother blamed me for the accident that took his life, I buried my grief. I had just gotten accepted into Julliard, so I knew school would need my focus. I didn't deal with my grief. Even after the assault, I pushed my pain away. I just couldn't face it. I focused solely on dancing. Once I graduated and had a few small jobs under my belt, it seemed that dance was no longer a good escape. I couldn't keep the bad stuff pressed down any more. It welled up like a tsunami and drowned me. I went home and just ... broke, and I wanted to shut out the world, make the hurt stop. I knew my mom didn't mean what she said, but I started to blame myself. I started drinking, but when that didn't help, I reached for a razor. I just wanted to shut off the pain and the loss. I didn't want to hurt myself. It helped. The pain, the release of it, helped me cope at the time."

Gavin grazed his lips up my face, pressing a kiss to my temple.

"Was that the only time you did it?"

I nodded, snuggling deeper into his embrace.

"You have to know none of those things were your fault. Your mom was grieving and I'm sure she didn't mean what she said. And what Bryce did … you didn't ask for that."

I knew he was right, but in a way, I still blamed myself for those things that had happened in my life.

"I know. I miss Jeremy, though. And I miss my mom. She changed after Jeremy died. She buried herself in work. And then Bryce …" I shuddered.

Gavin tucked my head under his chin and kept me close. His warmth comforted me.

"Shhh. Give your mom time, beautiful. She'll come home when she's ready."

I nuzzled my face into his neck and whispered into his skin, "I hope you're right."

He stroked his hand up my back and smoothed my hair from the back of my neck. I was so lost in his touch that I almost didn't hear his whispered words.

"Are you okay?" Gavin's fingers wrapped around my middle, holding me close.

I sighed, resting my hands over his forearms. "Yes, now I am."

Having him to lean on meant so much.

He tightened his hold on me and lifted one of my hands to his mouth, kissing it softly.

"Tomorrow is the anniversary of his death. I don't want you suffering with your grief anymore, baby. If you'll let me, I want to be here for you."

Something in his voice stirred me and I turned in his arms, placing my hands on his chest.

"Thank you," I whispered, touching my mouth to his jaw twice before I dropped my face to his neck. I breathed in his heavenly mint scent and something else that was distinctly HIM.

He tugged my hair gently so I lifted my head. I smiled back at him as my heart raced at the look in his eyes.

"Babe," I whispered, my hands clutching the fabric of his shirt as his breath parted my lips. He ran his fingers down my cheek as he slowly dipped his head toward mine.

I was already breathless when his mouth closed over mine. His lips treasured mine gently, stealing my breath and sending tingles across my skin when he grasped the back of my neck with his hands. His tongue ran along my bottom lip, his teeth nipped at it hungrily. I moaned as desire pooled in my core. My body yearned for him.

A soft kiss turned into an urgent one. My hands tangled in his hair and my mouth opened to his. His tongue ran along mine, exploring, tasting, touching mine as we passionately ate at each others mouths.

"I want to make love to you so badly right now."

I pulled away from his lips, breathless and wanton for him.

"Yes …"

He chuckled softly and began to kiss my jaw, his mouth trailing down to my ear and the sensitive spots along my neck.

I moaned, moving closer as he grasped my hips and ravaged my neck with soft nips and teasing kisses.

"I have a meeting with Techtronic's in twenty minutes," he whispered as he kissed down my shoulder and unzipped my hoodie before pulling it off my body, tossing it to the floor.

When his lips grazed my nipple through the fabric of my polo shirt, I groaned, opening my legs eagerly.

"That's plenty of time."

"Aria, baby, wake up."

My eyes fluttered open to see Gavin beside me, his smile lit up his ruggedly handsome face. He wore a pair of faded Levi's and a button-down white shirt. His chest filled out the shirt perfectly. My fingers itched to touch him. His mouth swept over mine tenderly.

"Hi, handsome."

He laughed against my lips, eyes filled with love.

"Good morning, beautiful."

It was then that I saw the tray of pancakes, scrambled eggs, and bacon. My stomach grumbled at the sight of the delicious food Gavin made. I smiled, biting my lip as he winked down at me.

"You made me breakfast?"

His lips tilted up in a smile that could make any girl swoon. It made my heart race.

"Wasn't that our deal?"

I nodded, took a bite of the heavenly food he had made me.

"Do you miss him, beautiful?" Gavin murmured as he leaned over where I laid, tracing a hand over my bare hip.

God, I missed him so much. How was it possible I had lived without him for seven years?

"Every day," I whispered as a tear escaped.

I remembered that night so clearly. He was so happy for me that night. He always wanted the best for me.

Gavin's hand closed over my shoulder so he could pull me towards him. He gazed down at me. I felt his heart through his shirt, beating a steady rhythm.

"He'd be so proud of you, baby." I nodded, tangling my fingers in the hair at his nape. Touching him was a balm for me.

"I know."

Gavin leaned back from me and grazed his knuckles over my cheek. "I'm here for you, whatever you need. I know today is going to be hard for you. What do you want to do today, baby?"

"Um, actually there is something."

His eyebrows rose as he sat across from me. "I want to go see Jeremy's grave site."

I meant to go yesterday, but it slipped my mind and I hadn't been in a long while. It was time.

"Of course. Can I come with you?"

I smiled, brushing my lips against his. How did I deserve him?

"I'd love that."

His grave was just as I remembered, a handful of lilies were in front of the stone. They were Kel's favorite. Jeremy always gave them to her on special occasions. I wondered when she was here.

I knelt in front of the stone and laid down white roses like the ones Jeremy had given me one Valentine's Day after Bryce had ditched me on our anniversary. My fingers traced the words etched in stone.

Gage Jeremiah Morgan

Beloved son and brother

We will miss you

The feel of the stone under my fingers brought tears to my eyes as I remembered the moment he slipped away from us. He was such a kind-hearted person.

Why had he been taken from us so soon? Why not me?

I felt tears well as emotion overwhelmed me.

Be strong for him. For Jeremy. I told myself.

I sat cross-legged, feeling Gavin kneel behind me. His hands ran up and down my arms and I found the words I wanted to say to Jeremy, not knowing if he could hear me.

"I'm here, Jer. I'm sorry I haven't come to see you lately, I kind of lost my way."

I hadn't come to his grave since before my stay at the hospital. I hated that, but I knew that I needed that time to come to grips with my grief and the pain that his death had caused not only me, but all of us. My family. I hadn't dealt with when I should have. But now I was.

My kind, gentle brother had a hold on each of our hearts and when he passed, we didn't know how to go on. Each day that had passed since then was hard without him, but with Gavin by my side, I was getting stronger.

As if he could read my thoughts, Gavin slipped his arms around my waist and rested his chin on top of my head. Just having him close gave me strength.

"I miss you so much, Jer. It's not the same without you, but I've found some happiness again. It's been seven years since your accident. I'm finally accepting what happened. I'm still dancing, and I've found love, just like you wanted for me."

Gavin kissed my temple, running a soothing hand up my back.

"Jer, I hope wherever you are, you're happy. You deserve that. I … I love you, Jeremy. Always."

I pressed a kiss to my left hand and laid it on the tombstone above his name.

I felt a sense of clarity; he was at peace now. And finally, I was too.

"I miss him so much," I whispered, more to myself than Gavin.

He pulled me to him, wrapping his arms around my middle as his lips lingered on my forehead.

"I know."

I sniffled, turning into his embrace. His eyes filled with love, and I immediately lifted my lips to his. It was a slow, inhaling kiss that gave me butterflies.

"Thank you for being here," I whispered into his neck.

He smiled a soft smile, cupping my cheek in one of his hands.

"I told you. I'm not letting you go, beautiful." His hands clasped my face so lovingly.

My heart yearned for him as my body relaxed against his. I loved him so much. I don't know how long we sat there, Gavin holding me with my head on his shoulder.

"Jeremiah was his middle name?" he asked, lifting my chin to meet his clear gaze.

"Yes, Gage was my grandfather's name, but he never liked it. Everyone called him Jeremy. I think it fit him."

He nodded, helping me up and grasping my hand in his. This man was always so gentle with me, knowing exactly what I needed even when I didn't.

"Are you okay, Aria?" he asked, placing a kiss on my knuckles.

I gazed up at him and nodded, tightening my hold on his hand.

"Better now, babe."

We stepped onto the sidewalk. Down a little way, I saw St. Luke's Lutheran Church, the church where I had my First Communion. A wedding was going on and the sight of the wedding party gathering made me realize something. I wanted that. I wanted him. I wanted to marry this man. How was that possible? Marriage was something I hadn't considered in years.

"Aria?"

"Oh, sorry."

"Daydreaming?" he whispered in my ear, his hot breath grazing my cheek.

"Maybe," I bit my lip to hide my giggle.

"Come on, baby." Somehow, he saw right through me.

Chapter 11

"I miss you, sweetie," Farrah whispered the following day when she opened the door to her apartment on Eastern Avenue. She hugged me tightly then pulled back, her eyebrows going up when she noticed my expression. Ever since Gavin left for work, I had this pit in my stomach. I'd come to rely on him so much in the last few weeks and it terrified me.

"Aria, is something wrong?" Her soft voice was traced with worry as she pulled me into the entryway and wrapped an arm around my shoulder.

"I knew something was up with you at lunch the other day. Did Gavin do something?"

I hastily shook my head, knowing how well they hit it off that day.

"No, he's wonderful. Actually, I think I've fallen for him."

As I said the words, I gasped at how true they were. I longed for his touch, the sound of his voice, the way he said my name. I needed him. When I was sad or happy or anything, I always needed him.

"Have you told him?"

"Well, no."

"This is good, isn't it?" Her forehead creased with worry, bright eyes narrowing.

"I don't know. I vowed to guard myself, to keep from getting attached, falling in love, and inevitably getting hurt. But Gavin, he just sees right through me. He doesn't let me hide. He feels so good … God, I'm so confused!"

She took one of my hands and gave me a small smile.

"Sweetie, it's okay to let yourself trust him. I saw how he couldn't keep his eyes off you. He might not realize it yet, but he loves you. It's written all over his face! Trust me, this isn't one-sided."

I took a deep breath, hoping she was right. But how could he love me? My thoughts scattered as Farrah pulled me into a hug.

"What should I do?"

She sighed, pulling back and giving me a knowing smile, reminding me how lucky I was to have her.

"Just listen to your heart, Ari."

I had to tell him how I felt. I should have told him already.

I smiled, thanking her with another hug. My stomach settled and my mind cleared. Now I realized the strange look Gavin gave me this afternoon wasn't concern or pity, it was bright, filled with care. *Oh, my God, it was love.*

Suddenly, Jaden bolted into the room, a phone pressed to his ear and his face looking surprisingly stressed. He usually looked so at ease, but now his eyebrows were drawn together and one hand clenched his black hair.

"She's here. Yes. All right. Bye."

Who's here? My worries disappeared and were replaced with confusion.

"Your boyfriend is worried about you. You should really help a guy out, Aria."

Gavin? Why would he be—oh, no!

My scalp prickled when I realized I still had my phone off.

"What are you talking about? I saw him earlier."

He folded his arms over his chest, agitated.

"That was Gavin. He has been frantically trying to reach you. He got Farrah's number from Kel when he couldn't reach you by phone. Did you guys have a fight or something?"

"No …"

Farrah walked around me and stepped up to Jaden.

"Relax, Jay. It's all right. She's here. Give him a call, Aria."

I reached into my pocket, hastily turning on my iPhone. Once my home screen popped up, I dialed Gavin's cell and pressed it to my ear. I bordered between worry and nervousness.

"Aria!" he answered, his voice laced with worry.

"It's me," I whispered.

"Why did you turn your phone off?" his voice strung tight.

"It slipped my mind. I was just talking to Farrah. Why were you so worried?"

He exhaled, obviously at war with something.

"You're still at Farrah's?"

"Yes."

"See you soon. Don't leave."

"Gavin … I can just meet you at home"

A low chuckle of laughter emitted from him, but it had no trace of humor. He must be really mad.

"Jaden gave me directions, Aria. I'll be there in a few minutes."

"Okay."

His voice had such a dominant bite to it that when he hung up on me, I just stood there staring at the screen for a good two minutes. What the hell?

Farrah came back in and took a hold of my shoulders.

"What did he say?"

"He's on his way. I have no idea what's going on with him."

She chuckled and dragged me into the kitchen.

"Welcome to the world of men and dating, sweetie!"

"We're going to go to a movie and let you two have some time. Text me, okay?" Farrah announced as she followed Jaden out the door.

I don't know how long I sat there, trying to make sense of things. His overprotective nature was making me crazy, but it made my heart race, too. If he didn't love me, he wouldn't get so worried, would he? There were so many things I loved about him. His eyes, his crooked smile, his voice, and God, his kisses. Could this be right? I just didn't know.

Okay, I did know. But I was scared.

A soft knock at the front door had me rushing to open it. I sucked in a breath as soon as Gavin's stormy eyes gazed down into mine. His forehead creased as he let out a breath, looking me up and down for injury. Tentatively he touched my cheek.

"Are you okay?" he whispered, pulling me to his chest and winding his arms tightly around me. I pressed my face to his neck and nodded, feeling the tension leave his body as I clutched onto his collared shirt.

"Yeah. Why the overreaction, Gavin?"

He pulled away and ran both hands through his tousled hair. Stepping into the apartment he paced the length of the living room a few times in silent contemplation. When his eyes finally shifted back to mine, they were filled with a cloud of uncertainty.

"You can't do that to me, Aria. I couldn't call or text you, you weren't at your place. Do you have any idea what time it is?"

I gaped up at him, at a loss for words. I hadn't noticed the passage of time while I was here.

"It's almost six, Aria. I was worried." His voice filled with anguish and it tore at my heart knowing I caused him to worry. I went to him and cupped his cheeks in my hands. My breath caught at the concern and maybe love in his eyes.

"I'm sorry I worried you. But why were you so worried? It's not like we've been together long." That last part just slipped out. *Crap.*

His eyes hardened at my words and abruptly he pulled away from me.

"I've been having one of my security guards detail Bryce Williams. He was seen in the Downtown South End. I thought … Christ, Aria. I was afraid he got to you!"

Bryce? Security detail? Oh, God. It felt like the bottom of my world dropped away in those long seconds when I heard his name. I couldn't move. I couldn't breathe. I clutched the counter behind me and gasped for air as the memories flooded my mind. His dark eyes. His grip on my chin when he got angry. The cold look in his eyes that last day when he took everything.

"Wait, how did you know his last name?" I asked in a broken voice.

"The police reports are a matter of public record, Aria. I had to protect you. This is the only way I know how." He paced some more, wearing a hole in Farrah's kitchen floor now.

"B-Bryce? He was ... Oh, my God." The breath whooshed out of me and suddenly I felt lightheaded. I began to fall.

Gavin's eyes widened as he caught me in his strong arms. My body shook with a cold shiver as he cradled me against his chest. He kissed my forehead gently. His warmth spread through the cold, replacing darkness with white-hot light.

"Shh, it's okay. You're safe." His soft voice was the only thing I could focus on.

I shook my head. I was so angry at my own carelessness. Gavin had a fierce look on his face. He looked as if he'd step in front of a bullet to keep me safe. I knew he would. I felt my heart break open, letting in light and illuminating the truth I'd refused to admit until now. I loved him. I loved him. I couldn't lie to myself anymore. I was in love with this man. My Gavin.

"I'm so sorry, Gavin. Please don't let me go," I whispered, my voice heavy with fear.

He scooped me up and settled me on the love seat before kneeling in front of me. He grasped my hands tightly in his and his stormy blue eyes captured mine.

"I love you, beautiful. I won't let you go."

I gasped for precious air, losing my voice as those three words replayed in my mind on repeat. *I love you. I love you, beautiful.*

As the wheels started turning in my head again, my heart sped up. It all started to make sense. The look in his eyes, his gentle touch, his protectiveness. He couldn't stay away from me. *Oh, my God, he loved me.* And I fell for him that first day when he called me beautiful.

"Aria, are you okay?" Gavin asked, his hands linked with mine.

His eyes swam with everything I hadn't allowed myself to see until now. God, I was so much in love with him.

"Could you say that again?" I whispered shakily.

He slowly smiled, one of his hands cradling my cheek, eyes blazing with sincerity.

"I love you. I'm so in love with you. Ever since I saw you dance, I was smitten. And then your gorgeous green eyes looked into mine, and I was gone, baby."

My heart stuttered as his words seeped through me. Then I realized that he wasn't the only one. I was drawn to him the very first time I laid eyes on him.

Gavin shook his head incredulously, taking my head in his hands gently. His eyes filled with adoration, worry, concern, and love.

"I. Love. You. Baby. I've never been more sure of anything in my entire life."

I grasped his hands holding my face and felt moisture in my eyes. His admission seemed to banish all my doubts and insecurities. He loved me, all of me. I'd had no idea.

"God, I love you, Gavin. I love you so much."

The words tumbled out of me, my heart yearning for this man. He exhaled, his eyes brighter now. He shook his head once in disbelief before sitting next to me and pulling me onto his lap.

"Say that again, Aria."

I laughed a little, never taking my eyes off his.

"I love you." The words wrenched from the deepest part of me.

Then his mouth covered mine. He pressed his lips urgently to mine, parting them and holding me. One of his hands caressed my cheek. I moaned low at the back of my throat as I let go and gave my heart to him, knowing he'd forever be the man I loved more than anything in this world.

I wrapped my arms around his back and licked into his mouth, needing more of him.

"Jesus Christ, Aria," he whispered against my lips as he sucked on my bottom lip, drawing another moan from my mouth.

"Take me to your place, Gavin."

He groaned and attacked my neck with soft and passionate kisses.

"I'd love to, but we really need to talk about this. What happened with … ?"

I put my hand over his mouth, stopping him, and shook my head.

"We will, I promise. But right now, I need you to take me back to your place and make love to me on every surface in your penthouse. Can you do that?"

He chuckled, pulling away from me and tucking a strand of hair behind my ear.

"Yes, ma'am."

He helped me up and led out of the house.

My mouth never left Gavin's as he pulled me into his apartment minutes later. He closed the door behind us, pressing me up against it. I wrapped my arms around his neck and hitched my legs around his hips, moaning when he softly bit down on my lower lip. He slipped his hand under my shirt, touching my bare back and groaning when he encountered the lacy fabric of my Victoria's Secret bra.

He pulled off my shirt and regarded me with blazing eyes.

"I want you so much."

I smiled, my blood heating in anticipation.

"I want you, Gavin."

Without another word, he swept me into his arms and carried me to his bedroom. He flicked on the lights and set me on the comforter.

He stepped back and slowly peeled off his suit jacket, took off his shoes, and undid his tie. He stepped closer to me and I hastily knelt on the bed, undoing one button at a time on his dress shirt.

"You're so beautiful, Aria," Gavin whispered, kissing my neck and covering my body with his once he discarded his clothes. He kissed me hungrily as he slid my jeans and underwear down and looked deeply in my eyes.

"I was so worried today. I can't even think about something bad happening to you again, baby. I need you."

The vulnerability in his voice was my undoing as I kissed his chest and neck.

"I'm so sorry, I had no idea, Gavin."

He kissed my forehead, fingers threading through my hair.

"I know. I'm not blaming you."

I tightened my arms around him and kissed his jaw eagerly.

"I need you, too, Gavin. Now that I've had you, I know I'd be lost without you."

He kissed me softly.

"I'm going to make love to you now, my beautiful."

My heart stuttered as I opened my legs to him, desire pooling in my core as I felt him at my entrance.

"Yes …"

In every caress, every kiss, every softly murmured sweet nothing, he showed me just how much he loved me. And I was lost to him.

Chapter 12

The enrollment forms and a candidate handbook felt heavy in my grasp as I unfolded them and dropped my eyes to re-read the black lettering across them. I had gotten the papers in the mail today and excitedly, I rushed here to share my news with Gavin. When I found out that I'd been accepted, utter joy was all I felt.

This was my dream.

This internship could make my career.

I skimmed through the first few pages as I felt Gavin's arms wrap around me from behind. He pressed a kiss to my temple and then turned my face up to his.

"Hi, baby, happy birthday" Gavin whispered roughly against my lips, his minty breath wafting between us. It was a sweet inhaling of a kiss that left me wanting more.

"Gavin" I turned into him, leaving the papers on the kitchen island as he lifted me onto the counter.

"So, your enrollment papers came?" He ran his hands up my thighs and his eyes captured mine.

"Yes, I'm so excited! I can't believe I got the internship. It's such a good opportunity for me."

He smiled wider and placed a kiss on my knuckles.

"I'm so proud of you, beautiful. I do want to talk about a few things, though."

I nodded, my fingers coming up to smooth strands of hair out of his eyes. He gazed down at me and I just knew where he was heading with this talk. He was worried now that Bryce had been spotted around here. Honestly, I was afraid myself. He came so close to breaking everything I was. My soul, my being, my hope for a future empty of pain and loss. Still, I didn't want Gavin to worry, not about that.

"He isn't going to come looking for me, Gavin. If he does, he'll go back to prison. I'm sure he doesn't want that."

Unless he was here for me, to steal me away. That dark thought caused a shiver to roll up my spine.

Gavin pulled me into his arms, locking me against the firmness of his chest. He shook his head and closed his eyes briefly, obviously conflicted. God, I hated this. It took me so long to move on from what happened with Bryce, years. And now that I was truly happy, he showed up again and caused more trouble for me.

"I would feel much better if you stayed here with me, Aria. Please. Move in with me. If you are away from me, I'll worry. Besides, I live closer to the academy and the studio and we'll be together. Isn't that what you want?" His deep eyes met mine. I saw hope and fear in them.

I gasped, happiness and uncertainty soaring through me. *He wanted me to move in with him? Was I ready for that? Yes. No. God, I didn't know.*

"Gavin, I don't want you to worry about me and of course I don't want to be away from you. But, I … Do you think we're ready to live together?"

I chewed my lip nervously. He grazed his thumbs along my cheekbones. My skin tingled from his gentle touch. The devotion in his blue-gray eyes was my undoing.

"Do you love me, Aria?" His voice reverberated through me, heating my blood and squeezing my heart with need.

My answer wasn't even a thought in my mind. It wasn't a choice for me to love him, he just took my heart away with that smile and those eyes that read my every thought and emotion.

"Yes, Gavin. God, I do." I wrapped my right hand around the back of his neck, and caressed his jaw with the fingers of my left. His stubble was rough against them, the contact fueled a riot of emotions inside me.

Love.

Desire.

Need.

He smiled crookedly, making my heart skip a beat in my chest. His hand went to the back of my head, his fingers loosening the tie holding my hair back. Finally freed, it fell down my back. His eyes captivated mine as he ran his hand down my hair, before slipping the strap of my tank top down. His hand explored my skin. I gasped, my teeth closing on my bottom lip, desire churning in my core. His hand ran down the length of my arm to the sliver of skin between the top of my yoga pants and the hem of my top. Warmth spread across my skin and I couldn't stop the low moan that slipped out.

"Does my touch make you want more? Are you thinking about the other places you'd like my hand to touch your soft skin? Does this ... " He abruptly pinched my nipple through the cotton fabric, causing me to call out. " ... make you need me inside you, around you, consuming you completely?"

"Aaah ... Gavin, please ... " I whispered, my head falling back slightly as my eyes closed in anticipation of his body pressing against mine.

I couldn't form any thoughts right then.

"Open your eyes, beautiful," he murmured.

When I complied, I saw a heady mix of sincerity and love in his eyes. I wanted him, I loved him, this was right.

He grasped my hips and pulled me against his chest. My hands curled into his bare chest and my eyes to locked onto his blazing blues.

"Yes or no, Aria?" he whispered, repeating the words he said the first night he kissed me.

My head swam with so many reasons to say no, but when I saw the determination in his eyes, I nodded and whispered my assent.

"Yes, Gavin."

Without another word, he carried me to his bedroom and laid me on the bed, his eyes lit up with joy.

"I'm going to love you now, beautiful."

His mouth was only inches from mine. There was such sincerity in his eyes that it was impossible for me to look away.

Gavin spent the rest of the morning loving me, just as he always did.

Tenderly.

Roughly.

Lovingly.

And I soaked up every moment of it.

Once we were both completely sated and exhausted from a long, blissful morning of love making, Gavin's hand took mine and he led me to the bathroom for a shower.

Soft kisses fell over my shoulder as large, callused fingertips smoothed body wash over my fevered skin. I felt Gavin's mouth move against my skin as he spoke.

"Today is all about you, baby. What do you want to do?"

"This," I breathed, turning to lock my arms around his sculpted hips and raised my mouth to meet his. He planted a rough, sweet kiss on me.

"Let's do this all day. I can't think of a birthday present better than this."

A groan emanated from his chest as he took my lower lip between his teeth and tugged, creating a delicious warmth in my core.

"Done," he growled and then his mouth crushed over mine and he did just that.

And again, I soaked up every moment.

Chapter 13

Adrenaline pumped through me as Peter Piers and Justin Scott, the top coordinators in the program at Grayson Academy, flipped through their clipboards. They faced me and about twenty other dancers. Over the last three weeks I'd gotten to know most of them, but now they were my competition for a position. My dream job. I held my breath as I waited for Peter to begin.

"Our decision hasn't been an easy one to make because all of you are talented dancers. But unfortunately, we can't take twenty-two of you. We can only take three. So, we've chosen twelve of you to perform individually in our Summer Showcase. We will judge each of you on your performance and then choose the three lucky ones to join our company."

It felt like I was suspended in air as I waited to hear the names. *My name, please, my name.*

"If I call your name that means you're one of our twelve finalists. If not, know all of you are incredible dancers and these decisions weren't made lightly."

We all nodded as Peter flipped a page on his clipboard and cleared his throat. I pressed my lips together, clinging to hope and crossing my fingers behind my back.

"Dianna Ramirez, Jessica Lawrence, Sarah Kennedy."

The first three names were called and we all clapped for them. "Ella Marley, Georgia Calvin, Kasey Phillips, Maya Scott."

My hands shook, my body buzzed with excitement and nerves.

Oh, God. Only five names left.

"Beth Mann."

More applause. "Candice Anthony, Melanie Lopez, Jasmine Elliot."

My heart skipped a beat at the name I immediately recognized. I don't know why I hadn't noticed her before. She must not have ever been in my small group for practice sessions. I turned to see the blonde I recognized from the tabloid pictures I saw weeks ago. *Oh, my God, she was gorgeous.* Golden hair, sultry eyes, ivory skin and slender hips.

I barely heard it when the last name was called.

"And Aria Morgan."

The entire crowd burst into applause, from the teary-eyed girls who hadn't made the cut to the smiling faces of ones who had, like me.

I was pulled into a hug by Kelly, the girl I'd become the closest to. She squealed with joy as we hugged. I was in a state of shock. *Jasmine. Gavin's beautiful ex-girlfriend. How had I not noticed her before?*

"You're Aria, right?"

I turned away from Kelly to see Jasmine Elliott looking at me with a small smile on her face. Her bleach blonde hair and hazel eyes were all I saw as I took her in. I couldn't help feeling her smile was fake.

"Yes. You're Jasmine, right?" I practically stuttered, not sure how to act around the girl who'd hurt Gavin so badly in the past.

She was in the past, yet, here she was.

"You were great, by the way. Congrats on making the cut."

Her wide, unblinking eyes met mine and she tipped her head to the side. She was sizing me up.

"You're Gavin's new girl? I read something in the papers about him having a new love interest. I just put two and two together when I heard your name called," she said, judging me.

My heart dropped and I had no idea what to say to this woman that my Gavin, used to love. I didn't understand what he saw in her or why she was here now.

Why did it seem that our pasts were coming at us from all sides? First Bryce and now her. I took a step back from her.

"I ... I have to go. Sorry." I pushed past her, my mind reeling as I grabbed my bag and keys, heading straight to the door.

Once inside my car, I set my bag down and sucked in a breath, trying to calm down. I thought she was in Rome. And she was so beautiful. A small part of me wondered what he saw in me when he could have her. I shook my head. Where were these thoughts coming from? I knew who he loved.

My phone rang then and I took it from my purse, surprised when I saw Gavin's breathtaking face on the screen. As if he sensed that I needed him or something. *How did he do that?*

"Hi," I whispered, trying to regain my equilibrium.

"Hey. How did it go today?" The sound of his deep, smooth voice chased the rest of the chills away and my heart began to race.

"Good. I'm a finalist. I made the cut."

"Yes! I am so proud of you, baby. Why don't you sound excited about it?"

I started my car and eased out of the academy's parking lot.

"I think I'm just in shock, Gavin. I really am excited though."

I could tell that he sensed something was off, but I didn't know what to tell him.

"Aria, what's wrong?" he asked, his voice filled with concern.

I exhaled, not wanting to do this over the phone.

"We'll talk about it tonight, I promise. I have to go, Gavin."

I heard a loud screech in the background and then his rough breath across the phone.

"Okay."

When I heard the three soft knocks on the door of my apartment, I glanced up from the oven, shutting it with my knee and peeling off the apron I wore. I was beginning to cook more often, now that I had Gavin. He was bringing out something domestic in me.

My mind was still spinning over Jasmine, but I realized Gavin was right. We both had pasts. I just had to trust in us. My insecurities got the best of me today and that wasn't fair, since Gavin never gave up on me. Even when I told him about my past, my baggage, he still wanted to be with me. So why should Jasmine change anything?

"You're early," I said as I opened the door to him. He wore gray slacks from work and a brown dress shirt. The sleeves were rolled up to his elbows in a sexy way. His eyes locked onto mine in a trance as he gazed down at me and stepped inside. They were filled with determination, love, and some unnamed emotion I couldn't read in the depths of his eyes.

"I couldn't wait to see you, beautiful," he said, dipping his head and wrapping an arm around my waist. The other glided across my thigh as he hitched it around his hip. I moaned when he sucked tenderly on my lower lip, grazing his teeth along the seam, teasing it. Every thought left my mind as I melted into his arms.

"We should talk," I whispered, leaning against him as he sat us on the couch. I faced him in his lap. Curiosity and confusion filled his eyes, and I knew I should be honest with him.

"I met Jasmine today," I whispered.

His hand froze on its journey over my back and his eyes cleared with understanding. His hands ventured from my parted thighs up to my torso to my shoulders. His thumbs dug into the muscles of my shoulders and I almost lost my train of thought.

He knew my body so well.

"She was in Rome, I thought. Where did you see her?" He asked, his blue-gray eyes lifted to meet mine.

I skated my hands down his chest and under his dress shirt to feel the warmth of his skin.

"Actually, she is on my dance team. I didn't realize who she was until her name was called as a finalist, today."

Gavin nodded, his forehead creased with an emotion I couldn't place. *Worry? Maybe.*

"Did she upset you?" he whispered. His hand came up to settle at the nape of my neck, a finger tipping my chin up so I looked into his eyes.

"No, it just surprised me. I didn't know she was a dancer, let alone one of my competitors at Grayson." My voice had an edge to it, betraying my simmering feelings of jealousy and doubt.

I saw him run a hand through his hair and his eyes closed briefly. His shoulders tensed, the calm of a moment ago, gone.

"I don't know why she came back here. She hasn't really stayed in touch in the last four years."

His eyes betrayed his frustration and I cupped his cheeks with my hands. I just had to touch him.

"What's wrong? We don't need to talk about this. She's in the past, right?"

His eyes immediately softened as he leaned his forehead against mine. I rested my palms against his beating heart, needing the reassurance of his heartbeat. His heart began beating faster and I loved knowing I affected him. He affected me the same way.

"Absolutely, I'm just wondering why she's here now. There's nothing here for her. Her father and brothers live in Las Vegas and her only other family is in Aspen."

I took an uneasy breath. In my gut, I knew the reason she was here. Gavin.

I slid off his lap and went to the kitchen, leaning against the island. *Was it possible that she wanted him back?* I didn't know why, I just needed to think this through without the distraction of his touch.

"Could she be here for you?" I asked, dipping my eyes to his.

Gavin looked at me as he rested his elbows on his knees.

"No … I mean … I don't think so."

I narrowed my eyes at him, not sure how to take his evasive answer.

"I mean, it's been four years. Why would she come back now?"

I watched him move from his seat. He paced back and forth, shaking his head in disbelief.

"Does it matter? I'm with you, Aria."

I smiled, the sincerity in his eyes driving away my doubts about Jasmine's intentions.

"You're right. I'm sorry."

Moving back to me, he kissed my forehead. I nuzzled my face into his neck. His scent engulfed me immediately. He was silent for a few moments, holding me around my waist.

"Were you worried that she would change things between us?" he murmured after a while.

He read my mind. I met his eyes, nodding.

"Just a little," I admitted.

He lifted my chin and pressed his mouth to mine, causing my heart to race with a gentle kiss. When he pulled away, I saw the love in his eyes. Inwardly I scolded myself. He loved me. *Why was I doubting that?*

"I'm not going anywhere, baby."

I pressed closer to him and rested my head on his chest, enjoying the feel of him.

"I know, but what if she's ... "

Gavin's lips at my ear stopped me and he grabbed my hand in his.

"That doesn't matter. Aria, I don't want her. I want you, beautiful."

Emotion stung my eyes at his declaration. He pressed his mouth to mine. I immediately slipped my tongue into his mouth deepening the kiss. Passion jolted my body to life. And when he slanted his mouth over mine, grazing his teeth over my lip, I moaned softly. I clenched his silky hair in both hands and explored his mouth. Desire built in my core.

"I. Want. You." Gavin's whisper fueled my need.

I moaned, grabbing at buttons of his shirt. Then the oven dinged.

"Food's ready."

I felt his chuckle against my neck, his stubble grazing my skin, making me want him more. I groaned in frustration, pulling back and giving him a wink as I went to the kitchen.

We managed to eat dinner without any more talk of Jasmine or unpleasant things.

"You look so sexy in this apron, beautiful," Gavin said, wrapping his arms around my waist and kissing my neck softly as I washed the dishes and tipped my head back against his chest.

His mouth closed around my earlobe and nipped softly, making me ache more.

"Will you make love to me, Gavin?" I asked breathlessly, turning in his arms to see his heat up.

"That's the plan."

I tightened my arms around his neck and pressed my lips in a soft, lingering kiss. We laid in my bed, basking in the afterglow. Being in his arms relaxed me and made everything else fade away.

"So ... I was thinking we could move my things into the penthouse today. Is that OK? "

His eyes filled with wonder and he nodded, kissing my temple.

"Absolutely. Come on, let's take a shower."

Though moments ago I was sated, I felt my core tighten deliciously at that suggestion. I quickly followed him down the hall to my bathroom.

He turned on the shower head and turned to me, eyes heated with want.

He pulled me against his chest and planted soft kisses along my jaw. Then he sucked on my collarbone, moving his hands down my body until he reached the bottom of the over-sized t-shirt I wore.

"Gavin ..." I moaned as he dragged his hands up my stomach and across my rib cage, finally slipping the fabric over my head and dropping it to the floor.

"So, beautiful," he whispered, taking my hand and leading me into the shower. We stood under the hot spray.

"Turn around," he ordered.

I did as he bid. He pressed my hands against the tiled wall of the shower. Slowly, he covered my body with soap, while kissing my neck and teasing me. In time, he turned me back towards him. The suds rinsed off my skin. I looked up into his intense blue eyes.

"Lean your head back, baby. I'll wash your hair."

I smiled at his thoughtfulness and obeyed, moaning loudly as he massaged my scalp with his fingers. The pressure against my scalp mixed with the hot water and his touch stole my breath. I felt my body hum with desire.

"Oh, Gavin," I moaned breathlessly.

"I know."

He rinsed my hair, and then with a boyish smile, handed me the body wash.

"Wash me?"

I giggled as I nodded and squeezed some into my hand.

I pressed my mouth to his chest and glided my hands over his stomach, up toward his neck and then down toward his length. He groaned, eyes widening and lips parting.

"Baby, you're my undoing," he whispered as I ran my soapy hands from his neck, down his arms. I intertwined my hands with his.

"Same to you," I whispered reaching for the shampoo.

He tipped his head back, so I could stroke my fingers through his hair. I reveled in the feel of him as I worked the shampoo into his hair. I rinsed him before pressing into him. I wanted him.

"Gavin, you feel so good."

His eyes smoldered before capturing my mouth in a hard, wanton kiss. He licked along my tongue and wrapped his arms around me. He nudged me with his desire.

"Wrap your legs around me, Aria."

I did and he grinned, kissing me softly. He walked us out of the shower and set me on the counter. He knelt in front of me.

"What are you … ?"

Suddenly he ducked his head angling my hips up with his hands. He ran his mouth over my inner thigh and slowly licked my cleft in slow, hungry strokes.

"Gavin!" I cried out, arching into him, yanking on his hair as my head fell back.

Pleasure rocked my core in pulsating waves as he relentlessly kissed my cleft and licked inside me without stopping. I moaned again, feeling my release coming. It overwhelmed me, drowned me, surprised me.

"Gavin … please," I begged, needing something more but I wasn't sure what.

Then he pushed two fingers inside me, twisting them as he thrust them in and out, in and out. I struggled for breath as my body climbed, trembling with pleasure. I grasped onto him tighter and called out in pleasure as I shattered into a million vibrant pieces, closing my eyes in ecstasy.

"Wow," was all that fell from my lips after that.

After getting dressed and packing most of my things, we loaded them into his four-door Toyota Tundra. Gavin grazed kisses along my hand.

"Penny for your thoughts?" he whispered, pulling into the rear lot so we could enter through the back entrance.

"Just feeling lucky to have found you, Gavin," I murmured, leaning across the console to steal a kiss that only left me wanting more.

"Trust me, I feel the same way. Let's get you unpacked and then I'd like to take you somewhere, baby."

A small smile played along my lips as I remembered every delightful surprise he'd given me since we met.

"I love surprises," I said, biting my lip.

He smiled widely. His eyes were playful as he urged my lip from between my teeth with a lazy lick of his tongue.

"Good. I want to make you happy every day, Aria."

I gasped, not expecting his earnest words. I wanted to feel his love every day, too.

"You do, Gavin."

He winked at me, hopping out of the truck and helping me out a moment later. His eyes looked so blue in the sunlight, the blues overshadowing the grays.

"What?"

He gazed down at me, raising an eyebrow.

"I love your eyes," I whispered, dragging my teeth along his jaw and kissing the side of his mouth.

He groaned, chuckling lightly. It was such a sexy sound.

"I love you, Aria. And I love your smile, by the way."

My heart skipped a beat.

He took me around to the tailgate and began unloading the boxes stacked inside. He handed me my duffel bag and I went to unlock the back door with my new key.

"Wait, babe," he said, stepping in front of me. His shoulders tensed as he unlocked the door. "I just want to be careful. My security team is inside and I don't want to catch them off guard."

I looked up at him. I had forgotten his concern about Bryce. I cringed inwardly, not wanting to think about his whereabouts. I would rather pretend he wasn't a threat. I'd rather him be long gone like he was before.

Gavin tucked me close and pressed his lips to my forehead.

"Has something happened?"

"No, I'd tell you if something had. I promise. I just don't want to be careless."

I nodded, leaning into him as he let us into his apartment. He set the boxes down by the couch.

A dark-haired, slender man with the lightest green eyes came across the entryway. He had an earpiece in his ear and there were three other men behind him. Though they were dressed casually the way they carried themselves was anything but casual. The man in front stepped forward to shake Gavin's hand.

"Mr. Thomas."

"Spencer. Everything clear?"

"Yes, of course. This must be Ms. Morgan. It's nice to meet you."

I offered my hand and he shook it. He looked young, no more than 25. He had to be the security lead Gavin mentioned.

"Aria. It's nice to meet you, too."

Gavin wrapped an arm around my waist and looked back at Spencer.

Worry coiled in my gut as the concern filled Gavin's eyes and I leaned my head against his shoulder, my trust that he would make this all okay was stronger than my unease of the situation.

Later that day I unpacked my things, excited by how well I was adjusting to this home-style penthouse Gavin now shared with me. I set the picture of Jeremy and me on the bedside table. I noticed another framed photo sitting there. I picked it up and saw a worn photograph in a black frame. An older woman with soft gray eyes and wrinkles around her mouth smiled at the camera. She had, white hair pulled into a bun. I saw the resemblance in her face. Gavin stood next to her, a huge smile on his face and his arm around her shoulder.

"Hey, beautiful," Gavin murmured, stepping up to nuzzle my cheek.

"Who's this?" I asked.

"My grandmother from my dad's side. Tessa. We were really close when I was growing up."

I turned in his arms and pressed my hands to his cheeks when I saw the tinge of sadness in his eyes.

"When did she pass?" I skated my fingers across his freshly-shaven jaw.

"Last year," he murmured, almost to himself.

I wrapped him in my arms. Gavin pressed his face into the swell of my neck and breathed me in. He leaned back after a moment, his eyes were clear of sadness. Instead, I saw only the love he had for me.

"I love you, Aria. Always."

He bent his head to kiss me. When the kiss ended, I rested my forehead against his, trying to catch my breath.

"Can I take you somewhere, Aria?"

I smiled, nodding as he grinned that wide smile at me.

"Sure."

Chapter 14

Gavin took me to the beach for a picnic and swim. We didn't worry about the darkness that followed me, we didn't talk at all, actually.

We just held each other, swam together and shared a blissful time together.

It was amazing. I never wanted it to end. But as the sun set on the horizon above us and the wind in the salty air picked up, I felt Gavin wrap my pink towel around my shoulders and he tugged me into his side.

"Let's go home."

My heart soared at the sound of that one word. Home.

"I really like the sound of that," I whispered. His eyes filled with want as he carried me off the beach and set me beside his truck a moment later. He dried me off, wrapped the towel back around me. I grabbed another one and dried him off, placing a kiss quickly on his lips before hopping into the heated truck. The heat warmed my fingers, banishing the goose bumps covering my arms and legs.

"You're so beautiful, Aria. You take my breath away every time I see you."

His sincere voice and hungry blue eyes made my heart race with desire. He held one of my hands the whole ride.

"I love you," I announced as we parked, smiling as he dipped his head toward mine.

His nose ran along mine. The tender way he adored my mouth was heavenly. God, I never knew I needed this. But I did. His love had healed me in the best way possible.

"I love you, too, baby. Let's go inside."

I nodded, looking up and spotting a white Lincoln in the spot next to us with a figure inside. When Gavin opened my door, his eyebrows were drawn together in concern.

"That's Jasmine's car. Why is she here?"

He came around and opened my door with a frown on his face. He grabbed my hand and led me around the front of the car, his face tensed with frustration.

"Maybe she wants to apologize."

He shook his head, tracing a finger down the side of my face as we stood by the car. Her door opened and she stepped out.

"Gavin …" she said.

"Wait here," he commanded her and he walked me to the door of the building.

What did she want? Uneasiness spread through me the minute I saw her slender frame leaning on his car acting as if she belonged there.

"I'll figure out what she wants. Can you wait for me inside, baby?"

I nodded, trying to calm the worry etching my mind. I kissed him softly, giving him my best smile. He handed me my purse as he ran a hand through his hair, steeling himself to talk to his ex after four years of silence.

"I'll be waiting in our bedroom." I wrapped my hands around his broad shoulders and pressed my face into his neck.

"I won't be long," he said before kissing me deeply.

I sat on the edge of the bed, waiting and waiting and waiting. I was dying know what they said. The suspense ratcheted up my anxiety. Finally, I heard the front door close, and then footsteps down the hall.

Gavin opened the door and met my eyes, his brows drawn together in agitation. He sat next to me and gazed into my eyes, silently.

"Everything okay?" I asked when I couldn't take the silence any longer.

Nodding, he kissed my knuckles as I smoothed hair from his eyes. He looked tense, which only spiked my apprehension more.

"I'm sorry she showed up here, Aria. I promise you, I didn't ask her to come."

"I know."

He sighed, the tension finally leaving his body all at once. His eyes cleared as he gazed down at me earnestly.

"She won't be back. I made it clear who I want."

My heart stuttered, his deep voice and clear eyes penetrated my uneasiness.

I pressed against him and burrowed my face into his neck.

"Make love to me, Gavin."

His eyes filled with love and I moaned as his mouth came down to suck and lick my throat. His hands flexed against my bottom. All my insecurities were forgotten as he made love to me slowly.

Chapter 15

"Today's session might take a while since it's my last one before the showcase. Gavin, you don't have to stay."

Gavin opened the glass door of the building for me, a shadow of a smile on his handsome face.

"Only for a bit. I have an overseas conference call and a few meetings this afternoon."

Eli waved us over and I saw Gavin's shoulders tense when he spotted Eli's shaved head and piercing navy blue eyes.

"Eli, this is my boyfriend, Gavin Thomas."

"Nice to finally meet the man who's stolen Ms. Morgan's heart. I'm Eli Jenkins."

Gavin relaxed substantially and they shook hands, moving into easy conversation as I slipped on my ballet flats and went to the center mat to begin stretching. My limbs ached more than usual. I was sore from all the earth-shattering lovemaking we'd done over the last week. When I turned, I saw Gavin's adoring stare as the music began and Eli stepped by my side.

"Ready to practice the routine?" Eli asked. I nodded, stretching once more and pulling my hair into a messy bun. A slow, lingering melody began and my eyes fluttered closed. The notes collided into each other, creating a sad haunting mood as my first steps glided over the floor. As the dance ended, I kept my eyes closed, taking in a cleansing breath.

I could almost see Jeremy applauding, just as he always had when I performed. It calmed me.

When I opened my eyes, I locked onto Gavin's intense gaze. Stepping forward, he pulled me to him and I pressed my face to his neck, inhaling his distinct scent.

"What did I do to deserve a goddess like you, baby?"

I kissed the side of his mouth, my heart skipping a beat at his hungry gaze.

"You're stuck with me, Gavin."

He smiled wide, closing his mouth over mine, stealing my breath and creating tingles across my skin. His heady scent overwhelmed me and hunger smothered my senses. I moaned his name as he explored my mouth. I didn't think I'd ever tire of this. His touch, his taste, his hands. It was addicting to me. Then, his phone rang.

"Sorry," he breathed, gazing down at his smart phone and frowning. "I have to go, baby. You okay to get home?"

I kissed his lips quickly, nodding.

"I'll have Kel come, no worries. How about I bring you dinner later? Will you be free by seven?"

His eyes brightened and his mouth turned up.

"See you then, Aria. Don't turn off your phone, okay?"

I nodded as he walked out. "You ready to continue?" Eli called, forcing my gaze from Gavin's departing backside. My cheeks heated and I nodded, heading toward the mats once more.

I slipped off my ballet flats and looked up to see Kel leaning by the benches.

"Hey." She grinned and threw an arm around my shoulders as we headed out to the car.

"How's the wedding planning going?" I asked as we drove to Henry's Pub, our favorite spot in East End.

"Amazing! Everything's coming together. I can't believe in only two weeks I'll be married."

Her face lit up in happiness. I'd wanted to be with her every step of the way as she planned her dream wedding but with the showcase and my new relationship, my mind was elsewhere.

"Good. I'm so sorry I haven't helped more with the wedding. If you need anything ..."

She grabbed my hand in hers and gave me a knowing smile.

"I know you're here for me. You've had so much going on ... I completely understand."

I nodded.

"How's Gavin?"

"Well, things are... He's just so unbelievable. I told him I love him, Kel."

She parked in front of Henry's and gave me a shit-eating grin. Oh, goodness.

"Oh, my God! And what did he say?"

I blushed, remembering his heartfelt words.

"Like I said, unbelievable."

She squealed happily and hugged me tightly, too tightly.

"I'm so happy for you!"

She released me, smiling.

"I know."

We walked into the pub and my stomach grumbled. I moaned in appreciation at the flavor of the delicious triple stacked cheeseburger. Kel picked at her fries, telling me all about the details of the wedding.

"Are you listening?"

I looked up, nodding as my thoughts roamed to Jasmine and the uneasy feeling I had that she was not going anywhere anytime soon.

"Sorry, I was just lost in thought."

She gazed at me and shook her head as if I was crazy. I had filled her in on Gavin's ex and the little stunt she pulled when she visited his, no, *our* home. Even though I knew how strong we were, I still worried her re-appearance would change things.

A small, insecure part of me worried that Gavin may have been better off with a woman without a dark past and the loads of baggage I had. I wanted to be good for him, just as he was so very good for me.

But was that possible when my demons were threatening to break us in two?

"That man is crazy for you, Aria. You know that. If his ex wants him back, so be it. He loves you. That's all that matters."

How did she know exactly what I needed to hear? I relaxed, nodding. She was right. I was being silly. He loved me.

"Thanks, Sis. Actually, do you mind if I order something to go? I thought I'd bring him some dinner."

She grinned, popping a fry into her mouth as I waved over our waitress.

"Can I get an order of fettuccine alfredo to go? With a Blue Moon?"

She smiled warmly, a strand of her red hair falling into her eye.

"No problem. Anything else?"

"No, thanks."

We stacked our dishes as Kel's phone rang.

"I'll meet you in the car," she said, putting down her half of the bill and scooting out of the booth.

"Okay, Hun."

With a to-go box in hand, I checked my messages, figuring on at least one or two from Gavin.

Nothing. He must have been busy, I told myself. I got into the car as Kel ranted to someone about how this was her special day and she deserved the world. I bit my lip, feeling bad for whoever was on the other end of the line.

After a detour to Glendale Florist for an order change that Kel insisted on, she parked toward the front of Gavin's building.

"Your man is rich!" she whistled.

I giggled, taking off my seat-belt eagerly.

"I wouldn't care if he was a janitor, Kel."

She turned to me, smiling.

"I know, sweetie. Don't take too long, we've got plans tonight."

I grabbed the food and made my way into the building, amazed at its size.

I hopped onto the elevator, smoothing my sundress down my backside and pulling my hair out of the bun. My mind started to wander between floors. How was it possible to miss someone I was with a few hours ago?

I stepped off the elevator on the 26th floor, coming to an outer door that read Gavin Thomas, CEO.

Somehow seeing his name on the door excited me. I opened it and saw a long granite counter and a reception desk with a man behind it. He flashed me a charming smile.

"Good afternoon, how may I help you?"

"Hi, I'm Aria Morgan. I'm here to see Gavin. We have a date."

His grin was infectious and he told me to go down the hall to the first door on the right.

"I'm sorry, Jazz," I overheard the voices from the lobby, and I knew immediately who Gavin was talking to. My heart sank a little. Just hearing his voice laced with worry for her had my breath catching in my throat. *Why was she in his office? What the hell?*

Confusion and a haze of unease settled inside me. My gut told me to turn away and call Gavin tomorrow once I'd had time to think about the questions swirling in my head. But my heart kept me walking towards the open door to his office.

I heard his soft voice soothing her. *Jazz. God, he was talking to Jasmine.*

I felt sick. When I rounded the corner, I saw his office door open. His arms were wrapped around Jasmine, her long blonde hair pulled into a braid as she clutched onto him. His lips landed in her hair as he held her in his arms.

"I can't believe it, Gavin. I can't …" she sobbed.

The sight of them gutted me.

Jasmine was holding onto Gavin as she cried, her voice loud and filled with anguish. I watched as she sobbed into his dress shirt and he held her tighter. The embrace was intimate, and the sight of it was almost too much to watch.

"Shhh," he soothed her and when she pulled away, her hands gripped the collar of his shirt while one of his hands settled at the small of her back.

My heart thrummed a panicked rhythm in my chest and tears built in my eyes. I told myself to look away. I couldn't possibly be witnessing this. When I saw her lips pressed to his all the breath left my body. A sound, low and guttural erupted from my chest, the pain seared through me at the sight.

My Gavin with her. I hastily turned around, blocking the image from my sight. I couldn't take it anymore.

How could he? After everything we had?

I still was not enough for him.

The thought made me want to get away from them as soon as possible.

Was it all a sham? Did he ever truly want me?

I dropped the food on the floor by his office. Tears streamed down my cheeks as I ran toward the exit. Doubt and hurt and anger filled me. My heart was being ripped apart, my stomach lurched as I made it just in time to empty the contents of my stomach into a trash can nearby.

How could I have been so stupid? He was probably seeing her this whole time and I was just too blind to see it. I loved him... God, I loved him with everything inside me. I ran even faster away from the scene and then I heard footsteps behind me.

I heard his deep voice calling behind me. I tried to wipe away my sadness as I realized he saw me. He came for me. Gavin yelled my name louder and I halted at the sound of his voice. It was laced with something? Shame? Worry? Fear, I thought. I just didn't know why.

"I swear to God it isn't what you think, Aria. You have to know ..."

Anger seeped through me, replacing the crippling pain for a moment. I turned around and walked to him, my body vibrating with so many emotions I didn't have a prayer of stopping the words bubbling up my dry throat.

"I have to know what, Gavin? Please tell me because it looks like I've seen enough to know!"

I wiped my mouth, sweeping my hair away from my face as the tears kept coming.

"Baby, I …" Before I knew what I was doing, my hand flew out and landed forcefully against his cheek, knocking his face to the side. His eyes shot back to mine, his gasp audible. I saw the fear in his eyes now, along with the ever-present love in his gaze. I couldn't stand to see it, so I turned away from him, intent on walking away.

"Don't leave, Aria. Please listen to me!" his voice filled with panic.

I ran away from him but somehow still heard the words he yelled to me, his deep voice jolting me with the fierceness in it.

"You have to know you're my world, Aria!"

By the time, I got into my sister's car again, my entire body was shaking.

"Aria! Are you okay? What happened?"

I breathed in and out, struggling, and finally found the words.

"Please. Drive."

Chapter 16

Kel handed me a steaming cup of cocoa and knelt beside me on the couch.

"What happened?"

I sighed, turning to her. I tried to reach inside and grasp my inner strength but, honestly, I wasn't sure I had any left.

"I saw him. Jasmine was there. His ex."

She gasped, wiping my tears away. Her eyes filled with compassion.

"Why was she there?"

"I don't know. She was upset, I think. Gavin was holding her and then they kissed."

I took in a breath then let it out, trying in vain to keep my tears at bay.

"Oh, sweetheart, I'm so sorry. What happened next?"

I gazed up at her, shrugging my shoulders in response.

"You didn't talk to him?"

I shook my head. What could he have possibly said to explain himself?

"I couldn't. I knew she wanted him back. I just never thought she'd take him from me like this."

Then Kel pulled me into her arms and I let go. The tears came and my body shook with sobs. Unrelenting and uncontrollable sobs. The whole time, I asked myself how could he do this to me? How could the man I'd been falling for do this to me?

Once I cried myself dry, I occupied myself by practicing my showcase performance for the next day. My heart felt empty after seeing that slut kiss Gavin, but I refused to waste any more tears. After my body was pushed to the limit I sank down on the mats in the guest room and took a sip of water. For the first time, I really listened to the lyrics playing. It was Gravity by Sarah Bareilles. The song reminded me of what Gavin and I shared.

I remembered the moment I saw Gavin, he took my breath away. Even though I wanted to hate him, I couldn't, because I loved him. How could it all be over so quickly? I couldn't bring myself to believe it, yet.

"Come on, Ari. You need some rest before the showcase tomorrow." Kel shut off the music and rested her hands on her hips.

"Okay, I'll try. No promises, though."

I got up. She hugged me tightly, and closed the door behind her as she left.

I crawled into the full-size bed and curled into a ball. I closed my eyes, willing sleep to find me. I yearned to feel Gavin's strong arms around me, his chin resting against my shoulder as it always did as we fell asleep together. I ached to hear him whisper "Sleep, baby" just before my eyes drifted closed. And it was with thoughts of his sweet murmurs and love-filled eyes that I found sleep.

Residual panic forced me awake as I sucked in precious air. God, I had a nightmare. I hastily looked at the clock, worried I'd overslept. The bedside radio read ten-thirteen in the morning. I took a deep breath, remembering Gavin's soothing words the night he found me here having a nightmare. *Breathe, Aria. Just breathe.*

"You up, honey?" Kel called from the kitchen. I got up and began making the bed in an effort to get my mind off the dream. He left me.

"Yeah, I'm awake," I answered. I heard her talking to someone on the phone.

"I know, I'll try, but she's hurting right now. Gavin, she needs time. Okay, will do. Bye. "

Gavin called her? Why?

I grabbed my iPhone and saw twelve missed calls, six text messages, and three voice mails, all from Gavin. My hand shook as I contemplated listening to them. *No.* I'd surely fall apart hearing his voice right now.

She was right. I needed time to think, and to mend my heart if possible. I turned off my phone and got dressed in one of the few outfits I had left here, brown yoga pants and a white button-down shirt. Leaving a few buttons undone, I slipped my phone and car keys into my purse and went into the bathroom to fix my messy hair.

"Ready, Ari?" Luke asked as he made his way down the hallway. I secured the French braid at the back of my head and smoothed my shirt.

"Yeah. Can you grab my dance bag? It should be on the bed."

"Sure thing."

He hooked it over his shoulder as he stepped out. He placed a hand on my shoulder, squeezing gently.

"How are you doing?"

I shrugged as he hugged me to his side and we headed out to the car.

Focus, Aria, you can do this, I told myself, willing myself not to cry about Gavin anymore. I had to be strong, if only for a few hours.

Hours later, I sat with Kel after my warm up, her fingers threaded through my hair as she combed the black curls down my back, securing each one with a bobby pin.

"Ouch!" I yelped as a pin dug harshly into my scalp.

Kel laughed nervously and released the pin quickly, letting the curl fall from her fingers.

"Sorry, sweetie. You okay?"

I tried to laugh, but my heart seized painfully in my chest as I kept seeing the same painful image in my mind. Gavin kissing Jasmine. His ex. The woman he almost married. The one who just walked in from having just finished her performance sauntered into the room and cast her eyes my way.

"Sure, no worries," I said through gritted teeth as I tried to ignore the look on her face and the memory of her lips on my man.

Gavin's mouth, the one that adored me and pleasured me in the best ways, locked on another woman's lips. It was still so fresh in my mind.

"I really think you should call him, Aria. I didn't mention it earlier, but he showed up at the apartment last night."

My mouth dropped open and a mixture of anger and confusion filled me.

Why?

Kaelyn moved around my chair and her eyes were filled with worry for me. I hated that she was worried. I knew she thought Gavin was the one for me. I blinked my eyes furiously, not wanting to shed one more tear for him.

He had been kissing another woman, Aria. You're better off without him!

"I know you're angry right now, Ari. And I'm so sorry, but you need to talk to him."

I shook my head, cursing the fact that he'd gained her stamp of approval before he broke my heart in two. *That was exactly how it felt.*

She took my hand in hers and I blinked, looking down to see her worrying her lip between her teeth. Then I realized just how worried she was about all of this.

All my sister ever wanted was for me to be happy and that meant sometimes she had to convince me to grab hold of that happiness, even when it scared me.

And I had. I had been blissfully, *crazily* happy with Gavin.

He threw it away.

"Ari, you didn't see him last night. He was a mess. I've never seen a man look so utterly broken and shit, I didn't have the heart to throw him out. I don't know exactly what happened with Jasmine, but you need to talk to him. I don't think he can survive without you."

I sniffed as a sob broke through my chest and my heart beat faster at the thought that maybe I had hurt him by running away as I had.

"H-he hurt me, Kel. I can't see him. I can't even think about him because it just hurts too much."

Her arms wrapped around me and I felt her nod her head against my shoulder.

"I know. But I think you are both hurting. I just want you to be happy, Ari"

I wiped my tears away and pulled back from her, hoping my smile reassured her.

"I can't talk to him right now."

I really hoped she wouldn't push the topic because I honestly was not ready to hear Gavin's voice, see his face, or feel his presence any-time soon. It would just be too much for me. My heart couldn't take anymore fractures right now.

Before she could say anything, my iPhone rang a melody from the vanity in front of us. We both looked at it.

Oh, holy crap. Was it him?

"Hello?" I didn't recognize the number but then I heard Callie's voice.

"Hi, Aria?"

She hiccuped. I heard her crying and voices in the background. *Oh, no.* Deep inside me, my heart stopped as fear took hold.

"What's happened, sweetheart? Are you okay?"

She sniffed and after a moment she calmed down.

"Something ... well ..."

There was a rustling noise and my hands shook. She continued.

"Gavin's car ... He's been in an accident."

Oh, God. All the air left my lungs and I struggled to find words. *Gavin?*

"You're at Mercy West?" I choked out.

"Yes, Wing C in Emergency. Hurry."

I dropped the phone to my lap and sucked in a breath. My body was strangled in a sob. My skin felt like ice and my heart dropped into my stomach. I lost Jeremy and it all began with a car accident.

God, no. It was happening all over again.

Chapter 17

Gavin was admitted to the hospital, he was in an accident. Aria, he's in critical condition.

The words from the phone call repeated in my head. I clasped my locket in my hand like some sort of good luck talisman.

Gavin was hurt. Or worse ... God. If only I had been with him last night, if only I hadn't run away. The fear unfurled in the pit of my stomach and pushed against my ribs as I struggled for words.

"Come on Aria, let's get to the hospital. It's going to be okay I promise you, honey."

She turned me around in the chair and cupped my cheeks so, I had to look into her soft eyes.

"Do you believe me?"

I nodded, knowing she was right. I had to hold onto hope, Gavin needed me now. And God, I needed him so much. I couldn't lose him. I couldn't lose the man I loved more than anything. My thoughts never strayed from him on the ride to the hospital. It was a long drive through traffic. I must have zoned out because when I came to, we were parked in front of a hospital.

Panic gripped me once again and I threw open the car door and ran towards the double doors. My feet carried me across the parking lot so fast that I found myself struggling to catch my breath. I knew I should slow down. I knew I should wait for Kel to catch up. I knew all of those things, but all reason had fled my mind, I just had to get to Gavin. I had to.

"Ari!" Kel caught up with me and I forced my feet to slow. She grabbed my hand and looked into my eyes with such concern and love.

"I have to call Lucas to let him know what's going on, but then I'll come find you. OK?"

I nodded as we turned the corner into the ER lobby.

I sucked in a breath, trying to find the strength to think positive right now. *Did have injuries? Or was he going to be OK?*

I needed answers.

Unwillingly, my eyes were forced closed by the fear racking my body and I felt my sister's arms wrap around me. *How could this have happened to Gavin?* Whenever I'd been in his car with him, he was always a cautious driver. He wouldn't drive recklessly. That was very much unlike him.

Unless … unless he was going out of his mind after I ran away from him, from us. Maybe he wasn't thinking and all he could focus on was getting to me.

I hastily tried to rid my mind of thoughts like that. It was not like there was any possible explanation he could have given me that would make me believe him. Believe that my initial thoughts when I saw that woman in his office were wrong or misguided. He was kissing her. His ex. The woman that jilted him at the altar years ago. Gavin told me what that did to him. *How could he?* I felt the sharp glass of heartbreak in my chest from the memory of seeing him kissing another woman. I didn't think I'd ever forget it, but if I hadn't run, would we be here now?

"Oh, my God, this is all my fault," I whispered, a sob erupting from my chest as I buried my face into my sister's shoulder.

She rubbed my back slowly and tightened her arms around me as I sobbed quietly.

"Shh you have to stay positive, Ari."

I sniffled, nodding to reassure her I was okay. I took a deep breath as she released me and wiped my tears away.

"I'm okay, go. It's OK, I'll see you later. Thank you, " I whispered, faking a smile.

Kel leaned forward, giving me a kiss on my forehead.

"I'll be back soon, go see your man, Aria." She smiled warmly, hoping to lift my spirits.

I waited until she turned the corner before wiping my cheeks and finding the strength to walk towards the emergency room where I saw Callie sitting in a chair with her chin resting on her knees. Her eyes looked lost as she stared across the waiting room at a conference room; the door was open.

"Callie?"

She looked up and her eyes lit up as she got up to walk over to me.

"Are you okay?" I asked as she hugged me.

We sat in the waiting room chairs. Her eyes filled with tears. My own pricked with moisture at her sadness.

"I can't believe this is happening. My mom is in with the doctors now."

"It's going to be okay, Callie." I turned, grabbing her hand as my mind rewound the last few weeks.

The best moments of my life flooded my mind. Making love with Gavin, breakfast in bed, the joy in his eyes when I told him I loved him the first time, countless happy moments replayed in my mind. And then, the final heartbreaking image of his ex-fiance locking lips with him inside his office yesterday.

I didn't know how long we sat there, but eventually I started to fidget, restlessly in the uncomfortable chair.

"Sweetie, I'm going to take a walk."

She nodded, giving me a half smile and I released her hand to head toward the bank of elevators. I pulled out my phone, stepping into the empty car. I clasped the locket in both hands as I closed my eyes and took a deep, cleansing breath.

He was going to be okay. Gavin. My Gavin. He had to be OK. I loved him. My goodness, I loved him so much. Even though I was so hurt right now, I knew I still loved him.

The voice mail alarm signaled from my phone for the fourth time, and I couldn't ignore it anymore. Last night I missed him so much, I missed falling asleep in his arms. The feeling of his lips on mine as we laid in bed together. The heavenly sight of his face, relaxed and handsome as he slept in the early hours of the morning.

With tears building in my eyes, I selected the first message he left for me. I closed my eyes, leaning against the stop button on the elevator's control panel. The car slowed to a stop between the third and fourth floors as Gavin's soft voice came across my senses.

"Aria, please, call me. I know what you saw, but I promise you with everything I am that I did not kiss Jasmine. Just please call me so I can explain. I love you, baby. Please call me."

Oh, my. His voice sounded so raw, so wounded. And so, determined. The next message was a couple of hours later. I sucked in a breath when I heard his voice again.

"Aria. I need to talk to you. Please. I love you more than anything and I promise you, I would never cheat on you. But since you won't answer your phone, I must explain. Jasmine showed up at my office, she was upset …"

His voice was filled such despair, it tore at my soul. *Could he be telling the truth? Oh God, I should have just stopped to talk with him!*

"Baby, it isn't what you think. She was barely holding herself to-gether. She had a falling out with her dad. I knew how she felt. I tried to comfort her. She kissed me. I didn't kiss her back. I pushed her away. And then I saw you. Baby, please believe me. I love you and only you. Call me …"

Gavin's voice broke, cracking on the last few words and a strangled sob escaped me as my legs gave out. I slid to the floor, my back against the glass wall of the car. The tears escaped my eyes and I covered my face with my hands.

Oh, God. He was telling the truth, I could hear it in his voice. And I just … walked away. I didn't even let him explain, I just … left!

I listened to the third message. My heart felt as if it stopped as I listened to his voice again over my voice mail.

"Baby, I know you are OK. I checked in at Luke and Kel's to make sure you were safe. You looked so peaceful. I am so sorry for causing you pain. I can't imagine my life without you. Please let me explain. I love you so much."

My finger scrolled over to the last message, it had been left at 5:22pm, today. Only twenty minutes before I got the call from Callie.

His voice sounded more determined now, but was still laced with pain and sadness. Regret, maybe.

"Aria, this has gone on long enough. I've tried waiting for you to call me, or to show up at the penthouse, but I can't wait anymore. I'm coming to see you, baby. I'll see you soon."

He was coming to see me, he didn't kiss her. Oh, my God what if he blamed me for this? Or, my breath evaporated from my lungs as I realized my biggest fear. What if... I lost him?

Just like Jeremy, just like my brother. I couldn't, I wouldn't lose him. I pushed myself to my feet and I pressed the button to start elevator's car. But this time, I headed for the first floor, back to the Emergency Room. I had to see Gavin

After twenty more minutes of waiting, a doctor came out of the conference room. Immediately, I stood with Callie, who gripped my hand a little too tightly. Seeing the fear in her eyes brought me back to seven years ago, when I was the sister waiting for word about her brother. So, unsure of what would happen, so scared of the inevitable. But now, all I wanted was for Gavin to be okay. So, I shook the doctor's hand and tried to remain calm as I waited.

He looked down, wiping beads of sweat from his forehead and then his eyes met mine, filled with uncertainty. A tall brunette with round rimmed glasses and kind gray eyes identical to Gavin's came to Callie's side and they hugged before she moved to me and a surprised gasp left me as she wrapped her slender yet strong arms around my shoulders, pulling me gently into her embrace.

"Gavin has told me so much about you. You must be Aria."

I nodded, taking her hands in mine when she pulled back, unsure of what to say to his mother at a time like this.

"I'm so glad we've finally met, Ms. Thomas. I'm so sorry I wasn't here sooner. I- I didn't know."

Hushing me quietly, she wrapped an arm around my shoulder and it calmed me.

"Please, call me Elizabeth."

I nodded and smiled before she spoke again.

"My son loves you very much. He'll tell you that when he wakes up, OK?"

We turned back to the doctor and he gave me a small smile and shook Callie's hand in greeting.

"I'm Dr. John Lee. Mrs. Thomas told me you are his girlfriend, yes?"

I nodded, holding in the emotions threatening to erupt from within me.

"I'm … um … Aria Morgan. How is he?"

"Well, Gavin is in stable condition. He does have bruised ribs and a concussion, some cuts and bruising on his stomach from where glass from the driver's side window cut him. Where he hit his head, there may be brain damage. We won't know more until he regains consciousness. I doubt there is any damage, since there's no indication of any in the scans we've run, but it is a possibility you should prepare yourself for."

I let out the breath I was holding, my brain struggled to process all this information. He was alive, that was all I could focus on. *Gavin was alive.*

"If all goes well, he should make a full recovery. Would you like to see him?"

He took my hand, getting my attention and I nodded.

Stay strong, Aria, just a little longer.

"Yes, where is he?" My heart beat faster at the thought of seeing Gavin, my Gavin.

"Room 172. He should be awake within a few hours."

I rushed to follow the doctor, the fear still coursing through me, though now it was mixed with a yearning of hope. Callie and Elizabeth caught my hands as I walked away and I turned back, confused. I wondered why they weren't coming with me to see him.

"Aren't you coming to see Gavin?" I asked.

"No. You go first. They will only let one of us see him right now and I know he'll want to see you as soon as he wakes up. We'll go get some lunch and meet you later."

"Okay. Don't take too long. He needs you too."

Callie hugged me tightly and then I walked away, the need to see Gavin fueling my body. I just needed to know he would be okay.

He had to be okay.

"Gavin, baby, I'm here." My voice was strained with emotion.

I tried to take deep breaths through the fear coursing through me.

What if he didn't wake up?

God, I couldn't fathom being without him.

How would I survive it?

I clutched the hand that wasn't bound up in wires and tape, pressing his palm to my cheek in an effort to connect in some small way. I just needed him to open those gorgeous blue-gray eyes of his.

I thought back to that first night he held me, so long ago. He held me as I trembled in fear. He calmed me with a simple touch and just a reminder to breathe. I drew in a deep breath as I looked upon his broken form. I needed to just breathe now. I needed him to just breathe now, too. I wasn't sure how long I sat there silently remembering the comfort he brought me in my moments of terror. After a while sitting with him in silence, I remembered Dr. Lee said that Gavin might be able to hear me, to feel my presence.

Suddenly it made perfect sense to me. I had to give him a reason to wake up, to come back. I had to talk to him, tell him everything I'd been feeling since Callie's phone call.

"Gavin …" I pressed my hand to his chest where I felt his steady heartbeat beneath my fingers.

"I feel it. I feel your heart. It's still beating. Please, please come back to me."

Tears welled in my eyes and I dipped my head to his forearm as I silently cried. I was so scared, so, so scared that I'd lost this kind, passionate, beautiful man forever.

"I'm so sorry, Gavin. I left and I didn't let you explain. I was so hurt, so angry with you after what I saw in your office yesterday. I had no idea what to think, how to move on from you. I love you. I think I've loved you since the moment we first met."

God, the truth of my last thought struck right through my heart. I'd been so afraid to open up to him, to risk my heart. Afraid that I'd be all alone in this thing I'd found with Gavin. But I knew I'd fallen forever in love with him.

I kissed his hand and the tears didn't stop as I poured my heart out for him. He'd owned it ever since I fell in love with him weeks ago.

"Before I met you, I was so closed off. I was so determined to stay away from any attachments, knowing how deeply my heart could be broken. I didn't want to risk that again. But you, God Gavin, you got to me, you saw me and I couldn't stay away from you. I was afraid that you'd hurt me, but more than that, I was scared that I would lose you, Gavin. These last few hours have been the most terrifying of my life and I realized something. I'm completely and totally in love with you, babe. I'm so sorry I overreacted and didn't let you explain. Please, open your eyes. Wake up so I can tell you how much I love you, Gavin. Please …"

I looked tenderly at his face, waiting and waiting. Longing for that soft smile to spread over his mouth, revealing his dimple. For those expressive blue eyes of his to bore into mine. But he didn't stir, his eyes remained closed. I exhaled and pressed my face to his neck, breathing his intoxicating scent into my nose. I mashed my hands to his chest, crying quietly into his neck.

Gavin, please come back to me …

"I'm sorry, I love you," were the only words I seemed to be able to utter as the sobs erupted from me, my throat constricting as I released the emotions overwhelming my body.

Chapter 18

I came back to consciousness when I felt a hand on my shoulder. Gavin's doctor stood beside me.

Breathe, Aria. Just breathe. In and out.

"I thought you'd want these. Personal effects he had on him when he came in."

He handed me a small plastic bag and I took it with shaking fingers. I could see his cell phone, keys, and a brown threaded wallet through the clear bag in my hand. Was this all I had to hold onto? Everything he had on him at the time of the accident?

"Has he woken up at all?" the doctor asked, taking Gavin's chart from tray on the wall at his bedside.

It had been quite a few hours since they allowed me to see him and he hadn't so much as stirred. Both Elizabeth and his sister had come and gone a few times, along with Spencer and a few of Gavin's close friends from his business. But through it all, I had stayed.

"No, I've been here all night." I couldn't leave him; God I'd never leave his side again.

"That's normal in these circumstances, it shouldn't be long though. I'll be back in an hour or so to check his vitals," Dr. Lee stated, a hopeful look in his eyes.

His words made the heaviness in my chest lighten. I didn't know how much more of this I could take. He had to wake up. I needed him to wake up so I could tell him how wrong I was and let him know how much he meant to me.

I nodded as the doctor left us alone again.

I turned back to Gavin and kissed his hand, before laying my head back on the bed. I gazed up into the face that I fell in love with a short time ago. I was surprised at how tired I still was. Only a few more hours, I told myself and closed my eyes once more.

My sister woke me some time later to slip my favorite sweatshirt over my head. I tried to smile as she hugged me tightly. I spotted Lucas standing by the doorway, looking intently at the two of us. I could see how tired they were, but Kel's love for me and Luke's love for her brought them here at close to one AM.

"Are you okay? I'm sorry it took me so long to get back."

I could hear the worry in her voice. She had to be the most caring person I knew.

I gave her a half smile of reassurance. I couldn't stop myself from looking over at Gavin's gorgeous face. He looked so peaceful. The fear in the pit of my stomach was still there and it hadn't wavered since I got that call hours ago.

"As okay as I can be right now. I just wish he'd wake up, Kel."

She took my hand and squeezed tightly.

"Don't give up. He'll come back to you."

I knew she was right, it just felt so hopeless right then. He should have woken up by now. Hell—he should never have been in this hospital. If it wasn't for the fact that he was headed to me, Gavin wouldn't have been in that area of town.

"What if he doesn't wake up, Sis? I can't—I can't imagine being without him."

My sister stared into my eyes.

"Have faith, Ari. Just, have faith. He loves you and he's here, that's all that matters, okay?"

I knew it could have been so much worse. Gavin was still here, and I had to focus on that. I had to remember how much he loved me.

"Beautiful."

A low voice woke me the following morning, the sound groggy and roughened from sleep and some other emotion. Immediately, I lifted my head my eyes darting to Gavin. His blue-gray eyes met mine and tears swam in my own. This time, they were tears of joy.

"Oh! Gavin! Thank God." I pressed my lips to his hand repeatedly, reveling in the feel of his hand squeezing mine.

Relief coursed through me. There was an intensity in his eyes and … a hopelessness? But why? My heart yearned for him, this man had become so precious to me. The feeling of relief now that he was awake overwhelmed me. He came back. I couldn't quite believe that this wasn't a dream.

"Aria, you're here," Gavin whispered, his hand wiping away the tears falling down my cheeks.

My skin tingled from his touch.

"I came as soon as Callie called me, I couldn't stay away. Gavin I'm so sorry …"

He stopped me with an index finger to my lips. His fingers curled around mine, holding tight.

"Come here," he said, in a groggy voice.

I hastily sat beside him. I saw him tense in pain as he shifted to make room for me.

"Please be careful, Gavin," I whispered, but he didn't listen as he scooted forward, grasping the backs of my thighs and pulling me into his lap.

Taking hold of both my hands, his mouth came down to kiss my knuckles gently. I blinked up into the dark pools of blue and gray that undid me every single time. His eyes were filled with so many emotions, it took my breath away.

"Please don't apologize. I can't tell you how sorry I am about what happened, but I promise you I will find a way to prove it to you. Jasmine-"

I pressed my fingers to his lips, silencing him. I took his face in my hands. His rough stubble and warm skin letting me know this wasn't a dream. He was truly awake and here with me.

"I listened to your messages, Gavin. I believe you, I'm sorry I didn't stop and let you explain. I jumped to conclusions. I thought the worst. The image is still so fresh in my mind, but after hearing your voice mails I know I was wrong to think you'd ever hurt me that way. I'm so sorry, Gavin."

My voice trembled as I remembered the pain and betrayal I felt over what I thought Gavin had done. He shook his head. Tears trickled down my cheeks, and I closed my eyes in an attempt to control the emotion that poured out of me. I needed to be strong, for now, at least.

"Baby, please don't cry. Please." Gavin's deep voice made my eyes fly open. My hands clung to his neck in need, fear, and relief.

"Gavin, God, Gavin."

I was overcome with love as I lifted my mouth to his and kissed him. It was a kiss filled with our love, filled with tenderness. When we pulled apart, I panted for air. Our foreheads touched and Gavin pressed me against him. His hands held the back of my head as he gazed intently into my eyes. The tears still fell to my cheeks. When his mouth closed over mine again, my body shuddered in relief. He was here, he was alive, and we were together. *Oh, thank God.*

I could have lost him; I could have lost this. A sob erupting from the back of my throat, came out as a hushed whimper against his mouth.

"Shh baby, I've got you," he whispered as he kissed me again.

His lips engulfed me, his breath mingled with mine. His hand delved into my hair as his tongue slipped into my mouth. Need climbed through me, causing me to clench my hands in his hair and tug gently. The silky light brown strands curled around my fingertips.

My need for him overwhelmed me, unfurling in my core. I tightened my hold on his neck. His hands grazed my cheeks, so tenderly that it would have made me cry if I wasn't already. I lost my breath in the kiss. When he pulled his lips from mine, his eyes were filled with love, certainty, need, intensity,—God, so many emotions at once.

"Gavin…" I began to cry harder, my body shuddering with the overwhelming emotions breaking the dam inside me.

I needed him …

"Christ, no," he whispered, his lips coming to my forehead affectionately.

I buried my face in his neck, the warm skin under my nose comforting me. I breathed him in. His minty smell made my heart lift.

"I love you, Aria." his voice filled with heavy emotion.

I took a deep breath, and pulled back needing to see his face when I said what I had to.

He was really okay. Oh, thank you, Jesus.

"I was so scared," I murmured, placing my palms on his cheeks.

Understanding registered in his eyes. Gavin pulled back fractionally, his eyes leaving mine for the first time since he'd woken up.

They roamed the room, the ceiling and the machines beside his bedside.

"Do you remember what happened?" I asked, my hands running up his chest when I felt the tension in his body. I saw the realization tick in his eyes.

"A car, and a loading truck, I didn't even see them coming. Christ, it all happened so fast. I was coming to see you. Shit."

He ran his hand through his hair and gazed down at me with confused eyes.

I took his face in my palms, my thumbs skimming the yellow bruises across his jaw.

"Are you feeling okay?"

He nodded, pressing his lips gently to mine. Trying to reassure both of us that he was still here.

"I'll be okay."

I gazed up at him and leaned forward to grab the call button behind the head of his bed. I felt his eyes on me, watching me.

Suddenly he grasped my hand and pulled me back, his eyes looking softer now.

"Really, Aria, I'm fine."

"Please, the doctor needs to check you. They'll give you something for the pain. Gavin, I almost lost you."

My voice cracked and I bit my lip to control my emotions.

Gavin registered the fear in my eyes, and nodded. He ran his hands down my cheeks, wiping away stray tears.

I loved how gentle his touch was, as if I was a precious jewel that could break. It was just one of the many things I loved about him.

"I'm so sorry, beautiful."

Hearing him call me that again made me smile widely. There were moments during the night when I thought I'd never him speak again.

As we waited for the nurse, I couldn't keep myself from pressing my hands to his chest and kissing him gently on the side of his mouth. When I pulled away, I found myself wanting more. My naughty thoughts were interrupted by Dr. Lee coming into the room and waving me out.

I leaned forward and pressed a kiss to Gavin's forehead. He smiled that special mile reserved just for me and let our fingers slip from each others, just like the day we met.

Chapter 19

I waited outside the door of Gavin's room, knotting my hands in my lap. I had just left him with Dr. Lee ten minutes ago, and I already missed his touch. I was in awe that he was really okay. It was all I could focus on right then. My thoughts were interrupted when Dr. Lee came out and looked at me. His smile was much more convincing than the one he gave me earlier.

Pulling my phone from my pocket, I dialed Callie's number and pressed the phone to my ear as I waited.

"Hi, Aria!" her sweet voice came onto the phone.

I could still hear the worry etched within the sound. She was trying to be strong, just as I was. But she was scared.

I was scared, too.

"Your brother is awake, Callie. He'll want to see you and your mom."

"We'll be there soon. Thanks for calling."

"Of course. See you soon, honey."

Pressing end, I heard the door to Gavin's room open and then the doctor stepped out.

"How are you doing, Aria?" he asked and I tried to fake a smile.

I would be okay once I knew he was be healthy and we would have time to make up for the past few days.

I was so *stupid* to walk away from him without any answers.

"I just want him to be okay. He's going to be okay, right?" I heard the hope in my voice.

"He will, Aria. From what I can tell, all his vitals are stable and his scans all came back clear. He may have some pain in his ribs for the next few weeks. Maybe some headaches depending on how he reacts to the pain medications we've given him so, keep an eye out for that. Other than that, he's good to go."

All I heard was he was going to be okay.

I smiled, wholeheartedly for the first time since the accident and I took his outreached hand.

"Thank you for everything. When can he be discharged?"

"Soon, I'll file his papers now."

"Okay."

He stalked away, leaving me beaming. I just wanted to have Gavin back home with me. God, I hated hospitals. It seemed like yesterday in this very hospital my brother drew his last breath and was gone from this world forever. I still remembered the feelings of devastation, hopelessness, and confusion. I was lost in a sea of hurt, not knowing how to move on from Jeremy's death.

But Gavin, he healed me, he saved me, he found me. I was so very lucky to have him. He gave me a home when I thought I'd never feel that again.

Home. Yes, that sounded good.

Hastily, I went back into the room. He scrolled through his phone as he sat in bed. His eyebrows were drawn together in concentration, mouth parted in the sexiest way. I leaned my back against the door, watching him. His lips twitched with a smile and his eyes reached mine.

"Come here, baby," he beckoned, reaching his hand to me as I came around the foot of his bed.

"Miss anything important?" I asked.

He smirked. I sat beside him, running my hand over his roughened jaw. His eyes lit with something that made me want to swoon.

"A few meetings, a business lunch with clients from Seattle, nothing earth shattering."

Vaguely, I wondered why he never talked about his work; he was very vague about it. He should be proud of the work he did. He was well off and could retire already though he was only twenty-eight. But I could tell Thomas Innovations in Technology meant a lot to him. He enjoyed it, even though he hadn't admitted it.

"Why don't you ever talk about your work?"

The sentence tumbled out. I was horrified when I realized I actually said the words out loud. I bit my lip and continued exploring the skin of his jaw, gently tracing the bruises on his face.

Gavin shrugged. He quietly reached to pull on the ribbon holding my hair up letting it fall like a curtain down my back. I felt his fingers tease through it and I leaned into his touch.

"I love your hair."

He ran his fingers through the waves, tucking strands behind my ears. After long moments of playing with my hair, Gavin spoke.

"It's always felt like my father's company, not really mine. Don't get me wrong, I love Thomas and the business is thriving. My work intrigues me. I enjoy it, but it's not an empire I built; it's my father's. My father built everything, groomed the company to what it is today. I've only been a part of it for five years or so."

I ran my fingers over his chest, waiting for him to continue.

"The work he put in, Jesus, for half his life—it's been his legacy, you know? How can I just take over all of that without feeling a little indebted?" his voice was filled with vulnerability.

I knew in that moment, he trusted me more than before. I saw the intensity in his eyes and realized I'd never thought about it that way.

"But you should be proud of it, Gavin. Your father may have built it, but it's your empire now, and the work you do is completely your own. Baby, I'm proud of you."

In a flash, Gavin's eyes heated as he took in my words. He abruptly pulled me to his chest, grunting from the pain the motion caused.

Oh, shit, his ribs!

"Gavin, careful, your ribs." A slow smile crossed his lips and he didn't let me go.

"Trust me, it's worth the pain having you in my arms again. You have no idea ... " he didn't finish his thought.

I had no idea about what? What was he going to say? Before I could ask, he spoke again in a voice filled with promise.

"You amaze me baby, I'm in awe of you. Even after these past few hours, I should be taking care of you, making things up to you, but here you are, loving me as always."

I saw the love in his eyes and it brought tears to mine again.

"Gavin," I whispered, taking his face in both my hands.

"I'm always going to love you."

The words came straight from my heart. I knew I'd love this man forever. From the very moment, I saw him, he'd worked his way into my heart. There was no going back to my sheltered existence.

I gazed up into the endless pools of blue and gray. The smile he gave me was almost worth the pain of the last two days.

"I love you so much, Aria, baby." his deep voice made my heart constrict in joy.

Then his mouth crashed down on mine, fingers tangled in my unruly hair. I clutched onto him with everything I had. In his kiss, I found home. Our tongues collided, dancing together. He sucked my bottom lip into his mouth. I moaned softly in response. I felt him smiling against my lips.

"You are going to have to let me pamper you for the next few weeks. Doctor's orders, babe."

"Is that so? Now what did the good doctor say?"

He began to kiss down my throat ever so slowly.

I giggled, hearing the tease in his voice. Oh, he was so good at distracting me. His lips grazed my neck, goosebumps surfacing on my skin from his teasing touch.

"He said that you need to take it easy. Did he give you something for the pain?" I pulled back, meeting his eyes and placing my hands on his shoulders.

When he sat back he showed me the prescription slip Dr. Lee gave him and a roll of white bandage tape.

"Oh, good."

Gavin turned me so that my back leaned against his chest. I felt his heat in every line of my body. From my shoulders to my hips, I felt the hardness of his muscular frame against mine. I also felt roaming hands moving up and down my arms, soothing my goosebumps away.

"Mmhm." I pressed closer and turned to rest my head on his warm chest.

Time slowed as we just sat with each other. The silence was comforting and I had no idea how much time had passed when I heard Gavin's gravelly voice close to my ear.

"You're so quiet, baby. Are you still worried about Jasmine?"

I lifted my eyes to his and saw worry in them. Somehow, I felt a vulnerability now that everything was settled between us. My insecurities about Jasmine got the best of me and how was I to know it wouldn't happen again?

"Do you have feelings for her?" I whispered, my voice shaky with renewed doubt.

Gavin's eyes widened and before I knew it, he gently took my face in his hands. Those eyes I loved so much locked onto mine, seeing the fierce determination in them caused me to lose my words.

"Listen to me, Aria. When I met Jasmine, I was a sophomore at Georgetown. She was the first girl that ever held my attention. I loved her, in my own way and when she left me, I was heartbroken. After that, I focused on the business, my career, establishing myself in the world of technology. I never thought I'd find love again, not until you, Aria. I love you, baby. I have no feelings whatsoever for Jasmine."

I heard the honest emotion in his voice and my heart jumped. His words broke through my apprehension. I believed him.

I hugged him and rested my forehead against his, reveling in the feel of his thumbs stroking along my collarbone. I breathed in his scent for a long moment.

"Gavin." I leaned back, clasping his face urgently.

I covered his face in soft kisses until my lips brushed against his parted mouth.

"I love you, too," I whispered, seeing his eyes heat as he exhaled.

"God, Aria, I missed you."

His voice was deep with emotion and before I knew it, his mouth closed over mine hungrily and I was lost. His touch, the feel of his lips crushing mine, his hot breath against my mouth as he delved his hands into my hair. The passion erupted from within me, desperation coursing through my veins as I realized how wrong I was. I kissed him with every fiber of my being and when his tongue slipped between my lips, a soft moan escaped me. I was breathless, exploring him. He was trembling under my hands as he licked expertly into my mouth, nipping teasingly on my bottom lip.

"Oh God, I want ..." I whispered, my voice pleading but then his mouth hovered over mine again.

He chuckled, a low youthful sound that made desire pool low in my core. I loved that sound.

"You want me to make love to you, baby?" Gavin asked, looking down at me with blazing eyes.

A moan escaped me when he nipped along my jaw and then soothed the skin with his magical tongue before I could answer his question.

"Gavin."

It was a plea. For what, I wasn't sure. To continue this delicious torture or to stop?

Leaning back, he gave me a heart stopping, smile and I couldn't help biting my lip to hide my answering smile.

"When can we get out of here?" he whispered, running his hands slowly up my thighs.

The promise in those words was infinite and I slipped off the bed, settling myself in the chair beside him to regain my equilibrium.

"In the morning, I think. But you have to take it easy."

He shook his head, trailing his knuckles down my cheek. I had a feeling he was not going to follow the doctor's orders when we got home to our bed.

"Will you come home with me?"

His question surprised me and I heard a rawness in his voice. It took my breath away, making me realize how new all this was to us. We were teetering, still getting to know each other and now with this new-found fear of losing everything we'd built so far.

"Gavin, of course I will," I said, my voice just shy of a whisper.

I watched as he exhaled deeply and leaned forward to kiss the side of my mouth.

"I don't want you to worry about Jasmine."

His palm rested on my cheek, tipping my eyes up to his.

"I don't trust her, Gavin."

I didn't know why I needed to say it, but I did. She knew we were involved when she went to Gavin's office. She was upset, yes. I understood that part. But that woman had no right to make a move on him, especially when she was the very person to break his heart years ago. I could still picture her lips on Gavin's. God, I hated that she kissed him. His kisses were mine, solely mine.

"You have nothing to worry about. You're all I see, beautiful."

I looked up at him, then squeezed his hand in mine. I lifted it to my lips and kissed his palm.

"I trust you."

I trusted him completely. It was her I didn't trust.

"Then trust me to make sure she never comes between us again."

I nodded, then laid my fingers over his heart.

"I feel your heart beating," I whispered.

"It's yours, baby. It beats for you, only you. Listen to me."

I wrapped my arms around his neck and looked into his eyes as he continued. The intensity in his eyes stopped my heart.

"I won't ever hurt you. Never again."

My heart jumped in my chest, not expecting that. How did he know exactly what I needed to hear?

"Me either, Gavin. Me either."

After watching three hours of daytime television in Gavin's lap, he groaned a little in pain. He hid it well, but I knew he wasn't feeling the best. The doctor said he should take it easy and I fully intended to make sure he did just that. I would take care of him. The thought filled me with joy, though I hated that Gavin was in pain. My thoughts were rudely interrupted when he snatched the remote from me. I felt him smiling behind me.

"No way! What are you doing!?" I squealed, fighting to reach the remote.

His grin widened as he caught my earlobe between his teeth. My core tightened deliciously at the contact.

"I'm changing it. This is torture, beautiful. Three hours of damn soap operas!"

I giggled, leaning my head against his chest and looking up at him through my eyelashes. I pouted, hoping he'd let me have my way. I was just getting interested in the damn soap operas. His stormy eyes were soft and filled with amusement, gazing back at me as he bit his bottom lip to hide his laugh.

"I like them."

He grinned now, unabashedly and leaned down, running his lips along mine. His kiss was a gentle inhaling, a barely-there touch to my mouth. I groaned, wanting more as he pulled away and winked down at me.

"I can see the pain medication is kicking in," I said, unable to hide a smirk.

Deftly, Gavin flicked through channels, his eyes never leaving mine.

"Don't you want to watch something else?" he whispered, eyes dancing with humor.

Oh, this man. He was trying to distract me, and with his lips along the back of my neck it was working.

"Like what?" I asked.

Gavin's eyes were on the screen now and they lit up. Suddenly, he grinned, when I saw what he'd chosen to watch. *Final Destination 3,* he remembered.

"You approve, baby?"

I nestled my head into his chest and nodded, giving him a grin that held nothing back.

"Glad to hear it."

He leaned down, cradling my face in his palms as his mouth closed over mine, grazing his teeth over my lower lip with heartrending slowness. He brushed his mouth over mine gently, teasing me. I was breathless as I leaned into him.

"Gavin, please," I whimpered, moaning low in my throat when he sucked my bottom lip into his mouth, nibbling at it.

My skin tingled in desire for his touch and my breath faltered, wishing we were at home in our bed rather than here in a hospital bed.

"You taste so good. Are you wearing something new?"

He wiped my hair from the back of my neck and his mouth glided down, kissing and sucking as he went until his hot breath covered the top of my breasts just above the collar of V-neck shirt.

"Um, I'm not sure," I whispered, losing my train of thought as his index finger ran along the top of my breast, his hand unbuttoning the top button of my blouse.

I gasped, remembering where we were and what Dr. Lee said. He needed to take it easy for the next few days …

"Wait, you're supposed to take it easy, Gavin."

He ignored me, releasing the first and going to the second button on my shirt as his other arm tightened around my waist. I leaned back slightly, the exposed skin of my breasts feeling bereft without his touch.

"Gavin, we have plenty of time for this later. You're recovering. You are bruised and cut and Dr. Lee said you might experience some headaches. There's no rush."

I didn't know why I resisted his touch. The attraction between was like a moth to a flame, and I had no hope of staying away for long.

Gavin's eyes heated with want as he gazed down at me and ran his hands down my face.

Oh, I loved his touch.

"Aria, I missed you. I want you. Let me touch you."

His heartfelt confession knocked down my protests and I sagged against him, feeling his hands track up my thighs and then rest against my hips.

God, I missed him so much.

"I missed you so much, baby." The words echoed my thoughts and when I blinked up to his eyes, I saw the emotion in them.

"Oh, Gavin." I pressed against him, kissing his mouth briefly, then meeting his eyes again as tears built in my own.

"I was so afraid that I'd lose you. When Callie called me, all I could think about was how I just walked away from you and if that had been the last time … God, I -"

Gavin's eyes widened suddenly and he pulled me roughly to him, grunting low in his throat as he kissed me with such passion. His tongue slipping into my mouth as he held me tight against his chest. I felt his love pouring into me with each lash of his delectable tongue, each pull of his mouth against mine. His hands left my face and ran down my sides to slip under the hem of my shirt. His hands ran up my bare back, his tongue licking hungrily into my mouth. He cherished me with his kiss and I was mesmerized, grasping his neck in need.

"Baby, I couldn't leave you. I love you more than I ever thought possible and I promise, I'm not going anywhere."

He kissed my forehead and leaned back to wipe the tears that had been in abundance since his accident.

"Okay," I whispered, returning my lips to his as he deftly undid the rest of my buttons, his eyes filled with desire.

From behind me, someone knocked twice on the door. I pulled away from Gavin's arms and twisted to see his mother peering into the room with a grin on her face. I gasped.

Shit!

I slipped off his lap hastily once I was covered and stood at his bedside, my cheeks heated. She must have thought I was jumping her son while he was laid up in a hospital bed.

Oh, goodness, and I thought we'd hit it off at first, now who knew?

"Mom, I didn't know you were here," Gavin said, chuckling as she made her way into the room.

Without the cloud of emotion she had earlier, I saw how naturally beautiful his mother was. The shape of her face, the curve of her nose, even the gray eyes that complimented her ivory skin. She wore the same sweater and slacks from the day before. I could see Gavin in the way she moved and looked.

She kissed my cheek before leaning back and squeezing my hands. I smiled, trying to hide my uneasiness. I wanted her to like me, though I had no idea how to make that happen since my relationship with my own mother had never been smooth.

"It's nice to see some color in your cheeks, Aria. Sorry to interrupt," she smiled wider and gave me a wink before going to Gavin's bedside.

She sat beside him and took his hand in hers. She kissed his forehead.

"You feeling okay, sweetheart?" she asked, gazing down at him lovingly.

"Yes, Mom. I'm good now. When did you get here? I thought you were still in St. Louis meeting with Mr. Jamison?"

She shook her head. I went to the other side of his bed, where I sat in a chair, watching mother and son interact.

"I finished yesterday. I came straight here. I've been worried sick, sweetheart. Don't you dare scare us like that again!"

He nodded, squeezing her hand.

"I'll do my best, Mama. Have you heard anything about the other drivers? Is anyone hurt?"

She got quiet and looked down at him. Her eyes briefly shifted to mine.

Oh, no. There was worry in them? My heart constricted as a sense of dread coursed through me. What happened?

"The loader's driver, we don't really know. He left the scene almost right away."

"And what about the other driver?" Gavin's voice sounded calm and collected while I was freaking out internally.

Why would the driver hit Gavin's car and then just take off? Wasn't that against the law?

"Debbie Craig, yes, she's okay. She has a few broken ribs and a sprained ankle, but other than that she's fine."

Gavin tensed and he whispered something too low for me to hear to his mother.

"I'll take care of it as soon as I can. Dr. Lee said you're good to go so I'll call you tonight, OK?"

"Sure, Mom."

She kissed his cheek and leaned over to clasp my hand in hers, squeezing gently.

"Relax, honey. It's all okay now." her voice was soft, nurturing.

It immediately put me at ease.

"Thank you, Elizabeth."

I hugged her before walking her to the door. She smiled warmly and made her way out of the room.

Gavin was quiet beside me for a moment and when his eyes shifted to mine, they were guarded and darkened with worry.

"It's not your fault, Gavin," I whispered, running my hand over his cheek. He took hold of my hand, pressing my palm to his lips for a kiss.

"I know. It's just a shock. I asked my mother to make sure that the other driver is taken care of, physical therapy, hospital time. Whatever she needs."

My heart swelled, seeing the compassion in his eyes and his actions. It was ... sobering.

"What did I do to deserve you?" I whispered, watching as he carefully got off the bed.

"Because you're you, Aria." Though his voice was teasing, I knew his words were filled with meaning.

Gavin winced as he stood and I mirrored him, seeing plainly the pain he was in. I held him up as he took a deep breath, slowly letting it out.

"I'm getting you more pain medication before we leave," I vowed, my eyes flicking down to his bandaged forearm.

Some glass had gotten into his arm and the gash needed stitches. I saw the dressing needed changing.

"You okay to stand on your own for a sec?"

He nodded, giving me half a smile as I leaned over the bed and grabbed the roll of bandages.

"Aria, I'm fine," he said, reaching for his jacket.

I slapped his hand away and led him back to the bed. He sat in front of me holding out his injured arm to me.

"You spoil me, baby."

I grinned, biting my lip as I undressed his arm, carefully.

"Oh, trust me. This is only the beginning, I like taking care of you."

Once the bandage was off, I gasped at the cut in the middle of his forearm, stitched together intricately. My heart squeezed at the sight. God, I hated seeing him injured. I swallowed, reaching for the roll of dressing.

He blinked up at me. I worried my lip with my teeth, dressing his injury quickly and then exhaling when the cut was covered. My eyes closed as I reassured myself that he was OK. He was still here with me.

"Hey," Gavin whispered as he caressed my cheek.

He pulled my body to him, hugging me around my waist and pressing our cheeks together. His warmth was welcoming and I pressed a kiss to his collarbone.

"I'm okay, we're okay." Gavin's voice soothed me, chasing away the fears from the past two days.

I clutched his strong, taut shoulders and his mouth came up to kiss my temple. I sighed as he cupped my cheeks in his big warm hands.

"I love you," I whispered, reveling in the feel of his hands upon my face.

Gavin smiled big, causing joy to unfurl in my stomach. Then he kissed my lips softly.

God, I loved him. I sank my fingers into his messy hair.

"I love you. Unconditionally, baby. Come on, let's go home."

God, that sounded good, so good.

Chapter 20

I eased out onto the freeway as a familiar song came on the radio.

"This song," Gavin murmured as he took my free hand and lifted it to his mouth.

Butterfly kisses that lit me up from the inside feathered my knuckles. He turned up the volume. When I heard, the lyrics sung in a deep, throaty voice with base and guitar in the background, I was taken back to my party weeks ago.

Call it magic, call it true.
I call it magic when I'm with you
And I just got broken, broken into two
Still I call it magic, when I'm next to you.

I turned my eyes to Gavin's deep blue-grays, filled with nothing but love. Pure, unconditional love stared back at me. I'd been too scared to believe love like this existed for so long. I looked up and I knew the same love was shining in mine.

"You remember this song, baby?"

I smiled softly, putting the car in park outside the penthouse. I leaned over to rest my hand just above his heart.

"It's our song. The way you make me feel, Gavin. It's magic."

Gavin closed the small gap between us, wrapping one hand around my neck and another around my waist to hold me close.

"Aria." Gavin's mouth closed over mine then and immediately my lips fell open to welcome his passionate kiss.

The way he licked ardently into my mouth made my heart beat rapidly and my hands pulled gently on his unruly hair.

"Gavin …" I said when I had the breath to speak.

Then I kissed him again, and again, deeper. Desperation flooded me. I clutched him and whispered against his mouth.

"Let me get you inside."

Gavin pulled back and met my eyes, chewing on his bottom lip. God, my core tightened deliciously at the sight of him. So, sexy, so carefree, so mine.

"Are you going to have your wicked way with me, Ms. Morgan?"

"Um, no. I'm going to take care of you. You're recovering from an accident, Gavin."

I reminded him, and myself because even though I wanted him with every molecule in my body, we couldn't rush his recovery. God, the last thing I wanted to do was cause him more pain. When I looked into his eyes, he was still chewing on that lip, but now he pouted.

"Aria you can't be serious, we need …"

I cut him off with a hand to his mouth. I pressed a kiss to the line that formed between his eyebrows.

"You need to rest. Come on, let's go inside."

"I'm fine, baby. Stop worrying," Gavin reminded me for the third time.

Once inside, I pulled open the top drawer in the marble topped island.

"Shh," was all I said while I rummaged through the piles of papers and excess mess in the drawer in front of me. I remembered putting a takeout menu to Kel's favorite Italian restaurant in here before I left the penthouse the day before the accident. Before my world almost fell apart at the seams.

"I think," Gavin spoke in that low voice of his as he came up behind me and wrapped his strong arms around me from behind, "that you should cook for me, baby."

"No way. If I cooked for you, you'd be back in the hospital tomorrow. I have about exhausted all the meals I know how to make decently."

I chuckled, turning in his arms to see he was smirking already.

"You'll never get better without practice."

My brow furrowed and I hastily shook my head.

"I've tried, trust me. Cooking and I don't always mix," I said, turning back to the drawer and shuffling through more junk in an effort to find that menu I put in here.

Gavin didn't say anything else, he just cupped my nape and I pictured him smiling wider when I swayed against him at the skin on skin contact. He was trying to distract me. God, he felt so good and hard against me ...

"Hmm, Gavin," I moaned softly.

He kissed my neck, my shoulder and then one hand slid the strap of my tank top down so he could explore my skin with his mouth, lips and oh, his tongue.

"So, smooth, you have the smoothest skin."

He placed another kiss to my flesh.

"The most beautiful shoulders ... and these?" His hands came towards my breasts.

Suddenly Gavin turned me and lifted me to the marble counter top and stood between my thighs. He slowly lifted my top over my head and set it down somewhere behind him. A loud moan burst out of me when he cupped both my breasts in his hands, kneading gently. Instantly, my core flooded with arousal. Being touched after so long was magical.

"These. Are. Perfect."

When his mouth came down to tease and torture me, my head fell back in pleasure.

"Feels so good," I murmured, wrapping my legs around his hips and pushing my fingers into his long hair.

Gavin licked and teased my breasts, around the areola. Then he bit down gently.

"Oh God, oh my God, Gavin."

"So beautiful. So mine."

He took a hold of my hips and before I could think to stop him, he knelt in front of me and slowly peeled off my boy short panties.

When did he take my jeans off? I had no idea. He was the master of distraction. All I could focus on was that I was bared to him now. All I felt was my heady need to feel him inside me. I wanted to be consumed by him. I wanted to delight in the pleasure only he could give me.

"Wait, Gavin. You're recovering ..." I whispered, pressing my hand to his cheek.

Those gorgeous eyes tipped up to meet mine.

"I'm okay, baby. Let me love you. Please, just let me love you, now."

His soft, earnest words quieted my reservations about making love. When that slow, soft smile spread over Gavin's mouth, I nodded and sank my fingers back in to tangle in his hair.

Not another word spoken before Gavin wrapped his hands around my hips and urged me to part my legs wider for him.

"More," he whispered and I obeyed.

I opened to him and moaned passionately when he began kissing down my lower belly to my core. I ached for him so much.

"You are so fucking beautiful, Aria baby. I can't get enough," he murmured as his mouth met my opening.

He rubbed up and down, teasing me and then finally, God, he settled in to taste me. Slow, long licks and soft nips to my flesh almost drove me to the point of a crushing climax, almost had me tumbling over into the abyss—but not quite. Gavin hummed against my core, pressing two fingers inside me and rubbing in slow, deep circles. My skin lit up, my heart soared, and my sex clenched around him urging him to go faster. I need -

"Aah—yes!" I called out suddenly as Gavin licked and pulled and devoured me in that wonderful way of his.

I climbed higher and higher to ecstasy, so high that I knew this was going to be a high I'd never touched before.

"Please … Feels … Going to come, baby. Faster …" I moaned as the waves crashed through me, ripped me open and made me soar into orgasm.

"Let go, beautiful. I've got you," Gavin whispered and when he sucked my clit hard and fast,—I fell.

"Oh, Gavin," I whispered, letting my eyes fall open.

"Bed," he murmured into the hollow of my neck, as he scooped me into his arms and carried me towards the bedroom.

"Gavin … You're-"

"I'm fine, baby. I'm not straining myself by carrying you to our bed."

As he laid me across the cool sheets, my eyes wandered over him. From his sexy mouth to those deep eyes of his, to the light bruising that went down his neck and across his cheeks , to his delectable chest, taut stomach and lean hips. Gavin gave me a wide smile, warmed with affection and began to unbuckle his jeans.

"You're staring."

"Hmm." I ignored him and continued to explore him with my eyes. He was just so—sexy. So completely sexy.

"I love you."

The words came easily but were still thick with the honesty those three words incited. Gavin's smirk matched the humor in his eyes as he sauntered over to me.

"I have so much to offer, baby. But you just love me for my body."

Gavin teased, pushing me onto my back, resting his arms on either side of my head.

"Well, I love your body, how could I not?"

I kissed the side of his mouth softly, feeling his stubble against my lips. I pressed my hand over his heart.

"But, what truly made me fall for you? It's this, Gavin. Your heart. The way you love me, the way you believe in me, in us." I blinked up into his eyes and a warm smile tipped his mouth up.

"Aria," he whispered, grasping my hands and pulling them above my head where he held them in one of his own.

He caressed down my torso from navel to core with his other hand. A breathy moan escaped me when he dipped one finger inside and circled gently, around and around.

"I could touch you all day and never tire of it, beautiful. Your body drives me crazy with need."

I wrapped my legs around his waist and delighted in the weight resting against my belly.

"Then take me, baby."

Gavin smiled naughtily, grasped my hips and took me.

Chapter 21

My eyes fluttered open to the faint light of dawn coming through the large bay windows. I yawned and stretched my limbs happily, feeling refreshed after my first good night of sleep in days. Other than waking twice to make love during the night, I felt more rested than I had in a long time. I pressed my head into the pillow and let my eyes wander over to Gavin, was sleeping soundly beside me. His arm was stretched around my waist while he slept, as if he couldn't help but touch me even in slumber. His face was lit with the morning sun. I gently skimmed my fingers down his cheek where the bruising and cuts were barely visible. God, he was gorgeous. It still seemed unreal that this man was mine.

"Love you," I whispered into the hollow of his neck and pressed a kiss there.

"Hmm," he hummed in his sleep as I carefully slipped out of bed.

I moved softly across the hardwood floor to locate a pair of yoga pants and a tee.

Slipping into the bathroom, I heard my phone ringing from the kitchen. Hastily, I dressed and pulled my hair into a messy ponytail before heading to the kitchen

"Hey," I answered, seeing it was Farrah calling.

She sniffed on the other end of the phone, not answering me.

"Sweetie? You there?"

"I- God, I'm so sorry Ari. Jay came home from Seattle yesterday and we both turned off our phones to have a day together. I had no idea—Gavin, is he okay?"

She was so upset.

"Hey, it's okay Farrah. Gavin is home, everything is okay. Honestly, Kel was with me and so was Gavin's family. I wasn't alone."

I heard her exhale.

"What happened? All Kel told me was that Gavin was in an accident and that you were at the hospital with him for most of the night."

I sat at the kitchen table and ran my hand through my hair absent-mindedly.

"I was at the showcase for the academy. Kel was with me helping me get ready. Then I got the call from Callie. I swear to God Farrah, my world stopped."

Hell, my heart stopped in those moments in between. Not knowing if he was okay, if I'd lost the love I'd found … it was unbearable.

"But he's alright? Was he injured?" Her voice was filled with concern and I wished we were in the same room so I could hug and reassure her.

"No, he's—he's OK. We're fine, now. Stop worrying, Sweetie. Enough about me. How are things with Jaden?"

I wanted to talk about something other than the hospital.

"Wonderful, but I swear to God he has the stamina of a bull."

I almost choked on the piece of toast I was eating.

"Wow, Farrah! Warn a girl, why don't you?"

She laughed and soon I joined in, especially when she told me how many times she and Jay the Bull went at it last night.

"And then he showed me …"

I stopped listening as Gavin came out of the bedroom grinning at me. He was shirtless with a pair of loose-fitting blue pajama bottoms hanging low on his hips. A shot of desire coursed through me at the sight of him. He just rolled out of bed and I already wanted to drag him back there …

"Have to go, let's have lunch soon?"

"Oh, I see how it is. Gavin up for round two?" Farrah teased and I could feel her rolling her eyes.

My chair spun toward him. He stood in front of me, and those deep, deep eyes of his took me in.

"Bye, sweets."

I put down my phone and smiled slowly at my man. He looked too damn sexy in the morning.

"Morning, baby." I leaned forward and sucked his bottom lip into my mouth, tugging gently.

"Hmm," Gavin groaned, kissing me lightly and then tugged me to my feet without another word.

"Where are we going?" I asked as he led me out of the kitchen and back to the bedroom.

"Breakfast, I'm going to need my energy today." He started pulling out clothes to put on.

"Oh?" I asked innocently, biting down on my lip when he smiled sexily at me.

He slid his hand down my nape and placed a kiss at the top of my head.

"Because were not leaving this bed. All. Day. Long. So, get dressed."

Gavin held my hand as we walked to a small diner close to the penthouse. Even just the small contact of skin on skin kept the buzz of need alive inside me.

"You're blushing," he murmured, stopping on the sidewalk and cupping my cheeks gently.

"Am I?" I grinned, knowing he read my mind just now. He knew me so well.

Gavin skimmed his thumbs over my jaw, drawing small circles, igniting the skin underneath his touch and my eyes fell closed.

"Open, baby."

I opened my eyes and saw the softness in his.

"These," he rubbed his thumbs against my temples right next to my eyes, "made me fall for you, beautiful. So, bright, so expressive."

I smiled softly and kissed his palm. His words were filled with love.

"You're sweet." I tugged his hand to get us back moving. He wrapped one strong arm around my shoulders to keep me close. God, he felt good.

Ruby's was nestled between downtown and south-side Chicago. It looked like one of those fifties diners from *Happy Days* where the waitresses rolled around in skates. It was different and I immediately loved it.

"This is so cool, Gavin. Why haven't I heard of this place?"

He opened the glass door for me and placed a hand at the small of my back. The contact sent tingles up my spine.

A small petite woman with strawberry blonde hair and sky blue eyes greeted us.

"Greta! How are you?" Gavin said happily, obviously pleased to see her.

I wondered how long he'd been coming here. Years? Did he come here with his family? I flicked my eyes up to him as Greta went around a crowd of teenagers to get closer to us. She clasped his hand in hers.

"Greta, this is the girl I told you about. Aria, meet Greta. She's my mother's best friend. And she makes the best omelet known to man."

He winked at her, those blue-gray eyes warm with affection. I could see how dear Greta was to him, even after all these years.

"It's wonderful to meet you, Greta."

She pulled me in for a long hug, patting me softly on the back. Then to my surprise, she whispered in my ear.

"You're good for him, Aria."

I leaned away a bit and smiled at her.

"He's good for me, too."

Then she took my hand, leading us toward the back. I liked her easy-going nature and her devotion to Gavin. She considered him family.

When we were seated in a corner booth, Greta left us to look over the menu.

"I really like her," I said as soon as we were alone.

Gavin smiled widely and handed me a menu.

"Greta loves you already. Not that I blame her."

His eyes were smiling.

I looked through the menu, though I'd already decided on an omelet with everything on it. I felt his eyes on me as I flicked through the brightly colored pages.

"Do you know what you want?" I asked, reaching over the table to wipe a strand of his light brown hair away from his eyes.

Gavin leaned forward and grasped a strand of my hair, twirling it around his finger.

"Yes, I think I do"

Chapter 22

The moment I tasted Greta's infamous omelet, I moaned in satisfaction.

"Oh, my God, this is so good."

I took another bite and looked up from my plate to see Gavin watching me. The look in his eyes was deep, hungry and not for food.

"What? It's really good."

"They're the best known to man, baby. I did warn you."

I sipped my water and smiled at him.

"You did. Can we get out of here, now?"

I was eager to get home and have him all to myself again. Three days apart made me desperate to be with him, and he said we had all day. I fully intended to soak up every precious minute with Gavin.

Wiping his mouth, Gavin took my hand to help me out of the booth. After tossing two bills down on the table, we walked out of the diner.

"Let's go."

As we headed back toward home, my phone rang. I was tempted to let it go to voice mail, knowing that it couldn't be that important this early in the morning. Gavin nodded with a smile, urging me to answer it. I took my cell out and looked at the screen in confusion. I didn't recognize the number.

"Farrah again?" he asked, sliding his fingers through mine.

I honestly wasn't sure at first, but then I recognized the number. It was Mr. Pearson, as in Grayson Academy. I hadn't spoken to him since the day of the showcase last week.

Oh, no. Why would he be calling me?

"Hello?" I began, biting my lip, nervously.

A sliver of hope sparked inside that maybe he was able to keep my spot in the program. I told him I had a family emergency and I couldn't perform at the showcase. Maybe …

"Aria, this is John Pearson from the academy. How are you?"

I lifted my eyes to see Gavin silently watching me. I mouthed Grayson Academy to him. He nodded but frowned at the fear in my eyes.

"I'm—well, I'm good," I stuttered.

"Good. I wanted to let you know that the showcase did have to go on without you and I couldn't keep your spot open. I did try, Aria, but it just wasn't possible. We had to go with Ella, Beth and Jasmine. I'm sorry."

Immediately my heart fell into my belly and tears welled in my eyes. I had lost the opportunity I'd been working for these past weeks, hell months. But how could I have done anything differently when I got that call from Gavin's sister? I had to go, I had to be with him.

"Thank you for letting me know, Mr. Pearson, and thank you so much for everything."

"I didn't do anything. Ms. Morgan, anyone could see your talent. I wish you all the best."

"Thank you."

I clicked off my phone and stared at it for a long time before I felt Gavin tip my chin up to look at me. I sighed and opened my eyes to see his worried expression.

"You OK, baby?" He framed my face with his hands and all I saw were his deep blue eyes.

"I lost the spot."

The words were whispered, as if I was telling myself and not him. I didn't want to believe that I'd truly lost such an amazing opportunity.

The kind that could have made my career in dance. It was what I'd worked for all my life.

"How? What happened at the showcase, baby?"

I rested my hands on his waist and took a deep breath.

"The moment Callie called me, nothing else mattered to me. The only thing I could focus on was getting to you, to the hospital. And well, the show must go on. They filled my spot."

I saw understanding dawn in his eyes as he cupped my nape and dipped his mouth to my forehead. My breath whooshed out of me in defeat and disappointment.

"I'm sorry, Aria. I know how much you wanted that spot. It meant so much to you."

"I know."

I rested my cheek against his chest and we stood there a long moment, him holding me, my nose pressed to his neck. I felt so safe in his arms. It hurt that I wouldn't be able to work with the company, but there were so many other opportunities out there. This, right here, was what was important.

"Let's go home."

Gavin deftly untied my sneakers and pulled them off as he knelt at the foot of the bed. My eyes closed in enjoyment of the light touches he gave me as he undressed me slowly. He peeled off my socks, then glided his palms up my calves. I felt the comforter shift around me as Gavin climbed onto the bed and knelt between my parted legs. The buzz of anticipation made my body sensitive to every touch of his fingers.

"So smooth," he praised, skating his hands under the band of my yoga pants, slowly peeling them over my waist, down my thighs, and off my legs entirely.

"Please, Gavin. Love me," I begged, opening my eyes and reaching for his hand as he unbuckled his jeans. I watched as he pulled his belt off, dropping it to the floor with his jeans. I lost all the breath inside me as he stood in front of me wearing only a pair of boxers. Those blue-gray eyes of his were filled with wanton desire. For me only.

I bit my lip to stifle the moan that bubbled up in my throat when he slid the boxers off his hips and let them fall to the floor.

"I'm going to love you now, baby."

I smiled widely and tangled my hands in his hair. God, I loved how his messy hair went every which way.

"Finally," I whispered against his lips as he kissed me breathless.

Gavin's body hovered over me, both knees trapping mine. I felt the delicious weight of his want on my lower belly.

"I missed this." He placed a kiss against my throat, right under my jaw.

"Having you in this bed." Another kiss to my throat where he settled in to tease me.

"Making love to you." The words weren't teasing and I knew he was talking about our time apart.

"Gavin."

My legs wrapped around his waist and my hands smoothed up his chest to frame his gorgeous face. I had never seen eyes like his; they were my weakness for sure. I felt his hands close around my laced boy short panties. His breath hit my barely covered breasts.

"Oh, please …"

I begged and God, finally, he reached under me and ripped my panties from my body. My bra was next to go and then I was bare under him. His eyes were hooded with lust, bottom lip trapped between his teeth. And then he smiled that sexy smile.

"Stay," was all he said as he trailed light, teasing kisses down my nape.

His hands gripped my hips as he hovered over me. I felt the heat from his body, but not the press of his weight on me, not the toned muscles that flexed as he wrapped himself around me. I curled my hands around his biceps and blinked into the depths of his eyes.

I needed to feel it all. I yearned for the weight of him and the touches he'd give me. I needed it all.

"Please, baby. Let me feel you." I pleaded.

It had only been three hours since I felt him inside me but I felt bereft without him. I felt my core tightening in anticipation.

"Always," Gavin murmured into my neck as I pushed a condom onto his length and then he was pushing inside of me. He filled me slowly, inch by inch, allowing both us to savor the feeling. I felt my muscles stretch around him as he filled me up and then withdrew. He set a brutally slow rhythm that drove me insane.

"Gavin," I moaned, my head fell back in pleasure.

My thighs tightened around his lean hips once he was buried to the hilt inside me. I wanted to stay just like that, feeling him deep inside me forever, but when he started to move in and out, rubbing that sensitive spot inside me, I couldn't prevent the whimper that escaped me.

"My Aria, this is heaven. Being inside you, is the best feeling I've ever had. Don't ever leave me again."

The words were a plea. The softness of them made me tilt his head up so I could look him in the eyes. My breath caught in my throat when I saw the love in his stormy blue-grays.

"Never again," I vowed, lacing my fingers with his on either side of my head.

Then, he began to move again. We moved with a desperation that I'd never felt before and when I could no longer hang on to the cliff I was dangling from, I tightened my inner muscles around him. I simply couldn't hold the pleasure inside anymore.

"Come, baby."

And with one last cry of his name upon my mouth, I did.

We spent the whole day in bed, just like he promised, only leaving to grab quick bites of food from the kitchen. Finally satiated, we drifted off to sleep sometime after midnight.

Gavin woke me with a tender kiss to the temple. I felt his hands spread against my lower back. The feel of his hands on me was heavenly.

"Sleepy," I whispered, refusing to open my eyes for another few precious seconds. I heard the deep rumble of Gavin's chuckle beside me.

"Come on, beautiful. Open your eyes." He brushed his fingers over my cheek.

"What do I get if I do?" I teased, reaching up to his bare chest.

I moaned at the feel of it under my fingers.

"This."

The promise in his voice made me slowly peek one eye open and when I saw the platter of blueberry waffles, my favorite cinnamon raisin toast and more eggs than I could possibly eat, I moaned loudly at the sight of it.

"You shouldn't have," I said as I sat up against the pillows and reached for a large piece of toast.

"It was our deal, remember? And I haven't been able to do this for you lately so …"

He scooped some scrambled eggs onto a spoon and I moaned when they reached my mouth. The mischievous look in his eyes was worth the soreness I felt everywhere.

"Hmm, you're right about that. But you could have popped a stitch running around like that, Gavin. You should be taking it easy."

He shook his head slightly but the look of amusement didn't waver.

"I was standing in front of the oven, Aria. And I wanted to do this for you. You deserve to be pampered and adored and I'm going to do that and even more."

My heart melted at his proclamation.

"Thank you, baby." I rubbed my lips over his in a light kiss.

We ate the rest of the food. Then he placed a steaming cup of coffee in front of me. When I looked down I was happily surprised he remembered how I liked my coffee. Light with cream.

"You remembered." I took a sip and smiled at him.

"I remember everything about you, Aria. I couldn't forget even if I tried."

He laid back beside me. I savored a few more sips of coffee before I set the mug down and turned to face Gavin, our noses touching.

"Stay home with me again today, please. I am not ready to share you with the rest of the world just yet."

"I actually have …"

The words died in my throat when I remembered how close I came to losing him. It wouldn't hurt to spend one more day reconnecting with him and soothing all the hurt and fear away once and for all. We needed it. I could reschedule the meeting that I had lined up last minute. I was going to meet with someone about some dance opportunities now that Grayson was off the table. Kel had helped me line it up when I told her yesterday about the phone call. I needed to take the meeting. But as I looked at the man who was nearly taken from me, I knew it could wait. Gavin was more important. Only him.

I reached forward and pressed my cheek to his, embracing him. I felt the tension melt off him and I knew he must have been worried I would say no. But honestly, I needed this time with him. Our time.

"Let me get dressed and we can figure out what we want to do today," I said, pulling away and giving him a smile when our eyes met.

"Hell no."

Before I knew it, I was pulled back in bed. He hovered over me with that sexy-as-sin grin on his face.

"Where do you think, you're going, Ms. Morgan?"

"Um, the shower?"

The shake of his head was all I got before his mouth came down on mine. Immediately, my thighs clenched around his hips and my lips parted for him. I was lost in the kiss, the man and the weight of him between my legs.

Abruptly, Gavin stood and scooped me into his arms.

"Now, we shower."

I giggled and burrowed my face into his chest on the way to the bathroom. Once there, he set me gently on my feet.

"Make it hot," I said huskily as Gavin adjusted the dials on the shower.

"You make it hot, baby. In you go."

The hot, hot spray of water immediately soothed me. Gavin's eyes lit up with desire as he reached between our bodies to lift my hands to his mouth where he kissed each fingertip gently.

"Turn around."

He reached around me for my loofah and body wash. My need expanded in my belly and I recalled the last time he made love to me in here. It felt like ages ago even though it was just over a week ago.

"Oh, Gavin," I said as his smooth hands began to slide down the small slope of my neck, over my nape and to my shoulders.

His fingers rubbed and massaged the muscles there, soothing away days of tension and angst. I leaned into his hands, resting my head on his chest as he continued to adore my body with his touch.

"I love your skin." he whispered next to my ear just before his teeth caught my earlobe.

"Ahh." I turned and reached for his body wash to begin my own torture on his lean body. I was careful on his ribs and lower stomach, showing extra caution to the patch covering part of his forearm.

"Does it still hurt?" I asked, blinking up at him once he'd rinsed both the shampoo and my favorite Aloe and Chamomile conditioner out of my hair.

Being adored by this man was heavenly and I knew I could get used to it. I wanted it for the rest of my life. Somehow, it didn't scare the ever-living crap out of me anymore.

"No, and my ribs don't either. The pain medication did its job. Please stop worrying, baby. I'm OK."

He dipped his forehead to mine, resting it there for long seconds.

"Can we go to the Chateau?" I asked, referring to the small but absolutely stunning Italian restaurant Gavin's cousin owned.

His eyes lit up as he interlaced our fingers.

When he led me out of the shower, it was the first time in recent days that I was free of worry. I just looked forward to the rest of the day.

Chapter 23

After a restful sleep, I reached for Gavin's warmth but found cold sheets instead. I looked to the empty space beside me. Where was he?

I wrapped the sheets around me and shuffled down the hallway. I heard Gavin on the phone. He had to be in his office. I hoped he didn't have to go back to work yet, but his work was important to him.

So, I settled in to make some coffee. While I waited, I skimmed my fingers over the bookshelves lining the walls in the living room. I'd never seen Gavin with a book in his hands so it surprised me that he had such a large collection. Charles Dickens, Ray Donovan, Marie Barnes, Nicholas Sparks, the authors ranged from one genre to another. Somehow, I knew that most of these weren't Gavin's. I couldn't imagine him reading a full-length novel, like *Great Expectations*. He thrived on action, solving problems, making strides in whatever task he was focused on. Sitting with a book for any length of time would be a rarity for him.

"There she is," Gavin said as he wrapped an arm around my waist and kissed the side of my head.

His warm hands made tingles spread over my bare skin. I pointed to a Nicholas Sparks novel, *The Notebook*.

"Are you hiding a romantic side of you? Or is that Callie's?"

My voice was teasing and when he didn't answer me right away I turned in his arms. I skimmed my fingers down his arms to where he held me around the middle.

"My grandmother's. She loved to read. She always told me that whenever she was feeling down, she'd lose herself in a different world. It was her escape."

His voice was wistful and I heard how much he still missed her. I wanted to say so many things.

I'm sorry. She sounds so wonderful. You miss her, don't you?

But I didn't say any of those things; instead I wrapped my arms around his back and pressed my face into his bare chest. For a beat, I just held him. But then Gavin sighed and laid his cheek on the top of my head. He held me back, gently, but fiercely.

"She would have loved you."

"I would have loved her." I lifted my eyes to his and smiled shyly.

"I know, baby." He kissed me.

I nibbled his bottom lip, inciting a moan from his parted mouth.

"Bed." He growled, making my core tighten.

But I knew it was time to get back to the real world—work and my inevitable problem of a career. It was time.

"I'd love to, but I have that meeting today. You know the one I put off yesterday to spend the day in bed?"

Gavin pushed a strand of my hair behind my ear and grinned, his eyes on mine.

"It's time, huh?"

"I guess so. Shower with me?" I wrapped my arms around his neck and gazed up into those smiling eyes of his.

"Yes, beautiful."

Later, Farrah met me outside King's Bar and Grill with a big smile on her face.

"Hey, sweets! You look happy."

She came over to me linking our arms as we walked toward the entrance. It felt good to spend some time with my best friend after all that had happened recently.

"I am so glad that you found someone. I honestly think that boy is crazy about you."

I had so much to tell her about the past few days. I started with what happened with Gavin and Jasmine while we waited for our waiter. She listened with rapt attention as I described the scene I walked in on at Gavin's office.

She gave me a tight hug and said, "But honey, I have seen the way he looks at you. You have nothing to worry about with her."

"You're right. But every time I think about Jasmine and her lips on Gavin, it makes me sick. The wound, though accidental, still hurts. I felt so betrayed. I know the truth and I can't help but blame myself for jumping to the wrong conclusions and putting distance between us. Ultimately, if I had just talked to him then, he never would have gotten in the accident."

She looked at me, understanding.

"It wasn't your fault, you know that, right?"

I folded my hands in my lap and told myself that she was right.

"Yeah, I know. I was so scared, Fay."

"How—do you know what happened?"

"I guess a loader truck ran through a red light on I-22 and hit the driver's side of Gavin's car. Then another car hit him head on. The doctors said if it wasn't for the airbags … he could have been. …" I couldn't bring myself to say the rest.

The outcome was so unthinkable to me. Farrah clasped my hand across the table, her eyes filled with worry.

"Don't think about that. He's okay, right?"

I nodded, remembering his bright smile and heated eyes this morning. He was okay and we were stronger than ever.

"Very much so. Apparently, the loader driver didn't even stop after he hit Gavin. The police finally located him and have charged him with running a red light and hit and run."

"Have you talked to him about Jasmine? About what you saw?"

"I did. He told me that she kissed him and that's what I saw. I know he has no feelings for that girl."

That was one thing I was certain of. She eyed me speculatively, strumming a hand across the wooden table. I knew she wanted to say something. I sighed and tilted my head to the side.

"What?" I asked, knowing she had to speak her mind.

"You should make it clear to her who he belongs to, Aria. Girls like that don't care if he's taken. She might not stop unless she knows that you're not letting Gavin go."

Oh, my. I didn't think about this before, but I trusted him. If she became a problem, then I'd have words with her.

"I'll think about it. I just want to focus on Gavin right now. If I'd lost him—I don't know if I could have gone on." The devastation of that was still so raw for me.

Farrah's eyes immediately softened and she nodded, squeezing my hand.

"But you didn't. He is fine. Do you want to order? I'm just going to run to the bathroom really quick."

"Sure, you want a Pepsi? Or something stronger?"

She winked at me and slid out of the booth.

"A Blue Moon, please."

I watched her go and closed my eyes briefly, reminding myself to breathe as I recalled Gavin in that hospital bed. My phone rang in my pocket. Pulling it out, I saw Gavin's name flashing upon the screen. My heart lifted.

"Hi, handsome," I said, hoping he didn't hear the thread of uneasiness in my voice.

"Hey, baby. How's your lunch?"

"Good, Farrah's got some big news to tell me. I told her about everything. She's been pulling for you all this time."

He chuckled.

"Happy to hear that."

He laughed again, and I swore I could listen to that sound for the rest of my life. God, I loved his carefree laugh. I loved that it came from deep in his chest, never forced. I loved the sound of it against my ear when I rested my head against him at night.

"I love your laugh," I whispered.

I could practically feel his smile on the other end of the line.

"Is that all you love about me, Aria?" His voice was gravelly with that southern charm that always made me weak in the knees.

Though his family has settled in Chicago, he grew up on his grandfather's farm in Tennessee. Whenever I heard that slight southern twist in his voice, it was sexy as hell.

"Among other things, Gavin."

In the background, I heard his office phone ring and he sighed.

"I have a call, see you soon."

"Okay."

I hung up just as a waitress approached, smiling warmly.

"I'm Daniela, I'll be your server today. Can I get you something to drink?"

"Yes, can I get a Blue Moon and a diet Pepsi?"

"Sure, here's a menu. Take your time, I'll be back with your drinks shortly."

I smiled and took the two menus she handed me. Farrah came back moments later and flipped through the menu, snickering about the lovey-dovey couple sitting behind us.

"So, what's this news you have?" I asked, filled with curiosity.

She beamed at me and set her menu aside. Her eyes were bright and full of joy suddenly.

"Well ..." She took a sip of her Blue Moon.

There was none of the doubt or uncertainty that I used to see before she met Jaden. He was good for her and I knew she was happy with him. But it was hard for her to believe in happily ever after. She had never been that kind of girl. She deserved it, though. A happy ending, just like the rest of us.

"I'm moving in with Jaden. He asked me last night."

My jaw dropped open. I reached over and squeezed her hand.

"Oh, my God, and you waited all this time to tell me?"

She grinned brightly.

"Well, I figured I'd let you be wonder for a bit. Anticipation is the best part, isn't it?"

"Not on this! How did he ask you?"

She told me how Jaden put a key on her key ring and told her that he didn't want to be away from her anymore.

"I'm so happy for you, Farrah."

"I know, sweets. It's a good thing."

After a delicious BLT and over-sized portion of French fries, we split a smoothie. Once we were stuffed, we headed over to Gold's Gym to meet Kel. My meeting with the recruiter was at three so I had time for a workout with my two best girls.

"So, what are you going to do about Grayson?"

I look over to Farrah who's driving my car. I shrugged.

"Not much I can do. I lost the spot, Farrah. I can't expect another opportunity like that. I did schedule an appointment for three today with a recruiter Kel mentioned. Hopefully he'll have some suggestions for me."

"You'll find something, Ari. You live to dance, after all."

She was right. Dance was a part of me. I honestly didn't know what I would do without it.

By the time, I came out of the locker room, dressed in yoga pants and a stretch top I'd bought last month, I saw Kel was going double time on the treadmill. She looked up as I approached with Farrah on my heels.

"Hey! What took you so long?"

"Have you eaten at that new pub in the center? It's hard to say no to food that good!"

I went by her. She waved to Farrah who stopped to do some stretches.

"How's the man?" Kel asked panting as she ran.

I looked over to her, starting the treadmill beside her. I set it to walk for a while so I could warm up.

"Wonderful, as always. How's Luke?"

"Good. He's working on his thesis for school today. I swear that man is smarter than me any day of the week," she said on a laugh, her voice going soft with affection.

I laughed, happy to see my sister so carefree.

"That's only because you waste all your brain cells with little kids at that daycare."

She scoffed, waving her hand in the air playfully. I bumped the treadmill up to jog and started in on a run. It felt good to stretch my muscles and feel the burn of exertion.

"You're one to talk. You graduated with a 3.6 GPA from Julliard, yet you spend all your time at a dance studio, Ms. Morgan! And it's a preschool, by the way."

I stuck my tongue out and set the speed even faster as I popped my headphones into my ears. I teased her about being a preschool teacher, but inwardly I was proud of her. She loved those kids like her own. They were lucky to have such a caring person to teach them.

"You're just jealous you can't dance."

I flicked my eyes over to her while she pretended to ignore me. She really couldn't dance. My sister was good at many things, but dancing wasn't one of them. She turned and narrowed her eyes at me.

"But I can face-paint like a pro!"

Her snarky response made me burst into laughter. Kel stopped running to catch her breath and I could hear her laughing, too.

After a long workout, I was filled with energy for my meeting. We made our way to the locker rooms, chatting a little about the wedding while we changed. I brought a knee length white skirt and simple collared shirt to wear for my meeting this afternoon.

"I thought we could go over the guest list for a bit. Do you want to go back to my place or yours?" Kel asked, already veering me toward her car. I searched for my sunglasses in the depths of my large purse. I stopped short realizing I hadn't told her about my meeting.

"I have a meeting with the career adviser today. I can meet you after if you want?"

She looked at me then, her face spread into a proud smile.

"Oh, of course! Come on, I'll drive and wait for you, OK?"

I nodded, a little relieved to have the support. It meant the world to me that she believed in me.

We pulled up to the address Kel had texted me before. Innovative Solutions was on the third floor of an office building just outside of downtown. My stomach tightened with nerves. *What would they say?* Maybe I had lost my dream forever and they'd send me packing. I bunched my fingers together, telling myself it would be OK.

"Hey." Kel grasped my hand and squeezed gently.

I looked up and saw her brown eyes filled with understanding.

"You've got this, Ari."

Four words and she boosted my spirits. I smiled at her, knowing how much she still worried about me after everything that had happened over the past several years.

I pecked my sister's cheek and smoothed my skirt as I walked to the front doors of the building. As I made my way into the elevator, I felt my phone buzz with a text. Warmth spread through me when I saw it was from Gavin.

Good luck, baby.

His message brought a smile to my face. He could have said so many things, but I knew this was his way of telling me that no matter what, he'd be here for me. His faith in me gave me more determination. On the third floor I was saw a large sign with simple cursive words written over what looked like a crescent moon. Before getting off the elevator, I typed a quick reply to Gavin.

I've got this!

Soon, I came to a reception desk in a well-lit room.

"What can I do for you, Miss?" a young man, about twenty-one or so, greeted me.

"Hi, yes. My name is Aria. I'm here to see Scott."

He nodded and picked up a phone to make a call.

"Mr. Hayes? Ms. Aria Morgan is here"

I waited patiently while he spoke quietly into the phone. When he finished, he told me to go to the fourth office on the right. I smiled and thanked him. Then I headed toward Scott's office.

I knocked twice then opened the door. A blond-haired man with hazel eyes was intently focused on a stack of papers in front of him.

"Oh! I didn't see you come in. Please sit, Ms. Morgan. It's great to finally meet you." He clasped my hand and shook it as I came toward his desk.

I took a seat across from him and answered a few questions. He asked about my time at Julliard, what I was looking for in the future, what my dream job would be. It was so easy to talk about what I loved.

"I'll obviously have to make some calls, but there is an up and com-ing ballet that is looking for some new talent. It's called *Alas the Night*. Is that something you'd be interested in?"

Immediately I was thrilled. I'd done recreational dancing and pro-fessional dancing with a troupe I'd joined back when I was studying. But it had always been my dream to dance in the spotlight. The ballet. I hastily nodded my head and beamed a smile so wide it hurt.

"That's the dream," I stated simply and when Scott nodded his head, I knew he understood.

The moment I got back in my sister's car, she saw my smile.

"Things go okay?" She asked as she started the car. Her eyes were trained on me.

"Things are looking up," I said and winked at her.

I felt hopeful that maybe I hadn't lost my only opportunity in the dance world after all.

We stopped on the way to the penthouse to pick up my car. I tossed my car keys in my purse as we walked up the steps toward the pent-house.

"Why would you hesitate to move in here? This is so ..."

Kel stopped talking as we made it to the top level and could see through the glass doors into the penthouse. The hardwood floors and a big leather couch sitting in the center of the living room were all that were visible.

"Oh, my God, can I live here?" She gushed over how amazing it was.

Though, I was still getting used to the idea that this was home, I had to agree with her. The idea of making this my home with the man I loved, thrilled me. One thing that had always felt like home was being with Gavin. Wherever he was, that was home.

"Holy shit, this is nice. Show me around?"

She was salivating by the time we walked through the spacious living room and kitchen.

I grabbed my gym bag from her hand and nodded. How could I say no?

"Come on."

I led her into each room, and her eyes lit up when she saw the windows and fireplace along the far walls of the living area.

"He really likes the cherry wood, huh?" she asked, running her hand over the railing between the dining room and living room.

The style of this place surprised me, too, when I first set foot here. But now, I couldn't think of one thing I'd want to change.

"It's modern."

She nodded, setting her bag down by the couch and followed me toward the kitchen.

"I love it. Where is my favorite billionaire?"

I giggled, tossing her a water from the fridge.

"He must be in his office. Make yourself at home. I'll be right back," I said, making my way down the hallway toward his study.

I heard the faint strains of *Yellow* by Coldplay echoing from inside. I knocked twice, and opened the door. Gavin sat at his desk, phone pressed to his ear. His eyes flicked to mine and his face transformed from businessman to lover. Hanging up the phone, he smiled, and stretched out his hand to me.

"Hi, baby," he murmured and pulled me onto his lap holding me close.

I grinned, leaning down to capture his ruggedly handsome face in my hands. I traced my fingers over his freshly shaven jaw, reveling in the smooth skin.

"You still working?" I asked, sinking my hands into his mussed-up hair.

He shook his head, running his lips against mine achingly slow. Oh, he loved to tease.

"All finished. Did I hear Kel come in with you?"

I nodded and kissed the corner of his mouth. Gavin smiled wider and stood with me still in his arms. He set me on my feet, taking my hand in his and led me out of his office.

"You like Coldplay? I thought you were more of a Counting Crows man."

He grinned, kissing my lips softly as we walked toward the kitchen.

"I have many favorites. How was your lunch?"

I blinked up at him, smiling. Gavin dipped his lips to mine once more and I felt his smile.

"Good," was all I said as we made our way out of his office.

Kel sat at the kitchen island, sipping her water when we entered. She lit up seeing us together. She'd always rooted for Gavin, from the beginning.

"Feeling okay?" she asked as she got up and kissed Gavin on the cheek.

Oh, wow. Why did that make me feel just a tad jealous? Weird.

"Good as new. You like the apartment?"

She nodded, grabbing her bag and pulling out three binders filled with samples from her wedding planner.

Uh, oh. This might take a while.

"It's very homey, much unexpected. Care to help with some wedding planning?"

Gavin chuckled, winking down at me. He whispered in my ear, letting his breath fall across my face.

"Do we have a choice?"

"Uh, no."

"I'll get some beers, then. Aria, a Blue Moon?"

I smiled, taking two binders from Kel. This was going to take a while, we might as well be comfortable. My eyes didn't leave Gavin's as I bit my lip in an effort to goad him.

"With lime, please."

Gruffly ran a hand down his neck. I saw how I affected him just before he headed toward the fridge to grab three beers.

"Does it really matter, Kel?" I asked, taking a swig of beer as she flipped through samples of ballads for the bride and groom's first dance. She spent fifteen minutes on the same page.

"Of course, it matters! Gavin back me up here. Isn't the first slow dance the most important?"

He sat behind me on the carpeted floor, his legs around mine, his arm wrapped around my middle and his chin resting upon my shoulder. I felt his grin beside me, amused by my sister's bridezilla-like persona.

"It is, but it should be a song that tells exactly the way you two feel about each other. A ballad, maybe."

Surprised by his sincere word, I leaned into his embrace even more. He'd thought about this? But then it occurred to me, he was engaged before.

"Oh, my God! I can't believe I didn't think of this before, of course. It's the perfect song." She exclaimed, practically bouncing up and down with excitement.

"What song?" I asked, giggling when Gavin nipped on my earlobe, making my core tighten deliciously.

Just with that small tease, I was breathy and wanton for him again.

"*You and Me* by Lifehouse. It was playing at my senior prom when we danced for the first time. Do you think Lucas will like it?" Her voice was filled with excitement.

I smiled, remembering how happy she was that night. She came home on cloud nine after Lucas told her he loved her for the first time.

"Honey, that is perfect. He'll love it."

Gavin's lips running along the side of my neck were so distracting that I had to bite my lip to stop the moan trying to slip out. Meanwhile, Kel riffled through her last binder, filled with centerpieces.

"I just have to choose the centerpieces. Take a look."

She handed me the blue binder, opened to one of the last pages. It was full of pictures of centerpieces. I never knew there were so many centerpiece options. Some had flowers in the middle. There was one toward the bottom of the page with an open heart, plated in gold with roses surrounding the circular base. It was gorgeous.

"I like this one, you could even get your initials attached at the bottom of the tail. What do you think?" I moved the binder so Gavin could see it over my shoulder.

Gavin and Kel looked down at where I pointed. My sister's face lit up, slightly blushing. She loved it, I could tell.

"Perfect! Thank you, Aria!"

She kissed my cheek and then looked over my shoulder at Gavin, causing mine to flick up also. They were filled with amusement.

"I like it, it's thoughtful yet romantic. Definitely, the piece I like best. Good choice, baby." His voice was filled with praise.

I pressed a kiss to his palm as Kel hastily packed up her stuff and jammed it into her bag.

"I have to go meet Lucas. You want to meet up tomorrow?"

I got up and followed her toward the door, hugging her goodbye.

"I'll call you."

She smiled then hugged Gavin quickly before closing the door behind her, leaving us alone. I smirked. It was nice seeing her happy. She deserved it.

"Now what should we do with ourselves, hmm?" Gavin's husky voice whispered in my ear as he kissed my knuckles.

My eyes flicked to his and I bit my lip, a whole range of ideas going through my head.

"I can think of a few things, I'm sure."

I took his hand as his eyes heated with longing. It was crazy how being in the same room with him elicited such a reaction in my body.

"We only have forty-five minutes until we have to leave for dinner, baby."

I led him into the bedroom, my eyes never leaving his. I locked the door behind me, leaning against the solid wood frame.

"That's plenty of time."

And before I knew it, he dropped to his knees in front of me and slipped two fingers into the fabric of my flow skirt.

Oh! My legs felt like jelly as I took a small step toward him, seeing the desire in his eyes.

He undid the button and slid the zipper down slowly until the fabric hung loosely from my hips.

"I've wanted you all day, beautiful. I love undressing you."

His voice was deep with hunger. Everything south of my belly tightened in want.

"Gavin, take it off," I whispered, my hands on his shoulders as he glided the fabric over my hips, past my upper thighs and down my calves. The slow way he took them off made me breathless.

"Let me take your shoes off."

I stepped out of them. When his hands closed over the edge of my panties, his mouth ran along my lower belly. I moaned loudly, feeling desire pool between my parted legs. I clenched my core, needing to feel him inside me again. His tongue ran up my stomach and he slipped my panties over my hips, letting them fall to the floor effortlessly.

"Take your shirt off and then go to the bed and lie down for me, beautiful."

I drug my teeth over my bottom lip, hearing his voice filled with hunger. I looked down at him as I reached for the hem of my blouse. His eyes watched me eagerly as I lifted the fabric and slipped it over my head. God, I wanted him so badly.

"Okay ..."

I pushed away from the door and unfastened my bra before climbing onto the bed, laying down with my head pressed to the pillows.

"I love looking at you," he said, crawling over me and brushing his mouth to mine.

"I want you, Gavin."

He grinned, running his hands down my sides until they rested on my upper thighs.

"You. Are. Mine." The words were punctuated with kisses as he parted my legs.

My eyes closed in pleasure. His lips sucked along my neck, over my collarbone and kept wandering until they adored my breasts, drawing one of my nipples into his mouth.

I groaned, tangling my hands into his hair as he unleashed his tongue, moving lower, toward my belly. My legs parted wider, my hips lifting toward him in invitation. My hands deftly unfastened his pants eliciting a chuckle from him. He grazed his lips over mine as he kicked his slacks off. Finally, he pressed against my aching entrance.

Oh, my. I'd never felt this way before. I was drawn to this man with every fiber of my being. Almost as if he was my reason for existing, and maybe he was.

"You feel so good ..." I whispered, wrapping my legs around him and grasping his shoulders as he hovered over me, his mouth pressed to my temple.

"I know, baby."

Suddenly, he was inside me, slipping deep into my sex and gliding out easily because of how wet I was. He groaned when he was seated fully inside. He tilted my head back with a hand on the side of my face and dipped his head as he took my mouth hungrily. He pushed in and out while he devoured my mouth in a similar rhythm, back and forth. He created a steady pace, a heavenly tempo that had me climbing higher and higher. My core tightened and I clung to him in need. He moaned deep in his throat, the sound reverberating through my parted lips as he slipped out and pushed into me once more. Feeling him so deep inside me was intoxicating.

"Oh God, Gavin!" I called out, my mouth parting and my body tightening passionately as I found release. A quick forceful orgasm made my toes curl and my stomach flipped in pleasure. It went on and on, my eyes flicked up to Gavin's as he reared up over me, his mouth forming an O as he came, calling out my name over and over again, until he collapsed on top of me. He covered my upturned face with butterfly kisses, tenderly.

"Have I ever told you that you amaze me, Aria?" he whispered, pressing his head to my stomach as he hugged me tightly.

My hands tangled in his hair while my other arm wrapped around his middle. I drew precious air into my lungs, tears piercing my eyes at his heartfelt words.

"You have, baby," I giggled, breathlessly.

And then, with his arms wrapped around me and his mouth pressing to my belly, I was sated.

I heard his deep voice against my heated skin.

"I love you, Aria. Please don't ever forget that."

I cupped his cheeks in my hands and smiled his smile.

"I won't."

Chapter 24

Farrah and I went in and out of shops on Central Avenue in downtown Chicago, enjoying the sunny Saturday morning, searching for the bridesmaids' dresses Kel described to us—strapless, lavender, hanging just past our knees with black heeled sandals. We were cutting it close, trying to find exactly what she envisioned so close to the wedding. But with Gavin's accident and everything else going on, there just hadn't been time to get together and go. And today she had to work, so she had to trust us to find something.

As the day wore on, my feet began to hurt from all the walking. Crap, I forgot just how much I hated shopping. I remembered, when my mom used to take Kel and me; it was torture.

"Seriously, are we done yet?" I whined, grinning when Farrah gave me what could only be explained as the fuck-off look.

From experience, I knew that when she was on a mission, like now, there was no stopping her.

"No, we have two more stores to go. Come on honey."

I begrudgingly followed her inside Neiman Marcus, promising myself a pint of Ben & Jerry's Rocky Road ice cream afterwards.

After searching high and low, I heard Farrah squeal in delight as she held up yet another sleeveless dress, this one with a black embroidered sash that tied in the back. I sighed in relief, knowing it was perfect and Kel would love it.

"That's the one, Farrah. I'd bet my life on it," I said, going around the sales rack to find my size. There it was. Thank God.

"Kel is going to absolutely love these. Did you find your size?"

I held up the dress. "Let's go try them on."

I set my stuff down in the over-sized dressing room and took the fabric off the hanger. I saw Farrah grin at me in the mirror like a fool. What was going on with her?

"What's so funny?" I asked as I began to slip my clothes off.

"Nothing's funny," she answered as she hoisted her sundress over her head. "I just never really paid much attention to how tiny you are. NO wonder Gavin loves you."

Her voice sounded a little insecure, which shocked me. I removed my clothes and slid the lavender dress over my head, smoothing it into place. She was maybe three sizes bigger than me, if that. She was gorgeous and curvy. I had always been jealous of her curves growing up.

"Well, you know dancing is a constant work out. It makes it easier to stay trim. You know I have always been jealous of your curves. I bet Jaden loves them, doesn't he?"

She nodded, straightening out her own dress and turning towards the mirror as she tightened the sash behind her back. Her hips filled up the dress perfectly. And her long as sin legs were a knockout in the heels we found this morning. They were thin, maybe three inches tall and exposed her freshly pedicured toe nails. She still had a look of insecurity on her face.

"He does, but you know how I am. Maybe he's just saying that because our relationship is so new. Does he really want a curvy girlfriend with a less than perfect body for the long haul? I don't know."

She chewed on her thumb and looked away from me. I hated to think she didn't love herself like I always thought she did. The spunky attitude was part of her charm. I didn't say anything as I went to her. I gazed at our reflections in the mirror. There we stood in matching dresses and I couldn't see much difference between us, physically at least.

"You're gorgeous, honey. He'd be a fool to not see that, right? And you are so much more than what you look like on the outside. Never forget that."

Farrah ran her hand through her hair and nodded, but I could still feel her judging herself in the mirror. I clasped my best friend's shoulders and turned her to face me.

"There is nothing wrong with you, Fay. Jaden sees that. I see that. But if you don't see that, there will always be those doubts in your head. You have to believe in yourself, first."

I saw the moisture in her eyes and it tore at my heart.

"I'll try to see that, Ari," she finally said, softly.

I heard the vulnerability in her voice.

I pulled her into a hug, wrinkling the designer wear we were sporting but not caring. She was my best friend and I'd hate to think she was insecure wearing this dress on Saturday.

"Same here, sweetie. You look awesome, do you like the dress?"

She nodded, stepping back and clapping her hands as I turned in my heels.

"You so should have been a model, Ari. You have the body for it!"

I scoffed, remembering how mad my mother was when I decided not to follow in her footsteps. The thought made me laugh out loud.

"What?" Farrah asked as she undressed again and tossed me my clothes.

"You remember how mad my mom was when I went into dancing?"

My mom was a beautiful, talented model. Growing up, I always looked up to her. But once I started dancing, I knew that was what I was meant to do. When I'd told her that, it was the day of my high school prom. She went ballistic, said I could never make a career out of professional dancing. Now all that was in the past and I couldn't help but laugh at it all. Farrah laughed along with me, slipping her flats back on her feet as I sat to put on my thick heeled boots once more. I was still laughing when we opened the dressing room door and brought the dresses with us.

"See, now that was hilarious, she was crazy-mad!" Farrah exclaimed in her dramatic fashion.

We giggled like school girls and then my phone rang. It was Gavin. I sent Farrah a smirk and she took my dress, heading to the register.

"Hey, handsome."

"Where are you, baby? This bed is too cold without you," he whispered, his voice teasing. My heart jumped. Even though it had only been a matter of hours, I missed him.

"We're still in the plaza; I'll be home soon though. Just paying for these ridiculously expensive bridesmaids dresses. How was your morning?"

"Hectic, as always. You know you don't have to worry about checking prices anymore. I like spoiling you, beautiful."

I bit down on my lip to hide my smile as Farrah met me by the Neiman Marcus entrance to Central Avenue.

"I know, but I'm not used to spending this kind of money, it's just different for me."

He was silent for a moment and I started to think I'd lost him. Had I said something wrong?

"Does it bother you? My lifestyle? You can be honest."

Did it bother me? My family always had money because of mom, so it wasn't not new to me but still, I liked earning my way. I decided to go with my heart, knowing that Gavin liked to spoil me because he loved and cared for me, not for any other misguided reason.

"No, it's just different for me, Gavin. I'd tell you if it truly bothered me."

He exhaled, obviously calmer now.

"That's good to hear, baby. When will you be home?"

"Soon. I just have to drop the dresses off at Kel's apartment and drive Farrah back to North-end. Then I'll be home."

"You have Aaron with you, right? He's following you."

I looked behind where my car was parked and saw Aaron from his security team looking straight ahead. I was a little impressed by the Audi A3 he drove.

"Yes, he's here. We'll be safe."

"See you soon, beautiful"

His voice was low and full of promise, making me want him again. *How did he do that?*

"Bye, babe."

Once Farrah was home, I pulled out and headed toward East End again. I was eagerly looking forward to seeing my man after a long day of shopping, shopping and more shopping. The butterflies started again as I thought about how amazing the last few weeks had been. Gavin had either taken me out to eat or cooked for me every night since our wedding-planning session with Kel. He'd been so good to me; it sometimes felt too good to be true.

When I stopped at a red light, I spotted a gray Lincoln Aviator behind me. It was directly behind me, almost like it was tailing me. The windows were tinted. A sense of dread seeped through my veins as it followed me down I-22 all the way to the next light. I turned right, watching the rear-view mirror as it went out of sight. Aaron was in the next lane so nothing would happen to me, but God was I being followed?

I kept a steady speed toward the penthouse, but by the time I arrived in the parking lot at the back of the building, my hands were shaking.

I forced myself out of the car and grabbed my stuff.

Maybe I just imagined it. Was the Lincoln really that close to me? I wasn't sure.

I took a breath, holding it for a few seconds before slowly letting it out. I was still trying to shake off the uneasiness seeping through my veins when I made my way into the apartment and saw Gavin standing in front of the stove in the kitchen. A white button down shirt hugged his torso and upper arms and a pair of dark jeans hung deliciously loose from his hips while he cooked barefoot in the kitchen.

Oh, my.

I slipped my jacket off. The place smelled of garlic bread and pasta, making my mouth water.

"Smells good, baby."

Gavin turned smiling wide. He pulled me into his arms and kissed my temple. I grasped his wrists, needing him close for a little longer.

Oh, he felt so good.

"Thought we could have a dinner on the balcony tonight, what do you think?"

I pressed my face to his neck and grazed my hands up his back, reveling in the feel of him. The feelings of dread I had only five minutes before slowly evaporated, as they were replaced with the butterflies I always got when I was this close to him.

"I'd love to. How was your day?"

He stirred the pot with one hand keeping the other wrapped around me. His eyes flicked to mine, clear and blue.

"Busy, I might have to take a trip to Los Angeles for a few meetings."

I leaned back in surprise. It never occurred to me that he had to travel for work. How would I feel about being away from him? I would hate it. I'd miss him like crazy.

"Hey, don't worry. It's not for a few weeks and if I can get out of it, I will," Gavin said as he took the pot off the burner and laid the spoon beside the cooling plate.

He turned into me, running a hand along my cheek. I felt the skin tingle underneath his touch.

"Is that Italian I smell?"

That smile I loved spread across his face. He nodded as he cupped my cheeks gazing down at me, such care in his blue-gray eyes.

"Yes, and garlic bread. I'll save dessert for later."

His voice was full of unspoken promises. I smiled loving the feel of his arms wrapped tight around me again. I pressed my face to his neck and inhaled.

"Smells good."

I heard Gavin's chuckle before he took my face in his hands and looked at me with a devilish grin.

"The food?"

I pressed a kiss to his jaw and shook my head.

"Oh, no. You."

His eyes heated and he lifted my mouth to his until his lips brushed against mine ever so lightly.

"You are addictive."

I smiled against his urgent mouth, wrapping my arms around his neck and sinking my fingers into his silky hair. His hot breath surrounded my face in an intoxicating way.

"Am I?" I teased.

Gavin took my mouth, parting my lips easily with his tongue He kissed me with suggestive licks. His breath mingling with mine, stealing the air from my lungs as he kissed me with such ardent passion.

In seconds, I was breathless. When he took my bottom lip into his mouth, sucking voraciously, I moaned low in my throat in response.

"Hmm, do you want to take a shower?" he whispered, pulling back from my lips and tucking a stray strand of my curly hair behind my ear.

"If you insist," I whispered. Gavin scooped me into his arms and carried me to the bathroom without another word.

Gavin slid his hands down my back in a massaging motion as I sat on his lap. We went over to hang out after dinner. Kel and I were engrossed in a game of cards while the boys talked about the football game they were watching. Gavin pulled for the Colts while Lucas was an adamant Patriots fan.

"Aria. Earth to Aria Georgia ... " Kel snapped her fingers in a waving motion in front of me. I must have spaced out because she was trying to get my attention.

"What?" I tilted my face up to see her grinning.

"You're daydreaming again! It's your turn."

She winked and I felt Gavin stiffen behind me at what I might be daydreaming. About his hands skating along my skin, my back, my thighs, my shoulders. Oh, how I wanted them south. I ached for him.

"And who are you daydreaming about, baby?"

I turned my face into the hollow just above Gavin's ear.

"You. I want you, now." My voice sounded close to a growl as I whispered in his ear. Immediately he was hard behind me and I giggled.

"I'm sorry, Luke, but I think I've been neglecting my sweet girl, here. We'll see you at the church for rehearsal."

Gavin stood with me against his chest and nodded toward Lucas and Kel who were both smiling. They knew exactly why we were leaving. My cheeks heated in embarrassment.

"Have fun."

My sister practically sang and I laughed as she hugged me, whispering in my ear.

"It's good to see you so happy, Ari. See you soon."

Gavin took my hand and tugged me out into the cool night air. He immediately pushed me against the hood of his car. He dipped his head and began to rain kisses down my throat and neck.

"Oh, please take me home Gavin," I begged and pulled his head back with my hands so I could see the depths of his eyes.

"Home," he drawled, skating fingers down my face to grasp my chin.

Those eyes of his filled with tenderness that melted me into a puddle before him. I nodded and smiled shyly.

"Take me home."

It felt like it took hours to get back to the penthouse. The normally short ride up the elevator seemed to take forever. Gavin kept his arm around my waist the entire way and as soon as I closed the front door behind us I crashed my body into his, kissing him. Deep. Hard. Hungry. I felt wetness flood my core and Gavin's desire pressed against my lower stomach.

"Beautiful," he groaned against my mouth. Grasping the hem of my skirt, he pushed the silky fabric off my hips and legs. The next to go was his t-shirt, then the buckle of his loose-fitting jeans and finally my blouse. It took a matter of seconds for my bra and pink laced panties to join our clothes on the hardwood floor.

When I stood naked before him, Gavin's eyes took me in as if he'd never seen my body before. He didn't move to touch me, he just looked at me with hungry eyes.

"You are so sweet, Aria. I love that you're mine." Gavin pierced me with the intensity in his eyes and his words reverberated through my skin like sunlight.

I clutched onto his shoulders as he carried me to bed.

"Need you." I tangled my fingers in his hair and felt in my soul that Gavin was the only one I'd ever need.

As if he knew the depth of my need for him, he brought his mouth down to mine and whispered against my lips.

"I'm yours, Aria. But we only have an hour."

Despite his reminder, I pushed my body to his. I moaned passionately when I felt his hardness against me. I couldn't think through the haze of pleasure that I found myself in. All I could do was lose myself in the sensation. I wrapped my legs tightly around his hips and with one fluid thrust, Gavin buried himself within my aching center. He rubbed my clit over and over. I felt my core flood in response.

"Oh God."

I spasmed around him and met each thrust. Gavin dipped his tongue to my breasts and began to drive me crazy with that glorious mouth of his. He licked and nipped one areola before bringing the nipple into his mouth. I climbed higher and higher. My body was on fire from his touch, his mouth, his body pressing onto mine. Gavin slid out and thrust one more time so deep inside me that I was sure I couldn't hold the pleasure inside any more.

"Gavin ... Oh, God," I begged, clenching my muscles around him each time he joined with me and I could feel the waves of pleasure hit a crescendo.

"I'm right here, baby. Let go for me."

He nipped my collarbone, then soothed the skin with his tongue and mouth. I couldn't hold off any longer. I bit my lip and cried out his name as I shattered beneath him. Gavin whispered my name roughly and found his own sweet release within my flooded center. I felt his weight press against every line of my body. He framed my face, peppering my cheeks and nose with light kisses and then rolled so that I was on top of him.

"Amazing," he whispered.

Chapter 25

By the time, I looked up from my notebook, it was almost six. I sat up in bed and worried my lower lip with my teeth as I looked down at what I wrote to Jeremy. When dad brought me and Kel home from the hospital all those years ago, my mom had already left for some grand photo shoot in Milan. I was still reeling from the emptiness I'd felt when my world bottomed out. I couldn't eat, I couldn't sleep because every time I closed my eyes I saw Jeremy's face. His aqua blue eyes that used to soften when I needed a hug. His face when he mouthed "I love you, squirt" just before he was wheeled into surgery. Dad was at his lowest point, seeing both his daughters hurting and having no way to stop the pain we felt. But then, he gave me this journal.

"I know it's not the same but if you write to him, tell him how you're feeling and share with him, it might take some of this away. Just try, pumpkin. Please."

Sitting next to my dad, I knew Kel and I meant so much to him. I promised to try. So, I wrote to Jeremy. A lot. Not as much lately as I used to. I would tell my brother everything he was missing. Sometimes, it felt like I could feel him smiling down at me from above. When I finally brought myself to tell him about Bryce and what had really happened to me, I'd felt the gentle breeze of his memory surround me. As if he was in my room with me giving me one of those warm, toothy smiles that lifted my spirits all through high school and college.

Ever since I woke up this morning, I began to ask myself questions. Had I lost sight of Jeremy's memory? Had I slowly been forgetting my brother? With everything that had happened since meeting Gavin, I'd had this journal stuck between my two Julliard Alumni sweatshirts. I dug it out this afternoon while I was cleaning the bedroom, needing something to do since I didn't have anywhere to go. God, it felt good to write him again. It made me feel even closer to him than I remembered.

My thoughts, or more like my memories, halted when I heard the ring of my phone. Gavin's name flashed on the screen. A smile spread across my face when I saw.

"Miss me, already?" I purred into the phone, sitting down next to a hot cup of tea at the island. I heard a car engine and the rustling of a man's voice on the other end. I figured he must be on his way to yet another meeting.

"Where are you? I'm outside, baby," Gavin's tense voice immediately had my heart hammering.

Had something happened? It took a lot to rattle this man, what had happened?

"I'm at home, Gavin. What- what's wrong?"

"Thank God."

I heard him say under his breath a prayer instead of a statement. But before I could urge him to talk to me, I heard the lock turn at the back entrance as Spencer let himself in. I worried something had happened for the head of Thomas' security team to be here at six-fifteen on a Saturday night.

"Ms. Morgan, I need you to step out of the penthouse now. Gavin is waiting for you outside."

"I—is everything alright? Is he OK? He just called me." I asked, the pit in my stomach growing with worry the more time passed.

"You need to go, Ms. Morgan. I promise you'll have answers once you're outside."

The pleading tone in Spencer's voice made me hurry to slip on my gray flip-flops and pull on sweatshirt.

"Thank you, Miss."

He led me out the door and the moment I set foot on the sidewalk, he quickly ushered me away from the penthouse.

What the hell? What the hell was going on?

Confusion made my nerves spiral as I stood looking back at the building for the longest time, trying to understand what was going on. Then I felt him behind me. He didn't touch me, but I felt every fragment of his presence within me.

I turned and was immediately struck by the stormy intensity of Gavin's blue-gray eyes.

"Gavin, what's going on?" I asked.

He looked at me as if I was about to disappear. Without another word, he swept me into his arms. His warm, smooth skin urged me to wrap my arms around his shoulders.

"I'll tell you everything as soon as I know it's safe for us to stay here tonight. Can I just hold you for now?" Gavin placed his palm on my cheek and the worry I saw in his gorgeous face was palpable.

I nuzzled my face into the crook of his shoulder.

"Okay."

Gavin wrapped an arm around both my shoulders when Spencer let us into the penthouse later. As I looked around, I didn't notice anything out of place. But the hardened look the two men exchanged told me that something wasn't right. Confused, I backed away from both of them.

"What is going on? I deserve to know if something has happened."

My voice was filled with conviction, but that didn't sway either of them to answer me. Gavin gazed down at me and I saw the obvious concern and fear in his eyes.

"Spencer, thank you for everything. I need to talk with my girl, now."

Gavin shook his hand and led him to the door before shutting it with a silent click and turned to face me.

"Talk to me, Gavin," I whispered, taking his hand in mine when he stood in front of me.

"Come with me," he said, tugging me toward our bedroom.

I felt like I was being kept in the dark about something. I hated being in the dark, but I was also afraid whatever danger I felt was imminent from Spencer's visit.

Gavin guided me to sit on his lap. As I straddled him, I pressed my hand to his chest.

"Just tell me."

I felt his slow exhale. He started to trail a lazy finger down the slope of my shoulder.

"Spencer has been keeping tabs on Bryce. I had to keep you safe and that was the only way I knew how. Knowing where he is and what he's doing is the only way I can know he won't get near you, Aria. Baby, he can't get near you. I—I need you safe." The vulnerability in his voice tore through my heart and I nodded.

"I know you'll keep me safe. Why was Spencer here? Did you think he'd come here?"

Gavin leaned down and kissed the top of my head.

"No. He- Shit, I don't want to have to tell you this. I don't want any of this touching you, but Aria, he's been watching you. I saw the live feed and I can tell you he's probably been watching you, me, and us for at least the last two weeks."

Suddenly I couldn't breathe and my heart pounded so fast that I was sure I'd pass out. Bryce—God, the man that had haunted my dreams for years had been watching me. I clutched Gavin's hands holding mine and I saw the mixture of concern and fear in the blue-gray eyes staring back at me.

"How?"

Gavin leaned forward and cupped my cheeks with his hands. His warmth chased away the cold panic skating along my skin.

"Spencer found two hidden cameras, one in the bedroom and one above the front door. They're gone now, Aria. You're safe here."

I saw the fierce love on his face. I believed with everything I was that he'd do everything to keep me safe. I believed him.

"Gavin."

I wrapped my arms around his neck and lifted my mouth to his without another word. I tasted his minty taste. As he kissed me, I took all he had to give and gave the same in return.

Gavin sucked my bottom lip into his mouth and tugged in that way that I loved before he pulled away, cradling my face.

"I won't let him hurt you, Aria. I don't care what I must do but I promise you, you'll be safe. Please, believe me."

The shake in his voice made me squeeze him tighter. I pressed my lips to his throat.

"I trust you, Gavin. As long as we're together, I know you'll keep me safe."

A gentle smile spread over his mouth and he nodded.

"Can we go somewhere, baby?"

I nodded and kissed him once more instead of answering him.

Chapter 26

The sand warmed my feet as Gavin led me toward a small cliff south of the lake where we had a picnic weeks ago.

"I love that you brought me here, Gavin. It feels like this is our beach, our spot away from everything and everyone," I said, catching his hand in mine as we walked.

Gavin looked down at me and smiled gently.

"Just ours, Aria. I brought some food and that wine you love. I thought we could have a picnic before the sun sets."

I wrapped my hands around the back of his neck and drew his mouth to mine for a light kiss.

"I think that sounds wonderful."

I watched as Gavin set a sky-blue blanket on the flattest spot along the ridged cliff and placed a basket down by his feet. Then, he reached for my hand.

"When did you prepare all this? We left so quickly," I asked, sitting beside him and leaning back on my hands. He set two plates of fettuccine alfredo with basil and I gasped in surprise.

"Oh, Gavin. You remembered."

I could still smell the flowers from our date at his cousin's restaurant. I had this meal that night.

"Of course, baby. It's your favorite."

Gavin's eyes sparked with softness and mischief. A joyous smile spread over my mouth. Love surged inside me and I leaned forward to kiss his cheek.

"Thank you," I whispered, meeting his deep eyes with my own.

Even with the mixture of fear and confusion still coursing through me, I was thankful to have him.

I started in on the mouth-watering meal moaning when the flavors hit my tongue.

"Good?"

I took another bite while he watched me intensely.

"Oh, yes. Aren't you going to eat?"

I took a forkful of pasta and brought it to Gavin's mouth. He opened to me and groaned in satisfaction when he tasted it

"See? It's delicious."

His eyes become hooded as he traced a line down my throat.

"You are, beautiful."

Food and fear were forgotten when his full lips closed over mine. His kiss had a tenderness and desperation to it that made pulling away from him impossible. He needed me.

"Gavin, the food ..." I said between heated kisses.

He quieted me with a searing kiss across my lips. A moan tumbled from my throat when our tongues met and tangled. My arms clutched his shoulders as his deft fingers untied the back of my skirt, and pulled down my tank top to reveal my breasts. A small part of me thought about how someone, anyone could see us but somehow, that thought didn't stay with me long.

"God, Aria. I need you."

In two seconds, he had me cradled in his arms, lowering me to the blanket. With a flick of his fingers, my panties were gone from underneath me and I felt the cool air hit my core. I moaned against his mouth and wrapped my hands around his neck. Cupping his jaw, I looked up at him with all the love I could muster.

"Please don't worry, I'm safe with you. I know that's true."

His lips parted and his eyes drifted shut, I felt his breath whoosh out of him in relief at my words. Gavin pressed every line of his upper body to mine and when he opened his eyes, the darkness and worry were gone.

When he kissed me again, it was the gentlest of kisses. He slid the fabric of my tank top back into place, leaving me confused suddenly.

"Let me take you home to our bed. I want to make love to you so badly."

I pressed a kiss to his chin and nodded, letting him pull me up.

My thoughts wandered to the shadows of my past as Gavin drove us back in the Jaguar. I loved this car, so much like Gavin himself that I had to laugh. It too was sexy and sleek, drove fast and smoothly. But even thoughts of this car didn't stop my mind from remembering the fear that gripped me when Gavin told me about the cameras. God, what kind of crazy person did that? Put actual cameras in someone's home to spy on them!

I let out a shaky breath at the thought of what he must have seen. Gavin, me, our bedroom …

"Fuck, Aria, you're shaking!" Gavin's panicked voice threaded through my mind just as he parked and hurriedly unbuckled his seat belt, turning toward me.

"H-he was in our bedroom," I whispered.

I didn't know why I reacted now. I'd known the last couple of hours but just now I found my hands shaking with a gripping panic at the image of Bryce Williams standing in the sanctuary of our bedroom. The place where I gave myself to Gavin time and time again. *Would all our happiness be tainted by his presence? Would I never be rid of my haunting past? Would I ever be able to forget?*

Tremors wracked my body as Gavin took my face in his gentle hands, caressing underneath my eyes where wetness built. I focused on his eyes as he told me to breathe. In and out, one … two … three. By the third breath, the panic ebbed from my mind and I closed my eyes.

"Would it make you feel better if we went somewhere tonight, baby? I don't want you to be reminded of that man when you're with me. Just tell me what you want to do and I'll make it happen. Your safety and peace of mind is all I care about."

His voice was filled with concern and fear. I couldn't stand to think our time together would be haunted with the pain I'd endured at the hands of that man.

Somewhere deep inside, one word came to my mind. No. For so long I was afraid and unable to move on, to move forward, because of the fear that I couldn't overcome the abuse I'd suffered. But I was stronger. I was strong. Through dancing, my sister, my friends, Gavin's love, I had built a life for myself and I wouldn't allow Bryce to take that away from me.

"No. Gavin, take me inside. I know I'm safe with you. I won't let this change our life together."

I laid my hands over his holding my face. His blue-gray eyes darted between both of mine, searching.

"Are you sure? This is your home, Aria. If you're at all afraid here, I want you to tell me."

I nodded and looked up into his steely eyes.

"You'll keep me safe."

As he tugged me into the bedroom with him and put on the bedside light, Gavin pressed a kiss to the top of my head.

"With my every breath, baby."

Sleep eluded me as Gavin held me against him in bed minutes later. I pressed my face to his neck and inhaled his musky, minty scent, letting it soothe me.

"You're safe. Sleep now."

I closed my eyes and felt the press of his lips against my cheek before I fell into the deepest of sleep.

Fear gripped me when I smelled the cologne that I remembered from so long ago. I immediately tried to move but I was trapped against the headboard of an unfamiliar four-poster bed. My body was completely still, but I felt on fire with the need to move, to struggle, to do something to get away. I forced a deep breath out of my strained lungs and lost every particle of air when I heard the low, hollow sound of his laugh.

"You've changed, princess."

My whole body went rigid as Bryce neared the bed and his hands come down to the ropes binding me to the end of the bed. Fight, Aria. Move! My entire being screamed at me but for some reason, no matter how hard I tried I couldn't move even one finger.

"W-why can't I move? Let me go"

I strained to say those few words and they came out as a cry for mercy. I vowed I would never be a victim again, but what could I do? I couldn't move, I couldn't scream. God I couldn't even breathe.

"Why would I do that? You are my captive. And trust me, I fully intend to appreciate it, princess."

My skin crawled when he slid a finger around my ankle, which was numb like the rest of me. I opened my mouth to scream, but all that came out was a strangled whimper. A single finger moved around my ankle, to the clammy skin of my calf. I jerked helplessly, rolling my face to the side of the bed so I didn't have to look at the smugness in his darkened features.

"You forgot, Ari. You're mine."

Those words. Those words broke the damn on my immobility and emotions. I started to scream.

"No! Don't touch me! I'm not yours! I'm not yours!"

Fear gripped me, swallowed my screams and I felt the press of his hands against my sides.

Miraculously, I heard another anguished voice calling my name with worry.

"Aria! Aria, baby you're safe. You're safe here in our bed. You're mine, come back to me. Come back, baby."

I struggled to hear more, but my eyes closed and I seemed to lift from the weight of dread I'd been overwhelmed by.

"Aria? Open your eyes, now. You're safe now."

Gavin's deep and anxious voice lifted me out of the horrible blackness.

"Oh, no, no, no …" I whispered, shaking as my eyes opened and I found myself back in the comfort of our bed. Our room. Our home. My home.

Warm, gentle hands came up to my damp cheeks and Gavin slowly lifted my chin to meet his soft gaze. I saw love and adoration and fear in his eyes. Fear that still gripped my body and heart. I could still feel the grimy fingers of Bryce's hands and his scent surrounded me. Gavin took my hands in his and kissed each fingertip before pulling me into his lap. I buried my wet face in the crook of his neck. My chest heaved erratically, my body and hands shaking as I let the warmth of his body seep into mine.

"He- he said I was his. He wouldn't let me go. Please, please don't let me go."

"You were never his. A man like him could never know the treasure he held in his grasp. Aria, baby you are safe with me. I won't let go. Not ever."

I drew my face away and looked up into his blue-gray eyes filled with worry and tenderness.

"You promise?"

He nodded, drawing his mouth down to mine in the slowest of kisses.

"I promise." Even as he said that, the fierce and tender look in his eyes was his promise. His vow.

Chapter 27

Filled with a mixture of excitement and nerves, I made my way onto the stage where I hoped to find my passion again. It had only been a week since Mr. Hayes called me with the opportunity to audition for the part of Lena in *Alas the Night,* the up and coming ballet production he had mentioned in our meeting. I never dreamed I would audition for the lead. Kel drove me, but I went in alone.

I came to a table with three people waiting. The man in the middle gave me a welcoming smile and asked me to fill out the check-in sheet with my name and credentials.

My hand shook as I wrote my name and information down. I hastily found a seat next to at least forty other dancers who must be auditioning for lead.

Anxiety crept in as I looked around at each girl and one lanky male in the waiting area. I started to worry about whether I could really do it. *Was I a better dancer and performer than everyone here? Did I really measure up?*

As if she sensed my nervousness, the girl next to me leaned forward, looking at me with kind eyes.

"Don't worry about everyone else. Just focus on yourself. You've got to believe in yourself, sweetie."

She reached over and patted my knee. I did my best to smile at her.

"Nerves are getting the best of me, I think. Is this your first audition?"

She grinned and shook her head hastily.

"Oh, no. I lost count," she chuckled.

Then I heard my name called.

"Here goes nothing," I whispered, more to myself than her.

"Hey, my name is Jessica. Come find me when we're done. We can grab lunch?"

She had the kindest eyes I'd seen. I could use a friend.

"I have plans, actually. How about I get your number, though? I'm Aria."

We shook hands, exchanging numbers before parting ways. I turned to see the smiling man from earlier.

"I'm Leo. One of the directors. Come on in, Ms. Morgan."

I turned left, leaving the auditorium with a huge smile. I did it. I aced my audition. For the first time in weeks, I felt like myself again. My phone buzzed in my pocket as I walked to the small bakery I agreed to meet Kel at. I reached into the pocket of my sundress and didn't bother to look before answering. I had just gotten off the phone with Gavin and was waiting until Kaelyn was out of work to call her.

"Hey."

"How did it go? I've been on my toes all morning!"

I could practically feel Farrah's excitement. I laughed softly and wound a finger through my hair as I told her.

"I aced it! I mean, of course there's a chance they won't give me a call back, but I aced my routine. The scene I had to repeat for them was easy enough and even the director I spoke to said I exude the spirit of Lena. I can't believe I was so nervous."

"I knew you'd get it! Were there others auditioning with you or was it just you?"

"I wish. I wouldn't have been so nervous while I'd been waiting if it was only me."

"You've got the talent. You just have to believe in yourself."

Well if that didn't sound familiar …

"I know. I have to go, I'm meeting Kel in a bit."

She was quiet for a moment but I was not sure why.

"OK, see you later."

I clicked off and opened the glass doors to Hidden Sweets. Several wooden tables were set in the front. I didn't see Kel or Lucas right away. The white marbled counter top drew me deeper into the bakery. That's where I found Kel and Lucas. He was pressing his nose in her neck as they stood with another girl behind the counter.

"Hey." I walked over and felt a surge of happiness for Kel.

"Hey! This is Jenna, she owns the bakery!" Kel practically burst in excitement.

I laughed and stretched my hand to the petite brunette who looked at me.

"I'm only part owner, Kel. Remember?"

My sister waved her hand in dismissal. Luke laughed behind her.

"Sweetheart, she's right. Her mom does own half of the shop."

"And she lets me know whenever she can," Jenna said, casting her eyes down for a moment. I could tell she felt ashamed about her mother's being brought up.

"I know the feeling." I placed my hand on her shoulder and squeezed gently. She looked at me again and smiled.

"Let's get some pastries and sit," Lucas offered, going to the display case as Kel came over to me.

"So, this was the place you picked to cater the rehearsal dinner?"

"Oh, yes! Don't you love this place? I had no idea this bakery was even here until I tried Jenna's lemon Danish! It's to die for, Ari. To. Die. For."

Uh, huh. I just let her spiel on and on about the baked goods while I thought about my morning. My audition had been at noon so I got to sleep in with Gavin for a few extra hours. He woke before me, which was normal. I felt his touch before I was even awake. He tongued me to an amazing climax while I was still in a sleep-like euphoria. The best part? I woke up and the sexy man from my dreams was still there. I let him keep going and when he found out I'd been awake the whole time, he smiled and started all over again. I was beginning to think sleep sex was my favorite.

"And then he reached into his pocket and pulled this out! Isn't it absolutely gorgeous?"

Kel nudged me with her shoulder and I was pulled from my day-dream.

"Wait, what? What is that?"

I took hold of her left hand, my jaw dropping when I saw the larger stone set in the middle of her engagement ring. But, it wasn't a dia-mond. It was a ruby stone with small diamonds encompassing it. It was … breathtaking.

"Another ring?" I looked up to see happy tears in my sister's eyes.

"It was his mother's," she sniffed and I hugged her gently in my arms.

"You make him happy. Of course, he would give you something dear to his heart."

She laughed through her tears and I leaned back to wipe them away.

"Jesus, Kel, baby, what's wrong? Are you OK?!"

Lucas came toward my sister. His steps were quick, his face a mask of worry. His voice was filled with panic and I heard the tremor as he spoke. I let Kel go. When she sat, he dropped to his knees in front of her. The devastation in his eyes surprised me. I reached down and pressed my hand to his blond head. He must have seen her tears. My sister was a lot of things, but not a crier. She was the strongest woman I knew.

"She just got emotional for a minute. She's alright, Luke."

He nodded, but I could tell he was concerned about my sister. His hands grasped hers as his eyes pleaded with hers.

"Talk to me," his voice implored.

Kel smoothed away the stray hair that fell in his eyes. Her eyes dropped to the ring on her left hand and then slowly lifted back to her fiancé.

"This is the only thing you have left of her. What if I lose it or ..."

He shushed her quietly and wrapped his arms around her waist.

"Then I'll get you another, Kel. It symbolizes my love to you, my promise. That's what matters OK?"

I watched as the sadness lifted from my sister's face and she grinned shyly.

"I love you, crazy boy," she whispered just loud enough so I heard.

Lucas smiled wider and kissed her. I couldn't remember the last time I saw her really cry. It had to be when the accident happened. She was a mess that night. God, we all were.

In the span of a minute, Kel was back to her cheery self.

"Hey, stop pouting. I'm good. Let's eat!" she said, looping her arm through mine.

We sat at a nearby table as she dished out large cupcakes with vanilla, lemon, and chocolate frosting on them. My stomach growled in appreciation.

"Oh, yes," I moaned as I bit into the nearest one.

Chapter 28

I stepped inside the apartment and Gavin's roguish smile met me.

"You look beautiful." Gavin murmured when he reached me, grabbing my waist to pull me into his body.

"Thank you, it went well" I whispered into his chest. I felt him smile against my hair. Before I knew what he was doing, he spun me around in a circle.

"I knew it would, baby. Congratulations."

When he stopped spinning me, I tangled my fingers in his hair and pressed my mouth to his for a kiss. I felt his joy and hunger for me.

"It felt so good to dance again, Gavin. You have no idea."

His hand tugged me down the hall. As he laid me on the bed, he hovered over me and cupped my chin gently. He urged me to look at him.

"Trust me, I do have an idea. When you dance, it's nothing like I've seen before. Your free spirit, your innocence comes out and you shine. You shine."

God, when he said that to me, all I wanted to do was get up and dance for him right then. But my feet hurt and I really wanted to do something else.

"You really love me, huh?" I asked, running my hand down his chest toward his belt buckle. When I came in contact with his shaft he sucked in a rough breath.

"Unconditionally."

When I woke, I was still buzzing from Gavin's love making. I heard the shower running as I went to the kitchen to make breakfast.

The air seemed to shift around me when the bedroom door opened and light footsteps approached from the hallway. Gavin came up behind me and gave my behind a little squeeze.

"Sexy girl. Are you cooking? I thought that was dangerous."

I laughed softly and leaned up to kiss his cheek.

"Morning, Gavin." I turned in his arms and wrapped a hand around his neck.

"I can handle it, I think. Go have some coffee and I'll bring this out when it's done."

Gavin smiled warmly and planted a hard kiss on my mouth before sauntering off to find coffee.

"I promised Kel I would go back to the bakery today to choose treats for rehearsal tonight."

Gavin looked up from his plate and nodded.

Chapter 29

"So?" Jenna asked as I just devoured a sampling of red velvet cheesecake.

She had arranged for us to come sample various sweets for the rehearsal that night. I wasn't sure why we needed to taste everything to decide, but I was enjoying the cheesecake, so I wasn't going to complain.

"This is a definite yes. What about you Kel?" My sister bit her bottom lip and nodded between bites of her second cupcake.

"Um, I'm not sure …"

I threw Jenna a wink and finished off the cheesecake frosting.

"Awesome! Two down, three to go."

She pushed a tray of assorted cupcakes in front of us. There was vanilla, Oreo, apple crust, and Boston creme, all begging to be devoured.

God, give me strength.

Any more sweets in my body would not be a good thing. We'd only been here an hour and my belly was already full.

I threw my torso down on the love seat we sat on in the closed bakery and hid my face in one hand. Giggling, I shook my head when Kel nudged my hand with what must be another treat.

"I'm going to get sick from all these cupcakes, Kel! Just pick three out of the thirteen flavors we've tried."

I heard Jenna laughing and opened my eyes to see my sister well into her third Lemon cake.

We were going to be here awhile, I guessed.

Once we left Hidden Sweets, Kel's car was filled with assorted cupcakes and pastries Jenna insisted on offering us for the rehearsal. It was almost one by that time. I knew we were about to be seriously stressed for time with the rehearsal dinner starting at five.

"Stop stressing out, girl. I'll drop you off so you can get your dress, change and head over before four. We have everything set for tonight. Hell, Luke took care of most of it."

Her eyes twinkled when she talked about Luke. She had dreamed of marrying him for so long. She was finally going to get her happy ending. The wedding was tomorrow.

"Yeah, sorry. My mind is on overdrive today. You doing okay, Kel? Any jitters?"

My sister shook her head and laughed softly.

"Hell to the no. I've wanted to be Luke's wife since I was seventeen. I'm so excited."

I reached over and grabbed her hand in mine. Squeezing gently, I nodded.

"I know."

We turned into the parking lot beside the penthouse only five minutes later. I hugged her tightly before getting out of the car and waving her off. I could hardly wait to see her walk down the aisle tomorrow. She was going to be such a beautiful bride. My cell rang with Farrah's ring tone, *Wild One's* by Flo Rida. I reached in my purse and pressed the phone to my ear.

"Hey, what's up?"

"Where are you? We need to go pick up Kel's dress at the boutique!"

I would laugh at the haste in her voice if she didn't sound so stressed right now.

"Kel just dropped me off. We've got time."

I ran up the steps and fumbled my hand into my purse again, searching for the familiar rattle of the key Gavin gave me for the back door.

"Oh, OK. I was worried you hadn't left the bakery yet. How did it go, anyway?"

"She spent two hours trying every flavor before she could make a decision. I swear I thought I was going to have to kill her!"

I heard Farrah laughing hysterically.

"You home now?" she asked after her giggles stopped.

"I had to stop at home to grab my dress and change out of these sweats. I won't be longer than an hour or so." Longer if Gavin was home, already.

"Okay, you want to pick us up at three?"

I made it to the back door, finding it unlocked. It was odd for that door to be open. As I walked toward the elevators, I saw a bouquet of white roses on the foyer table with a lavender envelope sticking out. My heart stopped at the sight of my name scrawled across it.

"Sure, I have to go." I said in monotone.

I heard someone laugh in the background, probably Jaden.

"OK, you OK?"

"Yeah I'm fine. See you soon."

I hung up, and tried to move my legs, to go upstairs or run to my car. But I couldn't. I just stood there, frozen, my eyes transfixed by the oak-wood basket and the upturned white petals. Gavin had given me red roses, lilies and daisies, lilacs, but never, never white roses. There was only one thought in my head. These flowers were from Bryce. I knew it with every fiber of my being. First that text this morning and now, these flowers. *God, did he want me back? Was he here?*

In some far away part in my psyche, I knew I should run or I should at least look at the note, because it was possible I was over-reacting. But, I couldn't do anything. I struggled to breathe, my hands shook with panic and an overwhelming feeling of dread covered my skin.

I'd been so submersed in my happy little bubble with Gavin, I had been oblivious to everything else.

The Lincoln following me two days ago, I had let that go after my night with Gavin. It was so amazing being with him and I just … forgot, but what if there was more? *Had Bryce been here this whole time? Oh, my God, had he?*

Then, my phone vibrated in my hand, and I sucked in a breath, using all my strength to lift it to my sight. I gasped when I saw Gavin's name cross the screen.

"Gavin?" I whispered, steadying myself with a hand on the back of the couch. *Why couldn't I move my legs?*

"Baby, what's wrong? I can hear it in your voice."

Relief flooded through me at the sound of his soft voice and I forced myself to lean against the banister. Somehow, I formed words.

"I … I don't know, I might be overreacting but-"

He gasped, hearing the fear in my voice and I heard a loud noise that sounded like a door slamming shut.

"Where are you?" he asked, his voice soft with concern.

He sounded worried, and I realized I needed him here with me more than anything.

"I- I'm at home. I just got home."

He exhaled and I heard faint voices in the background.

"Stay there. I'm coming."

How did he know exactly what I needed? What would I do without him? I honestly didn't know.

"Gavin, you don't have to-" I started to protest, but he cut me off in the middle.

"Yes, I do. You need me. I can hear it in your voice. I'll see you soon, baby."

The concern in his voice thawed my nerves and I nodded, even though he couldn't see me.

"OK."

He hung up and I took a deep breath, unable to look away from the arrangement sitting three feet away.

While I waited, I tried to wrangle all my inner strength by distracting myself with thoughts of Gavin. His eyes, which were always so expressive. His mouth, oh, he'd made me feel so good with his mouth, his lips, and his tongue. His hands, I'd never been touched the way Gavin touched me. With just one touch of his hands I was always breathless. He conveyed his desire, his need and his love for me through his touch. I thought I'd loved a man before, but now, as I curled my fingers against my legs and closed my eyes, I knew these feelings were new.

After a few more minutes, I sucked in a breath. I looked in at the flowers again, trying to convince myself that the flowers were from Gavin. But if he sent flowers, they would be upstairs. I gasped in shock when I noticed a purple ribbon wrapped around the stems.

What—shit, no. It couldn't be.

I hadn't noticed that minor detail before, but now realization cleared my thoughts.

Bryce. It was Bryce, there wasn't a doubt in my mind now. That very first morning after he hit me, he brought me white roses in a glass vase. There was a purple colored ribbon wrapped around the stems of the roses. I remembered thinking how beautiful they were. The ribbon had shined in the faint light perfectly.

Fear pooled deep inside me. I opened my eyes, tears building quickly. *He was here, oh my God ... he was here at my home.*

My legs fell out from beneath me at the realization. Though he already had been here, at our penthouse, had he been following me too? Why? A sob erupted from my chest as my eyes closed and I struggled for breath. This couldn't be happening ...

When I heard a car door slam and footsteps, my eyes flew open to see Gavin looking disheveled, his face stretched with worry as he ran towards me.

"Aria?"

He dropped to his knees in front of me, his eyes filled with uncertainty.

My eyes filled with unshed tears. When he grabbed my face in his hands and searched my features for any sign of injury, the tears fell to my cheeks. With shaking hands, I pressed my fingers to his chest and felt a sense of relief. Thank God, he was here.

"Gavin," I whispered and clutched him, burying my face in his neck and inhaling his skin. He folded me against him. He held me close, with no air between us and kissed my forehead repeatedly.

"What happened, baby?" he asked, pulling back and grazing his hands over my face, wiping my cheeks clear of tears.

I pointed to the table the flowers were on.

"Those were here when I got home. I-I think he broke in. The door was unlocked. I might be overreacting but…" He stopped me with a tender kiss to my temple and pulled me deeper into his arms.

"Don't doubt yourself, Aria. Did you read the note?"

I shook my head. He went to the table and retrieved the square note paper.

"Fuck." He cursed, and immediately, my skin crawled.

I knew who sent the flowers and wrote the note. Bryce. My body trembled violently. I forced myself go over to Gavin's side as he kept his eyes trained on the paper.

"W-what does it say?" I asked when he squeezed my hand.

He exhaled, blatant worry in his eyes as he shook his head. His body was tense when he slipped the note out of my reach.

"Gavin!" I said, reaching for the note he withheld from me.

Gavin's eyes met mine and I saw blazing fire behind them. The same anger I saw when I told him about Bryce the first time. He wanted to protect me. Not reading the note increased my fear.

"Please, trust me Aria. You don't need to read it. How did you know who sent these?"

He caressed my cheek, banishing the immense fear away, but the worry, I just couldn't shake.

"Bryce used to always bring me white roses when he wanted to be forgiven, and they always had a purple ribbon wrapped around the stems. I just … froze, I'm sorry-"

Before I knew it, his soft lips pressed to mine and he cradled my face in his hands. He kissed me with passion and relief.

"I'm sorry ..." he apologized for the note.

His ardent words tore at my heart, but I had to know.

"Let me read the note, Gavin. Please."

Gavin pressed my body to his, as if he could protect me by doing so. He handed me the small square piece of paper.

With shaking hands, I turned it over and saw the slanted writing I'd recognize anywhere.

You forget, Ari.

You're mine.

My skin prickled with dread. I immediately dropped it, taking a step back as if it had burned me. *God, why couldn't he just stay in the past where he belonged?*

Panic set in my veins at the thought of Bryce getting to me, taking me. I gazed up at Gavin, feeling so many emotions I had no idea how to handle them.

"What do you need, baby?" he whispered, stepping forward and taking me into his arms again. His hand smoothed my hair off my forehead.

"You, Gavin. I need you. Just please don't let me go."

Gavin clutched my hand with his own. With the flowers in tow, he unlocked the door and ushered me inside without another word. As we rode in the elevator, I saw his tense muscles. He was on edge and so was I.

I thought the past was in the past and I could move on. But somehow, Bryce had made his way back into the present. He almost broke me before and as I leaned against Gavin's shoulder, letting him lead me into the penthouse, I prayed I was strong enough to handle this.

"Baby, are you hungry? I can make us something to eat while you go lie down for a while."

His tilted my eyes up to his with one finger under my chin. I swayed into his warmth, needing it in my frazzled state. My legs felt like jelly and the fear still shook my body.

"Will you lie down with me? We can eat in a few hours," my voice shook.

He took my hand, lifted it to his lips.

"Of course."

Once Gavin laid me down on the bed, he pulled me into the welcoming warmth of his body. I closed my eyes, focusing on breathing in and out.

"How did he …" my words were silenced when he leaned back and framed my face with his hands.

His eyes were full of worry.

"I have no idea, but I promise you I will find out."

I exhaled, trusting his words as I ran my hands up and down his chest to ease his tense muscles.

"My security team has been tailing him and as far as I know, he hasn't been within a ten-mile radius of Chicago in the last three months. When he was in the area, he only went to work at Jones and Harrison Law Firm in the north-end of the city or his home in Kennedy Park. I don't know how he got past us, but I promise, baby, I'll find out."

His words were determined. I nodded, pressing my forehead against his as I sagged against him. The fear, the panic, everything dulled in comparison to the love I had for this man. It was the only thing that mattered.

"Gavin, I'm scared," I whispered as a lone tear trailed along my cheek. I felt stronger than I'd felt in years and I didn't want to lose myself again if Bryce caught me. I knew, if he did, he might just break me.

Gavin's hands tensed momentarily in their journey down my back before they continued soothing my skin.

"Aria, I promise you I won't let him hurt you ever again. Please, trust me to keep you safe." I looked up to see his eyes, a stormy blue. I latched onto his waist and nodded, trusting him with my whole heart. He would keep me safe. I knew he would.

"I trust you, Gavin."

"I'm sorry you had to leave work, Gavin." I said.

His work was his father's legacy and was so dear to him. I hated to disrupt that. In one motion Gavin swiftly moved me beneath him so my hair splayed out onto the pillow.

His eyes were soft and endearing as he said, "You needed me, where else would I be?"

I smiled for the first time since coming home this afternoon.

"Thank you, I didn't know what to think when I saw those flowers, but you're right about one thing. I needed you."

The smile that spread across his face almost made the last hour disappear. As he pressed his body to mine, knees on either side of my thighs, it caused desire to spark deep in my core. Slowly he dipped his head until his lips hovered over mine.

"Let's forget it, baby. We'll talk it over with Spencer tomorrow but for now, let's go celebrate with your sister. I know she wants you there with her today."

I nodded, knowing he was right. I could forget about Bryce for a few hours and maybe we would even have fun.

"I'll give Lucas a call so they know what's happened."

I nodded and then moaned when his teeth grazed my earlobe. All thoughts of the past, the flowers and everything else evaporated from my mind. I needed to feel him right now. I didn't need anything other than this.

"Gavin."

The slow, soothing path Gavin's hand traced along my arms stirred the following morning and I found myself with a clearer head. I couldn't let fear get the best of me. I knew Gavin would keep me safe.

After calming down from the flower incident, we had gotten dressed for the rehearsal and I promised myself I would go and have a good time. Seeing my sister so happy and in love calmed my worry about the note, the flowers, the shadows of my past. Gavin was by my side the whole night and I found myself enjoying myself by the time dinner ended. I felt the bed shift as Gavin swept a kiss down to my forehead and the smell of his minty breath wafted over me.

"Hey, baby,"

"Hi," I whispered, leaning up to capture his mouth in a slow, sweet kiss that left whispers of it on my tingling lips.

He murmured against my parted lips.

"It's almost ten, I'm going to give Spencer a call and have him come as soon as he can."

My eyes widened at his tone. It was domineering and I heard the underlying worry in his voice.

"What are you going to do? I don't want to live in fear, Gavin."

He took hold of my hands and massaged them gently before he spoke again.

"We're going to talk with Spencer. I usually only use the security team for public events and company needs, but I'm not going to take any risks with your safety. I need to know you are safe; I won't be able to leave this bedroom with you unless I know that you'll be safe out there. I'm going to move them into the upstairs apartment, for the time being. If you're not at home, one of them won't be far, Aria."

I was taken aback and I pulled away from him, running a hand through my hair as my thoughts returned to the note Bryce left me.

You forget, Ari. You're Mine.

A chill raced up my spine at the thought of those words.

A cold, unwelcome shiver went through me. I'd never liked having security guards growing up, but with the constant media attention on my mother, I had no choice in the matter. But this was different. Back then, my mother used to always say, "I know you don't like it, but they're here to protect you, my sweet girl. If you ever found yourself in a swarm of reporters, they'll be the ones to guide you through it. It won't be forever, just for now."

I knew this had to be done for Gavin to protect me, but a part of me wondered could Bryce still find a way to get to me, regardless of the guards?

"Do you really think he's going to try and get to me?" I whispered after long seconds of silence.

Gavin scooted forward, cupping both my cheeks and pressed his forehead to mine.

"Yes, I do, and I'm not taking any risks with your safety, baby. You are my life now; you're the air I breathe. I love you, Aria."

Gavin's deep voice was raw with emotion. and I nestled my fingers into his hair and kissed his lips gently, trying to convey the love I had for him. It consumed me. Even though I feared Bryce finding me and taking me away, I was not running. I would not run.

"I'm so afraid that he's going to find a way to take me away from you." My voice broke on the last word.

I squeezed my eyes shut to stop the tears from building. I had to be strong. This time, I was not alone.

"Shh, beautiful. You're safe and I'm not going anywhere, I promise."

Chapter 30

I was still working on the last of my cinnamon raisin bagel when Spencer knocked on the front door. Gavin squeezed my hand gently before he went to answer the door. The two men shook hands. Spencer was dressed in faded jeans and a blue Dolphins tee, much different from his normal attire. But, it was the weekend and he couldn't work all the time. His piercing green eyes meet mine and one side of his mouth lifted in an almost smile.

"Good to see you, Ms. Morgan. Are you OK?"

There was genuine concern in his voice and I nodded. Gavin pulled me to his side and looked at me as he spoke to Spencer.

"We need to go over everything we're going to do to keep her safe. He should have never gotten in the building, Spencer. How did that happen?"

I heard the strain in his voice when he asked. I also saw the crease in his eyebrows that told me he was trying to reign in his temper.

"The security footage showed a delivery van arrived late morning and a man who could not possibly be Williams dropped off the flowers."

Gavin nodded, registering the information as he led me to the couch. Spencer sat on the ottoman angled towards us and continued to go over every detail he'd obtained from the security footage from both the front lobby of our complex and the back-parking lot. He had to enter through one of them and there was no sighting of Bryce on either. That fact lightened the fear weighing my chest. He wasn't in our home again. But he was still sent those flowers with the note to me and that was scary. If he had gotten into the penthouse, what would have happened? As that thought registered in my mind, a chill covered my skin.

"Aria, are you OK? Do you need to stop?"

Gavin urged me to look at him with a finger under my chin and when I did, I shook my head quickly.

"I'm good. Don't stop on my account. What can we do to make sure he doesn't get close again?" I aimed my question at Spencer though I didn't take my eyes from Gavin's. The intensity in them stole my breath.

"Well, both Mr. Thomas and I agree that making sure you are never—for any reason—left by yourself is a must. We already have Aaron following you, but I also want to bring on two more guards to stay in the penthouse when you're here on your own. There will be at least one of us, sometimes two if needed."

Was it necessary to have two men with me? My mind worked on overdrive trying to process the current situation.

"But, there is another option. One I think would work much better," Gavin whispered the words near my ear and I turned toward him, looking up.

"What?"

Gavin took my hands gently in his and smoothed his thumbs over my knuckles. He looked at me solemnly.

"Come away with me."

His wide, unblinking eyes pleaded with me. The determination in them stopped my breath altogether. He was serious. He wanted us to run away.

"Gavin, you can't."

He pressed one finger to my lips to stop me.

"I am serious. He is not going to stop until he is caught. This situation has to get worse before it gets better. The minute he gets too close, we can call in the authorities and bring him in once and for all.

But for that to happen, baby, he's going to get desperate. He wants you. If you think I'm going to let him come near you, you don't know me very well."

I clasped his face in my hands, knowing that he was afraid to lose me. But running? No way. I had spent years running from what he did to me and I refused to run ever again. Not from him.

"I love you for wanting to take me away but Gavin, I won't run. This is my life, our life. I won't let him dictate it. We will catch him. I'll do everything you tell me to in regards to my safety. You'll keep me safe."

I saw the struggle in his eyes as he stood and began to pace. I felt empty without his touch, but I let him pace a hole in the carpet.

"We can go to Paris. See the sights, find a small village to live in. We can make love every day. Just us. Please, run away with me."

His footsteps became faster he went on telling me everything we'd do in Paris, Milan and even Venice. My heart yearned to do those things with him. Travel. See the beautiful sights, places I only dreamed of. And someday, maybe we would. But not because we were running away. Gavin turned his eyes to me, holding me captive. A mixture of desperation, love and fear clouded them. He got down on his knees and took hold of my waist. I blinked through the moisture in my eyes. This man, my man, was afraid.

"I can't. Gavin, I have run from my grief, my fear, my past, him—for far too long. I won't let him think I'm afraid anymore. You have helped me find my strength and I know I'll be safe with you. We can get through this. Together."

I got up from my seat and slid to my knees in front of him. Wrapping my arms around him, I pressed my face into his neck. His mouth pressed to my forehead.

"I hate that I can't protect you from this. You deserve the world, Aria. I promise I'll give it all to you, but first we have to ensure you are safe."

His voice filled with raw emotion. I heard everything he felt, even the things he didn't want me to, in his voice.

Lifting my face, I pressed my mouth to his for a hard, desperate kiss.

"Thank you."

It was almost noon by the time Gavin walked Spencer to the door. I heard the door click closed and sighed.

"How would you feel about a bath? And then I'll let you get dressed."

Gavin helped me up, and when I stood I felt just a bit dizzy. I closed my eyes, and swayed into a warm, firm chest.

"Aria? Are you feeling alright?"

I nodded and smiled gently.

"Let's get you in that bath."

Gavin carried me toward the bathroom, kissing me the whole way. Though I knew he was still worried, I felt the tension slip from him.

He settled me in a warm bath with bubbles and lilac, my favorite. When Gavin went to move away, I clasped his hand.

"I thought you were coming in with me?"

He dipped his forehead to mine and pressed teasing kisses down my cheek and jaw.

"If I go in there with you, we won't make it to Kel's wedding."

His words made my blood heat and lower parts heat as well. I bit my lip and nodded.

"Well ..." I grasped the end of his shirt, but Gavin laughed softly and pulled away.

"Take your time, baby. I'll meet you in the living room."

And with that, he kissed my cheek and left me with my lust-filled thoughts.

I smoothed the lavender satin dress down my sides and stepped back to look in the mirror. I decided to leave my hair down, curled in subtle waves. My ivory skin appeared to be glowing and my eyes popped with the light shades of gray I used for eye shadow.

"Christ, you are so beautiful."

The moment I saw Gavin dressed to the nines in a freshly pressed black suit jacket, a blue shirt and tie, my heart stopped in my chest.

Oh, he was gorgeous. He looked like he stepped off the pages of Vogue. I met his intense eyes, grayer than I'd ever seen.

"So, beautiful," he murmured, coming to me as I secured the sash around my waist. He tucked a strand of my wavy hair behind my ear. His hand wandered down my back while I fastened my earrings, a pair of emerald green pendants my dad gave me for my birthday. I'd always treasured them.

"You're not so bad yourself," I whispered, reveling in the feel of his hand along my cheek.

Then his lips descended on mine. They devoured me, destroying my every thought so that I almost missed his hand going to the front breast pocket of his jacket. He pulled something out. My hands delved into his hair as he pulled his lips marginally away from mine.

"I have something for you, beautiful."

I leaned back, my heart beating fast in my chest. My eyes widened when he placed a rectangular box with dark blue velvet trim around it in my hands. It was a jewelry box.

"What's this?" I whispered as I peered down at it and then back up to his deep soul-baring eyes.

"This was my grandmother's. She gave it to me before she died. My grandfather gave it to her when he proposed to her and she told me to save it for the woman I fell in love with. Baby, that's you. I'm in love with you, Aria."

Oh, my God. My heart started to beat faster, tears pricked the backs of my eyes. Is he …

"Hey, relax please, baby. I'm not proposing to you now, not until I know for sure you'll say yes. But, this-"

He opened the box, displaying a beautiful gold chain, with a singular emerald green pendant in the center of it. Surrounding the stone were two heart shaped diamonds and two letters. On the left side was a cursive A, and to the right was a letter G. It took my breath away. A lone tear fell to my cheek as I felt the love in his eyes penetrating mine.

"This is an heirloom of hers and now, it's yours, baby."

Oh, my. He wanted to marry me one day, he was going to propose. Was this a dream?

"Gavin, it's so beautiful. Thank you, I love you," I whispered, pressing a kiss to his neck just below his Adam's apple.

"Our initials?" I whispered, joyful tears pooling in my eyes.

"I had them put in yesterday morning. I wanted to make this special to us."

"You amaze me," I whispered, leaning forward and pressing my mouth to his for a soft kiss that sparked desire in my core again.

I felt like this never-ending yearning to have him inside me would never cease. I prayed that it wouldn't. He smiled against my lips and chuckled as he pulled away. His eyes heated when I caught his bottom lip in my mouth, nipping softly until he moaned.

"If we don't leave soon, I'm afraid we might be terribly late for your sister's wedding," he teased.

Begrudgingly, I released him and turned to face the mirror. His arms wrapped around me, and he pressed a single, hot open-mouthed kiss to the base of my neck.

"Will you put it on me, Gavin?"

He removed the necklace from its box and laid it on my collarbone.

I gazed in the mirror in awe at the beautiful gem adorning my neck.

"Thank you. This is so special to me," I told him, smiling as he turned me so he could lift me in his arms. Again, he met my mouth with ardent, adoring lips. His tongue slipped into my mouth. I moaned, loving the feel of him when he pulled away too soon for my liking.

"Come on. You're tempting me," he murmured in my ear.

"Tempting you to what?"

His answering smirk was a promise that spurred my desire more.

"You," he leaned down to press a hot kiss to my throat as he spoke, "are tempting me to lock you in the bedroom and forget about this wedding you're so eager to attend, Ms. Morgan."

A delicious shiver ran up my spine. I wrapped my arms around his neck and my legs around his slender hips as he carried me through the bedroom toward the back entrance, his lips whispering against mine all the way.

I was so head over heels for this man.

Kel was near tears when I made my way into the bridal room on the second level of St. Mary's Lutheran Church. Seventeen years ago, my dad married my mom in this church. It was where I was christened as a baby. It warmed my heart to add another memory of this place.

"Aria! Thank God you're here!" she squealed, shimmying in her floor length wedding dress.

As she turned to show off the back, I saw an inked design I had not seen before. *Holy crap!* My jaw dropped open and I just gaped at her. I walked closer to examine the tattoo better. It was a beautiful intricate design of cursive writing and a single red rose underneath the words "and I love him." I ran my hand over it. When she turned toward me, her eyes filled with joy. Tears pricked the backs of my eyes. She was so happy.

"When did you get this?" I asked, kissing her cheek as she pulled me to the vanity.

"I wanted to give Lucas a wedding gift he'd never forget. Do you think he'll like it?"

She sat in front of the large oak vanity. Her makeup was light. Farrah stepped behind her, primping her curly blonde hair into a clip letting a few strands fall out, framing her face.

"He's going to love it, honey. You look beautiful. Are you nervous?" I asked as I sat next to her, squeezing her hand when it began to thrum against the wooden tabletop.

She shook her head, tear-filled eyes flickering up to mine.

"No, he's everything I've ever wanted."

Still, I saw the nervousness exuding off my sister.

"That man loves you so much, Kel."

She looked at me hesitantly for a moment and when I squeezed her hand, her lips curved up into a smile once more.

"I know."

She wrapped her arms around me in a hug. This was her day. Joy coursed through me for her.

"Love you," I whispered.

She leaned away. A knock at the door had us both wiping our tears away. She slipped on her sandals. She looked like a princess.

Dad came through the door, stopping when he looked at us huddled by the vanity. His green eyes filled with tears. He was dressed in the same black David Scott tuxedo that he wore to my graduation years ago. Kel came up to him. He smiled, the proud father exuding from within him.

"Oh, sweetheart. You look beautiful. Are you ready?"

She kissed his cheek, giving us both a smile as she hooked her arm through his. They made their way out of the room, closing the door quietly behind them. I sighed, a part of me wondering if one day, I'd be the one dressed in white walking towards Gavin.

God, I hoped so.

Farrah and I descended the stairs leading to the main floor arm in arm. The chapel doors were already open. Peering into the chapel, I saw that each pew was filled. Familiar faces were lit up with laughter as they talked among themselves. My eyes scanned the rows of seats and then, a pair of blue-gray eyes met mine. Gavin. He gave me a warm smile, eyes filled with adoration. I felt my mouth spread in a smile, my eyes taking him in. God, I had it bad.

"Ready?" Farrah whispered, as we lined up. I turned and smoothed my hands down the front of my dress, feeling the soft material beneath my fingers.

"Ready."

Farrah went before me walking slowly, her smile vibrant as she went. My eyes moved to Lucas, who looked ready to start his new life.

I took a deep breath and stepped into the aisle. I clutched the bouquet of lilies as I made my way down towards the altar. My eyes landed on Gavin's back and I felt the electric current of his presence. God, looking at him—stole my breath. Turning his head, his eyes captured mine. I saw his features change. They became softer, eyes burning with heat, love and lust all at once. It was cathartic. I smiled back at him and took my place beside Farrah. I blinked back the tears as Kel made her way down the aisle. I listened as my sister exchanged vows with Lucas.

"I take you, Lucas Jones, as mine. I will love you through good times and bad times. I will hold you up when you cannot stand. I will be your strength when you're weak, and I'll support you for always; withholding all others, for as long as I shall live. I love you."

Later as I watched them sweep across the dance floor later, I longed to have this dream with Gavin, taking him as mine, for always.

"What are you thinking about, baby?" Gavin whispered in my ear as he wrapped an arm around my waist and kissed my temple gently.

"You, always you." I whispered, lifting on my tiptoes to brush my lips against his.

His hands came up to my cheeks, his mouth opening as he claimed my mouth, adoring me, consuming me. I wrapped my arms around his neck, moaning when he bit down gently on my lower lip. His kiss stole my breath and created desire low in my belly as his fingers dipped into the silky strands of my hair.

"A dance, Aria?" he whispered, his eyes soft and filled with want as he gazed down at me.

I nodded as he led me to the floor. He brought me to him for a soft, tender kiss that rendered me breathless. His strong arms were around my waist and my hands glided up his chest to his neck. My lower lip trembled as he slowed the kiss until his lips just barely brushed mine.

"One day, I want this, beautiful."

His mouth dipped to my shoulder before he looked into my eyes. Mine widened, my mouth parted as I realized what he just said. Two marriage references in one day. He wanted to marry me … oh, my. My breath hitched in my throat as I gasped, and pressed my face to his neck. I wanted to be his wife. Oh, God I wanted it so much. But a small part of me hesitated, not knowing if I was ready.

"Gavin… I want to marry you," I said, lifting my head to meet his eyes filled with wondrous love.

At my words, they filled with joy. He placed a tender kiss on my lips. It made my heart soar.

"I know you're not ready, Aria. We aren't there yet. I just want you to know, that one day, this dream—this day, will be ours. And when that time comes, with all my heart I promise you, baby. I'll give you the world."

Tears fell from my eyes as I peered up at him, gasping at his beautiful words. Was this real?

"Oh, Gavin. I love you, so very much" I whispered and he held me a little tighter, lifting me.

He kissed me, slipping his tongue into my mouth and licking along mine. Gavin's body pressed to me as he moved us to the music, continuing to kiss me. He slowly lowered me to my feet never breaking our kiss.

"I love you. I promise you when I ask you to be my wife, there won't be a doubt in your mind. Do you trust me?"

I did trust him with my whole heart.

"Always," I whispered, pulling him down for another delectable kiss.

Chapter 31

By the time night fell, my feet ached in the heels I wore. I sat with Kel and Lucas. Gavin talked with the D.J. I wondered what he was up to. I didn't think I could dance another step tonight. His stormy eyes shifted to mine. He gave me a wink as he approached. My heart pounded when he stopped in front of me. Somehow, I found myself placing my hand in his once more.

"One more dance and then we can take off, okay baby?"

He helped me stand, leading me back toward the thinning crowds on the dance floor. His lips brushed over my knuckles before he swept me back into his arms. Every fine toned line of his body pressed to mine. I laid my head on his chest, just like our first dance. I listened to the steady thrum of his heartbeat. Then, the song began. It was a slow, romantic beat, the words a soft ballad. Gavin began to whisper the words in my ear, holding me close. A tear slipped down my cheek at his voice, raw and full of love.

All of me, loves all of you. Love your curves and all your edges, all your perfect imperfections. Give your all to me, I'll give my all to you.

By the time the song ended, joyful tears streamed down my face and Gavin cradled my face tenderly. He closed his mouth softly over mine. And I knew, there was no end to his love or mine, I loved all of him and he loved all of me.

"All of me, baby. I'll never give you anything less."

I looked up at him and smiled softly.

"Me, too. Take me home, Gavin."

He smiled against my lips and bent his knees to scoop me into his arms, kissing me once more.

"My pleasure, baby."

My head rested against Gavin's shoulder as we rose in the empty elevator car. My eyes drifted shut just as the doors pinged open.

"Sleepy girl," he murmured, wrapping me in his arms and guiding me toward the penthouse doors. He gave Spencer a nod before closing the door and tucking strands of my hair behind my ear.

"Turn around, Aria," he whispered and suddenly, I felt as if every surface of my skin burned for his touch.

I turned around, meeting his heated gaze. Gavin removed his suit jacket where it laid on my shoulders. His hands glided down my arms resting on my hips. Then, with achingly slow fingers, he slid the zipper of my dress down and ran his hand over my hair. His touch had me aching for him. I bit my lip to stifle a moan.

"You're so goddamn beautiful. When I saw, you walking toward me in this dress, you took my breath away."

I moaned, leaning back against his firm chest in silent invitation to continue. I wanted it fast. I wanted him to press me against the closest wall and claim me as his. He moved unhurriedly, taking his time with each cherishing touch.

When Gavin kissed me, it wasn't the gentle kiss from before. Passionate, desperate and all consuming, his lips treasured my mouth for long seconds before he lifted me with his strong arms, hitching my legs around his slender hips. His kiss claimed me. As he lowered me to the king-sized mattress, my hands knotted in his hair, silently pleading for more.

"Gavin …" I whispered when he pulled away, eyeing me as I laid beneath him in nothing but a purple strapless bra and panties, jewelry and the three inch black heels Farrah insisted I buy last week.

His eyes wandered down and I saw his arousal. He trailed his hands up my thighs to the lacy fabric of my panties. A moan slipped out, my eyes closed and desire pooled between my legs. My sex clenched in anticipation. Gavin lifted my hands to the headboard, holding them there.

"I want to do this slowly, I want to savor you, beautiful," he murmured and I nodded.

He lifted one finger, signaling me to wait. Warmth spread through me as he tongued his way down my navel, toward my hot sex.

Oh, yes.

But then, his mouth left me. When I opened my eyes, he was gloriously naked in front of me.

"I'm going to adore you, pleasure you, and love you. All night long. How does that sound?" he said, his voice filled with carnal desire.

And as his hands closed around mine again, I felt beautiful. There was no hesitation in my whispered answer.

"Amazing."

He chuckled, as he spread my legs wider and knelt between them. He softly kissed my hands. His eyes were fierce on mine.

"Please, I want you, Gavin."

As he slowly, teasingly, tasted and pleasured every part of my exposed skin, I fell even more in love with him. The night progressed maddeningly slow. I kind of floated after a while, but it was impossibly more than it had ever been with him.

"Mmmm, is it morning?" I asked, opening my eyes to see Gavin hovering over me.

"Yes, it is. Kel texted you. She wants to get cupcakes before they leave for New Orleans."

I sat up in bed and started to laugh. My sister was addicted to Jenna's cupcakes. But then I thought about the rest of what Gavin said.

"He's taking her to New Orleans?"

Gavin grinned and kissed the top of my head.

"Yep. Lucas said Kel always wanted to go there."

"She has. She almost went while we were in college, but couldn't go because of a bad case of the flu. She's going to love it!"

I could picture Kel's face when Lucas told her.

"I guess I better get dressed."

I pushed against Gavin's bare chest to get up, but he didn't budge.

"I was hoping I could convince you to stay in bed."

He began kissing down my jaw to my throat, heading further south. Desire pooled inside immediately.

"Gavin ... I need to see her off. She'll be so excited."

He let out a low groan and then pulled us up.

"Let's make breakfast first. I love watching you in our kitchen."

I wrapped my hands around the back of his neck and bit his lower lip gently.

"If you insist."

Later I met my happily married sister at our favorite bakery, Hidden Sweets. After indulging in pastries and cupcakes, I hugged her extra tight before I headed toward where I had parked my car across the street.

As I pressed the button to cross the street, I felt my phone ding in my pocket. I didn't get a chance to check the message before my phone rang. A smile crossed my lips as I answered.

"Miss me?" I pressed the button again as I spoke.

"More than you know, baby. You heading home yet?"

His deep voice made goosebumps cover my skin. As I waited for the light to change, I thought about the shower we had this morning. A mixture of steam, heat, and Gavin left me wanton for more.

"I'll be there soon, I promise. I was thinking we should shower again. I don't think I got very clean."

I could almost feel the heat I knew filled his eyes at my suggestion.

"I can get you clean, but it might take two or three tries. How far away are you, baby?"

The light changed and I moved towards the street, walking across.

"Five minutes, tops."

"I can't wait to see you," Gavin whispered in my ear. I looked down the street in front of me when I heard the roar of an engine coming toward the red light. All the breath left me as I saw a familiar gray Lincoln Navigator driving straight down the street toward me. It wasn't slowing down.

"Gavin!" I screamed, my voice dying in my throat as the vehicle got closer by the millisecond. Terror set in, but I was frozen. A small part of me knew exactly who was behind the wheel. It had to be Bryce. He'd found me.

I saw Gavin's smile in my mind just as shooting pain in my midsection stopped me from breathing. His face was all I saw before my eyes closed.

I slowly regained consciousness but my mind remained foggy. My arms and legs were heavy, and I couldn't seem to move them. It was almost as if they were restrained. How was that possible?

Unease laced my thoughts. My heart beat a mile a minute as I heard footsteps far away. It took every ounce of my strength to force my eyes open and keep them open. I scanned the room, my bedroom in the penthouse. But something was off. A sense of dread ran through my veins when I smelled the musky scent of Old Spice and the coffee.

What? Oh God, no. Bryce.

"Ah, she's awake. Hello, princess," a deep voice said.

Darkened brown eyes met mine, stopping my world. My whole body screamed "No!"

I reasoned in my mind, this had to be a nightmare. Somehow, though the sensations argued against nightmare. Pain emanated from my right ankle up my leg and ending in the pit of my stomach. Rope bound my hands and feet to the bed. There was no way I could untie myself. I was trapped.

My skin crawled with dread as my tormentor stalked toward me with a mug from the kitchen. It was black with a Chicago Bears logo across the front. Somehow, focusing on something so trivial made it easier to suck precious air into my lungs. My hands shook when I saw Bryce's unchanged face. His eyes scanned my body slowly. His mouth parted as he blatantly stared at my breasts.

I shook uncontrollably, pricks of dread covering my skin. A black sheet covered my body. I thanked God for that, though the sheet only covered my lower half. As he approached, I struggled against the ropes and opened my mouth to scream, but no sound came out.

Bryce stalked closer and stared down at me with lifeless eyes. I remembered the spark of mischief in them when I first met him in high school. How handsome and mysterious I thought he was back then. The man staring at me now was nothing but a heartless person that thrived on controlling others. I tried to take deep breaths, tried to pretend his staring didn't make me want to run as fast as I could. I would get away from him, but first I had to convince him to let me go. God, how did he get in here? Surely, someone would hear me if I screamed …

"Bryce, w-what are you doing here? Please, please let me go!" I almost screamed, as I struggled in vain against the restraints. Panic and fear consumed me. The pain of the rope breaking the flesh on my wrists was nothing compared to what I feared was next now he had me all alone.

This couldn't be happening now. I fought my way back. I climbed and suffered and finally found happiness again.

"Scream all you want, Ari. I told you, you're mine. No one can hear you now," Bryce said.

He produced a roll of duct tape from the bedside drawer. It was the darkest shade of green, almost perfectly matching his tie.

"I will quiet you if I need to, but what I have in mind, I want to hear you, princess. You got away from me before, but now, you're mine. Forever." he growled, and my stomach burned with nausea.

Gavin would find me; he had to find me …

I watched as Bryce got up and held the tape in front of my eyes. Then his hand forcefully grasped my chin and he forced my eyes to his.

"Will you stay quiet until I say so? Or do I need to tape your mouth shut?"

Hastily, I nodded my head as tears fell from my eyes. I was helpless. My only hope was Gavin. He would find me. He promised to keep me safe. I remembered his words so vividly in my mind. "I won't let him take you, Aria. I don't care what I have to do, but I promise you, you'll be safe. Please, believe me"

"Good girl, Ari."

The man who had tormented my nights for so long stood in front of me and unbuttoned his suit jacket, then the dress shirt underneath. Before I knew it, he was naked from the waist up. He climbed on top of me, his hand covering my mouth to stop my scream of terror.

No! Gavin! Gavin, help me! I screamed inwardly, as the sheet was torn from me.

I knew I had no power to stop him.

"Please, Bryce. I don't want this, you almost broke me before. Please let me go. I promise I won't tell anyone."

Suddenly, a large hand came down harshly across my face, slapping me with such force that I cried out in pain. He hit me again, again, again. One blow blended with the next and the pain was too much to bear. I tried to turn my face away, to curl into myself like I used to when his anger got the best of him in the very beginning. Back then I thought the beatings were my fault. Back then I was naive and young.

The blows didn't stop. Then he gripped my hips, fingers biting into my hip bones. I heard his zipper, deafening in my ears.

Oh, God, no! I willed myself to stop him, to kick and scream and I did. I fought his attempt to pry my legs open. I kicked against his hands gripping my thighs.

"No! God, let me go! Let me go!"

I finally managed to scream out loud. Hot tears streamed down my face as I cried, willing Gavin to come and save me from this monster. Then the darkness consumed me, silencing the paralyzing pain.

Chapter 32

I heard voices as the weight of darkness ebbed from my mind. Darkness was replaced with pain, throbbing pain in my face, hands, and stomach. I struggled to pull in one small breath of air into my lungs.

"Is she going to be okay?" I recognized Gavin's voice.

His voice was laced with fear. I longed to reach out and comfort him. But I couldn't. My eyelids were too heavy to open and my limbs were impossible to move. My mind was foggy. I felt Gavin's hand holding mine, squeezing tightly, keeping me from falling back into the darkness.

"She's been badly beaten, but thankfully you got to her before anything worse happened. She has cuts and bruises, but they will heal. It could be hours before she wakes. Then we'll be able to fully assess her injuries. So far, we haven't detected any head trauma or internal bleeding other than … We'll do some more tests when she wakes up."

I recognized the voice, Nurse Maggie who I met at Mercy West Hospital the night of Gavin's accident. My entire body wanted to sleep. My eyelids grew heavier by the second and though I yearned to stay awake, I drifted.

The sound of monotone beeping woke me from the heavy fog enveloping me. When I heard his voice again, I struggled with every ounce of strength inside to open my eyes.

"This is all my fault, Mom. I left her alone and now, Fuck, what if he-"

I heard the anguish in his voice when it broke. When I heard his muffled sobs, I couldn't take the sound. It tore at my heart. I struggled and fought the dark cloud of unconsciousness even more so I could find a way back to him.

"Shh, honey. She's going to wake up, I promise you."

With the last shred of strength I had, I lifted my heavy eyelids. The blindingly bright light made my head pound in agony. But then everything cleared and I saw Gavin, dressed in a white button down shirt and a dark pair of jeans, brown hair messy. His face was pressed into his mother's hair as she held him tightly by the door. I tried to clear my thoughts.

A million questions came to the front of my mind. *Where was I? How did I get here? What was happening?*

My throat felt as if I'd swallowed the desert. I opened my mouth, willing myself to speak, but all that came out was a choking cough that made my stomach flip and my head pound even more. I was lying in bed surrounded by machines, wires, needles. I had to be at the hospital. I tried to remember how I got here, but I couldn't figure it out.

I saw Gavin's mother whisper something in his ear. He lifted his head and turned to face me. His blue-gray eyes were filled with so many emotions- love, fear, guilt, worry, sadness- met mine and it felt like coming home. Love was so evident in his steely gaze that it banished all thoughts from my mind as we stared at each other for long moments. Inwardly, I rejoiced. He was here with me.

He ran to me, and dropped to his knees. His eyes stared fiercely into mine as he grasped my hand in both of his. The contact made my pulse drum faster and I barely felt the pain when he stroked my face with gentle fingers.

"Aria, baby, thank God, you're awake."

I gazed up at him. Tears ran down his handsome face. I yearned to reach out to him, but my free hand was captured in his. I opened my mouth to say something, but all I could do was squeeze his hand in mine infinitesimally and mouth "water" to him. Gavin nodded, his hands leaving me briefly as he poured a glass of water. I noticed his wrinkled shirt and wondered how long had I been out of it?

"Here, baby. Take it slowly, your throat is probably a little dry after not drinking anything over the last few days," he said, his voice laced with happiness and fear.

He lifted the cup to my lips and I drank, moaning at cool refreshing liquid.

"G-Gavin," was all I could get out before a sob slipped out of my mouth and I felt the dam burst open.

He looked shaken, but the love in his eyes was stronger than ever.

"Beautiful, no."

He leaned forward, pressing a kiss to my temple, wiping away my tears as I drew a deep breath, trying to grasp reality.

"Shh, please don't cry. I'm here, and I love you so goddamn much. Please baby, don't cry."

I clutched him as held me close. He breathed me in and a shudder went through his body.

"I am so sorry, baby," Gavin said, pulling back to cup my cheek.

The concern in his eyes made me want to close mine and hide from it.

"What happened, Gavin? Why am I here?"

He blinked as if he was surprised. He looked to his mother before answering me. She stepped forward to stand next to him.

"You don't remember what happened?" she asked.

I looked between them and shook my head. Confusion started to cloud my thoughts as I realized I was missing something major. I tried to decipher what I remembered. I was standing on the street. I was so excited to go home to Gavin. I remembered saying goodbye to Kel moments before. But after that? Nothing.

Not much. I had vague impressions of a gray SUV, a nightmare where Bryce had me, intense pain in my abdomen, a gunshot and blackness. But none of it made sense.

Gavin looked up to the ceiling for a moment, in silent prayer and then dipped his head to kiss the top of my head.

"It's going to be OK. I promise you, beautiful. After you left the bakery, Bryce hit you with his SUV. Thank God, I was on the phone with you the instant it happened. Spencer was able to access the traffic cameras in the area. Bryce had a vehicle we were unaware of. Spencer traced the registration to a cabin that his family owned. By the time we got there, you had only been missing a couple of hours. I'm sorry we didn't get there sooner, baby. He beat you pretty badly, but he didn't …"

He stopped, unable to finish his sentence.

"Didn't rape me?" I asked in a whisper.

He shook his head. Thank God, he didn't take that from me again.

"Where is he now? Did he get away?"

"Bryce was going to kill you. Spencer had to shoot him. He won't ever hurt you again."

Chapter 33

The ocean waves crashed on the lake shore. I heard Gavin approach from behind me. Then his warmth covered my skin. The shawl and the light sundress I wore wasn't warding off the chill the wind brought as the sun set.

"Hey, beautiful. I was looking for you," his voice, smooth as velvet to my ears.

Gavin pulled me gently to his chest and into his embrace. I sagged against him and tipped my face up to his stormy eyes.

"I missed you. Are you feeling okay?"

I turned fully into his embrace and rested my chin on his collarbone as I blinked up at him.

"Yes. Where were you?"

His eyes narrowed and I realized he was shirtless. There was a small inked design on his right shoulder. I moved a step back and read it carefully.

Never Forget
Tessa Lynn Thomas

Tessa. Who was Tessa? I looked back into his eyes and saw understanding staring back at me. He took my hand and led me toward a ranch style house seated right over the water's edge. It seemed familiar, as if I'd been *here before, but I was too focused on the name repeating in the recesses of my mind to try to remember when I'd been here before.*

"Gavin, where are we?" I asked, tugging slightly on his hand so he'd stop and look at me.

A small smile formed on his lips as he opened the front door for me. I stepped inside.

"We're home."

Home. This was where we lived? As I looked at my surroundings, I was filled with excitement. As my eyes scanned the living room, I was surprised to see small toys littering the carpeted floors. Barbie dolls and hairbrushes, pencils and notebooks with pink covers covered in doodled words I couldn't read. Like a little girl had just come tearing through here during playtime.

"What ... "

Gavin placed one hand on the side of my face and gave me the most loving smile I'd ever seen. His lips brushed my ear and he whispered gently to me.

"She's not so good at cleaning up when she's done. She's a messy little one, just like her mother."

I frantically looked up into his eyes, not knowing what he was saying, though a huge part of my soul already knew what he was telling me. We had a daughter.

"Look," he turned me to the right, wrapping his arms around me, almost as if to protect me from what I'd see.

"Tessa" I whispered.

I woke in a cold sweat, eyes shut tightly in an effort to try to remember the sight of her. Tessa. I could still see her light brown hair just like Gavin's. Her emerald green eyes were identical to mine. All I could think was she was our daughter. Our little girl.

Without opening my eyes, my hands dropped to my belly and then lower to cup my lower stomach where I felt a sense of emptiness. I never imagined myself pregnant, having a child with Gavin, my love.

But the dream, that dream—I knew it wasn't just a dream. It was my body telling me something I didn't or wouldn't let myself think about.

After Gavin's accident, had I missed a period? Would I have even noticed after everything? No, I couldn't honestly remember the last one I'd had. Silently, I counted the weeks since my last cycle and when I came to the conclusion- twelve weeks, my heart soared knowing I'd been pregnant with a child created from both of us, Gavin and me. Then, I opened my eyes. My heart plummeted to the floor. The vehicle that Bryce was driving hit me. Knocked me down onto the street. That alone could have hurt the baby growing inside my stomach. *But what came after?*

Though I couldn't remember some of the time Bryce had me alone, I remembered vividly what happened after I refused to go along with his sick and twisted game. He wanted me. He wanted me to surrender to him. I wouldn't. The beating that came after, left me with such pain that even now, I still felt the effects. I choked on the breath in my throat when the truth landed a blow on my heart that I was not sure I'd ever recover from.

I had lost our baby.

I sat up in bed until I heard Gavin's quiet knocks at the door. His eyes met mine when he came in. He looked so out of character, hair disheveled, eyes rimmed in dark circles, wrinkled clothes. I could hardly look into his eyes because I was afraid to see our baby staring back at me. He came over and grasped my hand tightly.

"I wish to God I didn't have to tell you this, baby. I wish to God I could just take you in my arms and promise you that everything is okay now that Bryce is gone. I want that more than anything, but I can't because I have to tell you this."

Finally, I summoned the strength to lift my eyes to his and when I did, I saw tears filling his blue-grays. I bit my lip trying to be strong for what was coming. I wanted to cover his mouth with my own and beg him to help me forget this ever happened. I wanted to pretend that I could live with the emptiness I'd felt since waking from that dream. But I tightened my hand in his and nodded.

His voice shook so badly, I thought it would break when he spoke.

"Aria, baby, the doctor told me you were pregnant when you were struck by the SUV. There's no way to know when …"

I struggled to contain the sob that pushed its way through my rib cage and out of my chest, but it was pointless. I stuttered the words to finish for him.

"When I lost our baby."

My eyes filled with all the sadness and emptiness I bottled up inside me. For the last several weeks our baby girl grew inside me. *How could I have not known? How could I have lost something so precious before I ever had the chance to love it?*

"I-I'm so sorry I lost her, Gavin. I wish I knew, but I lost her. I lost our baby."

Tears tracked my cheeks. I covered my eyes as the pain in my chest became too great to bear. It felt as if someone reached inside my chest and ripped my heart from my body. That would probably hurt less.

"Aria, baby."

Gavin was on the bed with me, reaching to pull me to him. I struggled against him. I didn't want to look at him because I'd see what we lost. I didn't want to hear his voice because I'd imagine what he would have said to her. I didn't want to let him hold me because I was afraid I'd never stop mourning the loss of what we could have had. So, I fought. I struggled. I pushed at his hands and screamed for him to let me go. I cried harder than ever and begged him to let me go.

Let me go.

Let me go.

Please, Gavin let me go.

Let me be swallowed up by this pain.

Let me drown in it.

Maybe then I'll understand how I could have lost our baby girl who had yet to take her first breath in this world.

Let me go …

"Listen to me, Aria. This is not your fault. We didn't know. We didn't know. I'm so sorry I ever let you out of my sight. I'm so sorry the events that I didn't prevent took our baby. But if you let me, I'll give you the world. Please baby, let me."

I didn't have any strength left to fight him so I laid my head on his chest and closed my eyes. He held me tightly, his body shuddering as he wept softly.

"I don't deserve any of that because I lost our baby."

The one truth that slipped out was straight from my heart. I didn't deserve his love or his care or his comfort after that. I didn't because I didn't protect her. My body didn't keep her safe.

As I drifted to sleep, I prayed I'd see our baby girl again.

"Tessa," I whispered and her head popped up from where she lined up wooden blocks on the floor in front of her. When her eyes locked with mine, she smiled shyly. The same smile I had when I felt shy or unsure. Warmth spread through me, the connection to this little girl was so strong yet so unfamiliar it would have knocked me off my feet if Gavin hadn't been holding me up.

"Go to her, baby," he whispered, urging me with a gentle nudge.

I didn't choose to go to her. I was pulled to her, my feet moving before I even told them to. It was like she was a flame and I was a moth. She was a magnet and I was a paperclip. I went to her willingly because how could I fight gravity?

Tessa watched me quietly with the brightest green eyes I'd ever seen.

"Mama?" she whispered, reaching to me. My chest filled with love, joy and awe at this beautifully perfect girl we created. I gently scooped her into my arms.

"Mama's here, Tessa Lynn."

She reached her hands up and put them on my cheeks.

"Mama."

That word was everything to me. It was home.

I woke just like before except this time I felt Gavin's hand on my back and his muffled voice crooning that I was safe. He didn't know that my fear upon waking wasn't due to Bryce or what he put me through. I was afraid that I'd never get the chance to love a child the way I knew I would have loved our baby. I moved my head to the crook of his neck and inhaled his musky smell. I loved his smell. If I closed my eyes, I could recall each time he'd held me like this. I wished to God it was enough to fill the gaping hole inside of me.

"I dreamed of her," I whispered, as if it was a secret.

He deserved to know the whole truth of what I felt. No less. Gavin leaned back slightly at my words and I saw the pain in his stormy eyes.

"I would have named her Tessa Lynn. After your grandmother. She had your brown hair and my green eyes and she was so beautiful, Gavin. She was our baby."

Thick tears filled his eyes as he nodded. My breath left me, as my hands curled into his and squeezed. I saw his pain, his anguish. The sight shredded me. I moved to pull my hands from his just as Gavin lifted them to his mouth. Gently kissing them, he allowed me to continue.

I reached up and held his beautifully rugged face in my hands as I said the rest.

"When I look at you, I see so much, Gavin. I see the man that brought me back to life again. The man that saves me each time he tells me he loves me."

He sucked in a breath and pressed a kiss to my forehead.

"I do love you, Aria. I don't think I'll ever stop."

"But I also see her. I see what we lost, our little girl. Every time I look in your eyes, I'll see that. I can't see the good because the pain inside me is too much and it hurts. God, it hurts so much. I can't, baby,

I can't be with you right now. Not now. It hurts too much and I have no idea how it will ever stop. Right now, it's all I can feel and you deserve better. More."

Abruptly he stood and covered his face with his hands. I heard a low sob and it tore at my heart in the worst way. Gavin's eyes met mine again and I sucked in a breath when I saw the desperation in his darkened gaze. The panic I saw made me want to say something to take his pain away somehow, but no words came out.

"I can't let you go like this, Aria. We need each other if we're going to survive losing her. Please, don't do this to us," he begged, eyes pleading with me.

The gray darkened with pain. Gavin reached his hand out to me, but with a low sob in my throat, I rolled over onto my belly and pressed my hands underneath me to keep from reaching for him. My love. Sighing, Gavin slipped beside me, squeezing me gently against his chest. After a moment of silence, he turned my face to his.

"Is this what you really want?"

His eyes implored me. I wanted more than anything to be able to say no, to just hold onto him despite the pain searing me from the inside out. But it would ruin what we'd shared all these months and I couldn't fathom that.

I nodded through clouded vision and clasped his hand tightly.

"Yes."

Kissing my cheek, Gavin gave me a sad smile.

"Only for now. I will only let you go for now. But us, we are forever. I won't ever give up on us."

The pain ceased for an immeasurable amount of time as I felt the love in his gaze and his touch.

"Me either," I vowed.

No matter how long it took, I'd find my way back to him. Gavin's hand came up to my neck and I closed my eyes in a plea as his lips met mine. The sensations of his touch exploded behind my eyelids.

"Aria, baby."

I surrendered to the love that Gavin put into his kiss and I gave him as much of me as I could. Tugging my fingers through his hair, I moaned when his tongue dipped along mine. In his kiss, I almost believed I could survive this pain, but somehow, I knew I would be lying to myself. I pulled back and shook my head as his mouth fell to my collarbone.

"I want to give you something. Then I'll find Kel for you, if that's what you want."

There was such regret and fear in his voice, but my mind automatically latched on to the positive part of his words.

"What is it?"

I sat up and watched as Gavin sauntered over to a drawer across the room. He came back and placed the necklace they must have removed when I was brought in. It was the one he gave me right before Kel and Lucas' wedding. He looked so handsome that night. It was hard to believe it was only days ago. It felt like a lifetime.

I clasped the stone and smiled for the first time since waking from my dream.

"Thank you, baby."

Then, he leaned forward and kissed me so gently I began to shake.

"I love you so much, Aria. I always will."

A single tear fell from my eye as I watched him walk out of the hospital room, never looking back.

Chapter 34

I laid in the hospital bed, willing myself to beg Gavin to come back. To hold me. To be with me. But in my heart, I knew if I did that, I'd only hurt him. I had to find a way to heal on my own and then maybe, just maybe, we could be what we used to be. When I could look at his face and see the love and contentment and not everything we'd lost. Everything I lost.

Thankfully, I had no tears left to cry over this heartache I had brought on myself by sending Gavin away. I curled into the lumpy mattress and tried to sleep. I laid there, eyes closed, feet burrowed into the sheets, willing a deep slumber to find me. But I couldn't seem to fall back into the darkness. I heard a faint knock on the door. I saw the young, tired face of Nurse Maggie. She smiled gently, the sympathy on her face was almost too much to see.

"There are a few people that want to see you, Ms. Morgan. Would it be okay if I let them in one or two at a time?"

She came over to my bedside and checked my vitals. Once she finished, I nodded to her. I knew Kel, Lucas, and Farrah must be out there worried sick. I didn't want to see anyone, but I owed it to them.

"Could you possibly send my sister and her husband in, first?" I asked her.

The kind nurse nodded and went back out. It was a few minutes before I saw Kel and Lucas step inside the room. I immediately felt a little less lonely. I gave her a small smile, and reached out to her.

"Oh, Aria we were so worried. Are you OK?"

She perched on the side of my bed and kissed my forehead gently.

"Physically I will be, Kel."

"I saw Gavin leaving a few minutes ago. He looked broken. What happened?"

"The accident, the trauma, something caused me to ..." I drew in a shaky breath before I continued. "Caused me to miscarry. I didn't even know I was pregnant, Kel. How could I not have known? Every time I look at Gavin, all I see is the baby we won't ever meet. The baby that my body failed to protect. I don't know how to be with him right now. I am more broken than I ever was. And I am not sure I will ever be OK again. So, I asked him to leave and give me space."

"Aria, honey I'm so sorry. The doctor told us about the baby. I can't begin to imagine the pain you're feeling right now. I'm here for you, so is Lucas and Farrah, Jaden, Dad, Gavin and his family. And ... Mom showed up last night. We're all here to help you through this."

I gulped at the news that my mother was here at the hospital. God. The last time I spoke to her was more than five years ago. The night Jeremy got into an accident and died in this very hospital. That was the worst night of our lives. The night we lost him.

I turned toward her and she helped me sit up. A shooting pain went from my head to my stomach, but I bit my lip, breathing through it. Once I was propped up, I sipped the water Lucas handed me. The smooth cool liquid slid down my throat like honey, soothing on the way down.

"When did she get here?"

"Last night around midnight. She wanted to see you, but you were still in critical condition so you weren't allowed visitors. Honestly, I didn't want her here, but Dad insisted we let her stay."

I didn't know how I felt about seeing my mother after so long, but I needed her. If I was going to get through this and heal enough to be with Gavin again, I would need a lot of support. I had family and friends here to help me. But I knew nothing would compare to a mother's love and support.

"I want to see her, Kel."

Her honey brown eyes seared into mine. Then she sighed and nodded at me. She leaned over, kissing my cheek.

"You're going to be fine, Aria."

As she left the room, Lucas trailing behind her, I doubted her words.

The sedative the nurse gave me began to set in while I waited. My hands curled in the sheets as a mixture of sadness and longing worked its way to the surface. The emptiness hadn't left since I woke and now it was accompanied with a longing to see my mom. It had been so long, why would she choose now to come back?

A small knock followed by the sound of the door opening slowly, let me know either my sister came back or …

"Aria? Can I come in?"

Her soft voice caused warmth to spread along with a pinch of apprehension. If she still blamed me for Jeremy's death how could I handle that on top of this? I couldn't. It would make the pain inside so much worse knowing my mother hated me for something that was never my fault.

"Yes," I answered, turning to face her.

Andrea Morgan, my mother and a famous model, looked worse than I'd ever seen her. Her short, dark hair was un-styled. Deep circles were under her amber eyes. A faint smile crossed her face as she stepped inside, coming toward me. I saw the worry lines etched above her perfect brow. I reached my hand out to take hers. When she folded her fingers over mine in acceptance, I felt just a little less empty.

"I can't believe you're here, Mom. Why?"

I searched her face as she sat beside me. Her eyes were warm with the love I remembered from my childhood. She loved modeling, but her heart was always at home with us. That's why when Jeremy died, her world fell apart. Somewhere deep inside me I asked the question she probably asked herself back then. Was the loss, the pain all I would ever feel? Or could I still let love into my heart?

"I got on a plane as soon as your dad called, sweetheart. How are you feeling?"

She sat beside me and wrapped an arm around me.

"I feel so lost, Mom. I lost … I was pregnant."

The words seemed so inadequate to describe the enormity of what I, what Gavin and I lost. I had to force myself to breathe once the painful truth was spoken. My mom's wide eyes filled with understanding as she nodded. She engulfed me in her warm arms. The tears came, and this time I didn't stop them. My cries were muffled into her blouse. She cooed reassuring words in my ear. The emotion erupted from the deepest parts inside and it felt like my mother's arms were the only things holding me up.

"Shh, I'm here now, sweetheart. I've got you. I've got you."

She repeated those three words over and over and let me cry out all the pain, the agony centered in my heart around the loss I still couldn't wrap my mind around. How could I? I hadn't even known I was pregnant, until I wasn't anymore. Now it felt like a vise gripped my heart and kept squeezing. I remembered vaguely dreaming about having children with Gavin. About a little girl that would be half me and half him. I wanted that so much and now, would it ever happen?

My mom felt my shudder, so she pulled back and looked at me.

"I'm so sorry I haven't been here, Aria. When Jeremy died, I couldn't deal with the loss. Everywhere I looked, I was reminded of what I lost. Your father told me to hold on to you girls. To not push away when we were all hurting so much. But it was like I couldn't stop myself. None of what happened was ever your fault, not this and not Jeremy's accident. Life sucks, but you are so strong, sweetheart. I'm just so sorry I left you girls to fend for yourselves all this time."

Light spread through my chest at her honest words. She never blamed me. A part of me always longed to know she didn't blame me for his death. With her confirmation, my heart felt a little lighter.

I kissed my mom's cheek in relief. After a moment, the question tumbling around my head tumbled out.

"I lost her, Mom. How could I not have known she was even in there?"

Sighing, she wiped my wet cheeks clear and pressed a kiss to my forehead.

"She was a tiny little thing. You wouldn't have known unless you'd taken a pregnancy test, but with everything that has been going on, it's no wonder you didn't realize you were late. This is not your fault."

My hair was swept from my face and the warmth in my mother's amber gaze made a sad smile cover my lips.

"I love you, Mom," I said into her embrace.

"I love you, Aria. I'll never leave you girls again, I promise."

I pulled back and nodded, knowing she would keep her word.

"Everything is going to be okay. We'll get you through this."

I sighed, partly in sadness and partly in acceptance of her words.

"I know."

When Lucas opened the door to the apartment Kel and I had shared, my heart cracked a little more. It felt so weird to stand here with my luggage in hand. I only brought two bags and my purse. Some clothes, toiletries and keepsakes mysteriously showed up in the doorway of my hospital room this morning. When I saw, the handwritten note taped to the front of one of the bags, I knew it must have been Gavin. He hated this, but he wouldn't let me go without the things I needed. His words made my heart beat just a little faster.

> Don't think for a moment that this is me giving up. I told you once and I'll tell you again. I won't let go. I won't give up on us. We haven't even scratched the surface of our lives together. I love you. Forever.
>
> Gavin

Now, as I stepped inside the place I'd lived happily before meeting Gavin, it felt like a lifetime ago. Lucas and Kel moved into a quaint home in Waverly Springs just outside of the city. The place felt empty now. I set my bags down as a pair of hands squeezed my shoulders from behind.

"I made an appointment for you this afternoon with that therapist the doctor suggested. I can drive you if you want," Lucas said.

Everything inside me wanted to revolt against the idea of going to another therapist. Over the past few years I had seen several therapists. One to help with my grief, one to help with my abuse and assault and more recently I had to see a regularly mandated therapist twice a week for my depression. Even though it made the depression and anxiety worse at first, it helped eventually. I knew I had to do whatever it took to help myself through this, if not for me or for my future with Gavin, but for Tessa. I owed it to her to keep trying no matter how hard the future ahead of me seemed. I nodded and turned to give him a weak smile.

"Thanks, what time is the appointment?"

He looked briefly at his phone and then back up at me.

"Four. I have to go pick up Kel from the school, but I'll see you at three thirty?"

I had completely forgotten that Kel had a training class this morning. She wanted to teach elementary school now that her future with Lucas was flourishing. Things were coming together for her.

"Of course. I'm just going to unpack and make some lunch. Say hi to Kel for me."

He nodded and kissed my forehead before heading out.

I turned and rubbed my hand over the center of my chest where I ached. I longed to be in Gavin's—our home, instead of here. Even after only two days away from him, I missed him.

"Hey, Ari?" Lucas called from the doorway and I turned.

"You've got this."

That vote of confidence made me smile genuinely for the first time in forever.

"I knew my sister was right for keeping you around, Luke. I really needed that, thank you."

He grinned and I saw understanding and pride in his green eyes.

"Anytime."

When he finally closed the door behind him, I went to the door. I locked both the chain and the doorknob. Out of habit, I guessed. There was no real threat anymore but I still felt safer with the door locked. Looking around, I sighed.

What if this was all my life consisted of? If I couldn't heal, if it wasn't possible, could I force myself to stay away from the one man I loved more than anything?

A few weeks, maybe even a few months I could withstand, but longer? God, I didn't know if I could do that. I guessed I just had to have faith that time would heal my grief over losing such a precious gift and my sadness now that our lives would never be the same.

Chapter 35

Three months later

The sound of my phone startled me from sleep.

"Hello?" I answered groggily without looking at the screen.

"Aria," I heard him say my name and it felt like home.

Three long, torturous months of missing him and trying to fix my-self had passed since I had heard it. I should be upset that he called instead of waiting for me to reach out. But I was so relieved to hear his voice. Three months felt like an eternity. I smiled to myself and exhaled.

"Are you OK?" I whispered.

He let out a sharp chuckle before answering, "No, beautiful. How are you? I know I shouldn't have called you ... "

His voice trailed off, unsure what else to say.

"Gavin, I'm so happy you called. I—I miss you."

The words fell out of my mouth as tears ran down my face. Tears of sorrow and loss still, but also mingled with tears of joy, relief and hope. My chest swelled with the connection being reestablished between us. But I still didn't think I could be who I was, or who I needed to be. I wasn't fixed yet.

"Christ, Aria. I feel like I'm going crazy without you," he answered with longing in his voice.

I sighed softly and tried to stifle the conflict in my voice. I didn't want to hurt him further. I had no right to ask more of him. But I had to.

"I know I'm asking a lot for you to wait for me Gavin, I'm so sorry."
"Aria, I'll wait forever for you. You have nothing to be sorry for."
"It won't be forever. Just a little longer?"
There was hope in my voice.
"I'll be waiting," he vowed, stirring my soul.
Then I said goodbye for what I hoped was the last time.

The final curtain fell as we curtsied and bowed to the thundering applause. I was elated we had pulled off a seamless production. *Alas the Night* was a success and I was proud to be part of it. The company had wanted me for the lead so badly that they had worked with me as I recovered from my accident.

The moment the second curtain went down, we all erupted in cheers. A few girls I'd gotten to know these past few weeks enfolded me in hugs. We all started to laugh. The weight in my chest felt a lot lighter today.

"You were amazing, Aria!" Becca exclaimed.

"So were you."

She was a more refined dancer than most of us, but she had such a bright personality that I felt no jealousy. Dance had been my life for so long and I loved being able to share it with all these talented dancers.

Leo, the stage director, clapped his hands. All faces turned towards him. Everyone buzzed with excitement.

"Thank you so much all of you; that was magic out there. Let's get out of here, shall we?" He smiled proudly and hugged each of us as we passed him. We all hurried to the dressing rooms to change out of our costumes and go home.

As the adrenaline, started to recede, I remembered the sound of Gavin's voice when he called this morning. He sounded so … I don't know. Sad. He missed me. I heard it in his voice.

I feel like I'm going crazy without you … he had said.

I hated making him wait for me, but what else could I do? The past three months had been long and pain-filled. I began rebuilding my cracked relationship with my mother, who was home for good. And I faithfully attended group therapy and individual sessions with Dr. Madison. Talking with her made me realize that nothing could have prevented what happened to Tessa. I may never know why I lost our baby girl before I even got the chance to feel her kick or to hear her tiny heartbeat. And I had to be OK with not knowing. I was getting there. I had come a long way. Talking to Gavin this morning had felt like a sign letting me know I was as ready as I could be to face him after everything. I owed it to him to try.

I made my way to my car and saw a note taped to my front window. Curious, I walked faster and I saw my mom's perfect handwriting from feet away.

I'm sorry I had to leave before I could see you, but you were exquisite and I am so proud of you for following your dreams, sweetheart. I'll see you tomorrow for breakfast.

Love, Mom.

I smiled at her note and tucked it under my arm before sliding in the front seat. The white flow dress I wore for Lena's last scene was made of a mixture of loose satin material for the skirt and thin lace covering my torso. It was gorgeous and if I tore it I was sure the theater would have my neck. It had to be worth more than my paycheck. I put the car into drive and just drove, no destination in mind.

I was ready to take back my life. I was ready to heal.

I pulled up to where it all began, Marley's Cove, and yanked the key from the ignition. I wasn't sure how I wound up there. I remembered that first night when Gavin brought me to that very spot; it was technically our first date. He showed up at the party Kel invited him to the day we met and afterwards he brought me here. I felt at peace here then. Calm. Like maybe I would be OK moving forward. Back then I never thought I would fall in love with Gavin Thomas. But I didn't regret even one moment of our time, even the part that led me to the unimaginable heartbreak I had gone through.

I got out of the car and leaned my hip against the door. I closed my eyes and stood there. I didn't think, I didn't feel, I didn't worry. I just was.

Behind my eyelids, I pictured Tessa. Her messy brown hair like Gavin's and her emerald eyes like mine, so bright that they looked almost yellow. Her first steps. Her first words. How would it have sounded when she said Mom for the first time? Would she have had Gavin's husky laugh that I loved so much? Would she have been like him or me or completely different from either of us?

I didn't know if it was this place, the sunset or the sense of peace I felt in that moment but my heart squeezed painfully in my chest. I opened my mouth and I screamed. I emptied my lungs with every ounce of strength inside me.

I screamed. For every lost moment. For every sad thought that had made it impossible to sleep at night. For the daughter, I could have raised with the only man I'd ever loved.

I opened my eyes and didn't realize they were welling with tears until they spilled over my cheeks and down my chin. I let them come. I let the emotions take over me for that moment in time. I sunk to the ground and let it smother me. Swallow me whole.

And then, after an immeasurable amount of time grieving the loss I could finally accept, I let her go. I took the necklace from around my neck that I had bought not long after my first therapy session. I had her initials engraved on it. I stepped to the grass covered ground. There was a stone set into the ground where I rested on my knees. It read:

Tessa Lynn Thomas

May you rest in peace.

You were loved.

I couldn't bury Tessa, but I needed a place to mourn her. A couple of weeks after I left the hospital, I started trying to find closure. That was a hard thing to accomplish without a funeral or a goodbye or anything at all to hold onto. I struggled until Lucas showed me the stone he and Kel bought for my daughter, it was the best gift I'd ever been given. She had a place now. She had a permanent mark on the world, not just my heart. She was at peace. As I stood and pressed a kiss to my hand, then pressed it to the stone, I felt at peace in my heart. I knew I may not have forgotten the loss I'd suffered and probably never would, but I was healing. It still hurt, it would always hurt.

"I love you baby girl. You're free now," I whispered before heading back, slipping my necklace into my pocket.

As I walked I vowed to live each day knowing that she was not lost, but in a better place. She'd live on through me and through whatever the future held for us. I backed out of the cove and headed straight toward the only place I'd ever called home, hoping I was not too late.

My hands shook as I knocked on the door to the penthouse. It was just after dusk and I knew he should be home, but I hadn't called him to check. Determination settled within me. I had to see him. I didn't care how long I had to wait to ask him this question.

I heard footsteps inside. I sucked in a breath as the door swung open, revealing Gavin dressed in a blue sweater, dark jeans and bare feet. His eyes widened as we stared at each other, the blues and grays of his eyes were all I saw. Joy, relief and love for this man tumbled through me. I didn't know who moved first, me or him. It didn't really matter. All I knew was we drew together like gravity. He pulled me to his chest and my hands found their way into his messy brown hair that had grown long again. His head fell against my neck where he breathed deeply. I wrapped my arms around his back so tightly that I was sure we'd meld into one person.

"Baby," he whispered, kissing the skin along my collarbone so gently it felt like a feather against me. "I missed you so goddamn much, Aria. So much."

I lifted my head from his shoulder just as he lifted his and our mouths met. We fused together in desperation. My mouth parted and I was completely consumed by him.

"Gavin … Gavin … God, Gavin," I murmured against his mouth, his tongue dancing perfectly with mine, his hands holding my face in between them as if I'd slip away at any moment.

I pulled away just enough to meet his eyes and smiled my smile for him. I saw the affection and wonder in his expressive eyes that I fell for so many months ago. Warmth spread through my chest where all my missing pieces seemed to fit together, filling my emptiness. I lifted my hands to touch his dear face. I asked the one question I came here for.

"Is it too late to ask you to spend forever loving me?"

Chapter 36

My eyes clouded with love and fear and hope as I waited for his answer.

He dropped to his knees and clasped my waist tightly in his hands. There were questions in his eyes.

"You never have to ask me to love you, beautiful. You are my everything. I don't want to eat breakfast without you again. I don't want to wake up before dawn without you. I don't want to spend this life without you for another second. Aria, baby will you marry me?"

I gasped as my eyes filled with joy and doubt. He reached up and took my hand in his. He kissed it gently before reaching into the pocket of his sweater. He pulled out a small box.

"I have had this box with me every day for three months. The day you asked me to give you space I bought it, as a promise that I wasn't letting go."

I began to shake in anticipation of what was in the box. He opened the box and placed it in my palm.

"Aria Georgia Morgan, will you let me make you breakfast every day for the rest of our lives? Will you love me again?"

My eyes filled with tears of joy as I nodded fervently.

"Gavin." I pulled him up to stand and threw myself into his arms, wrapping my arms around his neck and my legs around his waist.

"I never stopped loving you. You are everything to me, too, and I would be honored to be your wife."

He held me even closer and kissed me. On a soft sigh, my lips parted and he slipped his tongue into my mouth. We poured every ounce of love and regret and relief into our kiss that we could muster. I kissed him as if he had the last breath on earth and I had to take it from him. He kissed me as if we were never apart. He took my lower lip in between both of his and sucked. A soft, desire-filled moan came from my throat and into his mouth. I pulled away with a soft laugh and pressed my forehead against his.

"Wait, baby. I forgot one thing."

He gently set my feet on the floor and dipped to his knees once more.

"You are mine, beautiful," he whispered as he slipped the princess cut diamond on the ring finger of my left hand.

I laughed softly again.

"Forever?" I asked, my voice still breathy from our kiss.

"This is forever."

Then, he scooped me up in his arms and carried me into our bedroom.

The moment he set me down in the doorway of our bedroom, surprise filled my eyes. He took my hand and squeezed gently.

"I don't want you to live in fear ever again. He replicated our bedroom and I can't change that no matter how hard I try. So, I had my interior designer come in. Her name is Ivy and she's very talented. Now we can make new memories in a new room, this room. Do you like it, baby?"

My mouth dropped open.

"It's amazing, Gavin. Thank you so much."

He kissed my palm. He led me to our bed, and leaned forward and to whisper in my ear.

"Wait here."

I nodded and waited. He placed a note in my hand. I felt happy tears filled my eyes as I read the words.

> Avia,
> I feel like my love for you grows each and every day. From now on this is my promise. No more tears for us, only happy memories, baby. I'm going to give you my whole world, and then some. So, tonight is for you, I hope to always make you as happy as you make me every single day.
>   Always Yours,
>   Gavin

I looked over at him, biting my lip before falling back against the covers. I reached out to him and he came to me. When he was above me I caressed his cheeks achingly slow. I kissed his forehead and then the dimple in his cheek.

"Gavin, I love you so much."

"Forever," he vowed.

And as we made love, I thanked God for bringing me home.

I slid my eyes open the moment I felt strong arms tighten around my back. His warm breath was against my cheek causing a contented sigh to slip from my lips. I was momentarily confused, wondering where the hell I was. But then I caught the scent of mint and musky man. The memories, sweet memories of last night came flooding back and I couldn't stop myself from turning into Gavin's embrace and burying my face into my favorite spot, just below his jaw. I felt his heartbeat under my lips as I kissed his neck. This definitely wasn't a dream.

God, how many times over the last three months had I dreamed of waking up in our bed, seeing Gavin laying across the pillows with one arm slung over his head? That was how he slept most nights. Damn, even that turned me on. I felt his body stiffen a bit next to me. He wrapped one hand around my nape and pulled me closer.

"You're here."

I smiled, though his eyes were still closed.

"I'm here," I whispered.

After a few minutes, I realized he must still be asleep because he didn't respond after those few words. So, I rested my head next to his and drifted off again.

"Mom? Mom?" I heard a sweet voice call me and knew who it was. I stopped chopping vegetables at the kitchen counter, vaguely finding my surroundings weird. Our kitchen never had ceramic counter tops. I shook the thought off as I entered a small room off the kitchen. It was painted a soft pink color and Tessa Lynn, looking more like a teenager than a child, sat up in her bed as I entered.

"It's alright, Mom," she whispered and I took a step closer to her, confused at her words.

What was alright?

"It's OK, Mom. You don't have to mourn me anymore."

I sat down next to her and kissed her on the forehead.

"I don't mourn you, sweetie. You're here with me."

Her eyes seemed to lighten somehow. She got up from the bed and went toward her bedroom door. Opening it slowly, her face showed such love and sadness, it confused me completely.

What was going on? Was she going somewhere?

"I had to leave you and Daddy, Mom. But it's fine. I'll be with you in your heart, and I'll watch you be happy. He told me that he loves you so much. He misses you. You don't have to stay anymore, you can go be happy, Mom."

Suddenly it felt like everything was out of focus and I struggled to gain my balance.

"What do you mean? I want to stay with you."

Tessa walked over to me and crawled into my lap, resting one hand on my chest to feel my heart. All I remembered was—God, I loved her more than anything.

"Daddy needs you, they all need you. Go, Mom. It's OK to be happy again."

Her words were fierce with hope and sorrow and I heard the truth in them.

We'd lost her. I'd lost myself, but living again was the one thing I could do to honor our daughter. I had to, for her at least.

"I love you, Tessa."

I whispered, kissing her for the last time. I watched as her beautiful face disappeared before me.

"Aria? Wake up, I think you're having a nightmare."

Gavin's smooth voice broke through my haze of unconsciousness. I reached out my hand to calm him. My eyes slid open and they immediately caught Gavin's worried face above mine. I brought my hand to his cheek and the corners of my mouth lifted to reassure him.

"Not a nightmare, baby. I dreamed about her. She told me it was OK to be happy again."

As I said it, I knew in my heart it truly was OK. It still hurt. God, it would probably always hurt, the loss we suffered, but the fact was we had each other. Gavin had me and I had him. And someday, maybe we'd have more children and when that time came, I would tell them about Tessa and how much she meant to both of us.

Gavin skimmed his hand down my shoulder to my chest where my heart was beating.

"We'll miss her every day. Some days, it may be too much to cope with and when those days come, you'll have me. Our daughter will stay in our hearts always. We won't forget, baby. We can't."

As his eyes melted into mine, I wondered how I ever got so lucky to have a man like him fall in love with me. He had mourned her too. And I pushed him away when he needed me most. Though I knew it was what I had to do for me to start healing, I regretted ever causing him more pain than we'd already suffered. I never meant to hurt him. I knew how he had felt, because it was how I felt when my mom pushed us away after Jeremy's death. I understood now why she had done it, for her own survival.

"Thank you so much for never giving up on me, on us, Gavin."

I whispered, cradling his face in my hand. My touch was tender, my love for him transparent in my eyes. His blue-gray's heated with promise.

"I never gave up. I won't ever let you go, baby."

The fierceness in his voice made me remember a part of my dream and it warmed my still healing heart. I watched as he paused, clasping my left hand and kissing the ring on my third finger. His eyes were tender as he spoke again.

"Please come home."

I smiled widely; joy at those words coursed through me. As if I wanted to be anywhere else?

"Happily."

Chapter 37

As I unpacked my two small suitcases, I realized this place had become home to me. I hadn't realized it until I woke up without his warmth the three months we slept apart. My phone chimed with a text message. I placed the last items in the bathroom cabinet before walking back through the bedroom to retrieve it.

Come find me when you're done unpacking. I want to take you somewhere.

I smiled as I made my way to his office. I peeked my head in the door and saw him looking down at his cell phone. I knocked twice and his eyes swept to mine.

"That was fast," he said, coming around the desk and wrapping me in his arms. A contented sigh passed my lips.

"I didn't have much to unpack, actually. Most of my stuff was still here."

"Hmm," Gavin hummed under his breath and placed a kiss to the top of my head.

"Are you ready, beautiful?" he whispered and I nodded, eager for his surprise.

Gavin put my fleece jacket around my shoulders to ward off the harsh winds outside and led me to the garage. I expected to find the Lexus parked in its usual spot but instead, Jasmine was there. The sight of the sleek car brought back wonderful memories. I remembered how the engine felt like slow and passionate sex underneath me.

"I love this car."

Gavin took my hand and I saw the teasing smile he tried to hide.

I sat on the passenger side and left the door open as Gavin looked down at me with heat filled eyes.

"What?"

"You're turned on by this car, baby. Aren't you?"

His deep voice was the sexiest thing I'd ever heard. I felt the blush heat my face at his words. *Hell yes, I was turned on.*

"I don't know what you're talking about."

I heard the rich chuckle and I hastily closed the door before I admitted he was right. The moment I felt the engine come to life underneath our seats, my insides curled in excitement. Yes, I loved the hum and roll of this car, the smooth shift as Gavin took a turn. The leather seats felt perfect as I sat and toyed with my hair. But none of that was why I was filled with anticipation right then. I knew wherever he was taking me would be special and I was filled with curiosity as to what it might be.

"See? I knew it. You're blushing. Your cheeks have the most beautiful glow to them right now, Aria," Gavin murmured, reaching over to take my hand in his.

He grinned knowingly and kissed my knuckles as he drove.

"Well, I saw the car first you know. When we met."

I smoothed my other hand over his, tracing the lines in his palm.

"Oh, really? You love this car more than me, don't you?"

I pretended to think about it for a minute and then moved forward, kissing the dimple on his left cheek.

"I like the car, I'm not sure if I love it, quite yet."

His eyes took me in for a moment before they filled with amusement and he emitted a small laugh. God, I loved his laugh.

"There's one thing I want you to do before we get to the place I'm taking you. I want it to be a true surprise so close your eyes," Gavin said.

Before I did, I saw the slight shake in his hand against the wheel telling me he was nervous, too. After a little while, the car stopped and he turned the engine off.

"Turn around," he whispered low in my ear.

I complied, biting my lip. I felt smooth fabric, maybe a scarf, cover my eyes and he tied it loosely behind my head. He came around and helped me from the car. He kissed my temple and then turned me to him. I smiled happily and wondered how he could possibly top the night before.

"Gavin, I can't see!"

I squealed as he took my hands and guided me a few steps and then stopped short. He was silent. All I felt was his hand holding mine as he guided me. He chuckled and then lifted me into his arms before sitting me on a plush leather seat.

"Patience, beautiful. You'll love it, I promise," he whispered, kissing my cheek gently and then closed the door before I could say anything else.

I sat back and sighed, wondering how I ever deserved a man like Gavin Thomas.

"How much longer?" I asked for the third time in twenty minutes.

Gavin squeezed my hand and finally, the engine cut off and he lifted me out of the vehicle. He held me tight for a few seconds, kissing the breath out of me and then let me down. Wrapping his arm around my waist as we walked into what I guessed was either a meadow or a yard based on the grass and leaves I felt under my shoes. Gavin guided me maybe twenty-five steps, and then stopped, turning me to face him. He skimmed my jaw with his thumbs making my skin tingle at his touch. It was my undoing. And, it excited me more.

"Can I look now?" I whispered.

I could almost see the smile on his face through the silky fabric.

"Yes, but just keep in mind that this isn't all there is to see. You must use your imagination. This is just the beginning, baby."

I nodded and then undid the blindfold, allowing it to fall to the ground.

A gasp escaped me as I took in my surroundings. We were in an endless meadow of freshly cut grass. An old oak tree stood nearby. Directly in front of us was a beautiful white gazebo. It was huge. I couldn't help daydreaming about a wedding there some day.

I saw the image from my dreams lately. Gavin standing beside a white house with green shutters, a wraparound porch and endless grass as far as the eye could see on one side of it and on the other the most breathtaking view of Lake Michigan.

As I looked around me I could almost see the house materialize. I saw a beautiful little girl with brown hair and blue-gray eyes holding out a single red rose for me. She smiled up at me, wearing a yellow sundress with white sandals like mine. I turned back toward Gavin and pictured a little boy with his messy brown hair and my emerald green eyes running alongside him. *Oh, my God, a family. This, was ours.* I could see it.

Tears streamed down my face. Gavin reached for me and lifted my chin until I met his eyes filled with unbridled love. He gazed down at me trying to read my expression and I smiled, out of happiness and joy understanding the dream now. Us. Gavin, he was my dream.

"It's so beautiful, Gavin. Is it ours?"

He grinned, kissing my nose and then my lips softly before pulling away and nodding.

"I told you I'm going to give you my whole world, and then some. When I saw this property, the oak tree, the land, the meadow, the beautiful views of the lake I grew up with, I knew this was perfect for us. I want to treasure you, to make all your dreams come true, this is just the beginning, baby."

He wiped my tears away and then kissed me, covering my mouth with his. As I grasped locks of his hair, he parted my lips with his glorious tongue. This was forever.

"Gavin, when did you do all of this?" I whispered seconds later as we walked up to the gazebo.

Gavin stood beside it taking my hands and kissing each of my knuckles in turn.

"Yesterday. I've been waiting and waiting to do this ever since I laid my eyes on yours, baby. But now, the time is right."

Out of the corner of my eye, I saw people approaching from the far edge of the meadow and I turned toward them in curiosity. *What was going on?*

Gavin wrapped strong arms around me from behind, brushing a strand of hair off my neck as he put his lips to my ear.

"I want you to know that we don't have to do this now. We can wait as long as you want. We can have a big wedding with all the bells and whistles, but I didn't think that would be what you'd want. We've missed so much time together and I think this is the perfect winter day for me to ask you to marry me. Right here, right now, beautiful. Marry me in front of all our family and friends. My mom and Callie, your parents, Kel and Lucas, Farrah and her family are here."

His tender voice trailed off as he dropped his arms from around my waist and let me process all he'd said. I recognized everyone he names walking toward us. My dad, dressed to the nines in a black suit and tie. My mom, Kel, Lucas, Farrah, her sister Melanie and even Jenna with her younger brother, Damon, walked toward us. They were all coming. Joy and uncertainty filled my chest as the possibility of getting married today unraveled in my mind.

Did I want this? My head swam with questions, how had Gavin arranged this without me knowing, had my dad given him his blessing, who would officiate. All those questions disappeared the moment I turned around and met Gavin's hope-filled eyes.

"Oh, Gavin. We're getting married. What about a big affair or a reception? Your family and ..."

Abruptly my outburst was halted by the crash of his lips on mine, his tongue seeking passage into my mouth. His hands came up to hold my head and I felt his smile against my mouth.

"I want to do this, to take you to be my wife in every sense of the word so that everyone here, in our lives, will know with complete certainty that you are mine. I will love you for the rest of our lives and if it's possible, I'll love you past forever, Aria. Just say yes."

The sincerity in his voice and the unhindered affection in his gaze disintegrated all my doubts and questions, except for one.

"Did you ask my dad for his blessing? I know it might sound traditional, but respect is very important to him and for you to ask me without his consent, I—"

Gavin's face split into a warm smile and he lifted me into his arms again.

"I did. All he asked was that I never lie to you or hurt you intentionally. He also said that if I ever hurt you in any way, made you feel inadequate or as if you're not enough, he would kill me with his bare hands."

My mouth dropped open in surprise, though I knew how protective my dad had always been but especially since Bryce.

I was not all that surprised that he would threaten my future husband.

Tears pricked my eyes and I laced my fingers around his neck.

I loved him so much.

"I love you," I whispered and I felt him smile against my hair.

"Is that a yes, baby?"

I nodded eagerly and he gathered my mouth to his and kissed me breathless.

"I love you so much, beautiful."

Chapter 38

Kel pulled me out of Gavin's arms moments before I saw Elizabeth wrap her arms around him, speaking softly to him. I knew they deserved some time. And I knew I had to thank my sister and everyone else for helping make this wonderful day happen.

"Are you sure you want to do this, honey? You can always change your mind. It is sudden and maybe you want a big affair. I know how much you guys have been through and we all just wanted to help make this day as special as possible. I hope you're not mad at me for keeping the secret from you."

My sister's big brown eyes filled with worry and I shook my head hastily.

"No! Please, Kel this is so wonderful. But how? Buying this land, getting an officiant and everyone to be here, today. How did he do it all?"

I watched as she worried her lower lip between her teeth before she grinned knowingly and shrugged her shoulders.

"Honestly, Mom helped set a lot of it up."

She led me over to the opposite side of the gazebo where I saw the white tent off to the side. A bride needed her space to dress and feel beautiful before she walked down the aisle. *Would there even be an aisle?* Somehow, with everything Gavin made happen to surprise me, I knew there would be. I was really getting married today. Joy and nervousness curled in my stomach and I had no doubts at all. I knew today was the day I'd become Gavin's wife. The thought of that filled me with overwhelming happiness.

"Oh!" I gasped when Kel opened the tent for me. The first thing I saw was an ivory white wedding dress hanging on a hook in front of us. It had a laced bust and no sleeves. The fabric was satin. The detail in the stitching was exquisite and I knew had I gone to the bridal store, I would have chosen this exact dress. My sister kissed my cheek and her smile brightened her face.

"I'll see you out there. Daddy will come soon, OK? Any doubts?"

I pulled her into a hug and kissed her cheek.

"Not one. Thank you so much, Sis. I love you."

She grabbed her purse and gave me one last squeeze.

"Love you back."

Daddy took my hand slowly walking with me as my body hummed with excitement. The aisle was covered with red rose petals. Each row of chairs was decorated with white silk. Baskets filled with roses and lilacs completed the look. My dad held out his arm and I placed my hand in the crook of his elbow. He wore the same black suit with gray tie that he wore to my sister's wedding. He looked so handsome.

"Thanks for coming, daddy."

He smiled warmly down at me as we started down the aisle toward the love of my life.

"I wouldn't miss it for the world, pumpkin. You look beautiful today."

I kissed his cheek and then darted my gaze to Gavin's smoldering blue-grays. He wore a gray suit jacket over a white button down shirt that showcased every line of his perfectly toned chest and arms. His messy light brown hair was slicked back away from his face. His lips turned up in a wide smile the moment his eyes met mine. Simmering heat filled his eyes and I knew mine reflected the same love. My dad kissed my hand when we stopped a foot from the steps leading to the gazebo. A trellis adorned with lilacs and lilies made a breathtaking altar. It was dusk, and the sunset reflected in Gavin's eyes offsetting his blueish gray with hues of deep oranges and reds.

"Be happy, pumpkin. I love you to the moon and back," My dad murmured.

Tears built in his eyes and I couldn't help the moisture that threatened in mine. I grasped his hand and kissed his cheek.

"I'll always be your little girl. I love you back, daddy."

He sniffled and wiped his eyes before leading me up the steps and placed a firm hand on Gavin's shoulder.

"Remember what I said, Gavin. Take care of her."

My handsome man took my hands in his and lifted them to his lips.

"I will, Mr. Morgan."

The moment my dad placed my hand in Gavin's, electricity shot through me. His eyes captured mine as he took me in his arms and whispered into my hair.

"You are so beautiful, baby. You take my breath away."

I smiled and leaned back, squeezing his hands in mine. I mouthed "I love you" and his answering smile would have made my knees give out if it wasn't for my dad's strong arm secured around my middle. I smiled up at him and kissed his cheek.

My dad smiled and retreated to his seat as I stepped under the trellis with Gavin. We stood before Reverend Jones, Farrah's dad and the pastor who married Kel and Lucas. I was so happy that he was marrying us now. I looked up into Gavin's eyes and saw so much love in them.

"I love you," he mouthed.

His hand tightened in mine. A tear fell down my cheek. *God. How was it possible to love someone so completely like this?*

I took a deep breath as the pastor began.

"We are all gathered here today to celebrate the blessed union of Gavin Andrew Thomas and Aria Georgia Morgan. Everyone, please take your seats."

I heard the bustle of about sixty people taking their seats. The pastor asked for the rings. He blessed them and encouraged Gavin to say his vows. His answering smile was ruggedly handsome, just like when we met. I wanted him then, maybe I even loved him a little then, but now, I loved him even more. I couldn't imagine my life without him.

"I, Gavin Andrew Thomas, take you, Aria Georgia Morgan, to be my lawfully wedded wife. To have and to hold from this day forward. To love and to cherish, through joys and through sorrows, in sickness and in health, for as long as I shall live. I will love you unconditionally, I will laugh with you and I will cry with you. I'll support you in all things and I'll never stray from our love. Aria, I'll be your world as long as you'll be mine."

He laid a hand on the side of my face and it felt as if his love poured into me.

As he finished his vows, I gripped his hands in mine, squeezing tightly as he gazed at me with so much love I could burst.

"Please place this ring on her finger and repeat after me," the pastor said, placing the golden wedding band in Gavin's palm. My breath caught in my throat when I saw it. Emeralds encompassed the band. Its design was hued with golden swirls, all intersecting to become one. It took my breath away. Gavin smiled warmly at me, never taking his eyes off mine as he spoke only to me.

"I give you this ring as a symbol of my love and fidelity."

He murmured and slipped it on my ring finger right behind the engagement ring he'd placed there not that long ago. Tears coursed down my cheeks as I squeezed his hand. It was my turn. I spoke from my heart as I looked at the only man I'd ever loved.

"Gavin. I think I loved you from the very moment I saw you. And now as I stand before you and our families, I pledge my heart to you. I vow to honor you and to keep you. Through happiness and through sorrows. In sickness and in health, for richer and poorer. Through the rough times and the good. I will love you, cherish you, and I will never stray from the love you've given me. I promise to keep my heart open to your love, no matter what trials are thrown our way. And I'll love you unconditionally, along with any children we may have for as long as I shall live."

Tears fell down Gavin's face and he mouthed "forever" to me. God, I loved him more than I ever thought possible. I lifted one of his hands to my lips and kissed his knuckles.

Pastor Jones handed me Gavin's ring. It was a solid gold band. When I twisted it in my fingers, I noticed the word "forever" engraved inside the band. I wasn't sure who was responsible for picking out his ring, or how whoever it was knew that "forever" was the perfect sentiment, but I couldn't have chosen better myself. And as I slipped it onto his finger, I said the words with as much love and joy I could.

"I give you this ring as a symbol of my love and fidelity."

Gavin took a deep breath and then leaned his forehead against mine.

"Forever," he vowed and I whispered it back to him, knowing I was only seconds away from being his wife.

Wife. Mrs. Gavin Thomas, God I loved the sound of that.

"So, by the power vested in me, I hereby pronounce you man and wife."

Joy burst through me, out of me. I wrapped my arms around Gavin's neck and saw his smile, the same one that cut through every wall I built around my heart all those months ago. Gavin's eyes filled with pure affection for me as he dipped his head to capture my mouth in a slow, heartwarming kiss that I felt all the way down to my toes. I was his. Forever.

"My wife," he murmured, holding my face in his hands and I tightened my arms around his waist as I whispered back to him.

"Forever."

The breathtaking kiss he gave me was his promise.

Epilogue

Gavin

One year later

I slid open the glass door and leaned back against the door-frame as I watched my beautiful wife work in the garden she insisted on tending herself. Between her dance school for girls and my thriving business at Thomas our days were full. There really was no reason for her to spend countless hours planting and tending a garden. But soon after her mother came to see our new house, Aria had this idea of a large, complex garden that she could nurture as the years went on. It was something for her to do now that most of her summer classes were done and the weather was getting tolerable enough to be outside. Her determination amazed me. There was no way I was crushing her dream of this beautiful, colorful garden. I watched as her long dark hair swayed in the wind as she worked the soil. Her skin was flushed from the sun.

"I can see you watching me, handsome."

She called to me and I chuckled, surprised to be found out. I carried her a glass of iced tea. Aria dropped her shovel and gloves, standing and smiling warmly when she saw me approaching.

"Good morning." I handed her the cold glass and pressed a kiss to her forehead.

I heard her soft sigh as she wrapped her arms around my waist and leaned her chin on my chest to look up at me.

"What's wrong, beautiful?" I asked, seeing the cloud of sadness in her usually vibrant emerald eyes.

These past few weeks had been weighing on her and though I tried to lift her spirits as much as I could, it was hard because I couldn't control what happened when we went to Dr. Hines, her gynecologist's office today. It had been a long and joy-filled year since we pledged forever to each other in the gazebo only a few yards from our house. It had only been six months since we decided to start trying for a baby. But after months and months of failed pregnancy tests and seeing the disappointed look in my beautiful Aria's face, I insisted we make an appointment to find out what was going on. We needed answers.

"It's all going to be okay, baby. The doctor will tell us what we're doing wrong and then we can try again."

A small, sexy smile crossed her face as she lifted her hands to tangle in my too long hair and she bit her lip before she spoke.

"And try and try and try again?"

"Oh, yes. Maybe we're not doing it right."

I teased, though with all of the places and ways we'd made love this past year, I highly doubted it.

"I'm pretty sure we are, what if something's wrong, Gavin? What if …"

Her voice started to shake as her fear was spoken. I pressed her to my chest and dipped my mouth, pressing a kiss to the top of her head as she rested her face in her favorite place.

"We'll find a way. I promise you."

I felt her nod against my neck and I squeezed her tighter, suddenly afraid myself.

I held Gavin's hand in mine across the arm rest of the Lexus and smiled while I listened to him arguing with his sister on the phone. The minute she told me her plan to move in with her boyfriend instead of living in an off-campus apartment like her mom wanted, I knew Gavin would have something to say about it. He was very protective of her. And he didn't really know Jude very well. Hell, none of us did.

"Look, I know you care for him Cal, but to move in with him? I just don't think …"

His voice trailed off as it felt like my ears closed and suddenly my stomach flipped. I winced as I tried to shift to alleviate the stomach ache I was suddenly having. I had never really struggled with car sickness before, but suddenly the movement of the vehicle was getting to me. Maybe I had been in the sun too long or caught a virus from one of the kids in my dance class.

"Aria? You okay?" his voice penetrated my ears again and my eyes shot to his.

The worry clouded the grays in them and I knew he could see the discomfort in my face.

"I … God, I think I'm going to be sick. Gavin …"

My voice trailed off as my throat began to close with the need to purge myself. I racked my brain for anything I'd eaten that might have made me sick. I couldn't think of anything in the two minutes it took him to swerve into the breakdown lane. My stomach started churning, and I trembled as I tried to swallow the nausea rising within me.

"Wait, let me get your door, baby. Hang on," he said, his deep-toned voice filled with concern. I couldn't wait for him to round the vehicle. I flung open my door and tried to breathe through my nose as I rushed from the Lexus. I managed to make it to some lovely bushes before I began to heave up the contents of my stomach.

Gavin's hand soothed up my back and to my hair where he held it away from my face as I hurled for a few more minutes. I coughed and struggled to breathe even after the heaving stopped. I felt his hand capture my nape in support.

"Breathe through your nose, baby. In and out, okay?"

I did as he said and soon the pain in my stomach started to subside. I rested my arms against my kneecaps in an effort to catch my breath. *God, what was happening to me?*

"I'm taking you to the doctor." Gavin said as he helped me back into the passenger seat and I nodded, remembering where we'd been headed before I asked to stop.

"That's where we were going, you know. I hope we won't be late ... "

Gavin shook his head and I saw the worry in his eyes.

"You were just heaving for like ten minutes straight, baby. I want a doctor to examine you that can diagnose other issues. I'll worry if we don't at least let them check you out."

I met his eyes and nodded, though it was most likely a wasted trip. I could have gotten ill for any number of reasons; we probably had nothing to worry about.

"I really don't think that's necessary and I hate to miss our appointment with Dr. Hines. But if it would ease your mind ..."

"It will, Aria. Please, humor me."

A surprised laugh at his comment burst from my mouth and I nodded. Letting him help me up, my lips tipped up in a smile when I felt his mouth press to my knuckles.

"I always do, Mr. Thomas."

"Thank you, Mrs. Thomas."

Even after a year of being married, I still loved the sound of that.

A nurse ushered us into a room when we arrived at the medical center. After checking my vitals and drawing blood, the nurse told me to go pee in a cup. Once that was done, I returned to the exam room and grabbed the paper gown to put on. I felt Gavin's eyes scanning me for an injury he could see.

"What?"

He grinned slowly and came to stand in front of me as I lifted off the blue sundress and set it beside me. Holding up the flimsy hospital gown, he helped me put it on and secured his strong arms around my waist instead of tying it behind my back.

"You feeling okay, now?"

I nodded and curled my arms around him, pressing my palm to the base of his neck and pulling his head down to meet my waiting lips. My mouth melded to his, his tongue escaped into my mouth and I tried to show him how much I appreciated him in my kiss. A faint knock on the door made a low groan emit from Gavin and he rested his forehead on mine.

"I'll wait outside for you. Or I can stay, baby. Whatever you need."

I hastily shook my head and pushed him toward the door as I tied the gown closed. Gavin's eyes heated at the thought of taking it off me. I laughed as he opened the door for a tall, older looking woman who must be the doctor.

"I'll be fine. See you in a bit," I said just before he closed the door behind him.

I turned to face the on-call doctor. I preferred my own doctor, but she must have been called away.

"Hello, Aria. I'm Dr. Lione. Let's see if we can figure out what's going on. I have some of your test results here. Why don't you take a seat?"

Her voice was soft and inviting, but a little spiral of worry started its way through me as I sat down on the bed and the doctor sat in a chair.

"You seem to be perfectly healthy, Aria. So far, I have found no signs of sickness in your lab work. Your vitals are good and you don't have any kind of fever. Some of the lab results take longer to come back, but I don't think they will reveal that anything is wrong with you. It is standard in women of your age to conduct a pregnancy test. It came back positive."

Wait, what? That was not possible. At least I didn't think it was possible. How many times had I gotten a negative reading on a pregnancy test?

"I can see this is a shock, just take a deep breath. Do you know when your last period was?" She asked, reaching out to take one of my hands in an effort to calm me. I thought back over the weeks since the last test I took which was … two and a half months ago. I hadn't had a cycle since, two weeks after that. Oh, my God, it's possible. Hesitant joy coursed through me at the thought of being pregnant.

"It was more than two months ago, two weeks after the last negative test I took. My husband and I have been trying for this past six months and actually, we were on our way for a consultation with Dr. Hines when I started to feel ill. Gavin insisted on bringing me here to be looked at."

"Well, I'd say that was a good idea. Congratulations, Mrs. Thomas."

A smile burst across my face at that news and my eyes began to water.

"You're … you're sure? I don't think I could take another let down …"

Doctor Lione squeezed my hand and set the test results on my lap to read for myself. There it was in bold print. Positive.

I don't think I'd ever been this happy, but seeing those words in front of me banished all my doubts from the last six months of trying and failing so very many times.

I was pregnant. I was pregnant with Gavin's baby. I was having our baby …

"Thank you so much. I can't wait to tell him."

Joy filled me as I hugged the kind doctor and walked out toward the waiting room where I saw my worried husband wringing his hands together as he paced up and down the small carpeted floor. His hair was mussed every which way from him running his fingers through it worriedly.

"Baby, I'm fine. Let's go."

At the sound of my voice Gavin came right to me and pulled me against his chest, kissing my hair gently. His warm embrace made the joy even stronger knowing I was carrying his child.

"I'm sorry we missed our appointment with Dr. Hines. Her office will call to reschedule. What did this doctor say?" he asked, pulling back from me to cradle my head.

His eyes were filled with worry. It was the same fear I saw flicker through them when we realized we lost Tessa. He was afraid of something happening to me, losing me. I was terrified of losing this baby too. The idea of that, going through that again, was my one true fear in all of this.

What if I lost this baby, too?

No, I told myself. This was a gift, a blessing and I wanted to tell Gavin at the perfect time. I wanted him to be overjoyed and I knew he would be. I took his hands and tried to comfort him.

"She thinks it's a stomach bug. I'm feeling OK now. Take me home."

He nodded and began to lead me outside.

We had dinner at home with me seated between his legs as we ate Thai food. I prayed it wouldn't bother my stomach. The moment Gavin excused himself to take a phone call, I went to the bedroom and climbed beneath the covers. Then I slipped my hands down to my nonexistent baby bump. It was crazy that I felt a sense of closeness the moment I touched the area where I knew our baby was already growing.

"Hi, baby. I'm so happy you're in there. Please stay put. I love you so very much, already," I whispered, rubbing my belly tenderly, enjoying this new foreign feeling.

I stopped talking to my belly when I heard Gavin on the phone with his mom. She had been so supportive of both of us this past year and I was so thankful for that.

"I don't know, Mom. Maybe, Christ, maybe this isn't the right time. I mean, I'm in over my head at Thomas and she's still building the school up from the roots, maybe it's not the right time to have a baby."

Hearing him say that made my heart drop into my stomach and stupid tears welled in my wide eyes. Maybe it was not the right time to have a baby. But it was too late for that now.

I didn't know what to do or how to feel after hearing that so I closed my eyes and willed myself to sleep.

I twisted my fork over and over near the scrambled eggs, pancakes and hash browns that Gavin made for breakfast. I knew I should be eating, especially now, but I didn't have any appetite.

"You're not eating," Gavin said as he pushed a curl behind my ear.

I nodded, not really meeting his eyes. It wasn't the first time this morning I'd avoided his gaze.

The loud clattering of silverware made my eyes shoot to Gavin's angry ones. I didn't get a word out before he scooped me up from my chair before I could even blink.

"W-what are you doing, Gavin?"

He didn't say anything as he strode into our bedroom, kicking the door shut and sitting down against the headboard where he arranged me so I faced him. I crossed my legs in front of me and fiddled with my hands. The look in his eyes said plenty. He wanted to know what was going on, but what was I supposed to say?

Hey, baby guess what? I'm pregnant and I know you don't want to have a baby with me anymore.

That would go down really well. A part of me knew he would be thrilled, but the whole time, I would wonder if he had doubts. About us.

About having a family with me. Also, I was pretty sure my hormones were getting the best of me.

"You tell me what's going on right now, Aria. We don't have secrets between us."

I stayed quiet, hoping he'd let it go.

Nudging my face up with his finger underneath my chin, I saw the concern on his face. I took one of his hands in mine and rubbed my thumb along his smooth skin.

"I heard you last night."

He tilted his head to the side and I saw he had no idea what I was talking about.

"Last night, you were on the phone."

The blue-gray eyes, I'd memorized ever since I laid eyes on them for the first time, filled with understanding and then with sadness.

"Christ, I didn't mean for you to hear that, Aria, baby. Please let me explain."

I tugged my hand from his and nodded, though he was pretty clear last night. I heard what he said.

"I want a family with you more than anything in this world. I dream of a little girl just like you or a little boy with your eyes and your smile. They would be perfect because they'd be ours. But watching you go through a never-ending cycle of hope and disappointment these past few months is breaking my heart, baby. I want you to be happy; I want you to have everything you've ever wanted …"

A warm smile parted my mouth at the truth in his eyes. He never meant that he didn't want kids with me. He wanted them so much, but he was willing to put off having a family to give me back our life together. I catapulted myself into his arms and kissed him with everything inside me. For a few seconds, he just laid there, surprised, but then his hands grasped the waistband of my sweatpants and pulled them down just enough so he could slip a hand inside my black laced panties. He could feel how aroused I was. God, I always was. With a suppressed groan, Gavin pulled my bottom lip into his mouth and tugged, causing an ache in my core.

"You thought I didn't want a baby with you? You thought I would give up on our dream, beautiful?" Gavin asked, his voice deep against my ear as he plunged two fingers into my opening just as I tightened my inner muscles in an effort to ease the ache.

I called out in pleasure and fervently shook my head.

"I don't know what I thought, Gavin. I was afraid maybe things had changed."

"Never," Gavin gritted out, circling his hand in a way that reached that one spot that made me scream his name passionately. "I'm giving you the world. This is only the beginning."

"You're right," I whispered, taking his hand from my core and putting it on my lower belly.

Gavin's heated eyes shot to mine and I saw a cautious hope in them.

"This is just the beginning. Our beginning."

His eyes widened and he shook his head subtly as he struggled to speak.

"Please tell me what you're saying, baby. I don't want to jump to anything ..."

I smiled widely.

"Yes, Gavin. And I think it's going to be a boy."

His eyes filled with tears as he pushed forward, dropping his face to my neck as he kissed me. His lips skimmed from my neck to my collarbone and lower still until his lips pressed so tenderly to my abdomen where our baby was growing.

"I love you, so fucking much Aria Georgia Thomas. And I love our baby already."

I ran my hands lovingly through his messy brown hair and repeated it back to him.

He said my name over and over like a prayer as he made love to me and I knew he was filled with as much joy as I was.

As I laid in the afterglow of the most passionate lovemaking I'd ever experienced, I was crazily, blissfully happy.

Seven Months Later

A sharp pain traveled across my abdomen, jolting me from sleep. I rubbed my belly and tried to drift back off. Minutes passed. I wasn't sure how many, but another pain radiated from my abdomen. I sat up and water gushed onto the bed.

Was this really it? I didn't think I was ready yet. Oh, god. It was happening.

"Gavin, wake up."

He looked at me groggily.

"Gavin, I ..."

I didn't get any more words out before his mind registered the wet sheets beneath us.

"Did your water just break?"

I nodded.

"Let's get you to the hospital."

Panic, joy, elation- it all flooded through me. I let him help me out of bed and to my feet. He grazed his thumbs over my cheeks and his blue gray eyes melted to my green ones.

"Are you okay? How do you feel?

I saw the worry and love in his steely gaze. I grasped his hands and placed them on my belly. Our little bear began to hiccup as I pressed a soft kiss to Gavin's mouth.

"It's time. Are you ready for this?"

He smiled and nodded, kissing me breathless before he kissed my forehead and wrapped his arms around me.

"I can't wait to meet him. I love you both so much."

I lifted my hands to his face, memorizing the joy in his beautiful eyes.

"I love you too."

Gavin rested his head next to mine on the hospital bed as I ran my fingers through his hair. It wouldn't be long. I treasured these last few moments of quiet before we met our baby boy for the first time.

When I felt another contraction coming, I grasped his hand in mine and squeezed it through the pain. He wiped my tears away and pressed a kiss to my forehead.

"What can I do, Aria? I hate seeing you in pain."

I leaned my forehead against his and shook my head.

"Just having you here is enough, Gavin. Thank you."

He grazed his knuckles down my cheek and lifted one of my hands to his lips.

"For what?"

"For loving me, having your love is everything I've ever wanted, Gavin."

He kissed me then, long and sweet and slow, pouring his love into our connection until I was breathless.

"Always, baby. I'll never stop"

It seemed like hours before Dr. Hines came in and perched on the end of my bed. She smiled as another doctor brought the epidural. I insisted on it because I knew I couldn't give birth without one.

"Okay, Aria. Sit up and grab the railing at the edge of the bed. This might sting a little."

I nodded, and did as I was told. Gavin knelt beside me, squeezing my hand in his.

"Breathe."

I did and after a stinging sensation in my back, everything south of my waist numbed. Oh, that was better.

"Better?" he whispered.

I nodded as he laid me back onto the bed. The doctors and nurses left.

I didn't know how much time passed as Gavin read my favorite book to me, *Pride and Prejudice.* I breathed through the discomfort that built every eight minutes. Gavin squeezed my hand and told me how strong I was. I wish he knew that he was the one that made me strong. His love.

Finally, my contractions were close enough for the doctor to come back. Gavin cupped my cheeks and I knew how much he wished he could take the pain for me. He loved me more than anything. He always had.

"I've got you, baby."

I nodded, pressed my mouth to his and reveled in everything about this moment.

It was time to bring our baby into this world.

"I'm ready."

I pulled Gavin's head down to my lips and kissed him softly before whispering against his lips.

"Don't let go."

I heard the need in my voice and when he kissed my forehead and squeezed my hand, it was his promise.

"Okay, Mrs. Thomas. Time to push. I want you to focus on Gavin as much as you can. Don't be afraid to squeeze his hand. You won't feel the pain, just pressure and you'll want to sleep. But you have to listen to your body and push when it tells you to."

I pushed for what felt like forever.

Finally, she smiled up at me and said, "He's crowning, are you ready, Aria?"

Gavin grasped my hand in his and his blue gray eyes filled with emotion.

My body was wrung out. Physically exhausted and pushed past its limit, all I wanted to do was sleep. Gavin pressed my fingertips to his lips and kissed them. He anchored me to him and when Dr. Hines told me to push again, I felt the weighted pressure in my middle and I didn't think I had the strength in me.

"No… I can't. I'm tired, I can't …"

I whimpered taking in breath after breath, my tear-filled eyes meeting his tortured ones. He pressed his forehead to mine. I felt the tremors in his body, his breaths. He was suffering with me.

"One more push, Aria. And then you can rest, I promise," the doctor said, holding my legs.

I groaned, pounding my free hand against the handrail.

"You can do it, baby. I'm right here. Squeeze my hand, take my strength. Push for me, beautiful."

His voice filled with concern, love and excitement. I heard it all inside him and it gave me profound strength. I breathed in and squeezed his hand as tightly as I could and pushed with all the strength inside of me. I pushed and I pushed, yelling out in agony as the fight left me and I collapsed onto the bed. When I heard the loud cries of our baby boy, they were the most beautiful sounds I'd ever heard.

Oh.

My.

God.

Tears coursed down my cheeks as I sobbed in joy and relief. Clutching Gavin's hand, I let the tears flow unrestrained.

"He's beautiful, my sweet baby" he whispered, that endearment so tender in his voice.

I looked up at him to see his eyes filled with so many emotions. Gavin dipped his head and slanted his mouth over mine roughly first, then with tender lips his mouth whispered over my cheeks, my nose, my forehead, my eyes.

"I love you."

"Would you like to meet him?" a nurse asked, holding our little boy wrapped in a blue blanket.

God, he was so small.

"Oh, my God …" I whispered, a sob escaping me as she placed him in Gavin's arms.

"6 pounds, 3 ounces, 21 inches. Perfectly healthy."

I watched Gavin peer down at his son, grasping his hand where little bear grabbed his thumb in his fist, holding tight and I swore my heart burst with such joy.

"He's so beautiful."

He was enthralled by our son, counting ten fingers and ten toes then kissing each one. Our son began to wiggle and cry, but Gavin rocked him gently, holding him to his chest and supporting his head with his hand, whispering to him.

"Shhh, Daddy's here. I've got you."

I wiped my tears and sat up. Gavin laid our son in my arms. He looked so much like Gavin that my heart burst with love.

"I've waited forever to meet you. I love you so much." I cradled him to my chest and kissed his forehead gently.

Bright, unyielding love erupted from my heart and my soul. He was just perfect.

"Welcome to the world, Gage Charles Thomas. We love you."

We talked about names for weeks, but when it came down to it, we named him after Jeremy and my father for his middle name. It fit him perfectly.

The nurses left the room and we sat together on the bed just gazing down at our beautiful son.

"Are you happy?" I whispered an hour later as Gavin held Gage to his chest and rocked him to sleep.

He looked down at me and smiled.

"Yes, more than I ever thought possible, baby. I'll love you both forever," he declared as he kissed me.

I smiled, feeling the same way as I grasped our baby boy's hand in mine.

And as I looked down into that precious face, I knew, this was home. I knew this was true. This was real. This was our happy ending. For a while it may not have been filled with as much happiness as sorrow, pain and loss, but we got here. And it was worth every second to have this moment right here, right now. It was worth it all to fall in love with this man over and over again, every single day from that point on.

The End

Dear reader,

We hope you enjoyed reading *Finding Beautiful*. Please take a moment to leave a review, even if it's a short one. Your opinion is important to us.

Discover more books by Amanda Kaitlyn at
https://www.nextchapter.pub/books/finding-beautiful

Want to know when one of our books is free or discounted? Join the newsletter at http://eepurl.com/bqqB3H

Best regards,
Amanda Kaitlyn and the Next Chapter Team

Playlist

- *Say You Love Me* by Jesse Ware
- *Gravity* by Sarah Bareilles
- *Magic* by Coldplay
- *Paradise* by Coldplay
- *All of Me* by John Legend
- *You and I (Nobody in the world)* by John Legend
- *Love Song* by Sarah Bareilles
- *You and Me* by Lifehouse
- *Stay with Me* by Sam Smith
- *Not About Angels* by Birdy
- *I Will Remember You* by Sarah Mclachlan
- *If I Die Young* by The Band Perry
- *Emerald Eyes* by Paul McDonald & Nikki Reed

About the Author

Amanda Kaitlyn has always had a passion, more like an obsession with the characters she creates in her writing. When she doesn't have her nose in front of her computer or in her notebook, she's reading another story on her Kindle. Her contemporary romance novel, Finding Beautiful is her debut novel.

Would you like to know more about this author? You can sign up to receive news, event information and special giveaways on her website and social media.

http://romancebyamandakaitlyn.com/
https://www.facebook.com/amandakaitlyn
https://www.instagram.com/AmandaKaitlyn_Author/
https://www.nextchapter.pub/authors/author-amanda-kaitlyn

More by Amanda Kaitlyn

The Beautifully Broken Series
Finding Beautiful
Breaking Lucas
This Beautiful Love: A Novella
Dare To Love: A Lesbian Romance (Coming Soon)
Unwrapping Lucas: A Christmas Novella (Coming Soon)
The Black Harts MC
The Broken In Us
The Redemption Of Us: An MC Romance
The Heart of Us
Protecting Us

The Beautifully Loved Series: A Second Generation Saga
Torn From Love (Hope & Adam)
Taken By Love (Ashlee & Gage)
Forever In Love (Avery & Jason)

Read on for a special look at #2 in The Beautifully Broken Series, Breaking Lucas
This is Lucas & Kaelyn's story.

Breaking Lucas
The Beautifully Broken Series, Book 2

Prologue

Past

The delicate fingers that lay between mine felt too light, too much like nothing. I forced myself not to curse as I listened to her breathing; slow and shallow. The sounds of the hospital room were the only things that could distract me from the straining puffs of air she let out of her lips every eighth second.

Why did it have to be like this? Why had she been given this slice of hell on earth, why not the millions of other people in this world? Why did my mother ... ?

My thoughts tore into a deep part of myself and I couldn't help the unfiltered anger that flooded me. She was the glue, goddamn it! I shoved my seat back so hard I was sure the legs were broken.

Ever since I could remember, my mother had been the glue. She held each and every one of us together, raining kisses over our faces even after we were old enough to be embarrassed by the kind of easy affection she'd always given. It didn't matter how old we got, she would hold us, in her heart and with those strong and unwavering arms, whether we needed her to or not. The only time either of my brothers or I had seen her anything less than a goddamn warrior was the night our dad sat us down after my high school graduation ceremony. Her face had been streaked in dried tears, her legs barely able to hold her up. My father's words rang in my ears as if that day had only been yesterday.

"Your mother is very sick, boys. The doctors say there isn't much they can do aside from making her as comfortable as possible. We don't know how long she has left."

I'd never known true pain before I watched my mother, once beautiful and full of life and laughter, turn into a shell of the woman I'd known all my life. I couldn't remember the last time I heard her deep, soulful laugh or her lame excuse for stopping by my condo every now and then. She didn't want to intrude, she'd say. She was sorry, she'd say. But what I always heard was *I miss you*. What she told me on those late night visits was always the same.

"*I miss you, baby boy.*" I remembered her saying those words so many times, the woman who'd raised me to give, not take. The woman who'd always put her boys first, even after she was diagnosed.

"Fuck," I all but growled, finding myself pacing the length of her hospital room, my life filtered unbidden through my head along with the memories of my childhood. A choked cough came from the bed and worry instantly had me by her side. Her hand came up limply to cup my cheek as her eyes opened, looking at me with such love that I felt the emotion rise up inside of me. My hands shook as I took hold of her hand lying against the hospital bed with both of mine, squeezing gently as to not hurt her. Nothing had ever gotten to me like my mother's love for me. It was a weakness I would never be ashamed of again.

"I *miss you*, my baby boy," she whispered, her voice so quiet I had to strain to hear it. Yet I did. A fat tear slid from my eye as I pressed my face to the warmth of her hand and let her hold me the only way she could.

"I'm right here, Mom. We're together, now"

She shook her head vehemently, as if I wasn't understanding her.

"I ..." Her chest heaved up and down frantically as she coughed and I plead with her to stop talking and just rest. But my mom, she was stubborn. It was a trait that was iron nailed into the Jones and Cardie family and there was no stopping her once she started something. Fear flashed through me at the thought of causing her any more discomfort at the cost of saying something in her state.

"Breathe. Breathe. Anything you want to tell me, I don't need to know. I know you love me; I know that, Mom."

My mother's eyes began to fill with fear and that's when her breathing dropped back to a normal pace. I let out a breath of relief and gently took her hand in mine again.

"I will miss you, baby boy. Take- t-take care of Darren for me ..."

A sharp pain pierced my heart at her frantic words. Her hand curled around my own as I squeezed three times. Her words felt like a goodbye that I couldn't bear to face, but if these were my sweet mother's last moments, I owed it to her to be strong.

So many words filtered through my mind as I tried to hold back the overwhelming pain that threatened to break me all over again. But I didn't need to be strong for her, I realized. She was the strongest woman to grace my world and for that, she deserved nothing less than what I'd always given her—the truth, even when it hurt.

"I'm so afraid of living in a world that would take you away from us. I can't wake up every morning knowing I'll never get one of your kisses ever again. Mom, I used to hate them. But now, please, just don't leave me. D-don't leave us."

For the first time in my life, I cried for my mom and I let her hold my face in the palm of her hand as my strangled cries filled the room, smothering the sounds of beeping until I forgot where we were.

"I've got you, Lucas. I'll always be with you"

My eyes were closed when I heard her just audible whisper. My eyes flew open only seconds later as loud, hurried beeping filled the room. The deafening roar tumbled out of me as I watched the last breath leave her body. My once unstoppable and loving mother was gone. *Gone.*

My soul crushed against my ribs as I crawled onto the bed and held her for the very last time.

I've got you, Lucas. I'll always be with you. Her words were the only thing I could hear even after the doctors had announced her time of death and the morgue had been called.

I'll always be with you.

Chapter 1

Present Day

The minute I stepped inside the waiting room I wanted to run the other way. I didn't belong here. I belonged six hundred miles away in Chicago with my love, my Kaelyn, the only one who'd ever touched my heart. Besides my mom, of course. My eyes wandered around the room to the patients that sat in each corner, most with their eyes closed and looking as if they'd spent most of their very young lives here.

I tried to imagine my mother coming here, every month, sometimes for treatments that only ever made her weaker, sicker, less and less like the woman who'd raised me. A hand clasped against my shoulder and I heard the deafening click of the heavy doors as they closed.

"This place is so depressing," Asher said behind me, his voice filled with cynicism and I laughed, knowing just how right he was. This was where people came to die, wasn't it?

"Knock it the fuck off, Ash. Luke doesn't need any more stress today." Ben, the oldest of my two brothers, turned toward him and gripped his shirt in his fist easily. Energy was rolling off him, the worry and agitation we'd all felt in the car ride here coming out to play.

"He isn't going to fucking die, so don't say shit like that. Got it, Kid?"

I watched as Ash sized Ben up and in one move had him in a head-lock against the very door that made my flight instincts kick in.

"Fuck man. I'm just trying to ease the tension, OK?"

Ben visibly relaxed at that and wrapped an arm around him in a quick squeeze, a sad excuse of an apology falling from his mouth.

"Come on; let's check in before someone kicks us out."

Ben caught up with my wide steps as we neared the reception desk of the hospital.

Fuck, I hated hospitals.

"Sorry, man," he said, facing me then. I nodded, not knowing what to say. It was selfish really, wanting to run away from the demon that tore through my blood while my brothers took the brunt of my heightened mood swings and their own fear.

They were going to lose me, too.

I couldn't blame either of them for being on edge, even if I wanted to.

"Lucas, I'm so glad you were able to make it out. How are you feeling?"

Dr. Rhodes' booming voice hit my ears and I lifted my gaze to see him in front of me. A sharp laugh came from me at the irony. Here we were in a cancer research hospital, our last chance at some answers about my disease, and he was asking how I *felt?*

"I'm peachy, Doctor. Can we get this started?"

He took a step back from me and I could see him taking me in, trying to decipher where my animosity was coming from. Aggravated, I placed a hand over my cloth covered head, clear of all the hair I once had and forced myself to take a deep breath. My cancer wasn't this man's fault. Hell, it wasn't really anyone's fault. I had been marked a wanted man the moment I was born and this thing would have caught up with me whether I wanted it to or not. It was just a question of time. As I closed my eyes and dropped my head momentarily, a pair of chocolate brown eyes with little flecks of gold flashed beneath my eyelids and that image gave me the strength to push through the anger I could feel heightening inside of me. I was ready to explode from it. But Kaelyn had always been stronger than me and I told myself that if I could just make it through today, I would find a way back to her. I just needed to get through this day.

"I fucking hate hospitals, Doc," I gritted out.

He nodded, as if he completely understood.

"We're going to make you as comfortable as possible during your chemo and afterwards. There are also spare rooms for your family to stay close if they'd prefer it. Shall we go back to my office?"

The empathy I heard in his voice put me instantly at ease and I nodded. I felt both of my brothers' hands on either of my shoulders, silently telling me *We've got you.*

We stepped into a dimly lit room behind a white door with no window. A large mahogany wood desk was in the center of the room surrounded by four matching chairs. A long brown leather couch was pressed against one wall of the spacious room while the others remained bare besides a single plaque that held what looked like the doctor's diploma in a glass case. Doctor Rhodes sat down, gesturing for each of us to take a seat. I readied myself to face a tough conversation ahead, knowing that this road had been long and grueling for mom and in the end, it had won over her unyielding strength. The memory of that didn't give me much hope looking forward.

"Before we begin your chemo I wanted to sit down with you and lay out how this is going to happen." His voice gave no room for argument and silently, I was grateful for his bluntness. Over the last two years I'd been doted on and reassured, some doctors even straight out dismissing my wishes when it came to my own body. *Fuck, that.* I had told them. I may not have much control over what was happening to my body, but I did have control over the decisions I made. I needed to remain myself, Lucas Jones, a hardheaded asshole at times, during this process. I'd be damned if I was going to sit back and allow my body to be poisoned with no end result in sight. That was a huge reason why I found myself here now. MD Anderson Cancer Center had one of the best reputations around and that was worth it, to me, to give it another chance.

"I'm going to put you on a rigorous treatment plan, and I will also set you up with one of the best dietitians I've had the pleasure of working with. Fiona Mills is a miracle worker when it comes to strengthening the immune system. I would trust her with my own family."

I nodded, to my surprise I believed him. He seemed to be a man that didn't say something unless he was being truthful. It was a fresh change after what I'd heard from people in the past.

"And what about this experimental drug you told us about, is he going to be in the trial?"

It was Ben that spoke up, his hands gripping the chair on either side of him. I knew he hated this, maybe more than I did. He was the closest to our mom, being the oldest and it hit him the hardest when she passed. I gave him a quick glance, raising my brow to gauge his mood. Benjamin lips turned up into what kind of looked like a smile, though it was probably only for my benefit.

"Yes, that was a major reason I wanted you to come down here so soon. This drug has been incredibly effective with leukemia and lymphoma. The cases I've seen have been very similar to yours, actually. Early to late twenties, with previous diagnoses in the family. Unfortunately, you cannot begin the trial until your blood cell count is higher. I'm hopeful that we'll only need to do a few rounds of chemotherapy as I know you've already been through the ringer these past months."

I folded my hands in my lap and they instantly curled into fists. The feeling of frustration that had clung to me for the last two and a half years rose in my veins, my body rigid with tension.

I didn't want to fight anymore.

All I wanted was to live long enough to see my girl again, that was if she would even see me after the way I had left her.

Find out more at
https://www.nextchapter.pub/books/breaking-lucas

Finding Beautiful
ISBN: 978-4-86751-421-4

Published by
Next Chapter
1-60-20 Minami-Otsuka
170-0005 Toshima-Ku, Tokyo
+818035793528
15th July 2021